HOUSE
OF JAGUAR

MIKE BOND

CRITICS' PRAISE FOR MIKE BOND'S NOVELS

House of Jaguar

"A riveting thriller of murder, politics, and lies." – *London Broadcasting*

"A tough and tense thriller." – *Manchester Evening News*

"A thoroughly amazing book. . . Memorable, an extraordinary story that speaks from and to the heart. And a terrifying depiction of one man's battle against the CIA and Latin American death squads." – *BBC*

"A riveting story where even the good guys are bad guys, set in the politically corrupt and drug infested world of present-day Central America." – *Middlesborough Evening Gazette*

"The climax is among the most horrifying I have ever read." – *Liverpool Daily Post*

"House of Jaguar is based upon Bond's own experiences in Guatemala. With detailed descriptions of actual jungle battles and manhunts, vanishing rain forests and the ferocity of guerrilla war, House of Jaguar also reveals the CIA's role in both death squads and drug running, twin scourges of Central America." – *Newton Chronicle*

"Not for the literary vegetarian – it's red meat stuff from the off. All action… convincing." – *Oxford Times*

"Bond grips the reader from the very first page. An ideal thriller for the beach, but be prepared to be there when the sun goes down." – *Herald Express*

Saving Paradise

"Bond is easily one of the 21st century's most exciting authors... An action packed, must read novel... taking readers behind the alluring façade of Hawaii's pristine beaches and tourist traps into a festering underworld of murder, intrigue and corruption... Spellbinding readers with a writing style that pits hard-boiled, force of nature-like characters against politically adept, staccato-paced plots, *Saving Paradise* is a powerful editorial against the cancerous trends of crony capitalism and corrupt governance." – *Washington Times*

"Bond's lusciously convoluted story provides myriad suspects and motives... Bond skillfully adds new elements to the mystery, including several energy corporations and no less than three *femmes fatales*... In the end, readers may find it nearly impossible to guess the killer, but they'll enjoy the trip. A complex, entertaining whodunit." – *Kirkus Reviews*

"Within the first page, I was hooked... From start to finish, I never put it down." – *Bucket List Publications*

"A wonderful book... quite powerful... going to create a lot of discussion." – *KUSA TV, Denver*

"A fascinating book." – *KSFO, San Francisco*

"You're going to love the plot of this book." – *KFVE TV*

"He's a tough guy, a cynic who describes the problems of the world as a bottomless pit, but can't stop trying to solve them. He's Pono Hawkins, the hero of Mike Bond's new Hawaii-based thriller, *Saving Paradise*... an intersection of fiction and real life." – *Hawaii Public Radio*

"A wonderful book that everyone should read." – *Clear Channel Radio*

"Mike Bond's *Saving Paradise* is a complex murder mystery about political and corporate greed and corruption... Bond's vivid descriptions of Hawaii bring *Saving Paradise* vibrantly to life. The plot is unique and the environmental aspect of the storyline is thought-provoking and informative. The story's twists and turns will keep you guessing the killer's identity right up until the very end." – *Book Reviews and More*

"A very well written, fast-paced and exciting thriller." – *Mystery Maven Reviews*

"*Saving Paradise* will change you... It will call into question what little you really know, what people want you to believe you know and then hit you with a deep wave of dangerous truths... *Saving Paradise* is a thrill ride to read and pulls you in and out of plots until you don't know who to trust or what to do any more than the character. You trust no one, you keep going, hoping not to get caught before figuring out what is happening. Mike Bond is not only an acclaimed novelist, but an international energy expert and a war and human rights correspondent who has lived and worked in many war torn areas of our world. His intellect and creativity dance together on the pages, braiding fiction into deeper truths about ourselves, our nature, our government, our history and our future." – *Where Truth Meets Fiction*

Saving Paradise is a rousing crime thriller – but it is so much more. Pono Hawkins is a dedicated environmentalist, a native of Hawaii who very much loves the islands but regrets what they have become. Pono is a thinker, a man who sees a bigger picture than most, and Mike Bond deftly (and painlessly) uses the character to instruct the reader in Hawaiian history from an insider's point-of-view. *Saving Paradise* is a highly atmospheric thriller focusing on a side of Hawaiian life that tourists seldom see. – *Book Chase*

Tibetan Cross

"A thriller that everyone should go out and buy right away. The writing is wonderful throughout, and Bond never loses the reader's attention. This is less a thriller, at times, than essay, with Bond working that fatalistic margin where life and death are one and the existential reality leaves one caring only to survive." – *Sunday Oregonian*

"A tautly written study of one man's descent into living hell... Strong and forceful, its sharply written prose, combined with a straightforward plot, builds a mood of near claustrophobic intensity." – *Spokane Chronicle*

"Grips the reader from the very first chapter until the climactic ending." – *United Press International*

"Bond's deft thriller will reinforce your worst fears about the CIA and the Bomb... A taut, tense tale of pursuit through exotic and unsavory locales." – *Publishers Weekly*

"One of the most exciting in recent fiction... an astonishing thriller that speaks profoundly about the venality of governments and the nobility of man." – *San Francisco Examiner*

"It *is* a thriller... Incredible, but also believable." – *Associated Press*

"Murderous intensity... A tense and graphically written story." – *Richmond Times-Dispatch*

"The most jaundiced adventure fan will be held by *Tibetan Cross*... It's a superb volume with enough action for anyone, a well-told story that deserves the increasing attention it's getting." – *Sacramento Bee*

"Intense and unforgettable from the opening chapter... thought-provoking and very well written." - *Fort Lauderdale News*

"Grips the reader from the opening chapter and never lets go." – *Miami Herald*

"Chilling story of escape and pursuit." – *Tacoma News-Tribune*

"This novel is touted as a thriller – and that is what it is... The settings are exotic, minutely described, filled with colorful characters." – *Pittsburgh Post-Gazette*

"Almost impossible to put down... Relentless. As only reality can have a certain ring to it, so does this book. It is naked and brutal and mind boggling in its scope. It is a living example of not being able to hide, ever... The hardest-toned book I've ever read. And the most frightening glimpse of mankind I've seen. This is a 10 if ever there was one." – *I Love a Mystery*

The Last Savanna

"A powerful love story set in the savage jungles and deserts of East Africa." – *Daily Examiner*

"A manhunt through crocodile-infested jungle, sun-scorched savanna, and impenetrable mountains as a former SAS man tries to save the life of the woman he loves but cannot have." – *Evening Telegraph*

"Pulsating with the sights, sounds, and dangers of wild Africa, its varied languages and peoples, the harsh warfare of the northern deserts and the hunger of denied love." – *Newton Chronicle*

Holy War

"Mike Bond does it again – A gripping tale of passion, hostage-taking and war, set against a war-ravaged Beirut." – *Evening News*

"A supercharged thriller set in the hell hole that was Beirut...Evokes the human tragedy behind headlines of killing, maiming, terrorism and political chicanery. A story to chill and haunt you." – *Peterborough Evening Telegraph*

"A profound tale of war, written with grace and understanding by a novelist who thoroughly knows the subject...Literally impossible to stop reading..." – *British Armed Forces Broadcasting*

"A pacy and convincing thriller with a deeper than usual understanding about his subject and a sure feel for his characters." – *Daily Examiner*

"A marvelous book – impossible to put down. A sense of being where few people have survived. The type of book that people really want to read, by a very successful and prolific writer." – *London Broadcasting*

"A tangled web and an entertaining one. Action-filled thriller." – *Manchester Evening News*

"Short sharp sentences that grip from the start...A tale of fear, hatred, revenge, and desire, flicking between bloody Beirut and the lesser battles of London and Paris." – *Evening Herald*

"A novel about the horrors of war...a very authentic look at the situation which was Beirut." – *South Wales Evening Post*

"A stunning novel of love and loss, good and evil, of real people who live in our hearts after the last page is done... Unusual and profound." – *Greater London Radio*

HOUSE
OF JAGUAR

MIKE BOND

MANDEVILLA PRESS
Weston, CT 06883

House of Jaguar is a work of fiction. The names, characters, places and incidents are products of the writer's imagination or have been used fictitiously and are not to be construed as real. Any resemblance to persons, living or dead, actual events, locales, companies and/or organizations is entirely coincidental. Initially published in a slightly different form as *Night of the Dead*, by HEADLINE BOOK PUBLISHING PLC, London.

Published in the United States by Mandevilla Press

LIBRARY OF CONGRESS CATALOGING-IN-PUBLICATION DATA

Bond, Mike

House of Jaguar: a novel/Mike Bond

p. cm.

ISBN 978-1-62704-010-5

1. War Crimes – Fiction. 2. CIA – Fiction. 3. Revolution – Fiction. 4. Guatemala – Fiction. 5. Environment – Fiction. 6. Human Rights – Fiction. 7. Latin America – Fiction.   I. Title

10 9 8 7 6 5 4 3 2 1

Cover photo © Andrew Lam/Shutterstock
Author photo © PF Bentley/PFPix.com
Book design by Jude Bond @ BondMultimedia.com
Cover design: Asha Hossain Design, Inc.

Printed in the United States of America

www.MikeBondBooks.com

For Peggy, *compañera de mi vida.*

And to the memory of Dr. Jeanneth Mayra
and the million martyrs of Latin America.

Y que mis venas no terminan in mí
sino en la sangre unánime
de los que luchan por la vida

– *Roque Dalton*

They break down your door at midnight and shoot you while your children scream. They snatch you from the street at noon and cut your throat in an unmarked van. They torture you for weeks, sending you piece at a time back to your family.

You were hungry and wanted more for your children. Or you'd read the Sermon on the Mount and tried to do what it asks. Or you were young and like Roque Dalton knew your veins didn't end in you but in the one blood of all who fight for life and bread.

All we can do for you is speak the truth.

I

House of Jaguar

1

THE MOSQUITO hovered, settled on his cheek; the soldier raised a hand and squashed it, his rifle clinking on his cartridge belt. "*Silencio!*" hissed the captain. Another mosquito landed, another; the soldier let them bite.

From far away, beyond the wail of mosquitoes and the incessant chirr of nighthawks, came the snarl of an engine. "Positions!" the captain whispered. One by one the soldiers squirmed forward through wet grass to the jungle's edge where the road glistened before them under the rising half moon.

The engine noise came closer, a truck grinding uphill round a curve. The curve coming out of Machaquilá, the soldier decided. Not long now. He fiddled with a scrap of electrical tape wrapping the magazine of his Galil. Wings swishing, an owl hunted over the road.

They won't be expecting us, he told himself. They won't be ready and we can kill them quickly and there will be no danger. The truck neared; he tasted bile in the back of his throat; his hands were numb with cold. If you don't shoot they won't see your rifle flash and won't shoot at you.

A beacon steadied on the treetops, fell on the road before him. A single headlight, the truck's, was coming up the road. He chewed his lip and blinked his eyes to chase away mosquitoes, rubbed his bitten wrist on the breech of his rifle. But if you fire fast and hard you'll help make sure they die at once and then they can't fire back.

The truck clattered closer, its headlight jiggling. Everyone will be shooting for the cab, the soldier told himself, so you must shoot into the back. "Hold your fire," the captain called. Transmission wailing, stockboards rattling, the truck rumbled past and disappeared into the night, just another cattle truck driven too many thousands of miles over bad roads on bad gas. "*Silencio*!" the captain said. From the jungle a howler monkey screamed like a dying child.

THE AZTEC eased down through five hundred feet, the jungle sliding under the wing like the floor of an immense dark sea. "I hate it when you do this," Johnny Dio said. "Reminds me of that joke about the secret to safe flying is to avoid the ground."

Murphy trimmed one aileron, watched the altimeter till it steadied at four hundred, the plane bouncing and banging on rising waves of jungle heat. "It's so flat here there's nothing to fear, just the House of Jaguar at Tikal." He slapped Johnny's knee. "And it's probably east of us."

"Screw you, Murph. You know exactly where it is."

"Unless the Mayans've built another one since we were here last."

"There could be some kind of goddamn radio tower, TV antenna… Even a big tree."

"That's why we watch out. You and me."

"It's so dark I can't see a goddamn thing."

"Just as well. You'll never know what hit you."

"Will you cut it *out*!" Johnny Dio shifted in his seat, fingers drumming his knee, his face glistening in the yellow instrument lights.

"The way you don't like this, Johnny, you should let me do it alone."

"My gig," Johnny sighed. "My money."

"Mine too," Murphy said softly, and saw Johnny smile at himself, as if for worrying. That if you had to be doing this, Murph was the one to be doing it with.

"You're right," Johnny said, "to be packing it in."

Murphy stretched, rubbing his back against the seat. "It's just habit, now. Got all the creature comforts I want."

"You don't do it for money, Murph. It's because you don't have anything else."

The glimmer of Chetumal began to bloom to the south; Orion was sinking into the west, Scorpio riding a half moon in the east, the Yucatán below darker than a midnight sea, the stars above like city lights. Murphy rubbed his face, liking the raspy stubble sound, closed his eyes and massaged them with his fingertips, still seeing the instrument panel as if he could watch it directly from his brain, thinking of the lobsters he and Johnny had eaten in Merida – he shouldn't have harassed the man because they were small – "estan cubanas," the man had explained. And Tecates. When this was over he was going to come back down to dive, sit on the veranda and drink Tecates, lime and Tecates. He notched the yoke forward, the engine's pitch deepening in the soggy air, the altimeter sliding down to three hundred, two hundred fifty. Light widened in the southeast. "Corozal," he said. "Going under the radar."

"I swear you like it," Johnny sighed. "You like this shit."

The jungle reached up, solid rolling waves of canopies with taller bare ceibas clawing up like drowned skeletons, down to two hundred feet, a hundred eighty, tipping the wings now between the tallest trees. "One time in high school," Murphy said, "I was in a class play. Only had to say one word: 'No'. Can you imagine, I blew it? I got so afraid I'd say 'Yes' by mistake, that when the time came I couldn't remember which it was and said 'Yes'? Screwed the whole thing up. Or maybe I was supposed to say 'Yes' but said 'No'. Can't remember."

"You're not the brightest bulb in the box, Murph. Always told you that."

A river's great black serpent slithered under the wing, sparkling with starlight. "Río Hondo," Murphy said. "We're back in Guatemala."

"When we get out this time," Johnny said, "I'm going to bag it too."

"Figured you were."

"I really like being with Sarah. She's easy, she's amazing. She loves me."

"All that counts."

"I really miss the kids, Murph. You were lucky, when you and Pam split, you didn't have kids."

"Don't know what I would've done. What's Diana say?"

"She won't give them up, but if Sarah and I get married, she'll let me have more visitations."

"Fuckin world," Murphy said. The engines steadied, almost hypnotic, the jungle drifting closer, as if the Aztec hung suspended over the slowly spinning globe. Ahead the land steepened into towering ridges of black stone with jungle on their crests. Deeper into a box canyon the plane droned, its echo bouncing off the cliffs that narrowed toward its wingtips. An end wall of vertical stone hurtled toward them; at the last second Murphy slid back the yoke, powered the throttles and the nose lifted and the saddle swept beneath them and they floated easily into a wide valley under a bowl of stars.

"Fuckin cowboy," Johnny said.

SEVERAL TRUCKS were coming. Not from Machaquilá but the south. The soldier wiped dew from his barrel with his hand, took a breath and held it, hearing his heart.

Lights brushed the pine tops and darted down the road. Headlights glinted round a curve – two trucks coming fast. The first roared past, a dark Bronco with orange roof lights. Then a Ford pickup with a camper top passed the soldiers, halted and backed off the road onto the shoulder. Two men got out and began to unload something from the back.

Half a mile down the road the Bronco's brake lights flashed as it stopped and turned. One of the men at the pickup stood with a flaring lantern and began to pull crates from the back. From each crate he took another lantern and lit it.

The men placed a lantern on each side of the road. They ran up the road, stopping in front of the soldiers to drop off a second pair of lanterns, and turned back down the road toward the Bronco with the other lanterns. The Bronco was moving closer; it too was dropping off pairs of lanterns.

"DOWN THERE'S Xultún," Murphy said. "A whole Mayan city – temples, schools, farms, observatories – all drowned in the bush."

The jungle had flattened, tilting west from the Pine Ridge mountains toward the black defiles of the Río de la Pasión. "Suppose the Mayans knew?" Johnny said. "That it'd die someday, their civilization?"

"Maybe they were smarter than we are..."

Johnny laughed. "Can't lose what you ain't got."

"Radar again." Murphy dropped lower, skimming the trees, slid back the mini-window and the engine roar bounced up at him from the treetops. Little spots danced before his eyes, circles with black centers like the fuselage markings on British bombers. "Petén highway," he said, nudging the rudder to swing southwest along a narrow dirt road.

"There was a guy," he said, "in one of their myths, named Utzíl. He got tired of staying home so he wandered south through the desert, found an alligator dying of thirst and carried him on his back to a lake, went on to his enemies' lands and fell in love with the king's daughter."

"Kind of thing you'd do."

"The king's soldiers chased the two of them all the way back to the lake. He hid the girl in a cave and the alligator appeared and carried him on his back across the lake so he could get help."

"Would you watch that fuckin tree!"

"It was five feet under the wing! You want to fly higher, so the radar picks us up and we get A37s all over our ass?"

"So what happened," Johnny said, after a minute, "to the girl?"

"When they got back the girl had died and he threw himself off a cliff into the water. Lake Atitlán it was, southwest of here..."

Black pastures and tin-thatched roofs flitted under the wing, hearth smoke smudging the stars, the distant starboard glimmer of Dolores, the town named Sorrows; he swung west of the road to miss the Army outpost then SSE back over the road at Machaquilá, an Indian name for all Indian things lost, with its wan lamps and vacant streets, a sawmill and scattered tree corpses, the unfinished church gaping like a broken skull, the barracks school by the zipping road; and he banked right then left into the cleft beneath the two steep hills that always seemed like tits, ziggurats, like the temples of Tikal, air rushing like a river over the plane's skin.

No shear now, he prayed, no crosswinds. The yoke was hot, vibrating in his palm, sweat tickling his ribs. He checked the landing gear: all down. "There they are!" Johnny said. Murphy eased the engine into low pitch, dropped the flaps, notched back the throttles, lifting the nose, and flared in a near stall down through the trees toward two rows of lanterns with the rutted road between them.

2

AIRSPEED EIGHTY, then seventy, the Aztec came down between the outreaching pine boughs toward the first lights, a man waving up. One wheel touched, bounced, caught a rut, yanking the plane starboard, pine boughs slapping the wing; Murphy gunned the port engine holding the nose high to pull it back till both wing wheels settled and the nose wheel dropped with a whump of gravel. Pumping the brakes he reversed the props till their roar shook the cabin, taxied back to the first lanterns, where the Bronco and pickup truck were parked, and cut the engines.

Johnny let out his breath. He lifted a heavy daypack from between his feet and set it on his lap. "Halfway home."

Murphy leaned back in his seat and stretched, feeling the muscles snake up his thighs and back, and popped open the door. The air was warm and watery and smelled of rotten vegetation. So natural up there, he thought, the ground's a comedown. He hesitated in the seat, not wanting to leave the familiarity of the Aztec's instrument panel and its worn controls, its sheltering cockpit and comfortable seat. "Home's where the heart is." He patted the instrument panel offhandedly, as though closing switches. A mosquito whined, touched his cheek. He slapped it, climbed out and slid down the wing and stood unsteadily in the glare of the lanterns.

The engines smelled of heat and avgas. There was a dent smeared with pine sap in the starboard wingtip.

"Murph – *qué tal!*" A tall skinny man with a thick beard ducked toward him under the wing.

"Goddammit, Paco! You didn't fix the potholes!"

"The what?"

"The potholes – *los huecos – en el fuckin camino*! Now I got a dent in my fuckin wing!"

"Ah, them." Paco kicked at the ground. "*Los baches.* If we filled them the Army would've noticed."

"How many guys you got out?"

"Two at each end. Beyond the lights."

"You got my fuel?"

"Sí, aviation fuel, as ordered." Paco called over his shoulder, "Ernesto – *los depositos!*"

A man in a red bandanna and a Harley Davidson T-shirt pulled fuel cans from the back of the Bronco and lifted them up for Murphy to pour one at a time into the wing tank. Johnny Dio stood in the glare of a lantern inspecting large bags of grass that Paco unloaded from the rear of the Ford. Johnny broke open and smelled each brick, put it back in its bag and resealed the bag. He hooked a spring scale to the port engine cowl and weighed the bags one by one, writing down the weights on a notepad and passing the bags up to Murphy to load through the starboard baggage door into the cabin.

"Murph, he is getting crazy," Paco said, "seeing *huecos* – faggots, on this road here."

"He must be *hueco con sus ojos* – proud of his vision," Ernesto answered, pissing at the side of the road, "to see faggots where there ain't none."

"Maybe he means you, *hueco* – so zip your little mosquito back in your pants –"

"Fifteen hundred and twenty-three pounds." Johnny shrugged the daypack off his shoulders. "You can keep the twenty-three or throw it in..."

"What am I to do, *hombre*?" Paco said. "Smoke it going home?"

Johnny gave him the daypack. "One hundred thirty-five grand. All used twenties and fifties. *No hay riñas.*" Murphy bit a thumbnail as he watched Paco flip through the money in the all-encompassing hiss of the lanterns.

Paco came closer. "Listen, Murph – you doing deals with anybody else?"

"You asking me that *seriously*?"

"*Sí, amigo.* People have been getting it – Flores, Dolores, Izabal. They fly in, everybody gets *extinto.*"

"By the Army?"

"Carlos says so. So you be careful, if you're doing any other deals."

Murphy shook his head. "We're *uno a uno.*" He stepped up on the wing. "Anyway, I may be tying it up."

"No more?"

Murphy shrugged. "I'll let you know, through Lucia."

Paco closed the daypack and looped it over one shoulder. Johnny hugged him, climbed into the cabin and buckled his seat belt. "*Gracias, compadres*! Twenty-five thousand *norteamericanos* thank you also..."

Paco's grin, his hand half-raised, the daypack slung over his shoulder, were caught in a burst of lights; standing on the wing Murphy saw it instantly – the glaring jungle, white plane and green Ford pickup, Ernesto in his red bandanna with one foot in the Bronco's cab, the harsh affronted jungle. He dove into the cabin and punched the starter thinking the starboard engine will be slow to start but I can run her down the road on one; if it's soldiers they'll shoot from both sides and we'll have to duck low and hope they don't hit the wing tanks; even if they do we can get a few miles if there's no fire. Over the whine of the starter a bullhorn blasted from the jungle, "*Estan rodeados!*" and a shot cracked as the port prop lurched a quarter turn and halted.

White smoke puffed from the port manifold, the prop spun slowly; Ernesto lay on his back, one foot still in the Bronco; there was a hole in the plane's windshield and Murphy thought I have to stop or they'll kill us. The plane began to jerk forward but soldiers blocked the road. Johnny was yelling but Murphy couldn't hear over the crash of bullets caving in the windshield and the second engine catching.

The plane picked up speed and the soldiers scattered as a pink tracer leaped out from the jungle and hammered the plane, Johnny jumped up as if he would smash through the canopy, punched Murphy's shoulder and fell against the stick. Murphy shoved him aside, the plane was moving fast now down the road with the bullets crashing through the fuselage past his face and knocking out pieces of broken windshield and sparking off the props, his whole body reaching upward to break free of the ground; smoke and flame burst back from the starboard engine, the cabin was blasted white with heat; the huge bang made him think the plane had been hit by a shell but it was the wing exploding; the plane cartwheeled off the road smashing him against the roof and floor and stick, Johnny was on top of him with flames coming up his sides and the door jammed, skin peeling off Johnny's face.

He tried to pull Johnny through the windshield but one arm wouldn't work; his clothes were on fire and the pain was so awful he had to drop Johnny, grabbed him again but the seat belt was buckled so he crawled over him to unbuckle it and yanked him down over the plane's melting nose, bullets slapping into Johnny as Murphy dragged him toward the trees.

Johnny was screaming, then Murphy realized it was himself not Johnny; a machine gun round had taken half of Johnny's chest, bullets singing through the pine trunks, boots running and rifles crackling and the Aztec seething and sending up long spirals of superheated exploding air. His arm was broken – that's why it wouldn't work.

Clasping the broken arm against his ribs he ran into the jungle, seeing at first by the light of the burning plane, then deeper into the darkness. He smacked his face against a bough, behind him soldiers yelling, "*Por aqui! Por aqui!*"

He caught his breath, listening for dogs. Now that he knew the arm was broken it hurt horribly, blood spattering on the leaves. They don't need dogs, he realized – they'll track you by your blood.

He tore loose a liana with his teeth and with his good left hand twisted it round his right biceps above the bleeding bullet hole and the pieces of broken bone poking through the flesh. From afar, above the now-distant crackling plane and the yells and snapping brush, came a familiar flutter, a loudening chatter. He ran, vines snagging his broken arm, mangroves barring his way, lost a shoe in a bog but kept running, smashing into trees and branches, stumbling, falling, running again.

The chatter grew to a clatter of down-beaten boughs and branches as the chopper's rotors flattened the treetops and its light darted down the trunks. A bullet whacked a bough; he fell, tried to crawl under a bush, but there were too many branches and he squirmed on his belly, dragging the broken arm, into a thicket of saplings. The chopper's light leaped over the thicket, dashed away. Soldiers ran past, boots shaking the ground.

The chopper swung east, its rotor roar hardening briefly as it crossed the road. Between the sapling stems he could see the firefly wink of soldiers' flashlights and hear the swish-chunk of their machetes.

"Is that you?" Right behind him the voice, in English with a Spanish accent. Murphy tried to duck but couldn't, hemmed in by the thicket, his back expecting the bullet, the horrible pain. "Is that you, Lieutenant Gallagher?"

Murphy bit his lip. Anything to live, even a moment longer. "What you want?" It was another voice, American. "I'm over here!"

"It's Angel," the first said. "I got something!"

Now it comes, Murphy realized, the bullets crushing and tearing.

"Over here!" Angel said, still in English.

"I'm coming," Gallagher answered. "What you got?"

"Tracks," Angel whispered. "Hurry!"

Brush scraped and rattled as Gallagher neared. His flashlight danced round Murphy's thicket. But he did not seem to see, or he was waiting to swing round the thicket so he could shoot Murphy without hitting Angel.

"Where?" Gallagher huffed.

"Look down!" Angel whispered. "See that?"

Someone gasped, fell, rifle clattering. "No –" Gallagher gasped.

"*Sí!*" Angel answered. One set of boots stepped quietly away.

Seconds passed and no bullets came. Mosquitoes landed in Murphy's ear, on his eyelids, lips, cheeks, wrists, neck, and ankles. He did not move. The helicopter came and went. He rose to his knees and slipped from the thicket, tripped and fell over a soft log – a body, warm, blood spurting from the sliced carotid, a man in uniform. Murphy stood and found the Pleiades in a gap in the branches, and turned west through deepening jungle toward the Río de la Pasión.

3

LYMAN WOKE the instant the phone rang. He rubbed his face, cleared his throat, settled his elbows on his desk, and picked up the phone. "Yeah?"

"Colonel?"

"Shoot."

"Your Indian left Merida at 0215 hours." The caller's voice was tinny and indistinct from the scrambler. "He crossed the Guatemalan border, Hondo River, at 0307. TD the Flores-Morales road seven klicks Sierra of Machaquilá at 0357 hours. Hey, what you think of that 'Skins game?"

"Impeccable," Lyman said. "Any other action, that sector?"

"Couple Guat slicks. You see that interception?"

"What slicks?"

"One on the LZ – he'd be your people. The other Cobán to Sayaxché – some general, probably, going for a beer."

"Thanks, Lieutenant. I owe you one." Lyman fumbled in his shirt pocket for his Marlboros.

"Negative. Don't sweat it."

"I will. I hate to owe people." Lyman hung up, took out a cigarette, shook his head, put the cigarette back in the pack, picked up the phone and punched three numbers. "Get me Cobán."

The phone's distant jangle sounded underwater, slow and deep. It rang on and on. "*Sí*!" a man answered, sleepy and irritated.

"Identify yourself, trooper!" Lyman said in Spanish.

"Sergeant Almédio, Cobán Armed Forces Command, Sir!"

Lyman waited a moment to let the man's fear sink in. "Get me Vodega."

"*Momentino*, Sir, *momentino*!"

After a wait the man came back on. "Capitán Vodega's not here, Sir."

"What? Where the fuck is he?"

"I don't know, Sir."

"He on that op?"

"What op, sir?"

"Forget it." Lyman hung up, staring at nothing. Thousands of styrofoam cups had formed overlapping circles on the desk's mahogany veneer. Why would Vodega be on Gallagher's op?

He lit a Marlboro, remembered his resolve, stubbed it out and put it back in the package. He inspected his nails, brown in the quick and muddy yellow at the tips, evenly and tightly trimmed, fingers darker than the desk. He imagined nicotine travelling down his arm into the hand, staining the skin.

He reached for a styrofoam cup. The coffee in it was cold, the color of used diesel oil. He emptied it into another dirty cup and poured a hot one. His hands would not stop trembling. He held the warm cup in his frigid fingers; reflected fluorescent light shivered on it.

Five forty-two. Eighteen more minutes and he could have a cigarette. Make it last till six-thirty. Then one more driving home. Yes, it was working – he was cutting down.

DAWN PURPLED the treetops, erasing the stars. Macaws stirred, began to crow; parrots and toucans screeched and battered wingtips in the branches. Spider monkeys jeered and threw down palm nuts; the cacophony of howlers followed Murphy through the jungle, making it easy for the soldiers to track him.

His stockinged foot slipped on a mossy log and he fell trying to protect the arm but it smashed against a bough and he cried out.

The soldiers had heard, were coming. Vines blocked his way, creepers and thorns, branches and saplings and trunks, madrones so tightly grown he had to scramble up and over them, his feet breaking through, the ching-ching of machetes and the yells of soldiers growing louder. Ahead were scrub and saplings, then a clump of thick brush that as he got closer he saw were treetops at ground height, trees growing up out of a sinkhole, a black pool glistening at the bottom. He slipped down into the sinkhole, rocks, dirt, and leaves tumbling with him, slid feet first into the water, took a breath, and ducked under.

The pool's rock sides were slick, he couldn't get a hold, pushed himself lower, hungry for air. How many seconds? Twenty, maybe. Clouds of sediment rose slowly, began to settle. No, maybe thirty.

On the surface above him the leaves rocked slowly, stilled. Water stung his arm. Maybe sixty seconds now. You can do this. Dirt dribbled into the pool, shadows crossed it. The surface shivered as a hand cupped into it; a khaki knee rippled one edge. Eighty seconds maybe. The soldiers' voices echoed, pebbles dimpled the surface and hit his face as they sank.

Not even two minutes. When you were little you did this. Sitting in school, holding your breath at your desk, the clock hand creeping. He sucked in water, coughed it out.

You have to go up and they'll take you and that's better than this, can't hold out any longer – go up there they'll reach down and help you.

Another soldier drank, his oval face protruding down. Murphy tried to remember how long it had been then could not remember what he was trying to remember, the light dimmed as he sank heavily into a dark chasm. Then from the distance a beam of light drew nearer. It was true, he realized, at the end you can see pure light.

He rose up this brightening tunnel toward the light, no pain, no fear, and burst gasping and choking into another underground pool with a vaulted stone ceiling, sucking in pure sweet air, sweet lovely forgiving air.

A slit in the cavern ceiling cast down a column of clerestory light. Through it he heard the soldiers grunting as they climbed from the pit. He dragged himself half out of the water on an edge of stone and lay with his broken arm above water.

The light steepened; through the crevice came warm air perfumed with jungle, loud with monkeys and birds, the buzz of bees and cicadas.

He woke, confused, reached for the lamp on his bedside table, scraped his broken arm on the rock and screamed, the echo bouncing round him. Before him hung a phosphorescent green face with black eye sockets and purple lips, but when he tried to knock it away his hand went right through it.

His breath whispered off the dripping limestone walls. He sat up, head banging the roof. Just a cenote, this. A sacred Mayan spring.

The light shifted, dust motes tumbling in its sloping shaft. There was no sound of soldiers. The agony in the arm was unimaginable. You should have stayed in San Francisco, he told himself. You should have been happy with what you had.

The water dripping from the shaggy limestone ceiling into the pool was like countless tiny bells. If you pray for everything to be all right, he decided, then maybe it will be. It's just like you to pray only when things get bad.

He took a deep breath and dove back down the tunnel to the chasm, then back up to the surface of the sinkhole; he waited in the water but there was truly no sound of soldiers. He stood in warm sun, shivering; a lizard watched him from behind a trunk, darting its scaly head from side to side. His broken arm was swollen and vermilion like the lizard's throat, his hand a mottled claw. He picked out slivers of bone and washed the wound with water from the *cenote*.

The bullet had come from the front side and had snapped the bone, leaving a small hole in his biceps and a larger tear with bone chips at the back. He was able still to move his fingers, and with great pain to raise the arm. He climbed from the sinkhole, found sticks and tried to splint the arm but it hurt too much.

He focused his mind on the flight chart of the Petén as it had looked in the Aztec's instrument lights. The road where he'd landed ran up the middle, north-south. He must be twenty klicks already west of the road. If he swung northwest he'd hit the Río Machaquilá, could follow it to the Río de la Pasión. Maybe another fifty kilometers. On the *Río* he'd find a dugout, anything; then only another hundred klicks downriver to Mexico. If he were very smart and very careful he might make it.

The last pines died out in an impenetrable lowland of hardwoods and thickets. Lizards and small green vipers were everywhere; scorpions scuttled, blue tails raised, over dead leaves. A weasel scrambled from a half-eaten rat; a boa swung at him from a vine-clogged limb, then turned away. Bees buzzed in an irritated cloud from a conical hive in the crotch of a dead tree aflame with white orchids.

AGAIN A TELEPHONE woke Lyman. He sat up in bed, thick-tongued. "Nancy!" he called. It kept ringing and he realized Nancy wasn't there. He ran down the hall to the living room and grabbed the phone.

"Howie?" Curt Merck's voice was nearly solicitous.

Lyman sat down, the leather chair cold against his thighs, trying to see the clock over the television. "What's wrong?"

"They blew it, Howie. Gallagher's dead."

"This line, Curt –"

"It's secure enough for this."

"I'm coming in." Lyman hung up, sat with the phone between his knees. There was dog hair on the carpet; he saw Kit Gallagher throwing a tennis ball in a long arc, the ball bouncing over the lawn, the black Labrador bringing it back coated in slobber that Kit wipes on the grass before throwing the ball again. Who's gonna take the dog? Kit brushing dandruff from his tie, his rigid motions when he eats, jaws snapping like a trap.

Lyman went into the kitchen. Sun splashed the yellow flowered wallpaper, the ceramic trivet of a Dutch girl in a bonnet, the Mr. Coffee with the *Warm* light still on, the dishes in the sink where Nancy had put them before taking the kids to school, the wall clock – a Minnie Mouse seen from the rear, her tail showing the hour, her red-gloved hand the minutes. Twenty after nine. Blood flowing round inside your body then it stops. So many times you go out to meet death, and finally, one time, it's there.

He poured a coffee and picked up the *Post* from the breakfast bar, a corner of the first pages sticky with egg yolk. Words words words. If the assholes only knew. Does anybody? He returned to the bedroom, found a pack of Marlboros, lit one and stood in a patch of sunlight, sucking in the smoke.

4

A TRAIL. Before him through the jungle. No wider than his hand. He looked up with thanks to the towering trees, followed the path till he met a long column of red ants carrying leaf chunks in their jaws, and realized it was they and others like them that had made the trail. The ants were stopping to touch jaws with others returning along the same way. He wanted to fall down, give up, but checked the sun and turned west again.

Soon the sun was overhead and he could not tell the way. He lay beside a tree. A blue motmot hooted from a branch and he wondered if it would eat his eyes. Long-tailed ebony *sanatés* flapped their papery wings, rustling and clacking in the palm crowns. Mosquitoes hovered with elegant patience. A huge fly bit his ankle; he waved at it and it buzzed round his head. Noon heat layered down in thick malodorous blankets, choking the narrow spaces between the trees.

He dragged himself in what seemed a westerly direction, drank at a puddle thick with mosquitoes, noticed the tracks around it, dug a stick from the mud and hid behind a fern clump. A vireo pecked at the water; he swung the stick and missed.

A small iguana crouched beside the puddle, its red dorsal fan raised, its throat pulsing. In his good hand Murphy raised the stick. It caught on a liana; the iguana glanced at him.

Like a whip the snake struck. The iguana leaped, rolling over and over but the bushmaster held, fangs deep in the iguana's neck, using its long thick body for leverage, till the iguana quivered and lay still. When the bushmaster had stuffed the iguana halfway down its wide unhinged mouth, Murphy jumped out and clubbed its head again and again until it stopped writhing. The long curved pit-adder fangs hung open, one showing a tiny venom hole.

Murphy dug a stone from the mud and sawed off the snake's head, ripped its body lengthwise, tugged out its guts, held it between his knees to tear a chunk of body muscle from its back and swallowed it. It came up and he forced it down again. He pinched his nose against the rank raw taste and swallowed another piece. When the snake was half eaten he drank the puddle dry and lay beside it on the soft leaves.

Waking in darkness he sat up to check for stars but none shone through the high canopy. Breath whistled in his throat, smelling of burnt decaying flesh. His body was a vast hive of cells aching for water; water hissed on the wind and licked at his lips. He chewed the mud of the puddle; it only made his mouth drier.

Moon shadows slowly climbed the black trunks. The darkness paled; swifts and swallows tittered, trogons stirred stuffily in the high platy leaves. An ocelot screamed. Dawn came with slits of flame between the treetops, the birds chanting wildly with the joy of surviving another night.

His arm would burst, the red infection, toxic as copper, sluggish in his veins. His tongue stuck, his jaw would not open. He crawled in circles looking for water, faint-ed, awoke, stood, turned his back to the rising sun, and pushed on.

Somewhere he had lost his other shoe; his feet were swollen with thorns and bites and ripped by rocks. Flies chewed his arm, their tiny feet stuck in the black blood.

He awoke on his back. Something feathery brushed his face, was tickling his ribs: a trail of ants crossing his chest like a red bandolier. They were feeding on his arm but he could not feel it. He sat up moaning and yelling, wiped them off with his other hand and fell back again.

The underside of a leaf glinted like a diamond. How pretty and peaceful the sun was, the warmth, birds singing. Wind rustled at his cheek, stirred the leaf; the light danced. He pulled himself near, saw the puddle whose reflection had flashed on the leaf, and sucked it dry.

Ahead was a long low building draped in vines – a Mayan ruin, maybe – there could be water, a path made by robbers, archaeologists. Two eye sockets gaped through creepers. A great Mayan stone scorpion: water – had to be – somewhere.

Watching for coral snakes in the vines, he climbed one-armed up the front, looking into the sculpture's empty eye socket, where a fat red-bellied spider hung in a web strung across the caved-in skull of a skeleton dressed in combat rags, the black nylon cross-belts still strapping it into the chopper's seat, the collective pitch and cyclic control levers jutting up rusty between its capless knees. He backed away till he could see the Huey's remaining rotor blade hanging bent from the shaft, the M60 mount in the port door

He sat. It's true, he thought. You *do* get punished for every evil you've ever done. Your Huey, back from Nam. Waiting for you.

He jumped to his feet. A huge black jaguar stood ten feet away. Its yellow eyes watched him. He reached for a gun, a stick – there was nothing. The jaguar smiled.

Too far to the chopper. Nothing inside. Don't show fear. Smells the blood. Coming now. Your chopper from Nam, the black cat. Coming to claim you. Suddenly he laughed, had no fear.

The jaguar cocked its head, flicked its long thick tail. He saw himself eaten, inside the jaguar, bloody chunks. The jaguar circled him, sliding invisibly through the trees and brush, turned back and stared, unwinking.

He tried to go back the way he'd come but the cat slipped behind him, close again, snarling huge teeth. He backed away, the jaguar coming after him. It circled again and this time he followed it and it went on, just ahead, sometimes looking back.

The land began to slope. The jaguar stopped at the edge of mangroves by a wide, fast stream flowing west. Murphy had a sudden rush of understanding, wanted to reach out, touch the glowing black fur, the monstrous rippling shoulders, felt love, absolutely no fear.

The jaguar vanished in the mangroves. Murphy knelt and drank till he could drink no more, then waded downstream, the afternoon sun dancing on the current.

He killed a small turtle sunning on a log, tore off the back and belly plates, the beak and feet, and chewed down the lukewarm tallowy flesh.

Night fell like a curtain. He dragged a dead bough into the water and tried to float downstream, but it caught on roots and sunken trees and he waded on without it. He could not remember how many nights there had been, at times could not remember what had happened.

He lay on a grassy bank. The ache of his arm filled his chest and shoulders, crushed his lungs; his fever made the blackness waver and buzz; thirst burned his throat no matter how much he drank. Sometimes the pain was so great he wept; at other times the arm seemed separate from him, its fate unlinked to his.

A blue sky and hot white sun gleamed through the trees. On the opposite shore a large-bellied girl watched him gravely; in the clearing behind her a hut of creepers and palm fronds squatted among plantains and dead corn.

He tried to wave, his voice a croak. The girl ran to the hut. A small dark woman came out and peered across the water at him, then ran along the bank to a clearing with other huts. She came back with several women; they waded to him and carried him across.

There was the sweet smell of wood smoke, the murmur of women's voices, the hiss and crackle of a fire. An ancient, wrinkled face loomed down. "Where am I?" he asked.

"San Tomás." A hoarse voice, a strange dialect. "*Norteamericano*," she said to the others, turned down to him. "You're with the Army?"

"No – don't tell them!"

She smoothed a wool blanket up under his chin. He called out, tried to focus on the rain-stained thatch above his head, but the ground slid away beneath him and he dropped into darkness.

5

IT TOOK Lyman an hour on the Army C-34 from Guatemala City to Cobán. From the air the steep black-green half-jungled hills were peaceful and deserted, a miniature mountain landscape for electric trains. He tried to imagine *them* down there, the guerrillas, with their guns and fear and hunger.

The plane kicked up red dust landing at Cobán Airbase. Red dust coated the jeep in which Vodega and two sergeants waited. Vodega shook his hand. "How was your flight?"

Lyman sat up front, forcing Vodega to the back. "*Any* flight that means seeing you, Captain Vodega, is a lousy flight."

"It's not my fault, Colonel, that Gallagher couldn't protect himself."

"I *want* whoever did it."

"It must have been the pilot. He was the only one who got away."

"You *let* him escape."

"I've got a battalion tracking him in the jungle between the road and the *Río*. I got a platoon in three *lanchas* working up and down the *Río* doing a 'detailed inventory', as you call it in your manual, of every village. I have two Hueys on full alert twenty-four hours to intervene the first moment I hear of him. You think we *let* him go?"

"You're just like every other fuckup. Instead of taking the trouble to do things right, you fuck them up and then you take much more trouble trying to fix them afterwards."

"You are telling me you're different, Colonel?"

"Who is he, this pilot?"

"The deal that was to be made was out of San Francisco. His plane is too burned, no numbers. The flight plans out of Mérida were false."

"Why'd you fire on him, goddammit? It all burned? The whole shipment? The money?"

"Yes."

"You *fuck*ups!"

"When my men yell to him he's surrounded, he jumps in the plane, tries to take off."

"So you got no idea who they were."

"Just what we know from before."

"I want him *dead*, Angelo. But listen," Lyman forced himself round in the jeep, stared into Vodega's boyish, acned face, "*I* want him before he's dead."

"No one needs him going north, telling stories."

"You don't have any fuckin idea who they were?"

"We identified one man, Paco Alguenes, from Jarha, in the south."

"I know where Jarha is."

"His wife was pretty uninformed"

"Show her some pictures..." Lyman turned to grip the windshield rim as the jeep slid through a turn.

"She died too soon. The children knew nothing."

The jeep halted before the HQ, a broad yellowed building with tropical mold down its walls. Lyman got out, stood with hands on the fender, blocking Vodega. "Why were *you* on that op?"

"Same reason you would have been, Colonel."

"Pray tell what's that?"

"I was responsible."

"And now you're responsible that Gallagher's dead."

"No. I'm responsible for wiping out another outsider. It's *your* people who wanted Gallagher down here..."

"With good reason. And now I'm here to replace him."

"I hope you fare better than he."

Was there a ghost of derision in Vodega's glance? Lyman couldn't decide, filed it for later. "We've lost a man – you know our policy on that."

Vodega got out of the jeep. "We know. We'll get this pilot for you."

THROUGH THE HUT'S open door Murphy could see other huts, a boggy trail between them, a bit of stream bank. A rooster crowed; a baby wailed. Hens clucked; two donkeys brayed back and forth across the village. The air smelled of fires, rotten vegetation and dank soil.

He shifted position and the earth moved with him. Turning on his side he tugged at the banana leaves wrapped round his arm. The pain and stench were horrible. With his good hand he fumbled for the tin cup of water the old woman had put on the floor by the head of his hammock, but it was empty.

Sunlight poured across the red dirt floor and over three clay pots and a white plastic jug, glinted on a half-loomed rug hanging from the center pole. The old woman and a younger one crouched on either side of a fire pit, both barefoot, in black cotton dresses and red embroidered ponchos. As the old woman spoke she rotated an iron pan on the coals, her flat cheek and wide brow lit by the sun, her silver hair braided down her back. She poured the pan into his cup. "Drink," she said in Spanish. "Soon comes *la doctora*."

27

THE FINGERTIPS that touched his cheek smelled of jungle, smoke, and gun oil. The man's face was shadowed, only the long bridge of his nose, his thin lips and pointed chin visible. In the open collar of his shirt dangled a silver crucifix. "What happened to you?"

"Plane crashed."

"Who shot you?

"Don't know."

"Stop lying."

A second man crouched down, black hair long under a camouflage cap, a white scar up his forehead. Two others standing in the door, rifles, one chewing gum. "Why were you flying over the jungle?" the scarred one said.

"Taking a friend to Costa Rica."

"I think you're CIA. Coming back from the raid on Paxtún that killed eighty-four people."

The men stepped away. When Murphy woke again it was dark. Firelight tossed shadows across the thatched ceiling; green saplings hissed into the flames; the murmur of the river came with a cool musty smell through the door.

THE OLD WOMAN fed him bitter hot drinks, built the fire till it crackled, her shadow dancing like a garroted man against the thatch. His heavy blankets were sodden with sweat. A glaring eye hissed down and he tried to get away but a strong hand held him. "*Tranquilo, tranquilo!*" a woman said. A lantern was hooked to the beam over his head. Cool hard fingers touched his cheek.

The woman wiped his face with a cold cloth, then cut away the banana leaves and washed around the wound with water smelling of peroxide. "So you're a soldier."

"No." He realized she'd spoken English. "Who are you?"

"The doctor." Her voice neared. "This will hurt, but is necessary." She slit open the arm; he groaned as the black blood spurted out. "Who shot you?"

"I don't know – stop!"

The pain was unbelievable as she dug inside the wound for splinters and bits of dead flesh. "Rémito – Pablo!" she called. "Hold him!"

The one with the crucifix and the scarred one pinned Murphy down while she cleaned the arm. "Who were you meeting," she said, "on the ground?"

"Not here," he gasped. "Costa Rica."

"Don't give me that! You're a *narcotraficante?*"

"I don't care, what happens, on the ground. *Stop!*"

"I'm sorry," the doctor said. The backs of her fingers brushed hair from his brow. "Listen, gringo, I can't stay. I must cut off this ruined arm and we'll send you downriver to Mexico."

It surprised him he could move, sit up. "No."

She smiled, her face round and brown. "You can't save it."

Inch by inch he forced the arm up, made the fingers move. "I won't give it up."

Her clothes rustled as she stood. The hammock rocked, the rush-mat ceiling sliding back and forth. Across the room she was speaking to someone – "*Delirante.*" There was a silence, the fire hissing. Again she spoke. "But we'll try."

"WHO IS HE?" Rémito said.

Dona Elena Villalobos rubbed exhaustion from her face, looking down at the gringo panting with pain and fever. "Probably flying grass."

Rémito snickered. "Silly games."

"Even with as much sulfa and bactrin as I've got he might not live. Seven point six-three caliber, clean through, broken humerus, but not shattered."

"If you use the sulfa and bactrin now, one of ours will die later without them."

She stepped outside, let her eyes find the stars. "I don't have the right to refuse him."

"You don't have the right to give him *our* antibiotics."

In the dark she saw Rémito finger his forehead. The scar worries him, she thought; it interests death. "How soon can we get more?"

"Not soon."

"In five days I've lost two wounded who would've lived had I any place but these dirt-floored huts and water boiled over smoky fires. There's dirt everywhere, the flies feed on wounds while I work on them." Her voice was gritty with fatigue; there was lethargy in her cells, grime beneath her eyes, an empty ache in her legs. "Now these *campesinos* with their dying gringo. Did you ever notice, in our churches, all the angels have blue eyes?"

"He's CIA."

"If he is I suppose you should kill him. But then why is he afraid of the soldiers?"

"Failed them, somehow."

"He has old shrapnel wounds. In his chest and hip."

"We should kill him."

She inhaled the wood smoke, rotten vegetation, and human ordure smells of the village. "When I was younger, every odor had such meaning. Now they're just smells."

Rémito took a deep, weary breath. He caressed her temples, massaged her neck. "Whatever you do," he said, "do it quickly. So we can go. Before the Army gets here."

6

EVERY TIME Lyman came down to Guatemala he hated it. Till he got here. Back stateside he'd probably hate it again. He watched the rain fall in thick diagonal sheets across the parade ground, rubbed his shoulder where the holster had chafed it. Wet damn heat. Bugs chewing the rotten skin right off you. Worse than the Mekong. Didn't mind wearing this gun then.

Trouble's Nancy. Way she gets on you. In Nam at least there were women. Here what you got but monkeys? Those Nam girls'd sell you anything. But Nancy never gave you any space without enlarging hers.

And now Kit Gallagher in a black plastic bag. Just like the old days. Except now it's him. Always said he'd end this way.

Admit it, Lyman thought, you just don't like her fucking other guys. You should be happy Kit's dead. But you're not. *It*'s what's rubbing you. Or you'd be eating it alive, down here. Guns, choppers, fear so thick you can slice it with a knife. Taste it, smell it, spread it on your bread. Fear in the night – the best kind, fear out of every nook and cranny, every crooked little street. Fear keeping everything alive.

This pilot still alive somewhere. Fearing too. Can *feel* him, Lyman realized. Wanting to live as bad as I want to kill him. But always have to play *what if*: what if he made the road, at Machaquilá, got a ride somewhere? If he's in Chiapas already, on the MC-DC flight, hungry to tell his story to the world? What would he say? Who'd listen? What if Nancy's doing it right now, while the kids're in school, some guy's number in her mouth?

Forget Nancy. Let her get it off with other guys. If she does you'll dump her when you get back, go outside.

Nothing wrong with outside time. Set up your own deal. Anybody who has to show up five days a week can't call himself free. Can't call himself brave either: only a coward denies his own needs. I used to tell her that, Nancy. But anybody who has to explain things to his wife certainly isn't free.

The rain hammered into pools flooding the parade ground. With revulsion he went down the steps into the downpour that coated his face like warm syrup and melted instantly into his clothes. How had he forgotten a poncho? Now he'd have to ask Vodega for one – Vodega'd love that: "Army of Guatemala", made in New Jersey.

He started the Jeep but it wouldn't shift into first, the synchro busted. Nam relics. Ghosts of gook chicks spreading skinny thighs across the back bench, American kids screaming out their shattered guts. Oh the dance of life. He nudged it into second and moved off slowly, the Jeep's bald tires slithering in the crud. He had to snuff this pilot. When the pilot was dead he'd break it with Nancy, get his black ass outside.

But Nancy didn't give up that easy. And did he want to, if she hadn't been serving it around? She always told him. One way or another. He flicked on the wipers but the blades were gone, their brackets scraping miserably. Hunched over the steering wheel, he drove one-handed, wiping at the glass.

MURPHY sat in early sunlight beside a red achiote bush, his back against a warm adobe wall, cradling his splinted arm against his chest. Yellow chicks pecked at the dirt by his feet while the mother hen paced nearby. A little girl crawled into his lap, avoiding his arm, her long mahogany hair tickling his face. She tore bits of squash leaf and tossed them to the chicks, who scurried for them then spat them out. "They're not hungry," he said.

"Want corn."

"Give them corn, then, Ofélia."

"No corn."

He nodded up at the cornfield on the slope above the village. The stalks were brown. "Where's that corn?"

"They kill."

"Who?"

"The first people come from corn." She got up and moved away. The sun's heat danced between the huts. When I was young, he thought, I'd knock down a willow stem without thinking. Now everything seems holy.

The old woman carried her blue plastic bucket up from the *Río* and filled his tin cup. From the hut she brought a lime and squeezed it into the cup. "Keep drinking water."

Towering clouds blocked the sun. Murphy stooped into the hut. His arm throbbed; he moved it at the elbow. The pain was severe yet good. It was as if someone else wiggled his fingers. The old woman scraped *frijoles* from a *quake*, warmed them in a pan on the fire, spooned them into his dish.

"I'm not hungry, Consuela."

"How can you not be hungry?"

"What happened to the corn?"

"The Army poisoned it, and the beans and the rice in the *aguada* by the river."

"That's crazy! Why kill the corn?"

"To make us move to the camps where you live inside hot wire, and if you try to leave they shoot you."

"And if you don't go to the camps?"

"Sooner or later they kill you too, just like the corn."

A NONCOM brought coffee. Carusi, the general's adjutant, clicked a pencil against his thumbnail. Vodega smiled steadily. General Arena had a cold and kept blowing his nose into a soggy tissue. Under the table Lyman wiped his palm against his thigh to cleanse it of the General's handshake.

"It's been a week and you haven't found the pilot," Lyman said. "Shall I remind you he killed our man on loan to you?"

"He wasn't on *loan* to us." Arena tasted his coffee, wiped his mouth with his great dark paw.

"Shall I mention what this does in DC? You *do* read American papers occasionally? You *want* these jerks in Congress to smash us?"

Arena had a tiny, merry smile. "Whether you get smashed or not has nothing to do with me."

Outside the window, Lyman saw, the rain had stopped. "Imagine, General, where that leaves *you*. When we thought some day you might replace Mejía Victores."

"We have *your* democracy now, You can't just put me in or take Mejía Victores out, like in the old days. We have an 'elected' president, same as you."

"I mean Chief of the Armed Forces, General. The guy who runs things. To bring a little stability to this place."

"Please don't lie so badly, Colonel, it's disrespectful. Stability's the last thing you want here. And please don't doubt the effort we've made to find this pilot."

"I doubt everything, most of the time. Especially down here."

"That's your job," Vodega said, "to doubt things. We don't mind. We help you all we can."

"So then help me by reconsidering the contributions thing, as Gallagher asked you. And don't be so goddamned territorial about the Colombians – we work with them – they're good people."

"Your version of good and ours aren't necessarily the same." Arena blew his nose, loudly. "And, regarding this pilot – why do you want him so bad?"

"If ever once we leave a death unanswered, General, the whole thing begins to unravel. You know that."

Arena wadded the tissue and put it back in his pocket. "Then you'll be pleased to know that a few minutes ago I have word, one of our infantry sweeps, near Sayaxché, they turn up an old man who has sold corn to an Indian from Río de la Pasión. This Indian told the old man there's a gringo in his camp."

Lyman jumped up, slammed his chair against the table. "Then what are we doing *here*? Get the choppers, for Christ's sake! Are you people crazy?"

The General raised his hand. "Moderation, my dear friend! No one knows where he's from, this Indian. The *Río*'s two hundred kilometers long, thousands of streams coming in…"

"This guy, who sold the corn –"

"He's not wanting to explain. So it takes a little while. But we cover every way out, Colonel. My men, they are hitting every part of that river, anywhere some Indian shoved aside the bugs and snakes to build his filthy little hut. If your pilot's on the *Río*, no way he's getting out."

"I remember other people," Lyman said, "being so sure of things. I had a CO in Vietnam, once, he was so sure he'd cleaned out a valley he got himself and half a platoon killed. I'm glad the gooks got him. Otherwise I would have." He looked at Vodega. "At least we should be up there, Sayax-ché, somewhere…"

"That's in hand," Arena sniffed. "The next chopper north, you two are on it."

CONSUELA ducked into the hut, her hair and poncho streaming rain. "Placido's brought corn!"

Murphy stood, wrapped his blankets round his shoulders, bent to glance beneath the dripping lintel at the charcoal sky battering the earth with rain – the huddled huts, disheveled path, and bent-down jungle drowned in gray-green aqueous light.

"I'll make tortillas," Consuela said. "There'll be food when the father comes." From under her hammock she took a wooden mortar and pestle, untied the sack of corn, poured some into the mortar, and handed him the pestle. "You do it."

He held the pestle under his left arm and began to twist it with his left hand into the corn in the mortar. "Not like that!" she chided, "keep it closer." Gripping the pestle against her flat old chest she used the forward rocking motion of her body to crunch the corn down. "This you can do, with just the good hand."

He tried it, twisting the heavy pestle down into the kernels that popped back up the mortar's worn silvery sides only to fall under the pestle again. "What does it mean, what Ofélia says – the first people came from corn?"

"Not *the* first. Here, shove the pestle down and out. Push with your weight, not against it. In the beginning, the Creators wanted to have someone to thank them. They asked Coyote how to make people, and she said make them from earth. But these earth people weren't strong, they melted in the rain. No!" Consuela scolded. "Can't you see you're pushing too hard?"

"I'm crushing the corn."

"Not too much! So Coyote told the Creators to make people from wood, and *they* will praise you. The Creators whittled people from sapwood, and these wood people made many children and covered the earth."

With his left hand Murphy moved his splinted right arm to hold the pestle. "Don't use that hand!" Consuela snapped.

"This makes it stronger."

"But then the Creators find these wood people have no hearts, no spirits. They do not remember the Heart of Heaven. They do not praise the Creators. '*De acuerdo!*' say the Creators, and bring down a black rain of flaming pitch to destroy the people of wood. This time, Coyote tells the Creators to make people from the corn."

The rain was gone. Outside the door the village hunched stained and dripping under a slaty sky. Water splattered from the thatch and bled in ochre ribbons into the *Río*. "Do the Creators think that the people of corn have hearts and spirits?"

"Not enough." Consuela sat back on her heels. "We suffer because we don't care about God. We do not praise the creation of life."

Across the river the far dark shore loomed out of the mist. A tiger heron screamed, but he could not see it.

7

"I GOT ALREADY three House committees, two Senate committees, special prosecutors, all that shit, journalists, everybody, up my back." Curt Merck's Slovac accent was burlesqued by the squawk box. "And now you can't even find this guy what did Gallagher."

"I'll find him, Curt. But we cut a deal."

"Deal? The deal is you find him."

"After I get him I go outside. With no recriminations. No callbacks."

"After this you work the basement. In the library. You can cut the grass."

"I didn't screw this op, Curt. It was screwed long before."

"It's your ass now."

Lyman checked his watch. The round clock on the signal room's yellow wall said two-thirteen – nine minutes slow. "In eight minutes I jump the slick to Sayaxché."

"You think this time you got the pilot tracked up?"

"Tracked *down*, Curt?"

"Up or down, just get him!"

"We got ten, maybe twelve villages to check. Off the Río de la Pasión, the Santa Amelia."

"I don't need to know where, Howie. Just don't be visible."

"You can't even *see* me in the jungle. Long as I don't smile."

"You're never happy enough to smile. Just get this pilot."

Lyman shook his fourth Marlboro of the day from its pack. "I'm nobody's keeper, Curt. Not even yours."

CONSUELA mixed the corn flour with lime and water and broke the dough into chunks she flattened between her palms, flipping one piece at a time on to a flat tin sheet on the coals. The tortillas as they cooked smelled like cornbread and caramel; he sat beside her, watching the pale yellow turn brown, swallowing saliva and clenching his hands.

When the first four were done she shoved them at him and started four more. He gave her two back. "If I weren't here," he said, "you could eat them all."

The hot rich tortilla flavor choked him. Unable to stop he swallowed the second, tried to stand but the room spun, making him sick.

She finished the new ones and gave him two. "We'll save the rest for tonight."

Clutching the two new tortillas he stooped under the lintel and went down to drink from the Río. A girl was gutting catfish to hang over a rack of saplings. "*Hola!* – it's you, *Guapo?*"

He grinned. "Don't call me *Guapo*."

"But you are!"

"How can you tell?" he teased.

She felt in her basket for another catfish, slit its belly and pulled out its blue-red intestines. "Besides, Consuela calls you that."

"How'd you know it was me?"

"You walk like a tapir – thump, thump, thump."

"It's just the new sandals Danielo made me. They're loose."

The tortillas were warm in his hand. I need them, he thought. Every family got the same. "Did you get corn, Epifanía?"

"Yes."

"Did you make tortillas?

"My little brother's sick. We're saving it for him."

"You'll get sick, too, if you don't eat."

She smiled. "There's the fish."

"That's Jesús's catch from yesterday – it's for the whole village." The two tortillas were beautiful in his hand; never had there been anything so complete. Her face came up, lips parting as she smelled them.

"Here," he said, "I can't eat more." She took them, fingers running over their edges, ate one and tucked the other into her dress. "Is that for later?" he said, thinking maybe she wasn't hungry – he could have it back.

"It's for my little brother."

"We've kept out some of the corn, to plant tomorrow."

"Soon as it's tall I'll be able to see again."

"Don't joke, Epifanía!"

"I *will*! I haven't always been blind. Only since the corn died."

BENEATH THE HUEY'S open cargo door the jungle seemed to roll to the ends of the earth, the river down its middle like a great silver tree of many branches. Even at three thousand feet the smells of jungle growth and decay and wet heat were stifling. Sun glittered on the treetops that each seemed to cup a sparkling bead of water in every leaf. A string of diamonds broke from the river and Lyman saw it was a flock of white birds the chopper had scared up.

The chopper's chattering *thud thud thud thud* shivered its bent, stained khaki aluminum against its missing rivets. Beside his hand on the door frame was an ancient yellow decal: "Do Not Mount Machine Gun This Side". Overhead the rotor shaft shimmied and wailed against the Jesus nut bolting it to the engine housing – you could go crazy waiting for that bolt to snap – how many had popped in Nam? When the rotors suddenly flew off and the ship dropped like a stone. Funny if that happened to him now, after all these years...

Steep palisades jutted black and treeless from the green jungle. Maybe they'd put the dam here – find the place with the biggest topographic drop, the Army Corps of Engineers had said, with the biggest potential head. No, AID had told them, put it where it floods the most, to drive these people out.

Vodega was crouched like a bat in the side door, bony shoulders tensed up around his neck, the machine gunner in a black T-shirt standing over him like a bulldog on a chain. Five soldiers sat in a clump on the vibrating cargo deck, one chewing on an unlit cigarette. Sunlight through the rotor blades fluttered on their blunt, impassive faces.

DONA VILLALOBOS shook herself awake, leaned over the dugout's side to wash her face. Rémito gunned the motor and ran the dugout up the bank. She found the gringo sleeping when she reached Consuela's hut. Such innocent faces they had, these gringos. She shook him. "Time to go!"

He sat up instantly. "Where?"

"Mexico. The Army's looking for you, checking the villages." She gripped his hand. "Press my palm with one finger at a time; I want to see how strong you are."

Her hand was hard and smooth, cool. He pressed as strongly as he could, pleased when she winced. "I can hide in the jungle," he said.

"Too dangerous." Quickly she unwrapped the splint, peeled back the dressings. "It's amazing, how you don't infect." From a US Special Forces pack she took a pair of scissor forceps, cut the black stitches sprouting like thick hairs from the bullet wound, and pulled them out of the pink, mottled flesh. "If they find you they'll kill everybody. What's your word for it – *counterinsurgency*? – for shooting the men and women and driving the kids and old people off to the camps?"

"That's not *my* word."

"What *is* your word for it, then? What your country does to mine?"

"I don't give a damn about words! You're fools, all of you! On either side. On *any* side." He stood up, wanting to cut off the aching arm, lose it forever. "It's all the same, can't you *see*? Nobody's noble, least of all you."

"You don't believe in war?"

"No."

"Where did you get them, then, the shrapnel wounds? From loving peace?"

"You don't have..."

"I couldn't help seeing them. I was healing you, remember?"

"And I'll always be grateful to you." The sun brightening her black hair made his heart plunge. Didn't she see *she*'d die too? And how senseless that was? Already he could see right through her thin envelope of skin, the nerves pulsing red and green tracers round the armature of her skull. "I was a helicopter pilot, in Vietnam. I took out the dead and wounded. And brought the new ones in."

"To do your killing for you."

"A lot of them came right back, dead."

"I was sure you'd die. I don't know why I gave you bactrin, it was a lost cause."

"Some way I'll repay you."

"I had no choice. I'm not allowed to turn you down."

"By whose law?" He stepped into the warm breeze off the river. See everything in light of the eternal. Egret winging upriver above its own reflection, white cumulus in blue sky over green jungle, the light through strands of her black hair. What a jaguar must see, stalking through tall grass. She was so small and light-limbed, animated by a strange consistency. He could see through her, how no one can be replaced, should ever be forgotten.

"Is that what God is, for you?" he asked. "The one who can't forget?"

"Someone's coming for you. In two days you'll be past Sayaxché, in three days in Mexico. If you're caught you'll be tortured unspeakably, and when you tell them about this village everyone here will be killed, and everyone else who's helped you. When you cross the Usumacinta have this cast changed and the wound checked at Bonampak. The clinic there is used to Guatemalan wounds."

"If I get caught I'll make something up, how I lived in the jungle."

"They'll want to know who made this cast."

"I did. I was a medevac."

"Eventually you'll tell the truth. They always know. It's then they kill you."

"It's crazy, what you do. You just make things worse."

"For you?"

"No! For you, and everyone else."

"Don't you see it's not enough, just to live your own life?" Strangely, she took his hand. "Once I wanted to be a brain surgeon. I wanted to understand the mystery of thought, the genesis of life. And I wanted to live a good life. But soon I realized too many people were in pain or dying for the lack of the simplest medical necessities. That I couldn't turn my back on them. That living a good life means doing as much good as you can."

"We all have altruistic reasons for what we do."

"What are the altruistic reasons for what you do?" She stepped into the dugout, yanked the cord; the motor stuttered and caught. The man with the scarred forehead came down the bank, slipped his rifle over one shoulder and climbed into the bow. She revved the motor and the dugout pulled away, its wake still lapping at the mangrove roots after its noise faded round a bend in the river.

Conchita, Placido's granddaughter, was scrubbing clothes against the river stones and hanging them like multicolored parrots on the streamside branches. "She says you are better, *Guapo*? The *doctora*?"

"She's angry I'm getting better."

"Don't mind her. It makes her sad so many people have been killed."

"I told her to stop fighting."

"She doesn't fight, that one. Anyway, it doesn't matter whether you fight or not. The Army still kills you."

He sat next to Conchita beside the clear, soft-rustling water. What could he really do? If he was tortured, what could he forget? The *Río* rolled past on its way to the sea, and he saw how the rain made it and it made the sea and the sea made the rain, and they were all the same, each a symbol for everything, and how to harm one was to harm all. The many-fingered leaves of the *quiebrahacha* drew their mantilla of shadows across his shoulders; a fish leaped, momentarily mirrored.

A change in the wind brought village smells, smoldering fires, drying thatch, ordure, mud. He thought he heard a chopper and tensed to grab Conchita, but it was a bee, bumbling in a flower. He remembered cars, noise, buildings, money, television, city crowds. How could I live like that, he wondered.

Conchita finished her clothes and walked up to the village. Jesús the son of the widow Sonora came down, took a piece of dried catfish, and crumbled it into a bottle. He waded into the *Río*, filled the bottle with water, and laid it on the bottom. Minnows crowded the bottle's mouth, darting one by one inside where they twirled among sparkling catfish scales. Against the far shore a heron flapped upriver, wingtipping the water. A flock of snowy egrets settled in the shore branches, their white reflections rippling among white water lilies. Jesús took the bottle full of minnows and set it upright in his mother's canoe and poled out beyond the shallows, a dark form against the river's verdant sheen as he baited hooks with the minnows and cast them out. A kingfisher cried as it skimmed the surface and looped up into the cobalt sky. Jesús tugged a line and drew in a bright, writhing fish.

8

FOG, alone and complete, from the edge of his skin to the ends of the world, cool damp encompassing fog.

In the center it grew darker. A shape, a *lancha*, the pillar of a man with a pole. Gold against the gray as the fog thinned.

The *lancha* slid into shore and the man drove it high up the bank with a final thrust of his pole. A hawk-eagle cried, and Murphy wondered what it must be seeing, high over the gray jungle and the fog thick down the low broad belly of the river. The man stowed his pole, shouldered a small pack and stepped onto the bank. "So," he said in English, "you're already waiting for me."

"*Como?*" Murphy stood, thinking should I run back through the village, he'll have no angle to shoot, don't run along the river, there must be others, where are they? "*No entiendo –*"

"You speak Spanish?" The man stuck out a hand. "I'm Father Miguel. The one taking you downriver."

"Now?"

"No, no," the priest chuckled. "After dark." He leaned back, hands in his pockets. "So you're the guy who crossed a hundred kilometers of impossible jungle, barefoot, with a broken arm."

"Seems long ago."

"What did you think of? What kept you going?"

"Nothing. It sounds funny, but nothing kept me going."

"Nothing doesn't exist." Ofélia came running to him and the priest swung her into his arms. "How is my *florita de Pascua*?" he laughed, bundling her against his shoulder. "By its name," he said to Murphy, "nothing cannot exist."

The fog was thinning. "The Army's coming," Murphy said.

"That's why we wait till dark."

"I won't have you risk it, just for me."

"I'm not." The priest swung Ofélia onto his shoulders and walked up into the village, the children flocking round his legs, the women running to hug and kiss him.

Dusk fell. Clouds of swallows skimmed the river; voices and fire-glimmer reflected over its sleek darkening surface. Monkeys hooted; doves chanted and nighthawks cried.

Murphy climbed the bank and wandered through San Tomás, trying to see it all for the last time, the huts with fires glowing now through cracks in their thatch, the chatter of children inside, the odors of corn flour, tortillas, chilies, squash, dried fish, rotten vegetation, mud, the crouching jungle, the dirt between his toes.

Ofélia's father Manolo sat by the door of his hut cleaning a black-powder shotgun, a gourd drum on the ground beside him. "It's a shame you're going, *yanqui*. I'd have taken you hunting tonight for *el tigre*!"

"What good am I with one arm, hunting for *el tigre*?"

"I need somebody to play this drum, to make *el tigre* come, while I sit in a tree to shoot him." Manolo held the gourd in his lap, the deerskin cover facing up, reached inside it and pulled his pinched fingers down a plaited twine of burro hair which, covered with beeswax, made a deep, reverberating growl. "See, it is something you can do one-handed."

"And that makes the jaguar come?"

"When he hears this growling sound, he is very angry and comes to see what new jaguar is roaring in his jungle."

"And in the dark you shoot him."

"*Claro que sí!*"

"And if you miss he eats me?"

"Powder's too dear. I can't afford to miss."

"And then you sell him?"

"I sell his skin in Sayaxché. The *yanqui* tourists in Tikal will always buy it."

"They're not all gone, *los tigres*?"

"For two years I do not see a track. Then since you came this one's been near. He's very rare, a black one. Like you, out of the east. Last night he slept in an *aguada*, a mangrove swamp where last year I kill a tapir. Tonight after the ceremony I go and call him. Then we'll have money for more seeds – black skins are the most valuable."

"How do you know he's black?"

"Black jaguars leave black hairs. Did you ever see one, when you were wandering in the jungle?"

"I saw nothing." Murphy's arm was hurting, and he stood, to move around. "It's dirty, your gun."

"I keep it buried, like the Bible, so the soldiers don't find it. Wrapped in deer hide, with a plug of coconut in the muzzle."

"They could come tonight, the soldiers."

Manolo glanced out at the fog coating the river and slinking up between the huts. "They come only in clear weather."

Murphy massaged his arm above the wound, driving the ache back down. "What does the Army care about the Bible?"

"You see that yellow flower? In our language it is *estapu* – very pretty. But in Spanish it is *flor de muerte*. Christ says to love and help each other. Why would the Army want us to do that?"

THE AMPHIBIOUS BOAT crossed the *Río* toward Sayax-ché, its front ramp throwing up a broad wake that sparkled in the town's lights. The ramp dropped with a muddy splash and two columns of men jogged up the bank, guns and packs clanking. Lyman's palms itched; pulse darted down his wrists like lightning. "*Usted!*" he shouted, grabbing a soldier.

"*Sí!*" the soldier yelled, startled, saluting. He peered at Lyman out of the dark. "*Sí, Coronel!*"

Lyman snatched the man's Galil. "Where's your goddamned bayonet?"

"Here, sir!" The man slapped his belt.

"Mount it!"

"Now, sir?"

"Goddammit it, yes! We're going into battle!" He spun round, glared at the others. "All of you, mount bayonets!"

"There's still the flight upriver," Vodega said.

Lyman glanced toward the voice, saw Vodega's slender form on the dark side, by some upturned *lanchas*. He wondered what Vodega had been doing there. "The men should be pumped. I want them hungry!"

"In your ardor, Colonel, don't forget they aren't your men, they're mine."

"I pay for them. I pay for you too."

"I pay my own way. Guatemala pays its own way."

"By cornering the weed market? That's how your Army pays its way?"

"That's why Gallagher was here. And that's what got him into trouble, isn't it? *Lieutenant!*" Vodega called. "Tell the men to dismount bayonets." His voice swung back to Lyman. "I don't want bayonets mounted in my helicopters."

"*Your* helicopters? Shit!" Lyman turned away, boots slithering in the riverside crud.

EPIFANIA'S FATHER José had set up an altar of lashed saplings at one end of his palm-thatched shed that stood between the village and the *Río*. On the altar an earthen bowl sat between two candles on a white cloth; in the bowl were three tortillas. Stars gleamed through slits in the palm fronds. "We're here to celebrate the life of he who was willing to give what is complete in him," said Father Miguel, "for what is missing in us."

Some of the people murmured; a sense of agreement seemed to ripple through them. "You have been gifted by a visitor to whom you gave the gift of life. Now he leaves but you live within him as he in you, although you may both forget this. Just as when he traveled injured through the jungle he says that nothing was with him, and does not remember. This is true of us all: we do not remember the gift of life."

Murphy walked down to the river where stars rippled among the black grass stalks and the wide ebony water mirrored the pulse of the universe. It would not come back. Only pieces – a scrap of terror, lash of branches, bare foot torn and bloody, the pounding asphyxiation down inside the *cenote*, the hunger, snakes, the Mayan scorpion that became a Huey with his own dead copilot still belted in, a black widow nesting in his cratered skull.

Had there been a feeling? After the first day, something balancing the pain? A waiting? A willingness to suffer? For what?

Genetic. The ones without fear of death were selected out long ago, he thought. The longer we survive the stronger is the urge for life.

"This is the body of Christ." The priest's voice was like the river. "The lamb of God who takes away the sins of the world."

After so many years, Murphy realized, it comes right back: the cold stone church floor against your kneecaps, wind sneaking like a cat under the door, stained windows patched with packing tape. Then door to door, the canvas bag of newspapers biting into your shoulder, snow like broken glass crunching underfoot, dawn turning purple over the black plains. But back then you thought God could take away your sins.

Now you're trying to bring yourself back inside. Like a reformed druggie teasing himself with the needle. A family man hungry for a hooker. Back inside the reason that has no meaning but the one *you* give it. But for you there's no reason at all.

The people gathered round the priest and he gave them each a chunk of tortilla. "The body of Christ," he said.

"*El cuerpo de Cristo.*" It was Erendria, the old woman, a great-grandmother whose men all were dead. Then Placido, who'd brought corn, who every evening gathered the children on the river bank to write Spanish words in the mud with pointed sticks. Then the children, ones who had sat beside Murphy in his pain and solitude, sung him scraps of song, told stories in Quiché, brought him limes and bits of melon saved out from their food. It seemed right to do it, silly as it was, and he waited in line behind the girl Conchita, thinking that even her name meant Little Immaculate Conception, she whose glossy black hair came up to his splinted arm; she bent and took her scrap of tortilla and moved aside, and the priest held up a tan chunk of tortilla and said *el cuerpo de Cristo* and he answered *Amen*, remembering *amen* means *it is true*.

The piece of tortilla came down in the priest's fingers and as he took it into his mouth he understood, and remembered that he'd understood before, that this *is* the body of Christ, that a chunk of corn flour in the skinny fingers of a priest becomes the son of God who gives himself to us so we can become a tiny bit more like him. Crossing himself he turned away, anxious to be alone.

In the north was distant thunder. Rain tonight, Murphy thought. We'll get wet, going downriver. But the thunder was familiar, wrong. "Choppers!" he screamed. "The Army! Soldiers!"

They clattered down over the treetops and settled on the new-sown corn, black scorpions with long black M60D machine gun stingers, jet engines wailing, flares sizzling down on little parachutes out of the night. "Get away!" the priest screamed at him. "If they see us they'll kill everyone!"

Soldiers running along the bank. In the flarelight Epifanía's fish rack tumbling. The priest shoved Murphy ahead of him, down to the *Río* and along its banks, boughs lashing their faces, the clatter of rotors and their huffing breath and the splash of their feet loud in the flare-bright night. They circled the village on the jungle edge. Another chopper roared over, frothing the river and battering down the mangroves. Under the glaring flares the soldiers circled, driving the people before them.

9

THREE CHOPPERS had landed; another circled. The soldiers forced everyone to the center by Manolo's hut. A small slender officer was taking the people aside one by one and asking them something to which they all seemed to answer no. A soldier came out of Manolo's hut holding up the old shotgun. The small officer took out his pistol; Manolo shook his head, pointed at the jungle. Two soldiers tied him to a tree. The officer stepped back among the huts and spoke with another, much taller, black, who leaned over to hear, cupping his hand over his ear against the choppers' roar. Rotor wash knocked off his fatigue cap and he ran after it, came back banging it against his knee.

Ofélia ran to Manolo and he shoved her away. The small officer was yelling questions at Manolo and smacking him with the pistol each time he answered. Ofélia clung to Manolo's leg; the officer bent and spoke to her, patted her head, motioned her back. "Even if they kill him," the priest said to Murphy, "do nothing."

The officer pointed at Placido and the soldiers tied him beside Manolo. Consuela knelt before the officer, her hands clasped, speaking up to him. "They'll shoot these two," Father Miguel said. "You must do nothing, or they'll kill them all."

There were forty soldiers, maybe, plus the chopper still circling, and no way to crawl closer without being seen. Guns snapped; Manolo and Placido jerked back against the tree and slumped, Manolo's heels digging the dirt as if still trying to escape death. Flames climbed the side of Manolo's hut.

Sonora shoved Jesús through the circle of soldiers; they ran after her and knocked her down, two holding her wrists and two her ankles apart as another unclasped his belt and fell on top of her, keeping his face above her snapping teeth till another thumped her with his rifle and she lay still. Jesús ran back at them; they knocked him to the ground and tossed him over the bank, his body slapping down into the shallows. Two soldiers cut Manolo and Placido from the tree and threw them into the burning hut; laughing, one wiped bloody hands on the other's back. The man on top of Sonora stood buckling his trousers and another replaced him.

"Stay here!" the priest whispered. He darted along the bank past Epifanía's fish racks, snatched up Jesús and ran back. "Take him downriver to the first rocks and hide him in the mangroves!" Whimpering, the boy tried to squirm free. "God keeps you!" the priest said. "Go!"

Murphy carried Jesús along the river in the shadow of the bank, then waist-deep around the mangrove roots, searchlights skipping over the water. A rifle chattered and he thrust the boy under; nothing hit near them. Where Conchita had been washing clothes he shoved the boy into a crevice in the rocks. *Stay* here!" He ran back upriver to the edge of the village.

He could not see the priest. Soldiers were pulling toward a hut but she broke free and sprinted across the dead corn toward the trees, her hair sailing out behind her, the stubble spurting with bullets as the flying chopper closed in. She sprawled but leaped up again, scrambled back toward the village, the chopper tilting to fire straight down but she zigzagged again for the jungle, a chain of bullets racing after her. As she reached the first trees they hammered her down, her limbs tumbling, her red cape windblown in the chopper's wake. Guns thundered, the people screaming; Murphy ran across the cornfield, smashed into a soldier and grabbed his gun but the gun wouldn't fire and he bayoneted the man in the groin then the belly, lunged at another, tripping him with the bayonet then jabbing it into his throat, but it stuck in his vertebrae and he couldn't pull it out; an M60 brayed, its roar smashing his ears; he grabbed the second soldier's rifle and fired at the M60; bullets hit beside him, shuddering the earth and spinning the bayoneted soldier. Soldiers were beating someone with rifles, forcing him into a chopper; Murphy saw it was the priest and ran after them. A white light tore into his skull and the ground came up and smacked his face but he rolled up and sprinted for the chopper, soldiers yelling and tackling him; the chopper took off, its lights caught him as he dashed through bright humming whistling bullets toward the village where Consuela crawled sideways dragging pink intestines, Ofélia's bludgeoned body lay in the flames, her hair sizzling, Erendría sat with her broken head clasped in both hands, Epifanía stumbled in circles, wailing. With the empty rifle he clubbed down a soldier, grabbed Epifanía and ran for the jungle, bullets riddling branches, splintering holes through black-white trees; he tripped light-blinded over vines, bodies, stones, dove into the river and swam out beyond the lights, holding Epifanía in the crook of his broken arm.

He reached the rocks. "Jesús!" he whispered; there was no answer. Epifanía clung to him. "Make them stop!" she screamed. "Make them stop!"

Rifle staccato erupted in the village, faded into the snapping crackling flames. Another chopper took off, the hum of its rotors deepening as the pilot changed their pitch. "Jesús!" Murphy whispered.

The fireglow above the trees made the river darker. He hid the girl in the rocks, swam downriver, called, went further, called again. He went ashore and ran back to the rocks, trying not to slosh. As he reached the rocks soldiers came wading downriver, their lights flashing. He ran up the bank; someone leaped, knocking him down, pummeling fists, "Jesús!" Murphy hissed. "It's me!"

He led Epifanía and Jesús back through the mangroves, his shins and ankles banging on their roots, the mud underfoot cold, mushy, and tangled with rootlets. Epifanía bumped into Murphy and pushed ahead, moving faster than he through the darkness, waiting for him and Jesús where the mangroves thinned and they scrambled through saplings where he could see nothing, not even the branches before his face, tried to stand but other branches held him down, their leaves rasping as he forced them aside.

A flashlight glinted off the trees, neared then died. Murphy forced the children under a fallen trunk. A stick snapped against his leg; he reached for it and felt a snake's tail, rattles, the snake's head pinned under his knee.

"What's that?" a voice said.

"It's you, pissing your pants," another snickered, hoarser.

Murphy pushed his knee down harder on the snake's head. "Ain't nothing here," the first voice said.

"That's why *we're* here." A match rasped and flared.

"Disgusting," said the first voice.

"More decorations for the *capitán*."

Murphy felt left-handed down the snake's writhing body to its tail and snapped the rattles. "Sickens me," the first repeated. There was the smell of marijuana smoke, a sigh, the spatter of urine. Murphy slid his hand up the snake to its neck. Beyond the downed trunk a cigarette glimmered in a cupped hand, disclosing a sloped, big-nosed face.

Murphy gripped the snake's neck behind the wing-shaped bones of its skull and twisted. "What *is* that?" the hoarse one said. The flashlight clicked on, its beam darting under the downed tree, boots crunching nearer. Epifanía tensed. Murphy tossed the snake over the trunk. "Aiee, *serpiente!*" yelled the hoarse one. Murphy pushed the children further along the trunk.

"Who's that?" someone said, in front of them.

"Snake," repeated the hoarse one. "I've got him."

Murphy led the children from the downed tree, behind them the soldiers' laughter and the thump of boots stomping the snake. Tendrils and vines dragged at the children's clothes; twigs and dead leaves rattled as small animals fled through the scrub. "That you, Mico?" a new voice said.

"I'm here," a gravelly one answered.

"Then what the hell's that?"

Murphy eased forward one foot, rustling a twig. A leaf snapped. He raised the foot, bumped a liana and side-stepped it. A tree was there; he leaned back and moved further right. Epifanía's hair caught on a thorn bush; the leaves scratched as she tried to free it. Murphy reached behind her and, holding the thorns, pulled her hair away. "You're going the wrong way, Mico," the gravelly voice continued.

"I'm over here, asshole! That's snakes you're hearing. Shine your light on them!"

Light shimmered through walls of vines, stems, trunks, and leaves, did not touch them. The gravelly voice and the one called Mico moved past. Murphy and Jesús followed the girl in a wide circle behind the village and upriver. Another chopper rose from the village and fluttered away, its throb fading. From time to time rifles fired like lone fire-crackers long after a celebration has ended. The blind girl moved steadily, as if she could see through the jungle night, Jesús behind her, then Murphy with one hand held before his eyes to ward off branches.

10

EACH TIME THE HUEY banked the priest's blood ran in streaks across the rattling deck; Lyman tried not to step in it. The scent up out of the jungle was like orchids, sharper than the jet kero vapor from the leaking fuel line or the charred cordite of the M60D.

The priest lay with his cheekbone crushed, his nose ripped open and bent to one side. His collarbone looked broken, too, one arm dislocated at the elbow and shoulder. The wrist was bent, too, clearly broken. Lucky for him, Lyman thought, that I was there to save him.

With his boot Vodega poked the priest's broken mouth. The priest pulled back his head; Vodega kicked him.

"Let it be," Lyman said.

In the weird downcast shadows of the crew light Vodega's muddy, bloody smile seemed painted on, a mask. His boot squelched into the priest's face.

"Come on, Angelo, let him be."

"It's between him and me," Vodega said in English. "He wants it – reliving the passion of our Lord…"

Lyman spat out the cargo door, the wind snatching it. The guy who'd run across the field, back there, what if he wasn't a *guerrillero* like these goons think? What if he's the American, the one who killed Gallagher? And we let him get away?

The priest will know. Once we get him in the confessional the priest will want to tell us. And these goons were going to kill him.

He leaned along the safety strap to the M60D and slipped his hands into its grips. They felt good and tight against his palms, his fingers strong around them. He pointed down and squeezed a burst at the river, the muzzle leaping, red tracers diving fast into the jungle. He lowered the muzzle more and fired again, digging a row of black geysers up the moonlit water. "Don't," the door gunner said. "Bullets are for people."

EPIFANIA LED THEM back to the *Río* then upriver in the shallows. A low moon bled across the water then fell behind the hills. Birds twittered, began to chant. The river brightened from mercury to silver as the stars died.

Over the din of monkeys, birds, and insects there came no sound of choppers. Jesús led now, Murphy last. An alligator slapped its tail on the bank and dived past him, clawing his thigh. The far shore took form out of the darkness, till every leaning bough and tall crown stood clear above its jade reflection.

Over their splashing footfalls he listened for choppers. If the soldiers had come for *you* then *you* caused it, he told himself. Or if they *saw* you. But they didn't see you till after they started shooting. What if you'd just gone forward, surrendered? Would they have killed them then? But maybe they came for the priest, and it wasn't your fault. Except the priest came to take *you* downriver.

If you'd gone out to them right away, maybe they wouldn't have killed everyone. Except the priest told you not to. You figured he knew more than you so you did what he said. Maybe he was just covering for you. But you took him at his word.

Mist was rising off the river like smoke from flowing lava. The treetops of the far shore floated on a band of white, then were gone.

No matter what, they were looking for you. That's why they trashed everyone. So it's *you*.

An eagle whistled, far and faint behind them. The children stopped, spun round, Epifanía holding up her hand.

It came again, up the dark channel of mist. Jesús tilted back his head and screeched, the high bitter cry of an eagle, and the other answered.

"He's coming," Epifanía said. "He hears you."

It was a dugout with an old man in the stern who jabbed his pole into the mud to stop. He spoke in Kekchi to the children and they answered simply, without emotion.

"He'll take us upriver," Jesús said. Murphy held the gunnel for the children to climb in. "Tell him I'm going back."

Jesús told the old man and he shook his head, clamped a hand round Murphy's wrist. "He's been to the village," Jesús said to Murphy. "Everyone's dead."

"Except the priest," Murphy said. "Tell him they took the priest."

Jesús told the old man, who did not answer, steadying the dugout with his pole while Murphy climbed in and sat in the bow. The old man backed the dugout from shore and turned upriver, poling along the shallows.

Mist rose around them. The mangroves along the near shore faded. The air was thick and white. Water rippled past the hull, up and down the old man's pole. The canoe's prow grew hazy, vanished, the thwart and Murphy's hand atop it indistinct.

"Epifanía?" he said.

"*Sí?*"

"What did the little soldier ask everyone, at the start?"

"He was asking if they had seen you. They all said no."

DONA ELENA VILLALOBOS snuggled down into her warm blanket, the hammock swaying gently. She raised her feet to swing the bottom of her tarp back under the blanket. The Galil lay beside her, its clip facing away, its barrel warm from her body.

Red sun streaked through the high, vaulting boughs. A drop of dew spiraled down layered beams of sunlight and hit her nose, spattering on her lip. She licked it, rubbed her nose against the blanket. How lovely to lie for a moment warm and peaceful, in the first magnificence of day.

11

BEYOND THE PROW a dark line cut the mist. The water turned pewter, molten; the dark line was the shore, tangled mangroves with sun bronzing their leaves. The sky turned blue; sun beat on the water. The old man poled the dugout up a narrow creek, leaves lashing their faces. When they could go no further he tied up to a root, spoke to the children.

"He says wait," Jesús said. "Someone will come."

"Where's he taking you?"

The boy asked the man, who said something then shook his head. "Can't say," Jesús said to Murphy. He came near and Murphy bent down and took him in his arms, then Epifanía. Jesús's eyes kept filling with tears and he wiped at them angrily.

"Can't I go with you, *Guapo*?" Epifanía said.

"Where I'm going it's too dangerous. Here there are people who'll look after you."

"You'd look after me too. I know you would. I'll be a good help soon, soon I'll see."

"He's going to fight the soldiers," Jesús said. "That's why we can't go with him."

He held them both, sensing that whatever he did it would be wrong. "I swear I'll come back for you. For you both. We'll go up north," he said to her, "and try to fix your eyes. And we'll go to Montana, Jesús, to the clear water mountains to fish for trout." He stood, dizzy and nauseous, not wanting to let go. "I swear it."

The old man spoke; the children pulled away and followed him through a path in the bracken into the jungle.

Murphy lay on the mud by the canoe. Blood trickled down over his brow into his eye, across his nose, blocking it when he breathed. He lay on his back but the arm hurt too much so he lay on his side, his head tilted back.

The day grew hot and heavy. His bloody scalp buzzed with flies. He crawled into the creek, drank, vomited, drank, and vomited again. Once a chopper went over, quiet as a dragonfly. Jets passed, high up; he could not see them through the treetops.

He contemplated the canoe. There was the knob of a bough cut off halfway down the side; it had thirteen rings.

He could not help these people. He could not let them help him. He could not take the canoe. He could not get downriver without one. It was too far, from here, to walk through the jungle to Mexico.

He could make a raft. There would be lianas, logs, sticks. He let his head fall softly into the mud. When he awoke he'd build a raft.

When he awoke the fog was back, the dusk. Was it only last night the priest had come? He looked round the hut for Consuela, listened for children's voices. There was no hut, no voices.

A round-faced boy with a rifle came through the bracken. He was dragging a dead baby by the hand. Then Murphy saw it was a monkey. The boy tossed the monkey into the dugout. "Let's go!"

"Go to Hell."

"Hurry!" The boy pulled him up easily by the good arm and made him sit in the dugout. He poled back down the creek and out on to the *Río*. A string of cormorants scampered downriver and lumbered up into the gloom.

The pole plunked, sucked free, plunked, sucked free, the *Río* churning at the prow. Ticks were climbing from the monkey up the dugout's hull. Murphy trailed his fingers in the fleeting cool water. A nighthawk screamed; a fish tail smacked.

After dark the fog lifted; the wind switched to the north, chilling his face. "Let me pole now, Niño," he said.

"Later."

From the east a towering wind came whipping the treetops. A wall of rain roared across the water, driving icy needles into their necks and shoulders, poured down their backs and cascaded into the hull. The boy yelled something and tossed him a can and he knelt bailing as the boat filled with rain; the rain fell harder, shattering the river, emptying the sky.

LYMAN TOOK A TAXI into Cobán and had a gin and tonic at the Hotel Excelso. The bar faced a dining room where no one sat. Beyond it was a half-lit garden where rain slanted across a Mayan pillar topped by four grinning jaguar heads. At the far end of the bar a tall, grim man in a too-wide gray suit and wet shoes stood with a fat, smaller man also in gray, their air furtive, as if even doing business together could get them killed.

Lyman downed another gin and took a taxi to the Little Pigs, a shack lit by two kerosene lanterns, smelling of tobacco and spilt beer. The bar girl was short with a round Mayan face and body and wore a yellow dress that made Lyman watch her breasts.

"Lousy night," he said to the barman.

The barman inclined his head.

"Can I get a beer?"

"Why else would I be here? El Gallo?"

"What else you got?"

"Nothing."

"El Gallo, then."

When the first was gone the man brought him another, a third and fourth. He watched the bar girl serving the four plank tables where a few peasants sat like cavemen waiting out the winter. He imagined holding the girl's naked ass in his hands. "I'll have some rum," he told the barman.

He raised the glass slowly, tasting the rim. Tonight one cigarette. He smiled, thinking how good that cigarette would be. How to make it *last*. How do you make *life* last?

Another fruitless day, he thought. Another meaningless night. At the end do we get punished for all our meaningless days? Father, one day, barefoot, trousers rolled to his knees, a red cap on his head, had walked up a greasy road through the Mississippi woods and had never come back. And we had sat by the pond, Aunt Ettah and Lila and I, not knowing. He'd gone because I'd argued with him, said talking to me was like talking to a block of wood. And they all blamed me. They all blame me.

The barman refilled his glass. "Nice here," Lyman said. Just keep changing – that makes life last. "I'm going to Petén for the temples. How's it up there?"

"It's fine," the barman said.

"Fine for what?"

"Fine for temples, anything."

"No danger of rebels?"

"Ask the authorities." The barman nodded his chin in the direction of the Military Base.

"I'm asking *you*."

The barman rolled up the wick of a kerosene lantern, stepped back to look at Lyman in its brighter light. "I have no idea."

THE RAIN STOPPED; the clouds parted; the last wraiths of mist slunk away across the water. At a bend in the river the boy turned ashore and tied up in the lee of a fallen tree. Bullfrogs croaked steadily. "I just want a place to sleep," Murphy said. The boy tossed the dead monkey over his shoulder and led Murphy uphill to a hut in a grove of banana trees. Lantern light shone through its rush walls; inside someone was moaning. The boy entered and someone came out. "Where are you?" she said in English. "I can't see in the dark."

"It's you! What are you doing here?"

Dona reached out and took him in her arms. "Oh, I'm sorry, so sorry," holding him tight, her voice against his chest. "I'm so sorry," she kept saying, holding him, swaying with him, her hair in his face as he bent down to her and finally held her too, the two of them together.

"I did it," he said.

She looked up at him. "You? What do you mean?"

"They were looking for me. Like you said."

"No!" She shook her head wildly. "They killed everybody because it was a reprisal, for an attack on a convoy. They picked it because it's a village that refused to go to the camps. It's not you."

"They were your people too."

She held him tighter. "It won't go away."

"Nothing ever goes away. And nothing ever stays."

She shook her head. "Only the two children? No one else?"

"The old man went back. He says no."

She reached up, held his face in both hands. "You're so feverish! This is blood! You're hurt?" Quickly her fingers traced the edges of the wound. "Come, let's get you into the light."

"No." He sat on the short, wet grass. "They came for me, the Army. And I didn't know it was for me. So I hid, like Father Miguel said. I should've surrendered."

She held his face as if to purge his thoughts. "If you had they would've killed everyone, just as surely." She held him one last time. "Come into the hut. I must see this wound. We will give you something hot."

"TWENTY QUETZALES," the bar girl said, cocky hope and fear in her eyes.

"Fifteen." Lyman put his hands in his pockets so she wouldn't see them tremble. "For all night."

The silky, black top of her head did not come up to his shoulder as she stood beside him while he paid for the room at the Hotel Excelso. He followed her up the stairs, watching her thighs for the dark place between them. The room was long and thin as a boxcar, a window at the far end, a single bed across the middle. Next to the bed was a chair with a lamp and a stub of candle in a beer bottle. He lit the candle and put out the lamp.

She stood with arms folded while he tucked back her hair and kissed her neck. She smelt like fruit, like passion fruit. He could see umber nipples beneath her low halter. There was a nervous taste in the back of his mouth. He reached into the halter and played with a wide, flat breast.

She dropped her dress. Her breasts swayed like pomegranates. Her pale, stringy underpants sloped into her crotch. Her skin looked oiled in the viscous light. He took off his clothes and lay beside her, caressed her. He could not will himself to harden. She would not touch him. He thought of Nancy's thighs around a stranger's neck. He stuck his finger up inside the girl; she sucked in breath.

He mounted her but could not enter. She stared sideways at the cracked wall where the candle cast spider web shadows. "Don't be sad," she said.

He paid her twenty quetzales and the taxi. The night had chilled. A crescent moon was going down, Hydra slinking west. He walked out of Cobán toward the Base, his stomach eerie as though his marriage had just died.

12

INSIDE THE HUT a fire hissed, a kettle on a pole across it. A woman lay on a mat, under blankets, knees drawn up. "What do you mean, a reprisal?" Murphy said.

"The guerrillas destroyed a convoy, last week, on the Flores road. We think the government attacked your village for that…"

"Can I use the kettle?" the boy said.

Dona glanced at the woman on the mat. "She'll need hot water."

"She needs food more."

"Put half the water in a bowl. Very soon I'll want the kettle."

With a machete the boy slit the monkey's belly. The woman on the mat made a clenched cry and Dona went to her. "*Qué hubo?*"

The woman writhed, could not speak. "*Nada,*" she said finally. "*Lo mismo.*" Dona felt the woman's swollen belly. "It's never *lo mismo, carina.* You're getting closer." She stood. "It's a breech birth," she said in English. "Caesarean, has to be. But I have no anesthetic."

"You'd do that here?"

"*Here* is not the problem. In the mountains, under a poncho in the rain, I have done brain surgery. Removing metal fragments." She sighed. "Why am I telling you these things? Come, let me look at your head!"

He sat by the fire while she washed the wound with hot water that stung unbearably. Each time the woman had a contraction Dona went to her. The boy finished skinning the monkey, laid it over a log to disjoint it.

"The bullet glanced off this place where the two sutures of your skull come together," Dona said. "So maybe it's just broken the edges. I can feel them move."

He pushed her hand away. "It was fine till you messed with it."

"That's true, it was. You just *don't* infect. Only a little, here, up under the hair." She soaked the blood and scab until she could pull the hairs free. "Amazing you didn't break the arm again. Tomorrow, in the light, we'll make a new cast. But you have a monstrous concussion, I'm sure. You feel dizzy, very weak?"

The boy finished chopping up the monkey and set the innards aside. He poured some of the hot water from the kettle into a clay bowl and set the kettle back on its pole over the coals. He put the monkey's head and all the chopped pieces into the kettle, added fresh splits of wood to the fire, and took the innards outside. The woman writhed, relaxed, panting. "It's coming, *cariña*," Dona kept saying, wiping the woman's face.

"There's nothing you can give her," Murphy said, "to ease the pain?"

Dona moved from the woman back to him, cleaning the wound. "You think if there was something I would not give it to her?"

"I don't think it was a reprisal, my village."

"They came because they were looking for you, but they killed everyone because of the convoy."

He looked up at her kneeling above him, one half of her face firelit, the other shadowed. We all have two sides, he thought. "Then we share the blame."

"If you're hungry for blame there's always plenty to be found."

"The government has its army, and you have yours. But it's the people who suffer."

"Every person in your village was part of the *guerrilla*, fought for it every way she could, he could."

"Even the children?"

"If you were a child seeing your parents killed, losing your older brothers one by one?"

"It keeps war going, that kind of thinking."

"Every village in the Petén's the same. Everything the Army does just makes it worse. There'll be war till everyone's dead."

"You like that?"

"I'm a doctor. I wish the war would stop. I think it's better to be a slave than dead. But the war's going on anyway. It won't stop. So do I go away and never think of it? Or do I stay and try to help?"

The boy came back with roots and the innards he had washed in the *Río*. He cut up the intestines on the log and put them in the pot with the rest of the innards and the roots.

"But you're *not* trying to help," Murphy said. You're a *guerrillera*. A maker of war."

"And I say to you, everyone here who thinks and dreams, everyone who has known pain, is a *guerrillero*."

"Dreams always fail."

"I have no bandages but will wrap this in a strip of clean *india*. You must wash the wound twice a day, with hot, boiled water." She tied off the colored cloth, pulling the last hairs free from under it.

"Why are they hunting me? At least ten grass planes fly out of the Petén every week."

"The Army's attacking other drug flights too. They're even killing the people who pay them for protection. But they are not suddenly against the *mariquana*, because they're still flying it themselves. Your friends, the ones killed when your plane got burned – they paid protection?"

"Every month ten thousand dollars, right to the top. Some General named Elena. Every shipper from Guatemala pays him the same."

"Elena? There is no General Elena. Arena, maybe?"

"Arena? Arena. Yes. That's it."

"He's the Director of Counterinsurgency. If an attack was ordered on your village, he was the one. Soon he's to be Chief of the Armed Forces."

"Where is he?"

"He's in Cobán, sometimes in Guatemala City. But you won't find him. Better you go back to America, to the television, tell them what happened to your village. The Indian villages are napalmed, the people driven into camps to starve behind electric wires. Children shot in the street, women in the fields. For nothing. Because they are Indians. Tell them it's happening everywhere in Guatemala. That America must stop paying for the Guatemalan Army."

"Their guns are Israeli – I saw them. Galils."

"America passes money to Israel for Guatemala, to get around the ban of your Congress against sending too much money to Guatemala. Israel built a Galil factory in Guatemala City, sends all the napalm, other explosives. Israeli pilots teach the Guatemalans how to make low-level bombing runs on villages. Mossad taught the Army how to run the IBM computers it has in Guatemala City."

"It makes my head hurt – your propaganda – everybody's."

"It's even in *our* newspapers, and they're certainly not free." She turned to the boy. "Soon I'll need the kettle, Pollo."

"It's not half done," Pollo said.

"There's the bailing can," Murphy said. "In the canoe. I'll get it." The air outside was cool and fresh after the smoky hut, the stars a vast explosion of light. He went across the clearing down to the *Río* and knelt to drink, the water rising up his wrist as his hand sank into the mud. He filled the bailing can, went back to the fire, and set it on the coals.

When the water boiled Dona put her instruments in it. The woman kept crying out. "Sorry, *Doctora*," she gasped. "Can't stop."

"We must choose, *cariña*. The baby's still blocked and I can't get his head down. He'll die if he doesn't come out soon. I must cut you open, the stomach, as I showed you. But there's nothing I can give you, for the pain."

"*Aguardiente?*"

"No, there's nothing."

"Do it."

"You will help me, gringo? First use a little of this soap to wash your hands with some hot water. Then give me the instruments I ask for. And Pollo bring the water, when I say."

The woman's belly was enormous. Murphy tried not to look at her swollen, bleeding vagina. Dona washed the woman's stomach with a piece of *india* and the tiny chunk of soap. She traced on the skin with her finger, changing positions and looking at it from different angles. The woman twisted up her body, clawing the mat. "*Momentino, cariña,*" Dona said. "*Momentino.*"

She took the scalpel and cut a steady long diagonal down across the belly. The woman shrieked, tears pouring across her face, fists against her teeth. "Take her hands, Pollo!" Dona said. She made a second cut, blood spurting out black in the dim light and pooling against the cloths she kept rolled round the cut. She pulled up the skin, cutting beneath to separate it from the muscle, then slit down into the muscle, the little cords popping back. "More cloths," she said, tossing the blood-soaked ones aside. "He's moving, *cariña*, your baby's moving."

The turgid womb beneath was purple-colored. The woman's mouth was bleeding; she's bit her tongue, Murphy thought. "Check her pulse," Dona said.

"Steady. A little faint."

"Keep watching it. Give me the number three scalpel now – quick – wash this off before you put it in the water, hurry! And string the big needles now, like I showed you!"

The scalpel blade sank into the bursting flesh. It's thick, the uterus, Murphy thought. The fire hissed and Pollo went to it, came back. "It's almost done, the stew."

The woman's hand in Murphy's was hot and weak, her breast throbbing. In the pool of sweat and tears in the corner of her eye the rush mats of the ceiling were reflected. Her whole body trembled; I've seen that, he thought, the tremor mortis. "I have him!" Dona gasped. "Slowly now he's coming."

She raised a clump of bloody organs in her hands and he thought it was the placenta then saw its wizened Mayan head, the tiny gaping mouth, the twig arms and taut belly with the umbilical cord plunging down. "It's a girl, *cariña*! A cloth, Pollo! Hold her, gringo, while I get the rest."

The baby weighed nothing in his hands, a bloody bitter face choked with horror. This is what it is, he thought, making love. Where did you come from?

"Quick!" Dona held the baby's head down, sucked out her lungs and spat; the baby jerked, convulsed, wailed a high, tiny cry. "More cloths," Dona said.

"No more," Pollo answered.

"My coat then, by the door."

She wrapped the wailing baby in her camouflage jacket. "A big needle, now, gringo. You're sure you've threaded three of them? And then the little ones. Remember, the light thread not the black one. Take her, *cariña*, quickly, she needs milk!"

The baby gummed a nipple, took a breath and wailed, sucked again. Everyone's sacred, Murphy suddenly understood. Everyone's been through this mystery. Up out of the water into the air. Gasping, stunned, dragged like an innocent fish from the sea.

"The smaller needles now, gringo." When she had finished suturing the uterus Dona gathered the muscles together one by one and sutured them with lighter needles and the same pale thread. Pollo took the afterbirth down to the river and then the cloths to wash them. "The stew's done," he said.

When she had finished the muscles she sewed up the skin with the black thread. Now that the woman's belly was less swollen the incision seemed smaller. Pollo washed her face and hands with the last of the hot water and brought her a cup of broth from the stew.

Murphy sat with Dona and Pollo by the fire, the bailing can half full of stew, chewing the last shreds from a shoulder bone. The woman lay silent, the baby whimpering at her breast. Out of the kettle the monkey's eyeless skull stared up at them.

13

LYMAN KICKED at a stone, heard it skitter along the gravel and hop into the grass. You should've stayed with the girl, he reminded himself, stopped to piss by a clump of cedars, holding a branch for balance. Behind the cedars rose a broken stone wall. Ahead were more cedars and a white fence, then dark scrub, a moonlit meadow. Take away color, he thought, you still get black and white.

The piss spattered on the rocks, sparkling. Rum and beer. Bad fuckin combination. And your combination doesn't fuck at all. But gets high thinking of other people doing it. People you know.

If your fly won't zip what if you leave it down? Why have a fly at all? To cover up your rod. Why have a rod? To make sure you're a God. Rocks stumbly underfoot, don't let 'em trip you. Halfway home. Fix the fuckin road, Lawd,

"Why don't they fix it in the road, Lawd,

"Why don't they fix the fucking road?

"Why don't they cover up their God, Lawd,

"Why don' –"

Horrible compression of air whizzed past his skull. He dove into the ditch as the sound of the shot crackled and banged up through the hills. In the ditch no cover, every stub and leaf sharp-cut. Clear ground uphill, a few bushes dark against the milky slope. Ahead a bare grassy channel, ditch shallowing to pale empty ground. Any way you go he's got you.

The pilot. He's followed you. Wants you to fear before you die.

Close-cropped grass, a boulder, the far dark hollow of the road to town, distant streetlights on the church face. He'll hit you before the boulder. Even if he misses he'll pin you at the boulder and you're worse off there than here.

Not a Galil, an M-16. Wind crossed the road, odors of mud, trees, cattle. He's in the cedars, behind the white fence. With a perfect field of fire.

You're going to cross the road and kill him.

"HE'S NOT THE ONLY PRIEST in a Guatemalan jail. And even if he's still alive, there's nothing we can do."

"I'm not going to leave him. In a sense he gave his life for mine."

"That's what priests do. You can't change that." Dona took a bowl of stew and sat across from Murphy at the fire, cross-legged. "You're very good with bandages and sutures. Where did you learn it?"

"The medics. I'd go in, to get some wounded guys, I'd get pinned or the chopper'd get hit, there'd be no medic or the medic would be dead or there's too many wounded coming in, so you learn what you can. While they die all around you."

"And in hospital?"

"I was only there a month. Hawaii. Soon as my wounds closed up they shipped me back. They were short of chopper pilots just then." He looked at the dirt floor, seeing the ward, the boys paralyzed from the neck down, the blind, the maimed, the ones with brand new steel skulls begging to die. "I learned there, too, how to care for people."

She reached out, squeezed his leg. "You see, you're just like me."

He shook his head. "I've learned every time you try to do good you just cause more pain."

"And now you want to find Father Miguel. Isn't that trying to do good?"

"No. That's just settling scores."

She sucked the marrow from a wristbone and dropped it in the fire. After a moment it began to hiss. "Before Vietnam, what were you?"

"A kid from west Texas. With a grin and a pickup truck. At least that's how I look in the photos."

"And now you're a drug pilot."

"Was. I don't have a plane anymore."

"You must have insurance?"

"They don't sell insurance for my kind of work."

"And you liked it, that work?"

"It kept me alive. Like the signs on the cement trucks in San Francisco: 'Find a Need and Fill It'. Like vodka or Valium or baseball or politics or television or anything else people want."

"But what people want can hurt them."

"Cars kill a thousand people every week in my country, maim ten thousand more. And nobody says a word. Grass never hurt a soul. It's like music, it makes people happy."

"And now?"

"That village was no different than my family. I didn't want to leave. I've walked into something I can't find my way out of."

She held her ankles, knees up under her chin. "Sometimes I think I've walked into something that even if I found a way out I couldn't leave…"

"That's war – you stay with it because you won't desert the ones you're with. But they're only there because they won't desert you."

LYMAN ROLLED TO HIS FEET, dashed up the ditch, spun round and sprinted down it then swerved sharp right across the road where moonlight snared every pebble and the thud of his boots was like thunder and the rush of his breath the wind, feeling the bullets whack against his ribs, smashing his skull, the loud blunt roar tearing out his lungs, then he was across, no shot, smashed down the fence then soft creeping on fingers and toes, close to the moss, the dirt, a breeze in his face, nobody, roots, stalks, lianas, creepers, bristle of pine tree, dead needles loud, creeping round it, still no human odor or gun or uniform or sweat smells. He laid his hand softly on a root and it recoiled and slid away.

MURPHY LOOKED AT HER across the pale fire, her small body, her long hair, her lovely face with full lips and dark arched eyebrows with the lines of fatigue in the corners of her eyes. "You look so tired."

"Every death takes you with it."

"Do you ever fear?"

"I used to fear for me; now it's that I can't afford it yet –"

"Afford it?"

"Death. Once you're in *la lucha*, you've don't have much time."

"How did you start?"

"I was in love, with an intern at medical school. They arrested him for going to the *barrios* to heal the poor. They shot him and six others the day the Pope came to Guatemala City. To show the Pope he needn't worry about liberation theology here. For three years afterwards I lived like a nun, finished medical school, did my residency in Mexico. When I came back I realized there was nothing else except this I could do."

He wanted to lie down beside her, hold her. "You're lonelier than I am."

She smiled. "In Vietnam you weren't afraid?"

"All the time. Even on leave, I'd know what was waiting when I got back."

"It doesn't bother you now?"

"I had some bad times and everybody I really cared about died, but now I hardly ever think about it."

"That's a lie."

A rock in the fire cracked and he felt he could hold it together, keep it from breaking despite the heat, the pain. "It'd drive me crazy. If I really saw it how it was."

"Then you are already going crazy. You just don't see it."

His back was aching; he sat up on his heels. "Maybe I still live it, all the time. Yes, I admit it – I do." His ankles were tingling from his having sat too long cross-legged. "After I came back from Nam I went down to Mexico, lived by myself in the desert, did a lot of drugs, thought things through. I learned there's no good in going over pain." He took her hand, warm from the fire. "Can't you see that?"

"It's not like that, *la lucha*." She looked down at her hand in his, up into his eyes. "Don't condemn what you don't understand."

The fire was like a friend, softly rumbling to him in its red-golden depths. It doesn't matter, the fire said. You can choose to die and be with her. What else better could you do? "Nothing's worth dying for," he said. "Except someone you love."

"Then it just depends how far your love goes."

LYMAN HELD THE PISTOL against the palm of his left hand to mask the click as he pushed it off safety. Moonlight behind him, making him black and his enemy light. A stick twinged underfoot – *how* can I let that happen? He backed off, stepped round the stick. Shall I go to you, my friend, or wait for you to come to me?

"I NEVER SLEEP in a hut. It's one of my rules. Nowhere they can surprise me. I always sleep in the jungle."

Her skin felt so near, her eyes in his and his in hers, no distance between them. "It doesn't spook you?"

"It did at first. I hate snakes. But if only once out of a thousand nights you avoid danger, it's worth it." From her US Special Forces pack she took a cotton hammock, two blankets, and a camo tarp. She lifted the freshly boiled instruments from the bailing can, wrapped them in dry *india* and put them in the pack. She handed him a blanket. "Pollo will make you a place by the fire." She felt his brow. "You must terribly need sleep." Her hand came down, caressed his cheek. "Thank you for all you've done."

"Done? What have I done?"

"You fought the soldiers at San Tomás. You saved two children."

"Out of twenty." His eyes stung and he looked down at the fire, away from hers.

"You have to let it pass." She squeezed his hand. "If the woman has pain, or if the baby cries too much, Pollo will get me. You must sleep."

He took up the camo vest and draped it round her shoulders, pulled it close around her neck. Her hair was fine against his fingers. It's true, he realized, only once do you really fall in love. And right away you know.

She took up her rifle, but he slipped his fingers under the sling and eased it from her shoulder, bent down for the blanket she'd given him. "I'm coming with you."

14

TO HIS RIGHT between the cedars Lyman saw patches of starlit meadow. That meant the road was to the left, beyond the thicker wall of trees. Ahead the cedars must narrow to a point fringing the road: his enemy couldn't get away. His fingers touched stone – no, three stones, one still muddy on the edge, just now overturned.

He put down the stone and checked that his knife was still secure in its sheath at his ankle. A moth fluttered in his face.

An owl whirred down through the branches, swerved and flapped away. Ahead was a big tree darker than the rest. Under his hand the land sloped slightly left, toward the road. Was the enemy still by the road? Or back in the trees?

The pistol caught in a spider web and he tore it free, heard the spider scuttle away. His fingers bumped a stinging plant. In the darkness just ahead someone breathed out softly.

TO STEP out of the hut was like falling into space; the stars vaulting up over the jungle were thick as atoms in a sea of light. Wind came up from the water, tasting of fish and stone, rustling the leaves of the banana trees.

They went down to the *Río* and drank. He dug mud from the shallows and washed his hands and face, feeling the skin come clean. Everything you give, he thought, you only get it back.

"I saved Ofélia's life once," she said.

The name made him flinch. "Nobody told me."

"She had diphtheria. I waited it out with her, three nights. There were no drugs but a bark tea we use, a salicylic compound, to bring down fever. She came back –"

"You mustn't –"

"All during the Caesarean tonight I was seeing her, your people, what the soldiers did. Over and over."

He tugged the camo vest closer round her shoulders, the smooth skin of her jaw against the back of his hand. "You brought another life into the world tonight."

"And I regret it."

He kissed her temple smooth and cool from the *Río*, the thud of her pulse against his lips. "You'll drive yourself crazy. For nothing." He massaged her back; the muscles hardened then relaxed, her eyelash tickling the corner of his mouth, her cheekbone hard against his chin, her small breasts pushing into his chest, her hair soft over his fingers as he squeezed the muscles of her neck. "You're hard as stone."

"The muscles get like that – from carrying the gun."

"Don't carry it."

She shook her head, her face against his neck, her breath down his chest. Her arms were strong around his back, her hands gripped his shoulders. "If I put down the gun it wouldn't change a thing."

"It doesn't help anyone if you die."

You don't see what life *is*, in Guatemala?"

"It's still life."

"It's what happened to your village – poverty, sickness, death squads, hunger. If you had children."

"I'd get them out of here. Mexico, Belize."

"They get sent back, and all the men and boys are shot."

"Can *you* get out?"

"Of course, I've got Mexican papers. But never –"

"How long, here, do you give yourself?"

"It could be tonight. In a year."

"All those years afterwards you won't be alive, to heal people."

Her shoulders slumped. The *Río* was like a drumbeat, steady and deep. "I'm sorry I was rude to you," she said, "when you first came."

"You weren't rude; you saved my life."

"No, but calling you gringo, and all that."

"I barely noticed."

"I say it sometimes now, but just to tease you." She held the curve of his face, giving it form in the darkness. "So many villages. San Tomás, Santa Teresa, Puychíl, Aguateca, San Juan Sayjá. . . I can see them all, every person dead and burnt, the children's bodies – all the hundreds of villages and towns destroyed, and I can still see all their faces."

He hugged her tighter. "You can make it go away. Everything goes away."

"You're saying you don't care?"

"I'm saying I no longer care that I care."

WITH A RUSTLE of cloth the enemy stood. A click of magazine against the buckle of a sling. Black metal grazed by moonlight.

A beetle crawled up Lyman's calf. He did not make a noise breathing or licking his lip or shifting his weight as he dropped his left hand down to the knife. He held his thumb over the snap and slid his fingers under the flap and popped it free. The knife's ebony handle was soft and warm, the tang up each side cool against his palm. The knife slid by itself from the sheath.

With a crunch of cedar twigs the enemy turned to go. Doesn't know I'm here: a ravenous joy surged in Lyman's chest. He holstered his pistol.

The enemy was stepping lightly away, heading toward the cover of the trees, shouldering his rifle – doesn't even know I'm coming.

He switched hands with the knife, darted up behind and grabbed the enemy across the eyes, yanking the head back to slit the throat but long hair was in his way and the sentry screamed and Lyman twisted the knife aside, yanked the enemy down and fell atop her, the knife at her throat. "Where's the others?"

"No one!" A girl, eyes wide with terror, flimsy hands at his wrists. "Please no!"

"Why'd you shoot?"

"Just a warning, *Señor*. I'm supposed to warn you!"

"Warn me what?"

"Not to come up the road. We're stopping the road-"

"Who? *Who*?" He grabbed her hair and slammed her head against the rifle barrel underneath. "*Who*?" Pinning her arms under his knees he jammed the blade against her trachea. She coughed, gasped a breath. "The *compañeros*. I didn't mean to shoot you. I wouldn't shoot anyone. It's to warn you to stay back!"

"Why?"

"There's danger ahead. You were singing in a foreign language. I didn't want you killed, you're not a soldier."

"I'm a goddamn tourist, and you shot at me!"

"I shot to *miss* you!"

The whites of her eyes and her teeth gleamed with fear and pain from his holding her hair and her neck jammed down on her rifle. Still pinning her arms he felt down her sides: no revolver. He pinned her right arm, shoved his left under her head to hold her left wrist. "Where's the other *compañeros*?"

"Please, *Señor*, don't kill me, please?"

"Tell me and I won't hurt you."

"They're up ahead."

"How far?"

"Beyond the hill, where the road turns."

"How many?" Knife clamped in his teeth, he felt her breast pockets then down her thighs – no knife, a scrap of tortilla in one trouser pocket. He raised his hand up the inside of her thighs, clamped it there.

"Please, *Señor* – I was warning you only."

"How many?"

"I don't know – I was told to stay here, warn off anyone who wasn't soldiers."

He slipped the knife under her rope belt, twisted the blade and slit the trousers open to the knees.

"Please, *Señor*."

He slid the blade under the front of her shirt, drew it down, cutting the buttons, gripped the knife again in his teeth and pulled the shirt apart. There was a black line down her right breast where the blade had nicked it. "Please, *Señor* – I'm just seventeen…"

"You *tried* to kill me." It was a stallion rising in him now, the delicious stinging joy, the hunger to absolve it. She wore nothing under the coarse trousers, her mound little and warm as a bird in his hand.

"I could have killed you," she cried. "I didn't want to!"

"STOP MAKING so much noise!" Dona whispered. "You're like a hippopotamus!"

"I'm trying to keep up with you! Wait – I'm caught. There. Goddamn snakes. Don't know how you stand this."

"The hammock's safe. Once you get in it."

In the darkness ahead an even greater blackness. "This the tree?

"The ceiba?" She moved ahead. Yes."

He put down the gun and backpack. "I can hang my own hammock," she said.

Her face was near; he could sense her form against the darkness, reached out, knowing exactly where she was, her arm already familiar in his hand. Maybe it was your healing me, he thought, engraved you on me. "You got this god-damned thing on safety?"

"Of course, gringo – you are so crazy!"

"I hate it. I hate them so much it makes me sick just to see them."

"Just because you had to fight for what you didn't believe in, now you think no one should fight at all."

"You have guns – *they* have guns; you're just inoculating yourself with their disease."

THE GIRL WAS FIGHTING to keep her legs closed but he jammed a knee between them, rammed her legs up and shoved in, her channel dry, too small, the rubbery membrane tearing, her cry, the channel slicker now with blood, and that's what it always takes, he thought, a little sacrifice to get things going, couldn't shove in deep enough with her writhing and flinching; it reared up like a stallion crashing down her velvet walls, driving far up, her insides imploding, in the sweet slick hot delight of coming to this and nothing more.

You could've made a baby. You always know. He drove the blade deep into her throat, blood spraying in his face, her body frantic then rigid then finally quiet beneath him. He grew huge again – I should have kept you, he thought, but it's better this way – and finally it soared out of him long and deep, from back there, the beginning, from way behind it, life, the end. He pulled out and rolled aside, wiped the knife and his hands and face on her rough-woven trousers. Oh Jesus, he thought. You bastard. But then again – she tried to kill me. He heard Nancy playing a Beethoven sonatina, the mantel clock ticking out its years, saw his son Joshua tossing up a tennis ball, not high enough, not hitting it at the drop. Joshua leaned forward, into the serve, and the pain of his death drove again through Lyman like a sword, Joshua beneath the huge tire of the cement truck, half a boy's body in a lake of blood. Sheathing the knife and pistol he took up the girl's rifle, a battered M-16, short clip, only three shots left. He crept slowly to the edge of the starlit meadow and knelt looking for the best way across it and around the hill ahead, where the road turns.

DONA LAY with her head on his left arm, her breath against his neck, her hands up between his arms and chest, the rifle lying at her back. He pulled the blanket down a little to see the angle of her cheekbone and the extra darkness of her hair. "Your feet are too big," she said. "You'll pull out the blanket."

He kissed her forehead; it smelled of smoke, jungle, and river. Already she was sleeping, the barrel of her rifle cold with dew against his knuckles. Through a tiny high gap in the branches the Pleiades shone down. When he looked a moment later they were gone. But it seemed a good omen as he drifted off to sleep.

15

HIS VOICE came from the light. "You can put it down."
She held the weight tighter, was suddenly conscious of how it cut into her shoulder, made her back ache as if she carried concrete. She slid it from her shoulder and it thumped to the ground. She raised her arms, could see the jungle below and realized she was flying, dipping and diving naked through the winds, veering with the turn of a hand, air rushing past her body.

There was a warm tingling between her legs. Must have to pee, she thought. I'll have to get out without rocking the hammock, not waking him, and walk barefoot in the snakes to take a pee. But the feeling was hotter, radiating, a magnet between her loins and his, urging them together. For a moment she let herself imagine it. But maybe he doesn't want to. I'm heartless, wanting this, even thinking of it, after what's happened.

She recalled the woman in the hut, in pain but not crying out, the baby wailing at her breast. If I have to pee I'll check on her, she thought, though Pollo should be watching unless he fell asleep. Maybe she's hemorrhaged or the baby's sick and here I lie thinking about sex.

She slid one foot over the side. "What's the matter?" he said.

"I was trying not to wake you. Must check María –"

He sat up. "I'll go with you."

"It's only a hundred meters through the jungle. Sleep."

He slipped into his sandals, tossed her pack over one shoulder, took the gun. "I'll go before you."

From the clearing the *Río* was a canyon of stars. The coals still glimmered through the hut's rush walls. Pollo stood when they came in. "She's been awake," he whispered, "but now she sleeps."

"And *la chica*?"

"She drinks and sleeps. She's happy."

Dona touched the backs of her fingers to the baby's face, the back of the woman's hand. She beckoned Pollo outside. "*Bien*, you know where to find me?"

"*Sí, Doctora.*"

"I'll come again at dawn."

"Sleep well," Pollo whispered, catching Murphy in the corner of his eye.

In the jungle she took the rifle from Murphy. "Meet you at the ceiba." When he'd gone she slid down her clothes and crouched, the wonderful feeling of it coming out, its warm smell rising up from the leaves. The rasp of cloth as she pulled up her clothes made her skin tingle. It was still there, the itchy feeling of having to pee, hotter than before. She bit her lip, saw the stone slabs she'd climbed as a girl, up Antigua's temple stairs. Yes, we called it church, she reflected, but it was *ours* from before, long before there was a church, when the stones that now make the church then stood in another form, for a different God – the sense of all this history *was* like God, this column of power. And he must like me a little bit, she thought, for he likes lying down beside me and kissed me and it's true as he says that I saved him… though maybe he would have lived anyway for he seems to live through everything, and in her hand she could feel how *he* would be, could not close her hand all the way around him. I will do it, she decided. I give up, he can have me. The Galil snagged on a creeper; she bent and tugged it free.

She was coming to him across the starlight filtering down through chinks in the rain forest night – he could sense her, felt where she was, the motion of each limb, her face, each step turning, bending toward him through the trees. I've always loved you, he said to her inside himself. You're all I've ever cared for.

Just to brush her lips once with his was enough to last a lifetime but made him need to taste her mouth, her teeth against his lips, her odor washing him through mouth and face and hair and hand and every pore, her tongue like an orchid he'd seen once in the jungle deep in the crevice of a tree, her body hard against him like the Galil, her nails digging into the back of his neck, as if they were twins, two halves of one, dying of thirst for each other, drinking each other in.

She lay beside him naked, the hammock swinging softly and there seemed forever, always, to do all this. To be naked, naked against her naked – how small, how lovely how slender how complete –

"This can't matter afterwards," she whispered, as if someone could hear, "we can't do it anymore, just this once. Just this once I so need to, oh if you could understand how I need you."

No wall between them, one skin, one blood, one body, to kiss her the only thing now, had ever been the only thing, wetting her rough smooth lips, his tongue inside them, against her teeth, her tongue warmed and curved and curled and wrapped his, drew back came forward and took him in again.

He reached down her slender body over the curve in her hips and between her thighs and she raised up one leg so he could touch her there, rub her there, anything he wanted she wanted, the two were one, and she held him, held his power, had forgotten how big, filling her hand as if it belonged there, completed it, her hand aching to envelop it and go up and down it and her fingertips around the tip and everything she did she knew how it felt for him as if she had the same sensation.

How small inside she was opening out, deep resonating petals, how slender her hips how small her breasts against him, and he saw how she would be heavy with child, everything, all time, was this, her body rising beneath him, her eager lips and teeth and tongue and breasts and belly reaching up, sucking him in, her knees locked round him, and he was coming into her, an arrow to pierce her so she could die and be reborn and this time I'll live forever, she thought, in the glory of it deepening inside her, widening her, wedging her apart until its point hit high inside her, dead center, making it all come true, she could not tell the smell of him from hers, his breath or hers, his skin or hers. We're twins, we just got separated young, for he was her body and she his, the great white sheet of night washing her away, and she saw that everything is twinned, has its reflection, is doubled.

She saw a rabbit crouched in the grass. It's mistaken, she realized, to think the eagle watches over it.

He could see all around as if the night weren't there, then realized that it wasn't, the raw boughs spiring into gray, skeins of creepers cascading down, bulging leaves and bracken, the fading stars. The jungle thinned with light, the trees tapered to carbon spars and blew away on centuries of wind, the soil chased after, flake by scurrying flake, the earth was bare – the entire earth – he saw how everything had gone, inhabited the stars.

16

THROUGH A CRACK in the floorboards between his boots Lyman could see muddy ground. Roll a few grenades under these barracks you'd get everyone inside. Curling his toes against the morning chill he sat thinking how he'd attack the Base, as a guerrilla, how to draw strength to the northeast perimeter. But you wouldn't really be there, you'd fire across the middle, cutting it, hit the southwest from their back then when the northeast turns on you, you hit them hard from the front, where you'd started in the first place. It was pure sense, pure guerrilla, and he thought lovingly of it for a moment, realized his toes were cold and slid on his boots.

His body was stiff and sore, as if he'd played football, then he remembered he'd been drunk, had gone to town; his head was hurting, God what a fucking headache. Then he remembered he'd banged his forehead with hers, the girl when she was trying to escape, fighting him, and he remembered how easily the knife cut the trachea, the jugular, almost automatically, her body quivering one last moment in his arms. Was it true, he wondered, stood and lowered his trousers to see the blood in dark flakes on his penis, saw his shirt, the backs of his hands. "Oh Lord Jesus Christ," he said, rubbing his neck gently and shaking his head. But the headache wouldn't lessen, and he wandered toward the latrines to wash his face in cold water.

"THIS CAN'T happen again. No more after this." Her voice was hoarse, as if from too much talking.

"I won't let it stop."

On her side, she drew one leg up over his hip, seeking him. "*La lucha* - won't let me. I don't want to."

"To hell with *la lucha*."

"You'd love someone who'd do that, leave those whose lives might depend on her?"

"And in *la lucha* people don't love, get married?"

"Married, yes."

"Then we'll get married."

She put her fingers over his lips. "You mustn't even say that."

With the swing of the hammock he rolled on to his back and she pulled up on her knees and knelt over him, the blanket sliding from her shoulders. She kept coming down and down and down atop him till he hit the place where he could go no more and she winced and pulled up slightly.

"You like this?" he said.

"God yes I like it. I'm not crazy." Her hair slid up his chest as she came forward to kiss him, fell over him, breast to breast, skin to skin and sweat to sweat, her nipples hard against his ribs.

The dance of life was this, the yin and yang, the going in and coming out, one body and one blood, one core, one understanding - not thinking, far beyond it, the *body* doing this, the *body* knowing what is right.

"YOU LOOK LIKE you fall in a pit," Arena said.

"Too much *aguardiente*."

Arena took the coffee pot and served it around. He put it down and brought round a plate of biscuits. He's learned this at Langley, Lyman thought. This convivial serving of his guests. To lower their defenses.

"Since when does rum scratch your face?" Arena said.

"I fell downhill."

"That was very much rum."

"That's all there is to drink in this Christly place."

"Come now. There's El Gallo."

When he's being convivial that means he's planning an attack, thought Lyman. Or has figured a new way to use me. Or knows how he can lose me. But when he is being convivial he's also at risk because he doesn't expect me to attack. "You're still wrong, General," he said. "It *was* the pilot, at that village, who shot your men."

"My men get shot by many people, Colonel."

"And it's the same one who killed Gallagher. I saw how he moved, how he got in and out. He's a soldier, General, and a good one. I want him. And *you* still can't find him."

"If that *was* him. This we don't think yet."

"Just because the priest says it was some Kekchi. Trouble with you people's you can't drop the habit of believing your priests. No Kekchi looks like that guy. Kekchis aren't that tall – he knew how to use a gun."

"You think Guatemalans don't know how to use guns, Colonel?"

"Not these farmers you keep killing all the time. Most of them can't even handle a plough. Excuse me for being blunt – I've got a hangover – but I could run Guatemala with a lousy military academy. How come *you* can't with a whole army and equipment up the rectum – excuse my Spanish – and all the counterinsurgency training you can swallow and a fucking spy satellite and twenty-four-hour infrared overflight and six hundred million in military aid and three billion in slush funds and another ten billion you make off the grass and coke flights?"

"Talking to you, Colonel, is like talking to a recorder. We don't think the man at that village who shot our two soldiers was this pilot you are so hungry for. The priest has been to the point of death three separate times and this is what he begs us to believe. He has said some other things we know are true, so we are disinclined to disbelieve him."

"Like what?"

"He has admitted he sympathizes with the revolution."

"What priest *doesn't* sympathize with the revolution? Half your fucking Army and *all* the *campesinos* do! Probably even *you* do."

"You're an expert now, on our society?"

"I'm paid to be. I'm not very good at it but I'm better than you. You don't have the fucking faintest idea what's going on."

"And you do?"

"Give me a *lancha* and ten men, General. I'll show you how easy it is to find this sky pilot."

Arena nodded slowly, watching his hands folded on the table before him, like the stubby fat prow of a ship, Lyman thought.

"Why not take your ten men and go up to Sayaxché this morning?" Arena said. "Angelo Vodega will go with you."

II

House of Obsidian Knives

17

POLLO blew on the coals and added resiny *ocote* twigs that flared up quickly. God give us peace, Murphy thought. Peace is love, came the answer. They heated the monkey stew, gave some to the woman, María, who was able to sit up and eat.

Globules of fat floated in the stew, between the bones. The monkey's flesh was wiry, the hairs nearly human – short, dark, and strong. The baby's wizened face seemed fuller, less frightened. You're getting used to it already, Murphy thought. Pollo took up his machete. "I'll find some roots for María."

Mice were chasing each other in empty corn husks by the door. Fog came up from the *Río* and under the hut walls.

He was conscious of every move she made, every breath, the pressure of her hand on his shoulder as she stepped past, how the light touched her black hair, the curve of her cheek. She stood beside him, warming her hands over the fire, and he held the inside of her thigh and kissed her there, between the thighs, smelling her through the worn jeans, her fingers combing his hair. Never, he realized, have I *ever* felt like this.

No matter how many times you see something it's never the same: now from the Huey the river with its coat of fog reminded Lyman of an old drunk sleeping over a heat grate, like a goddamn python, its jaws sucking in the world. He smiled at Vodega – in the company of villains and fools. I could've done anything, and look where I've ended up.

He waved the door gunner aside and took the M60D, the great gun swinging loose on its mount, grips tight in his palms. Truly nothing like this gun, nothing ever. No sense of power, purpose, like this. Treetops tipped past, birds scurrying. They're in among the fucking trees, the guerrillas. Millions and millions of trees. But their highway's the river. He punched the gunner's shoulder. "Tell Ramón drop down, follow the river."

"*Es claro que es muy peligroso*," the gunner said.

"I don't care how fucking *claro* that it's dangerous. Do it."

"WE MUST GO," Pollo said, "before the fog rises."

"Unless you can wait, let her rest here till tomorrow," Dona said. "That would be better."

"Here it's too dangerous. Better she's among her own people. We can cross here and go up the Santa Amelia."

"Go, then," Dona said. "Quickly while the fog's thick."

"And if there's monkeys I'll shoot one to feed her." Pollo took his Galil and went down to the *Río*, untied the dugout and brought it alongshore. Dona led the woman carefully down to the dugout.

"She's going to die," Murphy said. "She can't heal."

"She's got no fever; at Santa Amelia she'll be with family. I have to leave today – can't go with her. In a couple of days I'll check on her."

"*I'll* stay with her."

Dona shook her head. "You have to go downriver."

They settled María on her rush mat in the middle of the dugout, the baby quiet at her breast, inside her red shawl. Pollo poled away from shore, the dugout slipped into the fog, first the bow, then the thwarts, till only Pollo standing in the stern remained, a glimmer fading, gone.

"You're crazy if you think I'm going downriver," Murphy said.

She stood against him, warming her river-cold hands against his bare chest. He kissed her and kissed her, could not stop, get enough. Her body pressed hard against him. "I've got work today," she whispered.

He opened her shirt, making her hold him, her teeth nipping his lips, her breath fast. "We're going to do keep doing this and never stop."

"Let's go up there –"

"To hell with up there. We're going to do it right here." He was unbuttoning her jeans and she was pulling him down when he felt it suddenly on his back, his neck – the sun, the air suffused with sudden brightness. Fog rose like a curtain from the *Río*; Pollo was *there*, halfway across, caught in sunlight, using his pole like an oar against the current.

They heard the noise and Murphy sprinted uphill for the hut, grabbed Dona's rifle and ran into the open as the chopper came sideways down the *Río* spitting tracer fire that hammered the water like a great sheet of glass breaking, loud as the whole world breaking, the dugout spurting up and knocked apart, and Murphy led the door gunner by half the space between him and the door, down the black channel of the Galil's sights, on his neck to be sure to hit his chest; the rifle kicked and barked as the chopper swung away and then came round in a quick arc and Murphy fired for the turbine housing then the motor head, knowing he was dead now, that the door gunner would kill him, and Murphy saw a black man hunched over the machine gun, the officer who had helped to burn his village; as he fired the chopper swung away and he had to shoot at the engine housing; the chopper jerked and pulled up, and the black man was gone, I've got to lead them away from her, he thought, running along the bank, huge M60 bullets whacking and whanging among the *boloconte* roots, in the smell of burnt wood and dirt and the horrible vacuum that bullets leave behind. The chopper's whine retreated; it was fluttering north toward Sayaxché trailing blue smoke from the engine housing.

Dona dove into the *Río* and swam toward the shattered dugout. Murphy checked the clip – six shots. "I'll cover you," he yelled, but she did not turn her head. He wanted to scream, tear his face, ran out into the *Río* till he could see the point far downriver where the chopper had swung round a bend, its smoke trail indolent in the wind. The water was stainless steel in the brilliant sun. Dona swam back, grabbed her rifle and ran up to the hut.

"Hurry!" she yelled, tossing her pack and blankets out the door. Wiping her face, coughing and crying, she knelt at the fire, blew it alive, tossed in more kindling. "Watch outside – for more helicopters!"

"What are you doing?"

"Go!"

Outside there was no sound of choppers, no distant glint coming upriver. He stood in the hot shade of the banana palms, trying to catch his breath, the somnolent air searing his throat. He kept trying to check the rifle in his hands but his hands were empty. She came out with a torch of kindling and held it to the thatch. "What the hell?" he said.

"Quick!" They ran for the jungle, through the saplings and creepers and past the great ceiba where last night they'd hung the hammock, deeper into the jungle, up out of the *bajos* and into the hills.

THE SMOKE got thicker making Lyman lean out the door to breathe. The soldiers crouched on the floor, the dead door gunner between them. Lyman kept watching the engine housing but there was no way to know if it would hold, the Jesus nut rotating wildly, hot oil spattering the gunner's body. He stepped across the soldiers to the cockpit. "Get down close to the river!" he yelled. "When she dies we're going to drop like a stone."

"*Bajo demasiado peligroso!*" The pilot craned round. There were cuts like red paint on his face. "We tell you this already!" the copilot said in English. "Now we going to ditch, goddamn you."

Lyman made himself smile, nodded back at the Jesus nut. "She'll hold. Just bring her down, first open place you find, so I can get my men back to that hut. We'll find them, get them for your gunner."

"He's dead?"

"Through the head."

"Goddamn you!" the copilot screamed.

Lyman swung back to the crew deck, glanced down at the river like a glistening concrete skin fifty feet below the chopper's skids. Fools, he thought, to take it serious. But it was him, the goddamn sky pilot, the tall guy with the blond hair and beard, the one who'd been at the village the other night. The same one. He killed the door gunner and blew holes in the motor housing. He tried to kill us all.

18

ER FACE, muddied, torn and bloodied by thorns, seemed a stranger's yet infinitely near. "I didn't *want* you," she said. "We can't be together."

He tried to catch his breath. "Where're we going?"

"I must be somewhere tonight. That's why I couldn't stay, with María and the baby."

The mud on her face, he saw, was just tears and dirt. "I can get from here to Mexico. It's just jungle. But I won't leave you."

She shook her head scornfully. He felt a moment of such pity and love that the earth shifted beneath him. He slid his fingers under the rifle sling to take it from her shoulder but she wouldn't let go. "Everything you do – can't you see – just brings more pain?"

"Less than if I do nothing."

"For you, perhaps."

"That's cruel. And untrue."

"If you hadn't been there to help María, Pollo wouldn't have died."

She caressed his face, making him feel mean, selfish. "You mustn't try to talk me out of what I do. Not when we both know I'm right."

LYMAN KEPT the river on his left, a glimmer through the trees. It could only be another mile, Jesus, till they got there. He kept the pace steady, running, ducking, climbing, crawling, pushing aside the jungle at each step, elbowing and dragging his M-16 through the walls of trees. He looked back, panting, could see Martínez, the sergeant, then the first man behind him. "*Anda!*" Martínez yelled, pushing Lyman with his rifle.

Lyman ran onwards, going to lose him now, lose Martínez, lose them all, the bastards, do it alone, run, run lose them alone, the words steady in his brain like a beat, a heartbeat, and you can always beat exhaustion, just run, just remember the American pilot and how you're going to kill him for killing Gallagher and the door gunner, the two soldiers in the village, trying to kill you, thinking of how the bullet had skimmed past his head and whacked through the fuselage and sung off the rotor. Little piece of metal with your death on it. Run run run, with a little piece of death on it.

THEY CAME to a path going north and south along the first ridge above the *Río*. "The burro trail to Cobán," she gasped, holding his arm to keep from falling.

He felt the same sudden sureness he'd had the night before, going out with her to the hammock. He glanced up at the cracks of light through the canopy. "Choppers see us here." Thoughts blizzarded through his mind; he could see the tree canopy from above, as if he were looking down through the chopper's Plexiglass shell, as if with God's eye he could see how the trace of the trail cut through the jungle, how to pick out a motion, gun it down. Nam, how it was, shredding people under white hot metal hail. He saw her dead, torn apart by .50 caliber slugs, then saw her old, grandchildren round her, saw how that was false, would never be, saw the jungle crouching nearer, waiting for them to fail. "Give me that goddamn thing." He took the gun, swung it over his right shoulder, the backpack over his left. Sensing it might be the last time, he freed her lustrous hair from her collar, so that it fell down her back.

She wiped her face with both hands, a motion that seemed strangely like prayer. "It's for *you* that I wanted you to go to Mexico."

"How far do we go?"

"About an hour south. I'll tell you."

"You're going to follow me. About fifty yards behind. If I hit trouble, you beat it."

"The Army doesn't bother this trail, it's too far in the jungle."

"If you hear a chopper get into the trees. Try to get under a log. Same if you hear me shoot."

"TOLD YOU!" Lyman yelled. "Here it is!"

Martínez scrambled up to him. "There's fire."

Lyman tried to peer through the brush at the clearing. "Bastards're cooking."

"No. Big fire."

The men crept forward one by one through the jungle, exhausted, dirty, clothes ripped, faces bloody, Angelo last. "So what you want?" he said. "Cook lunch?"

"It's a big fire," Martínez repeated.

"Spread out, Christ!" Vodega whispered. "You want to get *extinto*?"

"They're gone, Angel," Lyman smiled, enjoying it that Vodega didn't want him to use his first name, not in front of the men, Vodega already angry about the chopper, about leaving it back there in the clearing instead of trying to make Sayaxché. Pilots not daring to take off again, waiting for a Shit-hook to pull them out. World of cowards.

The men were spreading out in a line, down to the river and up into the jungle. Lyman crawled forward to the edge of the open space with three charred banana palms and the cinders and burned beams where the hut had been. Too goddamn small for an LZ or I would've had him, the American, he thought. Why was he here? Who was that with him, that had looked like a woman? He back-crawled to Vodega and Martínez. "Burned their hut."

"Told you," Martínez said.

"I'm going around, find their trail. Hold your fucking fire."

Vodega smiled. "Think we'd waste *you*? Aren't you our ticket to Paradise?"

Lyman went up the line, Martínez's laugh behind him burning in his mind. "I'm going in," he said to each man. "Don't shoot."

He circled the open. His knees were trembling with fatigue and he forced himself to wait a moment till they stopped. Using the muzzle of the M-16 to prod his way between the branches and creepers he inched forward, waited, moved forward again. A khaki green and yellow bird hopped along the leaves before him pecking at twigs, fluttered away when he got close. The jungle was like the bottom of the sea, too thick to breathe.

Ahead a big goddamn tree, didn't feel right, danger. They could be here, he warned himself. He crouched in a fern clump watching the tree but nothing happened. Wind off the river brought the burnt smell of the hut. Why was he *here*, the American pilot? Figure that out and you'll have him.

He moved round the tree, closed in. Scuffed leaves, broken ferns. Rope burn round a trunk. Something was tethered here, a burro? Nonsense – never get a burro through this stuff. There was a second rope burn on another trunk nine feet away. Or someone slept here, in a hammock, not in the hut. Why the Hell'd they do that?

Unless there'd been some people in the hut, the two we killed on the river, and another one out here. On guard? Didn't make sense.

He followed the tracks from the big tree down to the still-glowing coals of the hut. "Angel!" he called. "Just you. Come on in."

Vodega came along the bank and up to the hut. "One of them went along the river," he said, "then came back."

"One of them slept up there," Lyman pointed behind him. "Under a big tree."

"We're chasing *espíritus, fantasías.* People who sleep under big trees."

"Who's your best tracker?"

"Chichito – the kid."

"Get him."

Vodega called and the boy came out of the brush, too small for his uniform, black hair in his face, his gun pulling down his shoulder, dirty toes out of worn sandals. "Five hundred quetzales," Lyman said, "if you can track them down."

Chichito dropped his eyes – he's too shy, Lyman thought. "Three people here," said, and Lyman realized the boy had just been checking the ground. Chichito circled the hut. "Maybe four." He raised his eyes, scanning the jungle wall, went down to the river, came back. "Two left in the canoe," he said. "Two went into the woods. One man, one woman. The woman is *Guatemalteca.* The other wears Quiché sandals but he's big and heavy and walks like a white man."

Joy cascaded down Lyman's spine. "You see, Angel?" he smiled at Vodega. "Oh thee of little faith?"

19

DONA FOLLOWED Murphy at a run south up into the mountains, the trail overgrown in thick scrub under the overarching boughs, tracers of day down through the canopy. It was crazy to let him carry the gun, the backpack. If he was killed how would she get her medical kit, the gun?

Murphy slowed to a walk but she couldn't see him in the brush, hunted his tracks through the snapped leaves and bent creepers.

She yelled in surprise as someone lunged at her but it was him, coming back. "Lost the trail," he said.

"Give me my pack."

He held her shoulder, keeping them standing. "No." His head wound was bleeding. I don't care, she thought. I don't care for anybody's wounds. The blood was bright on her hand. "I've got to sew this up again."

"No," he repeated, turned and spat into the brush.

"If they track us," she said.

"That big canyon we just went round – not far from the *Río*."

She nodded.

He took a deep breath, staring at the green wall of their back trail. "I should pick out a good place, wait to see if they come."

"With how many bullets?"

"Six, plus one in the chamber. You have more?"

"No." She felt a wild need to protect, hold him. "At the *Río* there'll be a canoe, to take you downriver."

"You're coming."

"Are you crazy? After all this? You think a quick fuck makes any difference? I have my job, other people here. They won't want you around. I have a man here, he'll be very angry if he sees you."

He was breathing deeply, wiping mosquitoes from his face. "You have some guy?"

"Of course!"

His face looked pummeled, defeated. She clenched her fists, the nails sharp into her palms. Do it now, she told herself, while you still can...

"The things you said, last night, this morning."

She could do it one more time, touch his face, making it seem like condolence. "I was heartbroken. The village, your village –"

"So you did it *for* me."

She shrugged. "Think that if you like."

"Bitch." He turned away, swinging the rifle ahead through the brush, and again she followed him, running harder, as he shoved through the thorns and scrub, shadowed under the great trees, this shred of still-unravaged earth, she thought, from way back, from the beginning. How have things gone so wrong, she wondered, why do things always go wrong? Go ahead, cry, he can't see you, he's far ahead, lost in his anger. That's why things go wrong, it's anger – striving causes pain, and striving's from a lack of freedom, the freedom not to die, and so it goes round and round and never stops and

I must not get caught up, she told herself, must stay free to help those who aren't, for what good's freedom when others are in pain? But that's an old lie and you must promise yourself no more lies, not even the lie of love.

CHICHITO'S BACK was bent as he ran, to watch the earth, sweat on his khaki shirt, the rifle butt like a brown animal under his arm, Lyman running behind, panting and trying not to show it, the others gasping and swearing and trying to keep intervals behind. Chichito halted, stood up; Lyman nearly ran into him. "Good!" Chichito pointed his small finger at a leaf splashed red.

Lyman wanted to hug him. "Head wound."

"*Sí!*"

"Which one?"

"The tall one."

"That's right." With a stab of pain Lyman saw Joshua in Chichito's face, the boy's calm self-assurance, of one born too long before his elders. He looked back into Chichito's black eyes: this time I'll protect you.

THE SKEIN OF THINGS unwinds, then you have nothing. She tripped, not taking her eyes from his back, how he ran surely and without fatigue for hours, the rifle easy, part of him. The skein unwinds and disappears. And when we're gone it never was. This is the decision she'd made long ago, after they shot Diego. To have nothing but *la lucha*. If you don't have it completely you don't have it at all.

The trail skirted a slope, half-clear, a view back over a hundred miles of jungle, the *Río* down its belly like a God. It's *all* God, she thought – and we betray it. "The trail goes down," he said.

"So do we."

He snatched her arm. "It's true, what you said?"

She looked at the ground. White rocks through the black soil, grass fine as a child's hair. "Yes."

She listened to him breathing. Sweat poured down her back. You'll never have this again, she told herself. And you're to blame. "When we reach the cutoff for San Pedro there'll be someone to take you downriver."

"I don't need anyone."

"Without help you won't make it. We have a way."

"I don't care for your ways."

"You're being spoiled again, gringo. It's nothing – a man and woman making love – you don't do this, sleep with someone then go away, the next day?"

"It's all I've done, for years."

"So what's so hard to understand?"

He smiled, shook his head. "Forget it."

"You'll go downriver? Or you'll be killed."

"And you?"

"We'll split up at the *Río*."

He grabbed her arm and knocked her into the brush, rolled up and crouched over her, scanning downhill. "Christ! You didn't see that?"

She tried to squirm free but he held her down. "What?"

"You're blind as a bat! Soldiers coming up the trail!"

Carefully she raised her head above the leaves. A string of soldiers coming at a run up the hill she and he had climbed ten minutes ago. "Give me my gun!"

"Go! I'll keep them. Easy here to pin them down. Tell me where to bring the gun."

"You won't keep it?"

"I don't want your goddamn gun. I don't want anything that's yours." He pointed the muzzle at her face, six inches away. "You don't go right now and you'll be the very first one I kill." He switched the selector off safety, jabbed the muzzle into her cheek. "Then I'll only have six bullets for the soldiers."

She had a throb of fear seeing his face white with anger. "In about ten miles the trail splits for San Pedro and Chinajá. There's a little valley. There'll be people there. They'll keep the gun. They'll take you downriver."

Watching where the soldiers had disappeared in the brush, he settled himself in position, wiping bark and dirt from the Galil's muzzle shroud. She gripped his shoulders. "Please?"

"What?"

She kissed him, tasting salt. "Go, goddamnit!" he said.

When he looked again she was gone. Six bullets. And one in the chamber. Too many soldiers. Kill a few and pin the rest. Or kill one early and try to get to his gun.

He crawled backwards through the scrub to the apex of the slope where the trees grew thick behind him and there was an angle of fire downhill where the trail cleared at a bend, enough to hit the point man, and if you had enough bullets you could rake the brush and try to hit the slack man. But he didn't, so the slack would reach cover and open up as soon as he shot, and they'd spray everything up here and he'd have to pull back, then when they came forward he'd be able to get the slack unless they circled. Of course they'd circle, but if he swung uphill he could flank them and in any case they'd get him, it was just a matter of how soon.

Again he glanced behind but she was truly gone. You're such a fool, he thought, an abandoned puppy ready to fall for anyone. This crap of all these years without anyone means that's how it should be.

The first soldier broke through the brush, climbing fast, a small man in khaki with his rifle slung. Murphy rested the Galil stock on his left hand, elbow well propped, settled his chest into the warm, soft ground so that the muzzle came up steadily, seeing down the barrel shroud to the center of the man's chest, adjusted for the slope, and slowly squeezed the trigger.

20

LYMAN HAD BEEN thinking of his sons, how Joshua had never lied, didn't need to, except when he'd been very young, and Lyman had taught him not to, that it was bad for *him*. But Jason lied constantly, almost a reflex. Have I made him ashamed of himself? Is he ashamed of himself because he's not Joshua?

The rifle's crack and Chichito flying back arms outspread were unreal because Lyman wasn't *there*, had to come back suddenly as he dived for cover and fired wildly uphill toward the sound and yelled for Martínez to spread the men. Someone was gasping; he realized it was Chichito. Behind him someone opened up, bullets shrieking over his head and whacking into the knoll above. The firing stopped, then from the knoll barked a single shot. Below Lyman a man screamed. Several Galils answered back; their fire wound down and again from the knoll the rifle fired once.

"Stop shooting!" It was Martínez, yelling at his men. "Eduardo, Camilio, Benito!"

"*Sí!*" one answered.

"*Who?*"

"Benito," the man called back.

It's the fucking pilot, Lyman realized. Up there with the *chica* I saw from the chopper. He doesn't have much ammo so he's letting us make the moves then picking us off. He's got the position and I've let us walk into what I said I never would.

Or he has the *chica* on his flank and when we try to circle she'll hit us. Or she's the one up there and he's waiting for us to come round. There was a faroff whine – Chichito, who must have fallen off the other side of the trail. There was no way to reach him without crossing open ground. Someone was thumping his rifle butt into the earth and Lyman was furious with him then realized the sound was his own heart.

THERE WERE THREE BULLETS in the magazine and one in the chamber. Murphy could not judge how much time had passed. Already soldiers were moving up through heavy cover to his left; he could hear them but couldn't risk a chance shot. When they got to the top they'd rush and he wouldn't get them all. He crept leftwards on his belly from the knoll into the dark jungle, down toward the soldiers.

A GALIL chattered uphill but not from the top. One of us, Lyman decided as he spun on to his belly and dashed across the trail and dived down beside Chichito who lay on his back, head low, feet splayed uphill. His mouth was full of foamy blood and Lyman sucked and spat it out, mouthful after mouthful, hammering his fist on Chichito's chest but not near the round wet hole in the sternum. Trying to stay low Lyman dug a compress from his pack and reached under the boy's thin body, pulled out his hand coated with lung tissue and blood. "Martínez!" Lyman rasped. Crumbles of earth bumped his knee and he saw they'd come from where Chichito's hands had clenched then relaxed. A breeze abraded the leaves.

"*Sí*," Martínez whispered, down and to the right.

"We got to circle both sides of that hill," Lyman called in Spanish, hoping the pilot wouldn't understand or maybe not hear.

"I sent the right flank," Martínez said.

"You and Angel go left, cut off the back."

"And you?"

"I'll stay with Chicho. Cut them off this way. Remember, there's two of them..."

A dragonfly landed on Lyman's wrist. The wind ruffled the boy's hair against his sweaty forehead. A spider web between a stem and branch cast prisms of sunlight. Lyman laid his ear against Chichito's chest, hearing only his own pulse.

MURPHY CREPT fifty yards downhill, found a depression with limestone boulders, all around thick with trunks, limbs, stems, shoots, saplings, creepers, leaves, brambles. Something hissed across the damp leaves, twanged a thorn, moved uphill behind him, a rat, maybe. He waited, counting out a hundred in pulses, forcing his heart rate slower while mosquitoes battered at his forehead and face, while the wind teased the leaves, masking the sound of moving men. Then he continued down, north, then up through ferns to a crevice of madrone that gave a view of the knoll where he'd been.

Leaves twitched across the slope below the knoll. A soldier bolted toward the knoll, another coming over the top through the trees. They met at the top and scrambled for cover; he hit the first and missed the second who ran back for the first and Murphy blew his head off, his helmet bouncing into the scrub. Murphy squirmed back from his crevice as bullets sprayed and sang through the trees. He checked that there was still one bullet in the chamber and crossed over the top of the slope and down its western side, away from the trail and the *Río*, then turned south, paralleling the trail.

"HE'S NOT DEAD," Lyman said.

"He will be. You're not going to save him by carrying him two hours in the jungle to an LZ."

"How come you don't have any fucking LZs? How come you don't *own* this country?"

Vodega came running up the trail and ducked down beside them, lifted one of the boy's eyelids, shook his head. "That's it," he said. "We're pulling back."

"*Back*?"

"We have five dead out of eleven. Or out of ten if we don't count you. That makes six you've killed today including the chopper gunner."

"You insubordinate little shit."

"You're not my superior, Colonel. You're from another world and you're screwing up ours. As soon as we get back I'm telling Arena to send you home. If *I* don't get back, any of my surviving men will carry the message." He turned half away to watch the knoll where they were bringing down the bodies one by one on a bough and poncho stretcher. "We're not girls," he spat, "you can't cut our throats."

THE RIDGE of the knoll continued south, bending eastward as it dropped toward the *Río*. Murphy kept to the heavy jungle below and west of the trail, halfway between the ridge and its valley. The jungle seemed to thicken, then he realized it was night coming, everything falling into shadow. There was a gray glimmer ahead and he pulled back to skirt it, turning east toward the river. The ridge had flowed down into the valley and he crossed a trail and could smell wood smoke and then the cool breath of the *Río*.

Voices were coming up the trail, several people running; he ducked into the trees. Now with only one bullet left he would pay for shooting the last two soldiers on the knoll, for shooting the one who'd gone back for his comrade. The first person passed, running hard. The second passed, lighter on his feet. "When we get to the fork," the third one called in Spanish, "we must spread out."

"Dona!" Murphy called.

The running stopped. There was a snick of metal as someone clicked off safety. "Dona! It's me," he whispered quickly in Spanish, before they could shoot. "I'm back."

"It's him!" Her voice neared out of the darkness, her hands snatched his wrists, clasped his face. "Oh God it's you," she said in English. "I was so worried, we came fast as we could. Where are the soldiers?"

"Went back."

"Pascual! He says they went back!"

A tall heavy man came to them, breathing hard. Dona dropped her hands from Murphy's arms. "How do you know? the man said.

"I hit several and they must have decided to carry back the wounded. After that I left the trail and went through the *selva*. They can't follow till tomorrow."

"How many'd you hit?"

"Two. Maybe more."

"*Mierda*!" the other man said. "Is it true?"

"If he says it," Dona said.

"I just wanted to give you time," Murphy said to her in English.

"I came to get a gun and found these two and brought them. I kept telling myself I must not worry because you are truly difficult to kill, but this time I was sure you were dead."

"And here I am."

She felt perfect within the circle of his arms, her shoulders a perfect shape and size, perfect the touch and smell of her hair against his cheek, her neck against his shoulder, lovely the feel of her arms around his back. She leaned into him, her weight suddenly on him. "Just let me stay here, a moment, like this..."

21

"YOU'RE GOING to die here."

"I *can't* go with you. Please, accept that."

"Your people need medics. I'll stay."

"You're too different, you'd be captured in a month. You'd give too many of us away."

Swallows were skimming the *Río* under the rising moon, darting and diving after insects, crying their harsh cries. "You're lying."

She glanced round at Pascual, who stood a few yards behind them. "Remember what I said, why I can't?"

"I don't care."

"He's the one."

"Shall I tell him what you said to me, last night?"

She half-smiled, embarrassed. "Go back to the States, tell the newspapers, everyone, what's happening here."

"Dona – I saw it all in Vietnam. Nobody cares, up there. Long as it doesn't hurt them."

"Tell them. *Make* it hurt them."

"It's coming," Pascual said. "*La lancha.*"

Murphy looked at Pascual, burly and bearded, hair curling down over his brow. "Why don't you protect her?" he started to say, but the question was crippled by too many differences. Pascual would not think a man should protect a woman, give his life for her if needed and never spend hers for his because she was the holy mother of his children, because she was life incarnate, because no cause was worth the death of a single woman. He thought of Inquisition priests killing Indian children to save their souls from Hell. They like Pascual believed in the efficacy of death. He saw how his whole life could be lived with Dona, and that it would not be.

"I'm sending a wounded compañero downriver with you," she said. "He was shot in the stomach two days ago. He's suffering horribly. We're trying to get him to Mexico, to the clinic at Bonampak. Please stay with him. You were a medic, do what you can."

From upriver a motor was approaching, a dugout canoe with two women in the stern, burlap sacks of corn stacked on planks atop the hull in front of them. In the shallows the women leaped out and shoved aside the front rows of sacks and lifted the planks, and in the moonlight Murphy saw a dark-haired man lying in water in the hull, under the planks. Dona bent over him, speaking softly, caressing his brow. One of the women grabbed Murphy's arm. "Get in!"

Dona was gone. Murphy squeezed into the hull, keeping his face above the water inside. The other man groaned, and Murphy saw his mouth was thick with blood that ran down his neck into the water. You're not going to live, Murphy thought. Planks clumped down over their heads, the corn sacks thumping on them. He could see nothing. The bilge of water, blood, and gasoline eddied back as the propeller dug into the river, then came sloshing forward as the engine steadied and the prow dropped. He twisted up his face and tried to back his body against the hull to avoid bumping the other man.

The hull banged and slapped the water, bubbles rushing past the wood beside his ear. There was no air. The man coughed blood down Murphy's face. "Water!" he gasped. "Please, water!"

SHE LAY IN the hammock pushing it slowly back and forth with a stick shoved into the ground. It was like moving in a womb, protected by the blackness, the silence, floating in an invisible world. Her mother's womb, dark, enclosing, warm, complete: was she truly remembering it? Could she go further back, to the fusion of her father's seed and mother's egg, back down the tunnels of their single cells?

The hammock rocked gently, its mesh tight around her shoulders. Unimaginable that *he* was here, in this hammock, what we did. The skin of her neck prickled, flushed. It wasn't even *here*, then, this hammock. Nothing was here but *him*.

Sex is God. *Why didn't I know that?* Sex brings life, and war takes it away. And look which one I've chosen.

THE CANOE'S motor slowed. Over its diminishing rumble grew a larger, heavier one, another boat approaching. Cracks of light flared down between the planks and corn sacks. The hull thudded into steel, the wounded man cried out as Murphy lurched against him.

"Where the hell you going?" a voice yelled down.

"To Sayaxché, Jefe."

"Where from?"

"Finca el Paraíso."

"Can't you see it's night?"

"The corn must be there by the morning! It's for the truck to Flores."

"How many sacks?"

"Twenty."

The prow dipped as boots thumped down on it. The wounded man sputtered as water sluiced over his face. "You troopers," the voice said, "move those sacks."

"You'll tip my boat!" one of the women yelled. "I'll lose my harvest! Who'll pay for that?"

The sacks groaned as bayonets thrust into them. Corn kernels sifted onto the planks. Lights darted back and forth through the cracks between the planks. Kernels plopped into the water. Murphy tried to raise his arms but the wounded man was jammed against him.

"Please, Jefe," the woman begged. "This corn is for the mill at Flores. To make tortillas. Everybody needs tortillas –"

"Don't worry, mother. Just checking you're not carrying something else in your sacks. Enough, men. Toss ten of them up here!"

"Please, Jefe! Everyone needs corn, everyone needs tortillas."

"We do too, mother. It's your penalty, for traveling by night. You're lucky we let you through."

Boots thumped back and forth on the planks as the soldiers lifted the ten corn sacks up to the patrol boat. Murphy tried to pull up his feet so that they would not show beyond the planks. Each time his knees bumped the wounded man's he moaned.

The other engine revved; the canoe's prow lifted as the boots rose from it. "It's no wonder," the woman wailed, "you soldiers have trouble with the *campesino.*"

"Have the sense to be quiet, woman, when you've come out ahead," the voice called down as the patrol boat pulled away. "*No critiquemos Guatemala!*"

"Water!" the wounded man murmured.

Again Murphy tried to free his own hands. "You can't reach it?"

"Water!" the other said. Murphy twisted his face down into the water and blood, took a mouthful, and filled the wounded man's mouth. The man swallowed, then with a burst of blood coughed it up again, face contorted with pain. "Water!" he gasped, "please water…"

NANCY JUST WON'T play by the rules, Lyman reflected. It's because of her I go to other women. Just like it'll be because of the Agency if I go outside. If the Agency's bringing the Colombians into Guatemala, who says I can't work for *them*? You can only take so much, when you're doing all the giving. Like with Nancy. She's too sharp, too independent. Trouble with her being so self-sufficient is that someday *nobody*'s gonna need her.

He shoved the pillow aside and rested his head on his folded arm. With one blanket he was too hot, with just the sheet he was too cold. Shouldn't even think about Nancy, times like this. Surrounded by cowards and dunces, ignorant Arena and insidious Angel. Nancy's the past, while I create the future. A field man, scouting enemy territory ahead of the tribe. Standing on peaks they'll never even see.

Today wouldn't look so bad by the time the Agency reviewed it. Fucking Guats afraid of the jungle. How they gonna catch guerrillas with their chopper at three thousand feet? Fucking Guats afraid of doing a little patrol. They hit hostile fire and they run. One thing to burn down a village of kids and old people, another thing to fight somebody who shoots back. When it was only that pilot, and maybe too the *chica*.

The way he fights, something familiar, how he uses cover. How he came through us and fired down from behind, got the two guys on the hill. Or was that the *chica*? Now I'll never know. Unless I find them alive, talk to them about it.

I can ditch Nancy and still stay close to the kids. No, that's just liberal bullshit. For the kids it's better if Nancy and I are unhappy together rather than being happy apart.

Can't ditch Nancy till I get back into the field. The Agency won't let me back into the field if I blow this pilot. And I won't find this pilot with these fucking Guats running away whenever things get hot.

If the priest would talk. A real confession. But Angel will kill him, out of misplaced zeal. No moderation, that's the problem with these people.

THE RIVER SLACKENED under the keel; the prow bumped mud. Feet splashed alongside the hull; someone dragged aside several corn sacks and planks. "Hurry!" one of the women hissed. "Here's the path to Sayaxché and the Flores road."

The night air was cool and sharp. Murphy tried to pull himself up but his legs were asleep. "The *doctora* asked me to stay with him!"

"It was her way to get you to leave. Now *go!*"

He clambered over the side. The *Río* was shockingly cold against his crotch. The gurgle of the canoe vanished in the raucous croak of tree frogs and the muted rush of the current along the bank.

He took off his poncho, shirt, and trousers, washed the wounded man's blood from his face, hair, and chest, wrung out his clothes, and put them back on. They sloshed and rubbed against his skin as he followed the bankside path north, downriver, till the half-lit hovels of what must be Sayaxché appeared on the far bank. Ahead the jungle thinned into a clearing where campfires flickered on the dun camouflage of armored personnel carriers. A few soldiers were clustered, talking, around the fires, their rifles stacked in pyramids. He backed away and circled them through the jungle till he picked up the two muddy ruts of the Flores road. He waited several minutes beside it but no one came, so he followed it north till it rose up from the riverside jungle and crossed a huge burnt forest under the vast bowl of the stars.

A charcoal dawn grew in the east. The road began to climb again and he left it to sleep in the scrub, awaking to bright hot sun and the nearing grind of an engine. It was not soldiers but a red Hino truck jammed with cattle, crawling up the last grade. As it downshifted to low gear he ran from the scrub and jumped on the rear bumper, climbed the rack, and dropped in among the longhorns' swaying haunches.

The truck jarred steadily toward Flores, the cattle staggering at each turn, staring round at him, rolling their white eyes and lathering their grass-stained liverish lips, huffing him with hot fetid breath. Beneath their bellies he caught flashes of rushing brush and cragged limestone. The brakes squealed, the axle shimmied and wailed, slowly the truck grated to a halt. Boots thumped round it. "What you got?" a man commanded.

"Can't you see?" a voice answered from the cab. "Twelve eunuchs spawned by El Negro, greatest bull of all Petén. On their way to Paradise, the San Benito abattoir."

"Seen anyone on the road?"

"Several girls coming out of Sayaxché. One of them had tits I could've licked all night."

"Beat it, farmer. You've never licked anything but yourself."

The truck lurched along the dusty rutted road, its crankcase clattering, stock rack rivets rattling, longhorns staggering and sliding on the manure-slick floor and slapping up at green flies on their bellies with dung-caked hooves. Three more times the truck stopped for checkpoints, the cattle lowing uncomfortably, the sun boring down like a blow-torch, crickets crackling like small-arms fire in the scrub.

The air smelled of charcoal and garbage; the truck wallowed from one pothole to the next; above the slats Murphy could see a radio tower, then lamp posts. He climbed over the back, hopped from the bumper, and walked into wide, gritty, unpaved San Benito.

Barefoot boys were playing tin can soccer in the street. A shady sidewalk fronted a string of shops. In one window were hammers with black rubber grips, yellow-handled chisels, saws with gleaming teeth, wooden boxes of shiny nails, zinc pipes, bags of seed, an orange diesel pump from Japan, machetes with flawless gleaming edges, and behind them the weird reflection of a man in a rag serape and threadbare trousers, skinny dirty toes out of home-made *caites*, his tangled hair and short beard thick with dust, who he saw was himself.

22

FIVE SOLDIERS turned the corner, sun glinting off their black rifles. Murphy drew his serape up around his face and stared down like a peasant at the broken stones and litter of the sidewalk, watching their dusty black boots as he stepped aside to let them pass.

Beyond town the road narrowed; the sun beat down. Dizzy hunger gnawed his guts. He walked and walked, but the distant hills drew no closer.

To the left the machine gun nests of Flores Airbase were like huge concrete toadstools with black eye slits watching him. A pickup truck took him to the junction of the Dolores road then turned south toward Machaquilá. He stood at the crossroads, the road to Machaquilá broad and dusty before him, and he felt it was the entrance to the path with heart, back into the time when he had flown at night over this same road, over Dolores and past Machaquilá and between the ziggurat hills and down between the lanterns to the bad landing on the pockmarked road, and he'd been furious because Paco hadn't fixed the potholes, and Paco had been right to fear the Army.

The dusty, still air blistered his lungs. If you concentrate, you can figure how long ago that was, he told himself. If you go down the road, it means you should go back to Dona.

You're going down the road to your end. It was September 13 when you left San Francisco. You stayed over in Merida and left the next night, the 14th. After midnight, the morning of the 15th. So you got shot up and hid in the jungle on September 15. It was two or three nights in the jungle, then a week maybe, in the village before Dona came. Then two weeks more till the priest came to take you downriver. Then the soldiers attacked and it was that night in the jungle with Jesús and Epifanía, then the next night was Dona in the hut with the woman having a baby and we ate the monkey the boy had killed.

The night with Dona seemed like all his life, not just one night.

His brain seemed impossibly clear and he could see his life as if it were a skeleton, bared of flesh. What if it were true that he'd spent his whole life with her, because the only time he'd *lived* was that one night? To think of her was to feel the pain strike to the bone, a rod of steel down to his core, the huge weight of sorrow.

It was truly the path with heart, as Castaneda called it, to go back toward Dolores and Machaquilá, back into the past. It called him so insistently it could not be wrong. But what would he do in Machaquilá? Go through the jungle again to the village? It was now burnt and empty. Yet intensely the road drew him: who was to say you couldn't figure out your future?

A heavy truck came grumbling up behind him and he turned, sticking out his hand. It was an Army troop transport, more trucks following, and he pulled in his hand but the first truck stopped. "Where you headed?" a soldier in the cab called down.

"Belize," he answered, not looking up.

"Come here!"

The man who had called down had a round face and a swollen jaw, as if he were chewing tobacco. "You're not Guatemalan!"

"I'm from Belize. Going home."

"Belize is Guatemala too. The *Ingleses* just stole it for a while. Hop in the back."

"Thank you but no. I've got friends to see on the way."

"Come on! You stuck out your thumb. We won't hurt you. We're going all the way to the border. Hurry or we'll lose first position and be eating dust all the way!"

A soldier leaned over the tailgate to help him up. The truck crunched into first gear and jerked forward. He sat down quickly against the tailgate, the soldiers shouldering aside to make him room. More sat circling him on the floor, others along two benches; they watched him half curiously. They do this, he reminded himself, pick people up then execute them in the hills. "Thank you, *compadres*," he said.

"*De nada*," one answered, turning to spit over the tailgate. He passed a sticky bottle. "Have a drink. It's good for the dust."

It tasted like jet fuel with a caramel odor. "Jesus, it's strong!"

"It's just *boj*, comrade." The soldier had hairy nostrils. Flecks of tobacco stuck to his teeth. "It's what the gods gave us when they took away our freedom."

The bottle clung to Murphy's palm when he passed it on. "Does anyone know what day it is?"

"Day? It's the Lord's day. You don't know that?"

"Yes, but what day of the month?"

"Luis, Franco, you hear?"

"It is 21 October," a soldier said. "Sunday."

"How far is the border?"

The man who had given him the rum glanced at the sky. "Till dark."

"Maybe," said a man with a bandaged eye.

"Since he got wounded," the first said, "Cíclopes here always worries about *la guerrilla*."

"You never know when you'll get ambushed," said the man with the bandaged eye. "Especially in the first truck. These pigs," he pointed at the other soldiers, "they laugh at me because I'm not afraid to fight, don't keep my head down like them!"

A soldier with a thick Mayan nose elbowed Murphy. "But soon comes the bad part!"

Murphy glanced round the circle of faces. The bad part is when these guys take you out and shoot you. "*Guerrilleros?*"

"It's when we pass the turnoff to Tikal. After that the road's no good. It's just paved between Flores and Tikal to impress the tourists."

"It takes a wise man to stick his head up in battle," said the hairy one.

"You should know, Valderrama. The only place you'll ever get injured is your ass."

The truck dropped with a bang from macadam to a boggy track that narrowed and twisted painfully up and down the rambling green slopes, the truck bed whanging and wailing on the bumps and ruts, one torn fender flapping like a broken wing. At times there were strips of un-logged jungle where thin waterfalls necklaced black mossy cliffs, trailing skeins of rainbow mist. Then came miles of slash-burned hills bleeding their cuprite soils into frothy brown torrents, the truck's dust coating the convoy behind it.

Checkpoint after checkpoint passed unheeded; Murphy sank down among his fellows, a chill breeze carving at his ankles. If they were going to shoot you they would've done it long ago. Unless they're playing with you. The road climbed through tangy pines flushed with sunset; he thought of chill

Novembers in the Texas Llano country, walking rocky ridges with his father through frozen juniper, a cold rifle in his hands, a scent of deer on the snowy wind.

LYMAN KEPT the telephone close to his face, his back to the Guatemalan soldiers in the Cobán signals room.

"You're not making things happen, Howie," Curt Merck was saying.

"You want a new deal with Arena, you work it out."

"What about this pilot, you're not getting him."

"It's the Guats, Curt. They won't let me. They won't fly low, they get freaked on hostile fire, and they're . . ."

"You're getting Arena pissed. We have too many irons in the fire for you to do that. I'm sending down some people, give you a hand."

"Listen, we brought in a witness, a priest. Theology liberation type. Vodega was gonna do him, but I saved him. Let me talk with him a while."

"How come you ain't already done this? You don't have your heart in it, being down there."

"I don't want any fucking D-team, Curt."

"Stop goading me, Howie. I'm sending down Vaughan, a dozen guys."

"You telling me I'm not cleared? That you guys got some other agenda?"

"You know what you know. When you get back here we discuss it."

THE TRUCK CRESTED a long ridge of pines and halted. The cab door slammed; a fist banged the tailgate. "Get him out!"

It was the swollen-jawed man. "Far as you go," he said. The second truck came grinding up behind. If they shoot me, Murphy thought, this is it. Below was a narrow black valley speckled with lights.

"Wait!" a soldier called from the back. "Come on, you guys, let's find him some food."

They bundled bread and a chunk of pork into a paper bag and handed it to Murphy over the tailgate. "Sorry we can't take you closer," said the swollen-jawed man. "But we're not supposed to take riders. Those lights down there are Melchor. Got your Belize identity card?"

"Yeah, somewhere." Murphy fumbled at his clothes.

"Just have it when you cross the bridge. Or you get a ride in another Army truck all the way back to Flores."

He stood by the roadside gulping the bread and meat as the convoy descended toward Melchor, mufflers banging and shooting sparks, headlights darting up and down the road cuts. Soon all was silent. Guatemala was empty and dark behind him; the western breeze carried across Belize's plains and piney mountains the dampness of the sea.

23

H E WENT DOWNHILL into the sleeping town. A
rusty statue slumped under a greenish street lamp;
huts and hovels straggled along the river bench. The
bridge and guard post gleamed with concertina wire under
yellow tungsten arc lights. He turned south into a pasture
past a clapboard hut roofed with straw, a pen smelling of
pig manure and rotten mangoes, a hutch where chickens
clucked fearfully.

At the pasture edge the jungle was a black impenetrable wall. He angled toward the river till he found a path
mushy with rotten leaves and occasionally the dung of donkeys. Fireflies were like shooting stars in the brush; mosquitoes whined in his ears; he kept wiping them from his
face. Something pinged underfoot and he dived expecting
a mine but nothing blew; he rolled away and ran, tripped
and sprawled; with a deep thump a flare burst overhead
trailing down radiant embers, cutting the jungle into black
and white staggering shadows. From the guard post came
the growl of a siren.

He ran along the trail, stumbling on sapling stumps;
another flare cracked, a third. The jungle was like day; he
pushed through it to the river; the bridge was hidden by a
bend. He slid into the water and began to swim across, com-

ing up for breath. It's easy, he thought, I'll make it. Then beyond the shallows the current snatched him, tumbling end over end, fighting up for breath and slipping under. The bridge swung into view, impossibly high and bright. With a crushing pain something huge and heavy hit him, dragged him down, he was caught in the boughs of a half-sunken tree; the bridge was overhead now, black under the flares; like a sea creature the tree churned over and spat him to the top and he clung inside its branches, hidden from the bridge.

The river swung to the left, the tree bearing hard against the Belize shore. He swam to land, pulled himself up a slippery steep bank and climbed a clearcut slope out of rifle range to a ridge overlooking the black river and the bridge gilded by the arc lights of the Guatemalan guard post on the far side, where up and down the banks soldiers were beating the brush, their flashlights winking.

Below him the corrugated huts of the Belize border post were lit by one lantern in whose wan glow a single unarmed sentry loitered. Murphy ran down a slash-burned cindery hillside to the road climbing up from the bridge, and ran east along it, away from the river.

After perhaps an hour he began to walk. The road traversed a small town where a few dogs barked disconsolately, then climbed into bowl-shaped hills where huge stumps of recent rainforest jutted up like menhirs. There were no birds, no snakes, no insects, only silence and the shuffle of his feet under the wheeling stars.

Toward dawn a narrow moon rose over a distant ridge capped by a dark pyramid he thought might be Xunantunich, where Mayan astronomers once calculated the exact trajectories of the stars. After sunrise a rancher let him ride in the back of his pickup to San Ignacio, then gave him a Belizean quarter, "for a roll, cup coffee" at a sidewalk vendor's. The hot jolt of black coffee and the sweetness of the roll made only *this* seem real, the rest seem a dream. So let it be a dream, he thought.

Beyond San Ignacio he washed his face in a ditch where gaily garbed women were cupping water into plastic buckets. He rode an empty cane truck to the outskirts of Belize City, then caught a lift north with a grass farmer in a new Bronco with quad speakers and fat steel tube bumpers for deliveries to the States. A warm breeze through the Bronco's window ruffled his beard and blew wisps of hair across his eyes. The farmer gave him a fragrant banana; he tossed the peel out the window and in the side mirror saw it alight birdlike in the grass. The farmer lit a joint and passed it to him; the rich sweet smoke filled his lungs; he could *taste* the air, see every emerald cell of every leaf of the hunched jungle and spiky bunchgrass, the algal pools and stooping egrets, the flysore Brahma cattle with their concave white flanks, the bleached towering skeletons of mahogany trees tied by green lianas to the chipped and chalky soil. The Bronco hit a hummingbird that exploded in a rainbow of feathers and blood against the windshield.

At Orange Walk's rotting Victorian square the Bronco turned east, and Murphy walked uphill through shady rubber trees till he caught a ride on a flatbed where strips of mahogany bark writhed like bandages in the wind. He sat on the back beside a broken-toothed Mayan who shared a handful of pumpkin seeds, their legs dangling over the end as they spat the pumpkin shells on to the road rolling away beneath them. "I just came from Guatemala," Murphy said.

The Mayan licked a white flake of pumpkin seed from his lip. "Guatemala? What is that?"

He got off the truck at Corozal Town and walked east along a dirt road fringing the Bay to a jungled spit with a white house in a grove of bananas and limes. A man was husking coconuts with a machete on a mahogany stump. "Hey! Lovejoy!" Murphy called, not wanting to startle him.

The man looked at him a moment, buried the machete in the stump. "What the fock happened *you*?"

"They killed my friends, burned my plane." Tears shot into his eyes. "Killed a whole village –"

"Who, mon, *who*?

"The Guatemalans, Americans."

Lovejoy grabbed his shoulder, walking him toward the house. "Let's get inside, get you a drink!"

"I don't need a drink. I want food, some time to think." They went into the cool, thatched, sea-scented shadows of the house. "I'm a little stoned, actually."

"I believe it."

"Had a few hits off a guy gave me a lift." He found a chair and sat. Safe now, he thought. Over. But she's still there. Going through it every day.

24

L YMAN CAUGHT a limo from National, tense to be home, hating and wanting Nancy. Languidly the lampposts sauntered past, the sleeping suburbs where once there had been farms and before that forest. Clumps of dead leaves were frozen to the streets; against the lights the trees lunged, black and spidery. "Been gone long, sir?" the driver asked, but Lyman didn't answer.

They passed a restaurant, a man and woman walking on the sidewalk, his hand on her shoulder, then another couple arm in arm. The walking wounded, Lyman thought, hobbling from the battlefield of life. He let the metaphor grow in his mind – as we get older, wiser, there's no more of this silly cuddling. We're the survivors, have learned that he who fights best fights alone.

His house seemed caught out by the limo's headlights, the Norway firs on each side of the door leaning away, hungry to escape, the lava chunks of the front walk loud like dry bread crunching under his shoes, the dry bread the children left but the birds ate it, and the children never found their way home. The doorbell rang in the distance, as if new walls had come between it and him.

The light flicked on. He felt thin and childish in its glare, holding his bulletproof attaché case like a door-to-door salesman, his duffel over one shoulder like an unexpected and unwanted visitor. Nancy's eye in the safety lens was huge and rotund. He held his breath, standing straight.

"Well, hi!" Frowsy and sleep-fragrant, her hair rumpled, her silk nightgown warm with slumber, she reached into his arms and he felt how slim and light she was, how evil it would be to hurt her, feeling also as always the need to be cool, steady, almost devoid of emotion because she seemed to prefer it. Who are you, anyway, he thought, to trot out your feelings?

"Why don't you ever *call!*" she said. "We've missed you."

"I've thought about you all the time." Almost all the time, he corrected himself.

She was rubbing her eyes and trying to wake up and he tossed his coat on a chair, took off his shoes and held her, her perfume irritating his throat, her hair tickling his unshaven chin, her lips against his neck. She pulled back. "Want something to eat?"

"No." He went into the bedrooms and hugged each sleeping child, the girl mumbling a dream, the boy waking instantly and holding him tight in his arms and not letting go till finally Lyman made him lie down, go back to sleep.

He padded in stockinged feet across the broad living room carpet, past the black stack of stereo equipment, the bookcase shelves of CDs in gleaming array, the leather couches, the marble side tables, the French watercolors and tall tapering plants; they seemed all to belong to someone else whose taste was good but excessive. He undressed in the bathroom, laid his clothes on his dresser.

"Just toss them in the hamper," she said.

"Not the suit."

"So how'd it go?"

"Standard stuff. Inspection, drills, exercises, troop reviews ad nauseam. Lots of nights to read and stare at the barracks' walls."

"What'd you read?"

"Oh, nothing. You know, magazines, that rot." The waterbed sank under his knee. "Detective novels, thrillers."

"Any good ones?"

"Not really. In one mind and out the other."

She smiled. "You really could've called."

"That's just it, Nan. I couldn't. Same old drill."

"Same old drill."

He lay down punching up his pillow. She held herself along him, and he wanted her badly, thinking you shouldn't, she probably doesn't want to, she's not awake, not expecting this, but he couldn't help himself, and she raised her hip so he could slide up her nightgown. She turned her face from his breath as he shoved into her, recoiling then trying not to show it, and he thought the pain of it, the pain of it for *them*, while in him the fire was building, the gorgeous explosion, and she got up and went to the bathroom and he felt rotten and empty, as if he'd just spilt the last five weeks.

"You must be sleepy," she said, getting back in bed.

He held her. "Not at all." Pretend she's a stranger, he told himself, tracing with a fingertip the line of her brow. Black hair, brown skin. "One bad thing –"

The muscles of her neck stiffened; she made herself relax. "What's that?"

"Kit."

She raised up, pulling free. "What?"

"He's dead."

She spun away and sat. Her claw came out and raked his face. "You bastard. You waited to tell me! Bastard!" She dashed out, nightgown sailing round her knees.

He followed her into the living room. She sat on the couch with her face in her hands. He wiped blood from his cheek and stared at it in the palm of his hand. "Are you sure?" she said.

"I saw him."

"Who did it? Which of you bastards is responsible?"

"He was killed by a drug smuggler, Nan. I'm not supposed to tell you that..."

"I don't *care* what you're supposed to tell! You and your goddamn silly rules!"

"The reason I was down there so long was to try and get the one who killed him."

"Which you failed to do!"

"It's not that easy, Nan."

"I don't *care* if it's not easy. I don't *care* anything about you!"

He looked down, realized he was naked. "I've done a lot you never see. I'm a lot more than you think."

She did not answer and he realized she was crying, quietly, into her hands. He felt cold and went back into the bedroom and climbed into bed.

MURPHY WAS WADING through a field of yellow flowers with a woman and a child. They were one flesh; he could feel what they felt and see with their eyes.

He was being hunted down a long hallway. He hid in the second story of a warehouse stacked with cases of canned sodas; he took a can. "Watch out!" Lovejoy yelled. "It's explosives!" He laughed and tossed it over a wall; it banged loudly, waking him up. Those flowers, he thought, they must be *flor de muerte*.

Breeze stirred in the white muslin curtains; through the window came the cries of gulls and mumble of bees. The room smelled of lime flowers, jasmine, and sea. The bees-

143

waxed pine floor squeaked under his soles. He walked out to the veranda and a flock of sparrows burst chittering from the eaves. He went back into the kitchen, drank fresh orange juice till the jug was empty then squeezed more juice and drank it. There was bacon laid out on the counter and he fried it with six eggs and ate them with lime pie. He mixed a big cup of Mexican instant coffee and sat out on the shaded terrace in the warm wind off the sea.

Lovejoy came and leaned his yellow bicycle against the terrace wall. He carried a plastic bag of red meat into the kitchen. The refrigerator door opened and shut. "You get enough to eat?"

"Just barely."

Lovejoy came out with four Tecates and sat. He popped one can and squeezed lime into it. "You slep' more, las' three days, than you used to in a month."

Murphy stretched his right arm over his head, testing it. "Feels good."

"Goin' stay a while?"

Murphy patted Lovejoy's shoulder, let his hand rest there. "Can't."

"I think you oughta wait, find another cargo, drive it up."

"Can't."

"You los' your plane, mon. How you going to earn a livin'? Better you let me front you a load, I'll buy you a van, you drive it up. Then you got money to buy another plane. Simple as thet."

"Don't need to earn a living any more, Love." Murphy's head hurt and he wanted to get out of the sun, realized he wasn't in the sun.

"Get yourself a camper," Lovejoy said, as if he hadn't heard. "Tie in with one o' them American groups thet drives their campers through Mexico together, the Wally Byams, thet what they called? American Legion, or some kinda religious group, Protestants – thet kinda thing. Go through the border with them, you be home free…"

Murphy opened another beer and squeezed lime into it. "I need you to front me a ticket and a driver's license so I can go home."

"Home don't sound like no safe place to be right now."

"They can't trace my plane, can't trace me anywhere."

"And what you goin' do when you git home?"

"Sort things out, maybe come back down."

"Revenge don't work, mon. It jes take you with it."

"I want to know why they hit my plane, killed Johnny and the others."

"You never will know."

"She said they're hitting other planes, even people who've paid protection. This General Arena's going to be head of the Armed Forces."

"That's his job, wipe out the others, keep it fo' hisself. He be doin' a good job at thet."

"And I want to know why that American officer was there, and why they killed him."

"You's too curious by far."

"Too curious by far!" Lovejoy's parrot repeated from its perch under a banana tree.

"If you fell for some woman like Dona," Murphy said, "you'd leave her?"

"Forget thet woman, mon. She not ever going to live for you."

"And the people who burned my village? You'd let that be?"

"Like thet woman say, the best way to fix thet is talk about it in the States. But the moment you do thet you blow your cover and these people goin' come looking for you. Now what's the good o' thet?"

25

"THEY'S A LITTLE too big for you, mon."
Murphy looked down at Lovejoy's flowered shirt huge in the shoulders and the purple trousers rolled up at the cuffs. "Your mother fed you too much."

"They'll do till I pop over to Chetumal, get you some right ones. Shoes, too. Today we takin' you into town, fo' a shave'n haircut."

"I'll keep it like this. Covers up the scar."

Lovejoy shook his head. "One more inch to the right and you was gone."

"Never hurt at the time. Only after…"

"Always meanin' to asks you, where you git thet star?"

Murphy glanced at the tattoo on his right arm, above the bullet wound Dona had healed. "The Lone Star of Texas. Got it in Hong Kong."

"Thet figures."

"I was on leave. Rest and Recreation."

"Thet's a trouble bein' dark black, can't do tattoos. You kin, but they don' show."

"You ain't missing much."

"Don't like Hong Kong. Use' to go there, in the merchan' marine. Didn't like it."

Murphy went to the refrigerator and came back with more Tecates and another lime. "Pick 'em off the fuckin trees."

"Wha's thet?"

"Limes. Sign of civilization. No civilization where you can't have fresh limes."

"Civilization's where the love's easy, mon. I thought a lot about it, seen a lot of places, and thet's the best indication I kin find."

"Always thought civilization was sex, drugs, and rock 'n roll. The Holy Trinity."

"We's a lot wiser when we's young. We sure git stupid, growin' older."

"All those days in that village, lying in that hammock, limes saved my life. Dona told me, said they fight off the infection."

"You believe ever'thing she say, this gir'l?"

The lawn in front of the terrace was fiercely white with sun. Through the beach palms Corozal Bay scintillated with blue fire. "People been dead twenty years, Love, they came back to me, alive like you and me. When I was lying in that hammock." Murphy stood at the edge of the terrace, the edge of the shade, breathing in the heat. "My two best friends in Nam, they got killed. We'd been living in death, seeing it all around us... there were days I remember seeing fifty dead or more, new ones, every day. But my friends – I would've gone crazy if I hadn't shut it down."

"Tha's the trouble." Lovejoy put an empty on the floor, opened another. "You shut *thet* down, pretty soon you're shutting it *all* down."

"For years I've hardly thought of them. Not thinking about what they've missed, since then. Every day they could be living, and do they still suffer, and I don't let it hit me."

"You lettin' it hit, right now."

"When I was in that village, my friend Okie who died in Vietnam, he sat on the floor beside the hammock and we talked for hours. I told him I've loved him like a brother all these years, down inside my heart. He said I had to pull through, that he had come back mostly for that, to help me. That I mustn't feel bad because I'd lived and he didn't."

"Yeah?" Lovejoy said.

"We called him Okie because he came from Oklahoma. He'd been a hippie, with a beard, before he was drafted. He would run right out in mortar fire to drag some guy in... bullets flying all around. He hated war. He just scorned it. So big and strong you almost thought he could take the whole war up in his fists and strangle it. He never let on, but it was eating him alive that his chick back home was screwing another guy. Some guy who was too sensitive to fight, had a family that paid a shrink to write the draft board a letter saying he was crazy."

"Then he probably was."

"What?"

"Crazy."

"Okie ran into a bunch of Cong on a path, he was going into the woods after a wounded guy screaming for help. He didn't have a gun or anything. The Cong just ripped him in half. I told him I'd kept thinking of that moment, how he must have felt. He told me it was pure terror when he saw them shoot and knew he was going to die, then being hit, horrible pain, being knocked back and you see everything close up and after your heart stops the brain keeps thinking for a while, sorting things out."

"Then what?"

"He said you can come back to the people who knew you. That you can help them, that the same battle between good and evil that goes on in life goes on afterwards. That evil's stronger and usually wins, which meant I had to harden my character, become more honest, think more about death and life."

"But what he say about *him,* since then? 'Bout where he been?"

"He just said you know what you know."

Lovejoy shook his head. "Shit!"

"He'd never known Clint, my other friend. Clint died before Okie came over. When I was in the hammock Clint didn't come as much as Okie, but sometimes they'd be there together and the three of us would talk, like sitting around a fire in hunting camp, thinking over past times. They became friends, while the three of us sat round together. Except they were both dead and I was in my hammock and it hurt to move and breathe and hurt even if you didn't and I was crazy with the pain and fever and they knew it and made allowances, and Clint used to tell me how to fight the pain."

Lovejoy got up, squeezed Murphy's wrist and stepped across the terrace out into the sun, across the blazing grass to the shade of a papaya clump. "Beer go right through you, on a hot day," he said coming back. "What he tell you 'bout this fighting pain?"

"He said you can't hold it back, gotta let it take you. That sometimes you can change it a little by moving yourself or breathing or forcing yourself to think of something else. Said he'd lain for three days on a little hill with a neck wound... I'd never known what happened to him, we could never find them. And during the third night their position got hit by B52s. Thousand-pound bombs." Murphy looked out over the terrace to the line of shore all green against the blue and white. "I used to get so full of hatred about what had happened. I wanted to go back to the States, take all the people who voted for that war, the politicians and the people who voted for them, wanted to kill them one by one, have them feel what my friends felt."

"And now?"

"I still hate them for being stupid. But now I think war's like an earthquake or something. There's no way we can control it."

"We jes' prefer war to other things, thet's all."

"Clint's daughter, she's twenty-one now, she was born after he died. I got wounded again at the end, never went to Maine, where Clint came from, never saw his wife. Years later, I never called his kid. So he asked me to."

"You going to?"

"Said I felt like one of those lousy fathers who never sees his own kid after a divorce, then suddenly when she's grown up he reappears, wants to claim her. He said it wasn't like that, that what keeps people apart is pain, not meanness. He said all meanness just comes from pain."

"I'M VERY PISSED you brought me back up, Curt."

"It's not your business to have emotions."

"How you expect a guy to do his best when you keep cutting his *cojones*?"

"I been behind you all the way, here. In this Agency, Howie, you got me to thank."

"I got *me* to thank, Curt. *I* got me where I am."

"With some help from your friends. Just like when I was coming up, I had people looking out for me. And what you got to remember is, afterwards you got to treat them well..."

The yellow of Lyman's fingernails irritated him, against the light chocolate skin, the fingers splayed out over the knee of his blue pinstripe. Spread fingers a sign of weakness, he thought, brought them together. Under the desk Lyman could see Merck's little feet hanging down from the chair, not touching the carpet. Little penguin feet.

"You got to accept when we wanted you out, down there, it's for good reason."

"You mean Latinos just don't like blacks."

"That too. But that's why I always pushed you down there, pushed you in their faces, because you're better than anyone else and I wanted them to have to admit it. Now instead you screw up and get a whole buncha guys killed."

"Six, Curt. Just six guys killed. And the reason the Guats don't take so many casualties is they're chicken. They'll burn a village, kill women and children, no problem. Just like us in Nam, the napalm raids. But at least *we* had the guts to go out in the boonies and hunt Charlie down. Blow his fucking ass off." Lyman realized his arms were quivering, made them stop. "You ask these Guats to get down on the ground, out in the bush, off the fucking trail? *Never!* A little recon? *Never!*"

Merck sat back, smoothed down one eyebrow, propped his elbows up on the chair arms. "Howie, there's policies being decided," his little hands came up and out, like a man rendering himself, Lyman thought, "far above my head. Like you, I got to deliver…"

"Don't pull duty on me, Curt."

"What you using your head for, Howie? Think *real politik*."

"OK, I think it's fine we jacked down the crude oil price and pushed up the ante on defense technology and forced the Commies under. And like you've said, we got a different ballgame now in Latin America because now, without the Soviets to turn to, the poor don't have any recourse but to eat shit. But bringing the Colombians into Guatemala – I don't see what it brings us."

"That's why I'm where I'm at, Howie, and you're going to stay where you're at. Until you learn to see."

26

"SOON'S Miss Pru and Desirée come home I'll cook up thet conch. You want fritters?"

"Do I want fritters? What kind of question's that? But we're gonna need more beer."

"Tecate he be all gone. Got to go back Mexico. They be jes' Libertad."

"Jesus!"

"You have'n too much anyways, mon. You been beat up, got to rest easy."

Murphy crossed the veranda and the grass underfoot now cooler in the late afternoon sun, stood barefoot in the water warm like warm tea. He stripped his clothes and waded in, sat letting the sea wash up against his chest. His head was spinning and he put it under the water and swam out underwater, the light pearly blue above and cool purple below, the rolling bay waves bubbling sunlight. You could drown like this, he thought.

NANCY took Lyman's coat and hung it in the hall closet. She glanced across the living room then came up to him, hands against his chest. "I'm sorry about your face."

"I know you don't love me. I know it and accept it."

"You don't need to hate me the way you do."

"I don't hate you, Nan. You're all I've got."

"You've got the kids."

"Yeah, and they come from you."

"They come from *you* too! Can't we live with some affection, till they grow up?"

"They don't need me."

"They'd need you if they had you. They just don't have you. And if you had them you'd need them, too. But you never spend any time with them."

"I been too busy, Nan. Trying to make things easy for them. For you."

"Let's make a new beginning?" She took his hand. "Pretend we like each other, like friends? Pretend we're just living together, two friends?"

"How many times we made new beginnings, Nan? You're just saying that now 'cause Kit's dead, you got nobody to fuck."

She twisted his wrist, nails in the skin. "You're the *bastard* that started that. You *wanted* me to!"

"Because I knew it's the only way you'd come alive. That you couldn't get it from me!"

"I *married* you, didn't I? What more do you *want*?"

He caressed her cheek, realized it was a slow slap and pulled his hand away. "We got married too many years ago."

"THE ONLY THING that counts is a man love a woman." Miss Pru put a big chunk of conch fritter from her fork into her mouth. "Don' matter 'bout nothin' else. Not to her."

"She's got to love him too," Lovejoy said.

"Of course. Otherwise she don' care if he love her or not."

"I don't want any man to love me!" Desirée said. "Who wants to have kids and everything? Horrible! When instead you could be free?"

Pru was cutting more conch. "Matters someday, honey. When you find you tired o' that 'ol freedom. When it wearin' you down. But you got years to go. You git to finish your school first."

"Then I'm going to be a doctor," Desirée told Murphy.

He almost dropped his fork, bit his lip, raised his Libertad to her, a mock salute.

She shook her head. "I'm *serious*."

He watched the thatch, watched nothing; the pain went away. "I'm sure there's nothing better you could do." It sounded false. "I mean it, honey."

Pru leaned forward, big black sweaty elbows on the table. "So I don' think you're right, Love, tellin' him forget her. He should go back there, *make* her come out here, to civ'lization, not live in the jungle like a monkey, like that gorilla!"

"He can't go back in there'n get her! They never let 'im back. They *kill* 'im if he try thet!"

"She won't go with me anyway, Pru."

Pru put down her fork. "Then she jes' a stupid gir'l."

"No, she's right."

Pru grasped the fork, shook it at him. "She right not to love you when you love her?"

"No, not that. She's got another love, that came first."

"You mean thet gorilla?" Lovejoy put in. "Thet one she said she loved?"

"No," Murphy laughed. "She loves what she *does*, what she does for people, making things better."

A wide incredulous *moue* creased Pru's face. "What she doin' for you?"

"I'VE BEEN THINKING we should buy the McCormack house," Nancy said.

Lyman poured the whisky into the octagonal glass and placed the one ice cube carefully so it wouldn't splash. Wait twenty seconds, just enough for it to cool the whisky not dilute it. The taste was like smoke, like fire, burning on the tip of his tongue then cooling backwards, oak fire flaring to ice up through his sinuses. He thought of hash in Vietnam, how the taste of it, the *feel* of it, had come up through his nose and into his brain. "We can't stand each other. You want us to buy a house?"

"You're exaggerating, Howie. I agree, it's been hard. But maybe if we shared in something new, something bigger, an improvement? It would say something about *us*."

"It would say we're out of our fucking minds."

"You'll never try, will you, darling? It's always got to be Howie just the way he is, he never *tries* to be better."

"I try to be who I am, Nan. That's hard enough." He took another swig of the whisky but it wasn't the same, too much water now. The thought of a cigarette made his lungs ache. "No, come to think of it, I don't try to be who I am. I never even know." If he had a cigarette in front of her she'd think he was weak, that he couldn't shake it. Nine weeks now, down to five a day. He could get up and go into the bathroom, or say he had to see something in the garage, have a quick one. But she'd figure out. Smell it. He went into the kitchen, dumped the ice cube, came back and took another, filled the glass up. The whisky was like piss, yellow and oily. He thought of all the Scotch bottles in all the stores in the world, all the wine, the beer, champagne. All waiting to be piss. All the fine pastries and steaks and gourmet foods, caviar at fifty bucks an ounce, waiting to be shit. "I bet if you try to learn about yourself, if *I* try to learn about myself, I bet I can."

She took his wrist that earlier she'd clawed. "I know you can, Howie. You do, and we can be together again. All the way."

THE THICK AIR was musky with star jasmine and citrus, the indolent breeze off the Bay, the sweet-smelling cane fields. "Coupla drinks at Mother Teresa's, Murph, then I'm takin' you home."

"I know the way back."

Lovejoy took his arm, as if holding himself up. "You liable to fergit."

"You don' have any fuckin *beer*. Here I come to see you and you don' even have any fuckin *beer*!" Each time I think of her, Murphy decided, it's easier.

"I didn't know you was comin'."

"Neither did I."

At the end of the street a white house with wide steps. "Them belly full but we hungry," sang the music inside. "A hungry mon is a hungry mon…"

They climbed the stairs, weaving between the men sitting with beers on the steps. Lanterns reflected inside off spilt beer on the table tops. Lovejoy got a cloth from the bar and wiped a table. Murphy sat; the table stuck to his elbows. Lovejoy took the cloth to the bar and came back with two beers. "Belikan?" Murphy said.

"Belikan."

"Jesus! The English ruined you people."

"Not me, mon. I's from Jamaica."

"I *know* that." Murphy drained his glass and watched the dancing bright-eyed slim-dressed girls clapping cheap gold heels and bare feet on the beer-spilt floor. "Going back, Stateside, I won't need a driver's license. Just lend me money for the ticket."

"How the *fock* you gettin' through the border?"

"Fly up, Monterrey, walk across."

"You crazier'n shit, mon. Border patrol going to have yo' *ass*. Then they going to start discussin' with you where you been..."

"You're afraid of the cops, Love. I really think you are."

"Course I am. When you livin' fine and easy why should'n you be? When any time they kin take it all away?"

"You've got good distance. You're not in it."

"The minute I stop paying I am. Or when they want to make an example. You always try to make sure they make an example of somebody else, but nobody ain't perfect." Lovejoy leaned forward clasping his beer. "How much you shoulda made, thet trip to Guatemala?"

"Bout fifty."

"You'll make more'n thet, driving it up."

"It's too dangerous. I told you."

"You's like I used to be, after twenty years at sea. I thought everything on land was dangerous. You been flyin' too long..."

"I don't want to go through no border with no half ton of weed." Murphy realized he was talking like Lovejoy. It's just the beer, he decided.

"It's 'emetic, mon, all welded in. The dogs can't smell it and even if they strip down your rig they can't find it. You cross at El Paso, like I said, with some Protestant missionary types, you ain't ever got a worry."

27

"JASON!" Lyman yelled. "This yours?"

The boy watched the transparent film canister in Lyman's hand. Inside the canister a golden butterfly, crumbles of wing at the bottom.

"I found it one day. On a hike."

"Well goddammit keep it in your room. Stuff like this all over the house, no wonder we're all going crazy."

"*We*'re not all going crazy, Howie," Nancy said.

"C'mon!" Lyman yelled at the boy. "Hustle! Hustle!"

"Howie," Nancy sat on the edge of the couch, hands clamped between her knees, "what's eating you?"

"*You're* eating me. *He*'s eating me. You're *all* eating me."

She patted the couch beside her. "Sit."

Despite himself he sat. There was an ache between his shoulder blades, all the way up his neck. He wanted to say he was sorry but wouldn't.

She put her hand on his knee. "I meant what I said, Howard. We're going to start a new beginning. I'm going to understand the stress you've been under and I'm going to make it better for you. And you're going to stop seeing me as some bitch, and instead as the person you love, the mother of your children."

He snickered. "I'm not even sure of that."

Her hand clenched. "You're going to stop saying things like that, Howie. That's part of our new beginning. If I have to, I'll do this all by myself. But I'd rather do it with you."

"You can't make me love you, Nancy."

"You already love me. I know that. The one you don't love is yourself."

"GOT IRISH WHISKY?" Murphy yelled over the reggae at Mother Teresa behind the bar.

She reached up a gold bottle. "Black Bush."

"That's Protestant whiskey, Bushmills."

"You prayin' or drinkin'?"

He took the bottle and two glasses to the table. "You goin' have a *bad* headache in the morning," Lovejoy said.

"Wouldn't feel right without one." He poured the glasses full. "Don't make no sense."

"It don' make any sense to me either, mon. So I jes' lets it alone."

Murphy drank a second glass, not tasting it. "You jes' love who you got," Lovejoy said, "an' you don' try to change the worl', 'cause the worl' been screwed up longer than you know."

Four men in uniforms came in and sat by the door, waving at the bar. "Those guys," Murphy said.

Lovejoy screwed round in his chair. "They's got a right to come in, get laid, jes' like anybody. On leave, prob'ly, from Honduras."

"They're Airborne."

"They's what? Hee, hee, I *know* they's born. Otherwise how they be comin' in here?"

"Like the ones who burned my village."

"Those was Guatemalans, you said."

"There was Americans with them."

The four Americans rolled up their sleeves, nodding and talking, the black girls gathering round them in the roaring reggae. One soldier, blond and broad-shouldered, beckoned to a girl in a lilac blouse and black shimmery slacks; she sat open-legged in his lap, drinking beer from his bottle as he bounced her loosely on his crotch, a cigarette hanging sideways from his red lips.

"Forget your troubles, and dance," Lovejoy sang with the music. "Forget your sorrows, and dance."

Murphy walked softly across the noisy crowded floor to the four soldiers. "Where you guys stationed?"

"Hi!" one grinned. "Have a beer."

"Where you stationed?" he said to the blond one.

"What's it to you?"

"I wouldn't have asked, motherfucker, if I didn't want to know."

The soldier watched him, chewing his cigarette. Murphy flicked it from his mouth. "Ever been in Guatemala?"

The soldier slid the girl from his lap and stood. "Well look at this. I come in here to get laid and I get some asshole in my face."

Murphy hit him square, the satisfying crunch of front teeth, agony snaking up his bad arm. The soldier went down in crashing tables and chairs, another's fist slammed into Murphy's chin and he flew backwards sliding on his back across the floor, tables and beer bottles tumbling. He got up and with a red flash of pain a bottle exploded over his head and he spun to hit the soldier who had the bottle, wondering is it blood or whiskey running down my neck, another soldier swinging a chair but it caught on a toppled table and Murphy kicked him and the blond one grabbed him and they fell, Murphy twisting to grind him backwards in the shattered glass, the others kicking his ribs and a boot hit his bad arm and he screamed, rolled free, grabbed a table, a single still-upright Belikan bottle on it ricketing absurdly as he threw the table and the other soldiers backed away swearing. The blond one got up and Murphy hit him again, under the ear, and he fell face down in the broken glass. "Get *out*!" Murphy screamed, a man behind the soldiers laughing white teeth, and suddenly Murphy saw everyone was staring at him, at the mess on the floor.

The blond soldier stood slowly. "You're crazy."

Murphy felt a sudden plunge of shame. "You get out of here. You get out of *everywhere* down here."

Blood was running down the soldier's forehead into his eye. There was blood in his mouth. "We were doing nothing, just having a..."

"You musta done something," Lovejoy said, "to make him so mad. Be smart, mon, move on. They be 'nother bar down the street."

"T'row dem white boy all out!" someone laughed.

Mother Teresa was sweeping up glass. People had set up the tables and were sitting again, laughing, animated. The barefoot girls were moving tentatively on the dance floor, watching for broken glass. Lovejoy grabbed Murphy's shirt. "Why the *fock* you do thet, mon? This be *my* place! Grace!" he yelled to a barefoot girl in a yellow blouse, "you take this crazy mon upstairs, see if you can *fock* some sense into him!"

Murphy rubbed blood out of his eyes. "Go to Hell, Lovejoy!"

"They soldiers goin' be waitin' fo' you! You git you white ass up thet stairs!"

Grace pushed him ahead of her upstairs to a low room with a wretched mattress on a broken bed and a dejected table cluttered with empty Belikan bottles. She unbuttoned the yellow blouse, dark shiny breasts popping out, slipped down her black skirt, nothing underneath. The bed squealed and slumped when he sat on it. She found a cloth on the table and stood before him, wiping blood and beer and pieces of glass out of his hair, her breasts warm and full against his face, her cunt smell tangy. After a while he put his hands round her and kissed her breasts, down her front and buried his face in her warm bush, the hair thick and silky, and she pushed him back on the bed and came on top of him, riding him slowly saying "Jesus", and his head was spinning and he was seeing strange places and dead faces and then it came out of him and he thought like pus, like purging some disease, and Grace a nurse, sister of mercy. How God was born, he thought, seeing the woman beside him, young and lithe, his seed inside her going nowhere, like all of us, seeing himself and Grace as God saw them, a woman and a man on a stained and sticky mattress, the floor with crushed palmetto bugs under a flyspecked bulb, mosquitoes clamoring through a torn screen, the laughter of drunks and reggae pulsing up through the boards,

He who seeks of only vanity
and has no love for humanity
shall fade away, fade fade
fade fade away

28

"WHY YOU GOT a picture of *him* on your wall?" Lyman said.

"You should hear his music, Dad."

"He was a traitor to your skin, Jason." Lyman sat on the bed, sneering at the Michael Jackson poster, a premenstrual hypnotic bitch. Had this man suffered everything, he suddenly wondered, just to make himself what people needed him to be?

His big flat hand felt strange on Jason's knee and he removed it, brushed the boy's fuzzy curls, *made* his fingers go into them. "He even straightened his hair, that guy."

"Like Christina."

"She can't help it. She's going to do anything I don't want her to."

"She's a girl, Dad. She can't be anything like you."

"How d'you think she's going to end up? Really?"

Jason drew up one knee, hands clasped round it, thinking. Lyman glanced down at Jason's sneaker to make sure the sole was not dirtying the bed. "Your mother has to wash that sheet," he said.

"Oh, yeah." The boy put down his foot. "Sorry, Dad."

"So what do you think?"

"About Tina? I think she's fine. She's nice to me a lot of the time. She takes me places, drives me to games when Mom can't."

"You don't hate her for yelling at you?"

"She only does that sometimes. Mom yells at me too, sometimes, and I don't hate her." Jason looked up at Lyman entreatingly. "Sometimes even you yell at me…"

'Don't let's talk about that now. Sometimes you deserve it."

"I got three goals last week."

"You did? In one game?"

"One against Harmondale Tuesday and two against Lincoln on Saturday."

"You play forward both games?"

"At Lincoln I played defense the first half."

"Shit! Why'd he do that?"

"Coach Larsen? He just did it, that's all."

"Well, you went out and showed him. You got two goals."

"He says everybody has to play offence and defense, that we're there to learn, not to win."

"That's liberal bullshit. Don't you ever believe that. The only people who try to teach you that are the ones who want to keep control over you. That's a white thing to do, Jason. All that counts in life is winning. Morals and laws are to keep most people in line so a few can do what they want."

"You've won a lot, haven't you, Dad? You've got this nice house and two cars? I don't know anybody else who has a BMW *and* a Mercedes."

"The Mercedes's old," Lyman smiled. "You can't count that." He leaned back, supported by his hands behind him on the bed. "You ever feel out of place?"

The boy took off his shoes and turned round to face his father, sat cross-legged. "With *them*?" He shrugged, pinched at the bedspread. "There's lots of others at school, Dad. I'm not the only one."

"You guys hang out together, all that?"

"Sometimes. I got white friends, too. I was just calling up Eric Baldwin, see if I can see him. Mom's going to drive me."

"What do they think of you, do you think?"

The boy pushed out his lips to show ignorance. Nigger lips, Lyman thought. He wanted to slap him. "I love, you, Son," he said. "Remember no matter what I do I loved you. That we all do what we think is best."

"I think sometimes they think because we can run faster than them we must be stupider. But I don't think that."

Lyman leaned forward, forced himself to brush the boy's hair. "They used to think we were slow runners, too. But we showed them. We're going to keep on showing them till they all end up as manual workers. Like we once were. One thing you got never to forget, is what we *were*. Unless you keep that in mind, all the time, you're never going to be different, not inside your heart." He punched the boy's shoulder, walked out, stopped at the door. "And no matter what you think of them, or what they think of you," he nodded up at the poster, "never water down your blood."

"YOU USE' TO SAY, we all pay for what we git."

Murphy tried to speak through the pain. "I'm fine."

"You look it."

"Just my hand. This damn arm."

"You head it look pretty nice too."

"I'm getting out of your hair, Love. Heading up north tomorrow."

"You going walk roun' the Belize border? I'll take you."

"I can find it."

"I'll take you. Go up Cancún, get a driver's license."

"How much?"

"Maybe three hundred. But you ought to take a couple thousand. To have for the ticket and expenses, all that. I'll give you some pesos, too, for the bus."

"Just give me a grand, some pesos. I'll send it right back."

"Thet Mother Teresa, she real mad at you."

"I'll pay her for the broken table, all that. Out of what you lend me."

"She don' care 'bout thet. It's the *reputation* of the place, to have white boys fightin' in it."

"They had it coming, those guys."

"You want a drink, or something? For your head?"

"My head just wants to sleep." Squinting against the sun, Murphy crossed the metal-bright lawn and crawled into the hammock in the dark green shade of banana leaves. The air was like a warm bath, with the perfume of fruit and many flowers, the warble of the parrot and the susurration of birds, the rustle of the wind. Like Clint had said when he returned from the dead, the best way to fight pain is think of something deeper. Like the last time you lay in a hammock. When she said all those things, acted that way. Like she was lonely and afraid and you couldn't have her but if you did have her she would be for you alone.

The breeze had died. Gulls slanted across the paling clouds. He went down to the Bay and swam out past the buoy and Lovejoy's boat nodding softly on the swell. A fisherman was stretching nets over the gunnel of his rowboat and killing the crabs caught in it with a stick, the dull thunk of wood on wood drifting over the water. The Bay was warm, buoyant, clear as green glass sinking into black, tasting sweet with salt and dank with river mud. To the south stretched the flat green line of jungle with the hump in its middle of a buried Mayan city; to the east a red-sailed dugout sat atop the silver thread dividing sea from sky; before him a coconut bobbed on its stalk. He swam far out till the water cooled and darkened, saltier, and he kept looking down for the white shape of a hammerhead out of the agate depths; a rainbow school of needlefish shattered like glass, re-forming beyond reach. To the west the Bay narrowed, the palms and tilting white rust-roofed houses of Corozal Town reflected in its northern shore, beyond them a dark filigree of treetops against the sunset coals.

"ALL YOU NEED is a wife and kids. Thet's all thet matters in life. Your money ain' worth nothin' without thet."

"You think I don't *know* that, Love? Why you keep telling me?"

"'Cause I don' think you *know* it. If you did you would'n act lonely like you do."

"So it didn't work out with Pam. It was too soon after Nam, I wasn't settled yet, in my head. But that don't mean I don't want to."

"Good you and Pam did'n have kids. Once you got kids you got to stay with them, no matter what."

Murphy watched Desirée setting the table, her long glossy girl's legs, the ease of movement. "I'd like kids."

"Whyn't you come down here, get a place outside town? Swim every day, sail, fish, do what you want. It's not crazy like up there, San Francisco. I *been* to San Francisco."

"How many times you told me about San Francisco? You think I don't know you been there? They *still* don't want you back."

"They don' treat you right up there. People aren't warm. You should marry some girl and come down here. There's good girls right here, too, no need to go up there to find one. There's Dorita's daughter. Hey, Pru?"

"Yo?" Pru called from the kitchen.

"What's her name thet girl – Dorita's?"

"Tha's Missie."

"How 'ol she now?"

"She be comin' eighteen, finish' school."

Murphy smiled. "That makes her less than half my age."

"She one pretty girl. Jes' as nice as they come."

Murphy stood carefully. There was nowhere that did not ache. He watched the last sunset slip from the violet sea, the first razor-sharp stars cutting through. He imagined this girl, Missie, pretty and slender with a white lace blouse and desire that burned all night. Dancing and singing her way through life. Loving her way, on every level. How much better. Instead there was Dona, the cold fire of love eating up his soul.

"Le's eat," Lovejoy said. "So you kin head you way up north."

29

THE FULL WHITE MOON rose huge out of the sea, blocked the black horizon, its canyons and crevices wide as the earth. The boat motor's snarl was entrancing, barred conversation, barred thought, left the dream of the senses where everything was possible and nothing was unreal.

The moon climbed, grew smaller. The oily sea sparkled with snakes of light. Lovejoy cut back the motor as the boat rounded a point and the electric bonfire of Chetumal leaped out at them, Murphy turned away, closing his eyes, opened them slowly. The water was like burning crude oil; the air smelt of asphalt, diesel, decay, and rain-sodden rot.

They passed to the north of Chetumal, the city lights behind them. Lovejoy angled in to shore and killed the motor, letting the hull grate on the gravelly beach. "You seen thet road? Going back to town?"

"That's the one?"

"Thet's it. You got maybe two hours' walk, jes' be at the bus station by midnight, for the las' bus for Cancún. Remember, take first class!"

"You're like a mother hen."

"I want you to come back 'n marry thet Missie gir'l. Be careful you don' get checked by some police before you get thet license in Cancún."

"I'll do my best."

"Take them new shoes off, goin' ashore. An' keep you feet dry."

"I have, for Chrissake." Murphy leaned over and hugged him. "God bless you, Love." He stepped over the bow onto the shallow shingle and gave the prow a shove out to sea. "I'll send the money soon's I get there."

Lovejoy started the motor. "Jes' bring it with you, when you come back!"

The beach was littered with plastic bottles and smelled of seaweed. He put on his shoes and broke through the brush up to the shoreline road and walked toward Chetumal, scuffing his feet on the gravel to scare away the snakes that would be basking on the road's stored heat.

Occasionally there were houses crouched down by the sea. Once a dog barked halfheartedly. Once there was the smell of something dead at the side of the road.

More and more houses. Lights. The city ahead in dark and bright patches. Telephone lines, the sounds of cars. Dogs behind gates, lighted windows, human shapes moving behind lace curtains. Smells of pomegranates, lemons, orchids, roses, guavas. Disjointed streets with pools of lamplight, strung with wires, the ghoulish blue glare of televisions, a woman singing "Y *siempre volveras.*"

The bus station said *Autotransportes del Caribe* in blue. People stood in lines or groups in clouds of diesel smoke to board their buses. He bought a first-class ticket to Cancún and found a window seat at the back of the bus. The seat was velvety and soft. The bus smelled of oranges, disinfectant, and diesel exhaust. People were talking quietly in the nearby seats; squat dark-haired women in flowered blouses, children with gleaming hair, young mustached men in dark jackets. An unshaven old man in work trousers and an ancient tweed blazer sat beside him, took off his straw hat and put it in his lap. "*Hola!*" he said. He had no teeth and kept his lips over his gums. He took two oranges out of a plastic bag. "Would you like one?"

"No thanks."

The old man put one orange back and tore the other open, separated the sections and chewed them carefully, one by one, a faraway concentrated look on his face. "It's a long way to go."

Murphy turned from watching the terminal, the people coming, going. "What's that?"

"Where you're going."

"*Como, Viejo*, how do you know that?"

"I was just asking. I have traveled too, in my life. I have been all over the Yucatán. Back then, it wasn't called that."

"What was it called?"

"It didn't have a name. It was where we lived. It didn't have a road. Where we went we walked, or took our canoes along the beach. We didn't belong to Mexico, to any other place. *Solamente estámos.* We just *were.*"

"It was better?"

"Of course. But that time's like a dead person. You can't ever bring them back."

The old man went to sleep and Murphy watched the last buildings straggle past, the road then thin, straight and bumpy, the black hands of the jungle cupping round it. The steady strong roar of the engine came up from the back, lulling and eternal, as if this spindly aluminum carapace were not hurtling down a dangerous narrow road but through safe and empty night. Doesn't matter if I die: the thought seemed maudlin but he realized it was true.

171

"Tulum," the old man said. "Only forty-five minutes to Playa." Murphy woke to look out at a scruffy station in the weak wash of a single street lamp. A clock said seven forty-five. That can't be true, he decided. Looking half-stunned and cold, a young man and woman with dirty long hair and variegated clothes waited for the driver to get down and store their backpacks under the bus. They gave him their tickets and climbed the stairs. There were no seats together so they sat apart. "Too bad you can't go back," the old man said.

"Where?"

"Playa."

Murphy smiled at the old man's forwardness. "That was long ago."

"You don't see her any more, though."

"See what – *la playa*?"

"That girl."

"Just because I'm a gringo doesn't mean I always travel with a girl, *Viejo*, or that I always go to Playa."

"What do you suppose she's doing now, that girl?"

"I couldn't care, *compadre*, let me sleep!"

"That's not a word to use that way, *compadre*, unless you share somebody's fate. It's in Guatemala they say that."

Murphy thought of the Mayan on the back of the flat-bed truck from Orange Walk to Corozal Town: "Guatemala," he'd said, "where is that?"

"I've never been there," Murphy said.

"Yet you wear a Guatemalan serape."

"Anything can be bought, *Viejo*."

"True." The old man took out the other orange. "I myself have been bought many times over. Many women have bought me, only to sell me at a lower price later. My price keeps going down. That way I am freer and freer. When I'm worth absolutely nothing I will be completely free."

Murphy woke again as the bus decelerated then halted to pick its way through the potholes and ruts of the Playa del Carmen turnoff. It drove down Playa's long straight *avenida* to the sea. Everything looked the same but there was nothing he remembered. The bus turned round in the *Autotransportes del Caribe* station and waited, rumbling softly.

"There's time," the old man said. "We'll get a banana!"

"I don't want a banana."

"Quick! Come!"

He followed the old man out into the chilly onshore breeze. The *avenida* dipped down to the beach with the sound of waves crashing against it. To the right the half-lit ferry dock; across the horizon Cozumel was a string of far bright lights.

The old man gave fifty pesos to a boy at a bicycle stand for a clump of bananas. "Why should I let you pay? he said to Murphy. "He would only overcharge you."

"Out here, four o'clock in the morning, he should." Murphy gave the boy a thousand pesos. The boy looked up at him, shocked.

"When you kill your love for one person," the old man said, "you kill it for everybody. I learned that when I was a boy like him, and the Mexicans killed my parents, and it has taken me many years to learn to love them and my mother and father too. He was right, Christ was. Love is the only way."

30

THE DAWN was clotted with black floating flakes, the air pungent with burning plastic and rotten garbage where a line of trucks was waiting to enter the Cancún dump. Clouds of swallows careered through the violet air, feeding on flies, the birds' bodies drumming like hail against the bus windshield. Half-naked children walked barefoot and old men rode burros or bicycle carts among tattered plastic, shattered glass, broken concrete, dead swallows, coils of rusty wire, and shards of derelict cars abandoned on the roadside. On the far, circling strand gray resort hotels were strung like half-illumined pearls.

Near the bus station a *jugatería* was already open; Murphy had two large orange juices, sweet rolls from a *panadería*, then in an early bar coffees and tequila. The sun had risen and heat was filling the streets. He took Avenida Tulum to a side street that became a path through brush to another street that he walked up and down but could not see the place he wanted. Three streets further he found a tile-roofed blue adobe office building that was the right shape, but its color was wrong. He knocked on its carved mahogany door. Jasmine flowers and dead bees lay on the steps. A bicycle passed, wheel squeaking; a jet rumbled over, gaining altitude. A sleepy-faced woman opened the door.

"Is this Nacimiento's office?"

"*Sí.* But he's not here yet."

"The Nacimiento that sells insurance?"

"The one. You want to wait?"

The low front room was painted the same light blue as the outside adobe and smelled faintly of bug spray and perfume. There was a large modern black desk with two telephones, a brass lamp, and family photos. On the blue wall was a Mexicana calendar of a beach with palms. At a second, smaller desk a computer hummed softly. "Can I get you some coffee?" she said. She had black hair and carmine lips and nails, wore a brown suit that emphasized her hips.

He drank the coffee and read *Excelsior*. She refilled his cup. The coffee made him need to piss but he did not ask her if he could use the *servicios*. A car stopped outside; its door shut and Nacimiento came in. "*Buenas días*," he said, shook Murphy's hand.

"The *señor* wants to buy insurance," the woman said.

Small and compact, his hair combed back, in a light green suit, Nacimiento stood like a welterweight. "How did you know to come here?"

"I've been here before."

"I don't remember you."

"A friend and I – three years ago. You found him a passport."

Nacimiento shook his head. "I remember that, but not you."

"We had a big sailboat out at Isla Mujéres. You got him a French passport, a good one."

Nacimiento's eyes widened. "That wasn't you."

"It's just the beard. I've been on the road."

Nacimiento took his arm, "Have you been in *cárcel*? Sit down."

"I've been sitting all night. I'm in a rush. I need a US driver's license, any state, but current. Dependable."

"If it weren't dependable I wouldn't sell it to you."

"I know that. That's why I'm back."

Nacimiento stood thinking, rubbing his palms. "Probably I can. Give me two hours?"

Murphy looked round, could not see a clock. "It's nine-fifty," Nacimiento said.

"If you can, how much?"

"You know better than ask me that – what was it last time, two grand, when we thought it'd be three?"

"Eighteen hundred. Instead of twenty-five. You remember that."

Nacimiento smiled. "It really *was* you. You're not the same man. A license, quick, even for you, it'll cost five."

"Too much."

"Times have changed. We're not the same little town. You want something that's been hot so long they pull you in first time you show it? For five hundred you get one so clean the owner still thinks he has it. All you have to do is change the picture."

"You get me a clean one, before noon, change the picture for me, I'll go five."

Nacimiento patted Murphy's arm. It still hurt, the broken bone, Murphy noticed. "Get some photos," Nacimiento said. "Go to the bus station on Avenida Uxmal – there's a booth. Four color photos."

On the way he stopped in the brush to piss. It spattered off the dry soil, ants scurrying round it. On Avenida Uxmal the sidewalk was clogged with tourists – Americans with sombreros and loud voices, pot bellies, Bermuda shorts and sunburns; French and Germans all young and slender, the men unshaven and the women's long hair bleached by sun and tangled by salt and wind. There were schoolchildren in white and black uniforms, boys in rags holding out their hands. The Avenida was six lanes of buses, trucks, jitneys, Volkswagens, and campers; their fumes blued the air and blended with the bright odors of gardens and fruit stands, the greasy tang of fried chicken, the sewery breeze from the Bay.

The angular, bruised face in the mirror of the photo booth was not his but simply a disguise. When he got home he'd discard it. The photos, too: four identical views of a tense, tanned man with a short beard, the cheeks sunken and the cheekbones far too high, the eyes receded, as if only to see out of and never into.

He took a taxi to the Hotel zone, tennis clubs and glossy cars, doormen, palm boulevards, and flashes of sea between shiny condo towers; in the Flamingo Mall he bought Levis and an ACA shirt and jacket and Nikes, a carry-on bag, underwear and socks, changed into the new clothes and put the ones Lovejoy had bought in the bag. He bought a cheap tennis racket and a can of balls, and opened the can and put them in the bag, then a beach towel that said, "I lost my –" with a picture of a cherry – "in Cancún", then a painted wooden fish with a green head, orange fins, maroon tail, a blue belly with a swan painted on it and a surprised look in its oval black-and-white eye. He bought shaving cream and a razor, toothbrush and comb, and shaved and brushed his teeth in a men's room reeking of urine, where a slim attendant paced, coughing quietly. He bought a cheap blanket and a kaleidoscopic shirt to fill out the carry-on bag, went upstairs and had a quarter pounder with cheese, fries, and a coke at McDonald's, bought a USA Today and a Newsweek and jammed them into the bag. He walked back to town through the traffic and harsh sea wind, scuffing the bag against palm trunks, rubbing his new Nikes in the dust.

"He doesn't look much like you," Nacimiento said.

It was an Arizona license, a reddish-haired man with a self-effacing smile and arched brows, ears too big and nose too little.

"Lamar P. Bultz," Nacimiento said. "That's who you are."

The name sounded funny with Nacimiento's accent. "Where'd you get it?"

"One of the guys working the dance clubs got it late last night. This Lamar P. Bultz, he's still sleeping it off at the Sheraton or somewhere – you'll be home before he knows it's gone."

"If it's no good, I'm coming back –"

"Never you worry." Nacimiento took Murphy's photos to the desk. With a drafting knife he cut carefully around the picture of Lamar P. Bultz and peeled it from the license. He cut one of Murphy's photos to match, beveling the cut so no edge showed. He glued it lightly on the back with plastic glue and ran a slight coat of glue around the edge, and laid it in place. From a back room he brought a hairdryer and cling film, heated the license and laminated a new layer of plastic over it. Holding it along the edges he waved it to cool it off. He counted the twenty-five twenties Murphy gave him and put them in his right jacket pocket. "You memorize the birthday and address, that stuff. So you know who you are – in case somebody asks."

Murphy took a taxi to the airport and booked a window seat on the next flight to San Francisco, Aeromexico at three-thirty, via Mexico City. He bought a book on Mayan ruins and sat waiting in the wide bright terminal. There were blond, tanned families, young couples holding hands, college boys with spiky hair and football shirts, old men sweeping cigarette butts, cigarettes hanging from their lips. There was a smell of jet exhaust and flowers; the marble floor was sticky.

San Francisco International was cold and misty. The customs man glanced at his license and nodded him through. He took a cab from the airport, lines of red tail lights ahead on 101. "Been gone long?" the cabbie called back.

"Couple weeks."

"Nothing beats coming home, huh?

"Nothing beats it."

He had the cabbie drop him in North Beach and walked the quiet midnight streets till he was sure no one followed.

San Francisco's cool windy streets were wet and nearly empty, a few buses wheezing on the upgrades, whores in leotards and fishnets chatting with two cops on a corner, men hand in hand under the tungstens, a bar disgorging laughing couples, a black dog running skinny and scared down a back alley past empty trashcans, once a gull coasting ghostlike downhill above the trolley wires.

He took another cab on Broadway out to the Richmond, got off at Twenty-fifth and Geary and walked down toward Sea Cliff, the trees dripping mist, lines of a song from the cab radio running in his head,

and the only sound that's left,
after the ambulances go,
is Cinderella sweeping up
on Desolation Row,

in the chill of sea, the rush of surf, and the hesitant rumble of a foghorn rising up from the Golden Gate.

31

25th AVENUE crossed Camino del Mar and narrowed to a lane between two great stone pillars, then swept down around a curve of broad lawns and Edwardian mansions. Between the houses came the boom of waves against the cliffs below. He went up the driveway of a white four-story late Victorian house with tall fluted columns and a great bronze knocker of a lion scowling at the street. The driveway followed the side of the house down to the garage; he climbed the steps beside the garage to a deck that swung out from the kitchen, then down the deck into the garden. Sea mist and rhododendron smells blew up from the sea. Under the back of the deck he popped a window and dropped down on to the floor of the garage.

It was absolutely black. He moved forward, banged his knee on a car bumper, swore under his breath, angled to the left till his hand touched a hanging cabinet. He felt around it to the door, opened it, and fumbled inside. At the back behind cans of polish and oil was a clump of keys. He climbed out of the window and walked back up the driveway to the front door with the scowling lion. He turned the latchkey then the deadbolt; deep inside the house an alarm began to whine.

He ran down the entry hall through the dark dining room, banging his knee on the double door into the sunroom, the alarm loudening its yowl, fifteen seconds and counting, thirty more till it lets go with everything – the old broad next door'll be fast asleep but this'll bring him back to life – found the alarm and punched in 32-42-47 but the alarm only whistled more menacingly, ascending through mezzo piano to mezzo forte, and he quickly tried 32-47-42 but fumbled the 7 and had to do it again as the alarm hit forte and suddenly halted; in the ringing silence he could hear the slow bong of the bell buoy off Baker Beach and the steady diesel thrum of a tugboat pushing a sludge barge out to sea.

The phone jangled. He went into the kitchen stubbing his toe on the edge of the freezer and dropped the phone on his foot, knelt and found the receiver. "Yeah!"

"Who's speaking, please?" It was a black voice, official.

"You call up in the middle of the fuckin night to ask who's speaking?" He stood rubbing his foot against the other calf. "Who the fuck are *you*?"

"Is this Mr. Murphy?"

"Who wants to know?"

"This's ADT Security. Your burglar alarm just registered an entry."

"Oh, sorry. The lights weren't on and I tripped over something. Thanks for calling."

"And you're Mr. Murphy?"

"Yes."

"Can you give me your mother's date and place of birth and maiden name, please?"

"Esther McCreary, Temple, Texas, May 21, 1926."

"Fine, Mr. Murphy. Thank you very much."

"No, I thank you. What if it hadn't been me?"

"That's what we're here for. Have a good night."

He put on all the lights and walked like an amazed peasant from room to room. In the living room he stood with his hands on the silken fabric of the couch back and stared at the ebony grand, the Pinchon of apple blossoms and the Seine hanging over the mantel, the endless meaningless books, the blood-red Kerastans on the gleaming oak floor. The ocean wind wailed down the chimney, stirring the ash; he went back to the front door and closed it.

The kitchen smelt shut-in and faintly of spices. Wreaths of mist dashed across the glass. He ate some pistachio ice cream and took a bottle of Dunphys upstairs and lay on the bed looking at the flat white ceiling, went out on the bedroom deck and opened the hot tub. It was swirling steadily, the water a little low but hot. He went back into the dressing room, rolled a joint, took off his clothes, and sat in the hot tub smoking and drinking the Irish whiskey while the mist flitted past like all the ghosts of history finally liberated from their graves.

"I DRINK WATER ALL DAY as you said, *Doctora*. Still she's dying."

"You've boiled guava root and mashed it for her?" Dona undressed the baby.

"As you said, with ashes of *Tusub cam* vine."

Dona took a cloth and soap from her pack, poured water from a jug and began to wash diarrhea from the baby. "In Flores this could be stopped with a bottle of Kaopectil from the pharmacy."

"You cannot get it, this miracle bottle?"

"We've lost two people this month trying to buy from pharmacies. The only way is to take it from the soldiers."

The baby wrinkled her shrunken face and whimpered. "If I had milk," Dona said, "I'd nurse her."

"To make milk you first need a man, *Doctora*."

"If there's milk anywhere, Roseta, I shall send it."

"If there's never any milk how should it suddenly appear?"

"If we take some from the soldiers."

Roseta waved her hand at the flies around the baby's face, and to Dona it seemed also a dismissal. "You must drink more water," she repeated, shouldering her pack and rifle. You must take more bone and tooth from your own body so your daughter may grow someday to feed her own frail calcium into her own daughter's mouth.

"Turn down the lantern, *por favor*," Roseta said, "when you go."

The moon three days past full hung in the middle of the sky. Dona moved up through the village to the last hut and knocked.

"*Sí!*" An old man's voice.

She went inside. There was a single candle, a thatched wall with a crucifix. "How is it?" she said.

"It was clear all the way to Concepción, *compañera*. Though some may have come since."

"Could you see any tracks?"

"It was too dark."

"And above?"

"One helicopter, very high, going south."

"No sound of guns?" She watched the old man's face in the faint candlelight, exhaling softly when his face did not fall and he did not say, "*Sí*, to the west", or "to the north", or anywhere.

"No, *compañera*, no sound of guns."

"Roseta doesn't know Bautisto's dead. No one must tell her now, the baby's too sick."

"The baby will soon die, *compañera*."

The moon gave enough light to see the trail as she followed it up out of the village and crossed a steep range then

183

down through thinning pines to the candlelit huts of Concepción perched on an eroded slope over a stream where stones rumbled and clattered. She entered an unlighted hut, rested her Galil by the door and dropped the pack from her shoulders. "God, I grow old."

"Your body doesn't show it."

"It feels it."

"Come, let me feel it."

"Stop, Martín. I have no stomach for it."

His hands clamped her waist, the hammock creaking as he pulled her to him, the pen in his pocket jabbing her breast, her face full of itchy beard as he kissed her eyes and cheeks and the tip of her nose, his mouth opening like a hairy peach against hers. He unbuttoned her shirt, his calloused hand flattening her breast. She backed away, buttoning her shirt. "I don't want it, Martín."

"Dona, it's *life* –"

"I want nothing to do with life."

"Life's just who you love."

"I don't love anybody!" She reached out in the darkness, took his hand. "It's soon time."

"I know the time." His voice softened. "That's why I wanted to."

She could hear the fabric of his shirt stretch as he breathed. "Forgive me, Martín. Another time."

"They are well, your patients?"

"You know they're not."

"And this plan, you think it's a good one?"

"There is no good plan for killing." She went to the door, feeling suffocated by this hut, this village. Why am I always the one who must give reassurance? she thought despairingly. Like Roseta, draining myself to feed the doomed.

32

AT TWO-MINUTE intervals they moved out of Concepción – first Manuel, a boy of twelve, no gun. Then Martín, then the Taliscá brothers – the tall skinny one, Gordo, and the smaller heavy one, Lupo – both carrying new Galils taken a week ago from the convoy at Quimalá, where their youngest brother had died. Then Margaríta from Chisapec, two women from Los Martíres, the teenager Solano, Dona, and last El Caballo, a small man carrying an M60 machine gun lightly as a machete on his shoulder. Ten in all, two minutes apart, they took the trail down the mountain and entered the black jungle on an overgrown chicle road.

Picking her steps, Dona tried to balance the Galil so it would not rub her shoulder. The mushy soil exhaled dank odors; the stink of lianas and pungent bunchgrass was unbreathable in the clammy darkness. Creepers and branches snagged the gun barrel and snatched at her backpack. She stopped, legs shaking with exhaustion, wanted to fall on the mud and cry. She made herself swallow. Snakes will get you, she told herself. El Caballo's coming up behind and he'll be angry. He'll think you're weak. She unshouldered one strap of the backpack, hung the Galil from that shoulder and the backpack from the other.

After two hours they broke out on a long ridge, the path dimly visible through the thinner overstory, the group tightening up now that they were far from villages and there was less danger of soldiers.

The ones ahead had halted; she came up to them, staying on the edge. A cool breeze rode across the ridge and dropped into the valley. She shifted shoulders with the Galil and backpack. Martín's watch said 2:17. As they walked onwards the image of the watch stayed before her eyes, three ghostly little numbers with two dots between the first and second.

After many kilometers the trail descended and circled a swamp where frogs croaked and insects chirred. It followed a stream from the swamp down into a narrow valley smelling of old damp cinders, past the charred spars of houses. An hour later they stopped where the trail dipped over a rise, in the south a cluster of lights. "Them!" she said.

"Them," Margaríta answered.

Dona dropped her pack and laid the Galil across it. Her body seemed to float. She lay down with her head on the pack. The night was spinning: one moment there was a tall tree before her eyes, then an open meadow, then the other *compañeros*, then the distant dangerous lights, the tree again...

Martín came up the meadow with another man whose glasses glinted from the lights. "Ready, kids?" he whispered good-naturedly, and they laughed quietly and gathered round him. "You've all heard the story..."

"They know it," Martín said. "We'll set positions before daybreak."

"The hole is the proper depth and all the dirt's been carried away."

"And every position is well protected," Martín added.

"Just be sure you're out of there on time. Six twenty-nine for everyone, except six twenty-seven for Martín and El Caballo because your position's more exposed and you have further to withdraw. And again, *don't* regroup afterwards. When it's time, disperse fast in twos and threes. Each of you withdraw exactly on your assigned pattern. Never more than four together or the American heat-seeking planes will track you by body heat till the Guatemalan Air Force finds you."

"You will overrun the Base?" Dona said. Her voice sounded hoarse, too quivery.

"If there's time, before the helicopters."

"I need *all* their medicines. Not just what you can grab easily but all of it. Look in all the cabinets and in the refrigerators and in any closets and everywhere you see –"

"Guns first, *compañera*. Sadly, a revolution's not won by healing children."

"Yes it is. Precisely by that. And each battle leaves more children to be healed."

"Perhaps you chose the wrong battle?" He turned to the others. "My squad attacks the Base from the east at five fifty-three, the moment the sun climbs above the ridge and its light strikes the Base: the soldiers will have it in their eyes as they face us. Like us, *you'll* be looking away from the sun – up the road where the rescue convoy from Dolores will arrive."

He half-glanced back at the ring of lights. "It will take between one and three minutes for the Base to radio Dolores they're being hit. It'll take Dolores eight to eleven minutes to get the troops into trucks and out the gate. It's going to take the trucks thirteen and a half more minutes to come round that curve below you. That's somewhere between six fifteen and six twenty-one. They'll be moving fast and looking for ambushes. But not where *you* hit them."

"Because there's no cover," Dona said. "Because we shouldn't *be* there."

"There's cover, *compañera*."

"The soil's limestone and the scrub's too low."

"If helicopters catch us," Margaríta said.

"The choppers'll be cold," he answered. "From the moment we attack, at five fifty-three, it will take the Cobras forty-four minutes to scramble from Poptún. It'll take the Huey gunships forty-seven from Cobán. So the soonest they can be there is six thirty-seven, and more likely six-forty. But you must be gone by six twenty-nine. El Caballo and Martín by six twenty-seven."

"I am to risk the lives of nine people to believe this?" Dona said.

"Ten people, *compañera*. Plus all mine. Listen – all of you: under no circumstances remain one minute longer than your withdrawal time. If you come under concentrated fire – and you shouldn't, given our approach – be sure to break before the choppers come, in no case later than six thirty-five. If you're pinned, watch the time and listen for choppers. When you hear them, no matter what, you run. Or you will die – do you understand that? You will absolutely die if the choppers find you."

"We're not fools," Margaríta said.

"When the trucks are below you the sun will be behind and above you, and in their faces. They'll be stuck on the road, with an open gully on one side and your slope on the other. You'll have a beautiful field of fire."

"Who's across the gully?"

"We're not playing it that way. Too hard to withdraw."

"If the convoy doesn't come," Martín said, "or if the firing stops at the Base, we leave, going in ones and twos as our friend here has reminded us. In no case do we stay a second longer than our withdrawal times. If anyone escaping from the Base comes up the road we ambush them just as we would the convoy, *unless* we hear the convoy coming. Simple?"

A line of blood began to spread across the eastern sky, above the Base's frail ring of lights. She felt the delicious coolness of death in her face, felt death coming down like Moses from the mountain with the engraved wisdom of God.

Reaching through the darkness, the man with the glasses touched each of them in turn, whispering, "*Vaya con Díos.*" It's like Communion, she thought as he squeezed her fingers, and she answered, "Go with God, *compañero.*"

33

FROM HER POSITION Dona could see the brushy opposite slope crowned by tree silhouettes against the lightening horizon, and the pale ribbon of road that curved round its foot with the open gully beside it then descended below her, swerving east toward the valley with the lights of the Army Base at its end.

The stones beneath her had grown warm from her body and she squirmed comfortably down among them. The rock on which her Galil rested was sharp and damp; the cold barrel stung her fingers. Thirty meters to the left was Lupo Taliscá's hunched form and the faint glitter of his rifle. To the right, from where the trucks would come, she could see neither Margaríta in her cover of spindly trees nor Gordo beyond, guarding the flank.

It's just me, she realized, and Lupo, whom I don't know, the two of us alone in this universe without time, without the sun which will never rise and the convoy that will never come and we will never shoot and that's what it feels like to be dead.

If it all goes well there'll be no bad wounds – she could hope for that. But all wouldn't go well and she mustn't even say it. If all went badly she had bandages and compresses for the easy bullet wounds. And if they could get the wounded out she could operate later. But a lung wound like García's, or Clemente's, and she'd lose them.

With machine guns in the trucks there'd be some big wounds, shearings and major tissue and bone loss and if the choppers came there'd be rockets and much worse, and if there were A37s she had nothing for the phosphorous burns.

A black jay fluttered down and pecked at the road's shoulder, ran a few steps, pecked again. She thought of when she was a girl and *sanatés* like these gathered at dusk in the church tower outside her bedroom window; leaning out of that window she had picked figs from the ancient tree with its roots deep in the graveyard below. It had always pleased her, this, the bodies of her ancestors feeding hers.

A red spot seared through the green dark east, widened, writhed up among the nest of branches into a white-orange ball whose heat came racing down the slope and slapped her face. Its light slipped down past the others' camouflaged positions, struck the opposite slope, and dropped onto the road where the trucks would come, then down into the gully, slid east past the rocks where Martín and El Caballo hid with the M60, then poured down into the valley toward the Army base, catching a line of yellow-leaved willows along an irrigation ditch, a pasture with two brown and white cows.

Once more she measured the distance below from the curve to where the first truck would stop: space for five trucks if they bunched up, or two if they didn't. Thirty-seven meters, Martín had said, from her position to where the first truck would be caught in the trench the other compañeros had dug last night; from that trench it was a hundred and ten meters to the curve where the trucks would come.

Behind her it was a hundred and forty-five meters to the crest of the slope where the real trees began. Till then there were only thin trunks, thin chalky soil with sparse grass to her knees. Crawl like a snake through the grass, Martín had said, if you have to.

She closed her eyes and tried to remember the position and curve of the road and the slope and every other detail, then opened her eyes to check, closed them again and again until the picture inside her head and that before her eyes was the same. Again she closed her eyes and dismounted the clip of the Galil and remounted it and did it again, reached out to memorize the exact location of the second clip at her elbow.

Light raced east across the valley toward the Base, the sun heating her face as if she were leaning down to a blazing hearth, and as she turned not wanting to be blinded there was a far *whammer-whammer-whammer* of a chopper nearing fast then suddenly rounding the hill. It banked away and El Caballo's M60 spat hard and the chopper's tail rotor flew off; the chopper swung round and round like a stone on a string, the pilot trying to bring it down fast but it dropped sideways into the jungle leaving a sudden silence then the boom of its crash and orange flames billowing up oily smoke and a flare of magnesium and chatter of machine gun rounds exploding in the heat.

"*Mierda!*" she screamed. "*Mierda! mierda! mierda!*" The Base gleamed silently in the new sun, columns of white smoke from cooking fires rising like the pillars of the sky. Out of the gully rose the smell of burning foliage, flesh, and jet fuel.

Voices came down the line; Lupo stood and yelled, "Stay put!" and she called it on to Margarita. Martín came running along the line. "The outpost will come to rescue the chopper – we ambush them – Miguel and his people attack the Base – reverse of the plan!"

"We must leave! This isn't the plan!"

"Fuck the plan! This is better!'"

"Choppers never come alone!"

Sweat fell from his face onto her hand. "They come, we retreat."

"You mean run!"

"*Sí*, run!" He glanced at his watch, then hers. "It's now five fifty-seven. You still have to be out of here at six twenty-nine."

"The choppers'll be here before then," she said, but he was gone to Margaríta, then up to Gordo on the flank, then ran back past her. From the outpost came the rumble and gear whine of trucks.

Clouds had thickened to the south; she kept hearing choppers in their thunder. But the choppers did not come; the sun inched higher; trucks came from the Base and stopped at the valley edge out of range, small and darkly backlit by the sun. Soldiers ran from them into the trees and up the slope toward the burning chopper.

El Caballo's M60 opened up; a soldier rolled like a corn-straw doll downhill, more running up the gully. She shot twice as they crossed the road; one fell then the other but the second scrambled for cover. A bullet flicked the bush beside her face. Another soldier fell in a burst from the M60.

Four helicopters in V formation dropped over the western slope, Cobra gunships with ugly jutting stingers; the M60 fired and one banked to spray it; Dona squeezed single shots at the side gunner and the Cobra turned on her, bullets shattering stones and spouting earth and she rolled up deaf and half-blind to fire back but her magazine was empty, the spare lost in rubble.

Her spine aching with terror as the chopper came at her, her legs begging to run, her fingers fumbled through the rocks for the magazine but it wouldn't mount and she saw it was backwards but now it jammed. A rocket battered her into the ground shrieking with fear and rage, the Cobra's machine guns pummeling brush and stone, the air filled with flying rocks and dirt and branches and a great white heat sucked her in and slammed her down in raging white silence.

There were cries like seagulls and the patter of dirt and stone coming back to earth; she realized it was herself crying, felt around but could not find her rifle, scrambled up and sprinted for Margaríta's trees. The universe was panting, a great roar rasping in and out and she looked down to see if her chest had been torn open, if the noise was from there, but she was not bloody.

Margaríta lay on her back, no head, just red roots sticking out of her neck. Someone was screaming, "Jesús Jesús Jesús" inside Dona's brain. She grabbed Margaríta's gun and ran through splintered trees along the slope as the chopper came back for her, bullets shaking the earth as she ran; she fell on her back to fire but it flitted past and she rolled up and dashed to Lupo dead beside a rocket's red crater then dove into the crater as the rotors came back, bullets shivering and spattering the singed, reeking earth, and she jerked and lay out straight.

Through her half-closed eyes and the black half-veil of her hair she saw the door gunner in his flak uniform and helmet like an avenging insect as he tried to steady the hail of bullets on her and the chopper slid past and dived downhill toward El Caballo and Martín.

A black rod dropped from the chopper and flared, dashed against the rocks, a sudden white shock of heat exploded the trees, great boulders soaring like foam through gyrating phosphorous clouds. She clung to the crater, the blaze burning her back, held her breath against the acrid smoke as she fumbled in the dirt for the rifle, waited till she could open her eyes then gasped a small breath that stuck to her throat like burning oil.

She waited longer not breathing, waited for the boiling white clouds to reveal the chopper hanging steadily above her like a snake over its poisoned prey. Still not breathing she aimed at the narrow black slot over the chopper's wiring channel and fired single shots that the chopper did not seem to feel till suddenly it lunged at her and she gripped the fractured earth waiting to die.

El Caballo's M60 rang out, metal hailing the chopper and it dropped away as two more choppers dived at El Caballo firing rockets side by side. The earth yanked itself from her and dropped her down ten feet away. She scrambled for the gun and fired at the new choppers till the gun was empty and she ran past someone's shredded body to El Caballo half-buried; when she knelt to him she saw it was just his head and torso, his pelvis and legs had been blown elsewhere, the M60 with them.

Martín had crawled beneath a toppled trunk, his chest and face red, his beard gone. No, not gone, for his chin had been blown away so that the roots of his upper teeth grinned out at her. Not knowing his chest was gone he tried to speak, his larynx weirdly working, bared ribs twitching.

A bullet tugged her sleeve; soldiers were coming uphill, their bullets snapping branches and sucking at the charred air; she reached beneath Martín's waist to the back of his ammo belt and yanked at the spare clip, the belt and part of his uniform and body coming with it. She knocked off the emptied clip and mounted this one.

A chopper was returning. She forced herself to check the clip then fired, a bullet hitting in front of a soldier but he fell anyway, perhaps from the ricochet, their bullets smashing bark and splinters from the fallen tree.

Martín pointed to her rifle then himself. She kissed his forehead and his eyes, his bloody upper lip. He pointed at the gun then his heart. She shot him in the heart; he convulsed, legs quivering. She ducked behind him and fired into the back of his skull, emptied the rifle at the soldiers, and ran screaming into the jungle.

34

HE WOKE IN a strange peace. A familiar sun spread diamond patterns across the ceiling. The rustle of surf drifted through the open window. The carpet was soft underfoot. He went down to the kitchen, the terracotta tiles cold, put water in the espresso machine, found coffee beans in the refrigerator, thawed a can of orange juice in the microwave, drank it, took a mug of espresso upstairs, set it on the sink and stood in the shower. Hot. Cold. Hot. Freezing cold.

The neighbor's poodle was barking. He finished the espresso, filled the mug with water, opened the bathroom window; the dog heard him and sprinted for its doghouse but the water hit it as it reached the door.

He grinned at himself in the half-steamed mirror, looked again, shocked by his rangy thin frame, the bony chest, skinny thighs with the long skinny pecker hanging down, the white puffy shrapnel stars across the gut and ribs... Touch them, honey, feel the metal move... The right arm looked funny, too thin, the discolored bullet scar like a hole left by a burning spike.

He rolled two joints, lit one and put the other in his right shirt pocket. He removed the innersole from one running shoe, took a razor-slim knife from the drawer of his bedside table, slipped it into the shoe and replaced the innersole. He found thirty-seven dollars and some credit cards in a drawer, and went down to the garage. You did right to come back, he told himself. This is the life for you.

The battery was dead and he pushed the car up the driveway and down the street, running alongside, jumped in to pop the clutch in second. It caught, spitting black exhaust, the engine running ragged all the way across Golden Gate Park and up past the Haight and over the top of Divisadero. By the time he drove out along Castro to Noe Valley it was running smooth, the streets half-bright with sun through the fog.

Number 729 Diamond was a tall narrow Victorian house with leaded glass and three-color trim. He picked the *Chronicle* off the bottom step, rang the bell. There was city scum on the Welcome mat. She smiled as she opened the door then her face turned hard and pale.

"Let me in, Diana."

"Oh Christ, oh please. You can't mean it."

He brushed past her down the hall into the parlor with its couches and doilies, its jade-colored marble mantel with the black marble clock, soft reflections of ferns and wall fabrics, the distant KGO – "your Bay Area news station" – she's like a lily, he thought, tall and pale and ready to bow at the first touch. "Don't give me that, Diana. You guys were split, you've got a new old man."

"How did you kill him?"

"We crashed. Hit a pine bough coming in. He never knew."

"You bastard. You fucking lousy pilot. You'd risk anyone to make more money."

"It was *his* life, Diana. *His* business. I didn't ask him."

"*You* don't have to ask people. They're drawn to you. You feed off them one by one."

"You want me to tell the kids?"

"You think *you're* going to tell *my* kids their father's dead?"

"Johnny had his own life. That's why you didn't love him."

"What the shit do you know about love?"

"Or that's why he didn't love you."

She gave him an upright look, coming out straight from deep inside, deeper than love or hate. "Don't assume you understand anything, Murph."

"You going to tell his folks? And he had a friend in LA –"

"Sarah Oldfield. The actress. He told me about her. You've probably had her too..."

He realized he was still holding the *Chronicle* and dropped it on a sofa and took her in his arms. "Don't be like this, Diana. Just feel the pain. That's all we can do, is feel the pain."

He sat in the car thinking of all the places he could go. He drove back down Market amid the traffic and the trolleys, white and black skyscrapers blocking off the Bay, through Chinatown to North Beach, parked on Grant, went into the Trieste, ordered Italian pastries and cappuccino. Sun beamed through the tall windows onto faces and chrome table rims, while the espresso machine rumbled and hissed through *fermate* in *La Donna e Mobile* and the wandering words of twenty conversations:

"He promised me Sri Lanka but we never got past Daly City."

"That's Bachelard's mistake, subsuming dialectics in pure phenomenology..."

"After one night with her she was out on the street again."

"I told him, 'Darling, the standard deviation's just the square root of the variance.'"

At the pay phone he called the *Chronicle* and asked for Melissa Maslow.

"I remember," she said. "It was at a party somewhere. You're the guy who races motorcycles."

"I used to, just for fun. Listen, Melissa, I've got a story. Something you could use."

"Everybody tells me that. It's why I hate this job."

"I've seen the most horrible massacre."

"You must've been on the Bay Freeway."

"Central America."

"People don't really care about Central America, Joe. Not like San Diego. But it's better than Africa. *Nobody* cares about massacres in Africa."

"The Army wiped out a whole village."

"Don't they do that all the time down there?"

"With American help."

"What kind of help?"

"American officers."

"Now that's interesting. You have pictures?"

"No. It was night. But I was there."

"Come see me."

"Now?"

"Can't."

"Lunch?"

"I've got a lunch thing. Two thirty?"

"Fine. But not at the *Chronicle*."

"Across the street, then. The Rathskeller."

"Till then who can I talk to?"

"You could try Cyndi Wheaton at BACCA."

"What's that?"

"Bay Area Committee for Central America."

He waited till the espresso machine stopped steaming milk and called the BACCA. Cyndi had a strong friendly voice. He imagined her in white tennis shorts, a racket in her hand. "I don't doubt what you've told me," she said. "It happens all the time."

"But the American soldiers –"

"What do you think our advisers *do* down there? Teach knitting?"

"I'm going to the *Chronicle*, the television."

"Before you do you'd better come see me."

The Bay Area Committee for Central America was one flight up over the Chevy dealer on South Van Ness. The receptionist was Latina but when he spoke to her in Spanish she answered in English.

Cyndi was beautiful, about thirty-five, long golden-reddish hair curling in at her neck, slender high cheekbones and appraising blue eyes. She wore a long pleated plaid skirt and a pink mohair sweater and had little pearl earrings. "It's too bad you don't have proof," she said.

"That's what Melissa said."

"But I'm going to get you together with our executive committee. And maybe some TV. Can you be back here at four o'clock?"

He drove home, dug through drawers in the dressing room and study, went down to the basement to a closet off the pool room and opened boxes till he found a worn brown address book. Under "Cunningham, Willard and Mary," was a 207 area code number. An old woman's strong voice answered on the second ring.

"Mrs. Cunningham?" he said.

"Who's there?"

"My name's Joseph Murphy. I was a friend of Clint's."

"I remember you. He used to write about you. He was very fond of you."

"I'm sorry I never got in touch."

"There was nothing you could've done."

"How's Mr. Cunningham?"

"We're getting along."

"Clint's wife… Wasn't she going to have a baby?"

"How'd you know that? He never knew."

"Somebody must've told me. Is she OK?"

"The wife? I suppose she's fine. She got married again, some trucker. The daughter, Sherrie, we don't see much of her."

"Where is Sherrie?"

"Out in San Francisco. At least she was when we last heard. That was a while. Two years, maybe."

"You have her number? An address?"

"Sherrie's? Probably not. Not one that works."

"And Clint's wife?"

"Lucy? She's over in Westbrook. Her name's Amato now. Married to this trucker."

"You have a phone book?"

"Just a minute." The phone clunked to the floor, grinding as it swung back and forth on its cord. "There's three Amatos in the Westbrook phone book. Got a pencil?"

He wrote them down. "If I get in touch with her I'll phone you."

"Clint was very fond of you. We have all his letters. We go over them. The time you landed in that lake, the time you boys went to Thailand... He always said he never would've made it through Fort Rucker without you."

Lucy Amato was at the second number. "Oh, hi," she said. "I remember 'bout you. That was a long time ago."

"I guess we've both kind of forgot about Clint."

"I'm married again. Been a long time. Prob'ly Clint's mom told you."

"I heard Sherrie's out in San Francisco. That's where I am. Would you mind if I gave her a call sometime?"

"Wouldn't mind at all. If I only knew her number."

"You got an address, anything?"

"Tell you the truth, Murph – that's your name, right, it's coming back to me now, that's the name Clint called you in his letters – tell you the truth, we had no end of trouble with that girl. She always hated her new dad, even though she never even knew the old one, ain't that something for you?"

"Happens."

"Hold on – I may have an address. It'll be an old one." She put down the phone. In the background he could hear the wet hum of a dishwasher and an Eric Clapton solo, the pure music making the moment a lesson, forever. "You still there?" Lucy said. "One fifty-four Alabama Street. That's all I got. Must've been six months ago, this. She wanted me to send some money. Said she was calling from a booth."

"Other than this, Lucy, how you doing? I'm sure Clint'd like to know."

"Not as if you could tell him, huh? God, what a time. But I'm fine now, me an' Mitch we got three kids. Good ones, not throwaways like Sherrie. I don't like to say it, Murph, she's my own daughter. But that's all she is. A throwaway."

35

154 ALABAMA was a tilting, unrenovated Romeo near the projects, Spanish names on the mailboxes. "Hey, *niño*," he said to a boy playing marbles in the dank hall, "*Donde vive la inglésa?*"

"Four," the boy said. "But she's got someone."

It was up one flight of sticky stairs with broken linoleum, a white door gouged by dog claws. The jamb had been split and repaired with tin. From other apartments came canned laughter and children's screams. He knocked, then again.

A creak of floor, a woman's sleepy voice, "Yeah?"

"Sherrie?"

"Who?"

"Sherrie Cunningham, I'm..."

"She's gone. I don't know where."

"I'm a friend of her dad's."

"She don't have no dad."

"She did."

The deadbolt opened, another lock shifted back. The door thunked against its chain. The girl had a long slender face with her father's palomino hair, a little freckled nose and wide lips in a wide mouth. "She didn't never have a dad."

"I've got something for her. From him."

Her face neared the door. "What was his name? Her dad?"

"Clint. Clint Cunningham."

She undid the chain, tugged her faded brown kimono tighter. The kitchen smelled of leaking gas, ashtrays, crack, and heat. She shoved beer bottles and dirty plates to one side of the table, motioned at a chair and sat. "I can tell her for you."

"Cut the shit, Sherrie. What the fuck you doing to yourself?"

Her hand searching for a cigarette among the dirty coffee cups was like a blind creature on the ocean floor. "Who're you to tell me that! I don't know you from nothing, asshole."

"I'm Clint's friend. He asked me to come back."

"You're just a little late."

"It was in an old letter. I was supposed to read it if he died. But I got wounded and the letter disappeared and I just found it. I just talked with your grandmother in Portland, Mary Cunningham, and your Mom, Lucy Amato..."

"You some dick?"

"My name's Joe Murphy and I live here in San Francisco. I was in the 101st Airborne with your Dad in South Vietnam and Cambodia."

"How's my grandma?"

"I think they all miss you. Want you to come back."

The girl smiled and shook her head, hair rasping on the kimono. She tipped cigarette ashes into a cup. "You got anything on you? Coke, anything?"

He shrugged. "A little weed."

"Give me a few hits?"

He gave her a joint and she lit it keeping her hair back from his Bic, sucking down and holding in the smoke. She held it out to him but he waved it away. "Your dad and me, we used to smoke that stuff all the time in Nam. They called our unit Celestial Airlines."

"That's where it got him."

He sat back. "So it did."

She waved the joint. "This is good stuff. I could sell some for you."

"It's my own. Not commercial."

"Everybody... should have their own... victory garden..." Her pale lemon eyes canvassed the wall above the sink, yellow paint with big curling blisters showing a greasy brown beneath, the ventilator gummed black, a black cord hanging down, the single shelf with a rusty can of Raid and three empty Colt 45 malt liquor bottles. The eyes drifted back to him. "What was he like?"

"He had hair like you and a small nose and broad shoulders. Kind of an awkward, muscular build."

"He was a runner, Mom said."

"Yeah. In college."

"I seen a picture of him and you standing in front of a helicopter, that place where you trained..."

"Fort Rucker."

"Yeah. You don't look too much like you."

"Reconstructive surgery by an Army intern. He had good intentions."

"It's not that bad. You're cute. You got class. Normally I'd charge a guy like you a hundred bucks."

"Because I'm white?"

"Because you look like you can pay it." She nodded at his Levis, the old shirt, the black jacket. "Not your clothes. You just *look* it." She fixed him with the yellow tiger eyes. "How you think my dad'd feel about me doing tricks?"

"I think he wants you to realize the magic of being alive before it's over."

"That's how he was?"

"That's how he was. But he'd want you to give up the needle."

"Who are you, cocksucker, coming into my house, criticizing me?"

"I had a friend who shook it. Took her three months. I'll help you."

"Jesus. You walk in here, total stranger, tell me how to live?"

"I'm close as you're ever going to get to your dad."

She stood, knocking back the chair. "Well just fuck off!"

The door was greasy from generations of hands. "Think about it. I'll come see you."

"Get out before I wake Reno, in there, and he cuts you up real bad."

Murphy glanced at the black man face-down on the bedroom floor. "Reno needs his sleep."

Down the hall the TV was roaring for breakfast cereal, or was it toilet paper? Over the screaming children he couldn't tell. He held his breath till he reached the street.

Lila, was that her name, the one who'd kicked heroin? Dark hair, so slender, purple bruises up the pale insides of her arms. Who three months later jumped off the Golden Gate.

He turned left on Bryant and parked on Fifth. The Rathskeller was dark inside after the bright street and smelled of bourbon. There were bronze cups and photos of reporters on a shelf behind the bar, a few people still eating in the booths. He sat at the back with a double whiskey till Melissa came in. She was wearing a red and white checked suit and a white silk blouse with an open collar. "You don't look like the same you," she said.

"Everybody tells me that."

"When was it, last spring? Why were you at Lily Tucker's party?"

"Friend of the bride."

"That's what I heard. But gossip's not my beat."

"I enjoyed talking with you. Would've called earlier, but like I said I've been gone."

"So what happened?"

He motioned to the waitress for another double Irish. "That's what I came to tell you."

FROM THE MOUNTAIN Dona watched Concepción but there was no sign of soldiers. She lay in the shadow of a broad pine tree on the soft scented mattress of its needles, the empty Galil beside her, her throat burning with rocket fumes and the singed stink of her hair.

In the village an old woman she didn't know carried a basket of clothes down to the stream and began scrubbing them against the rocks. A boy ran from the jungle with a dead wood rat and ducked into a hut. A little girl squatted on the bank; her pee trickled, glistening, into the water. On the hill above the houses a tan burro trotted in a circle, jerking at its tether.

Over her face a small brown spider had linked three pine needles with cables and was spinning a web between them. When the wind blew, shifting the needles, the cables tautened and relaxed, not breaking.

The spider did not know about the battle. She did not care about *la lucha*, the needs of the *campesino*. She was building a web so she could kill other animals to feed her children.

CYNDI WHEATON'S office was full of people. There was a television camera in the corner; its red eye flicked on when he walked into the room. She beckoned him into the hall. "This is for *now*, the evening news."

"I wanted to talk to your people first, decide the best way to find out…"

"Find out *what*?"

"What I keep *telling* you: who the Americans were!"

"That we'll never know. The best we can hope for is a little exposure, the best for Guatemala."

More cameras had arrived, more people with little steno pads and tape recorders, and it was easy to stand in their midst and look earnestly into the round black camera eyes with their blinking red lights, to answer the questions of the friendly men and women with the little note pads.

"Mr. Murphy? I'm Phyllis Steen of WFSF. What's your political viewpoint?"

"I learned in Vietnam not to care about politics."

"But you must have a feeling now about Guatemala?"

"We should get out of there and let them solve their own problems."

"Even if that means the Communists win?"

"I never met any Communists in Guatemala, just people."

"You don't see them as a threat to our way of life?"

Then it was over and he was no longer news, the reporters talking about the mayor's six p.m. press conference. Cyndi Wheaton shook his hand and looked into his eyes. "Stay in touch." He walked up Mission Street in the milky afternoon sun, a lacy fog dropping over Twin Peaks, bringing a trace of California winter.

36

HE WAS HOME before six and turned on NBC. At a corn auctioneers' meeting in Fargo George Bush was expressing his deep love for the people of North Dakota. Then came national sports; a left fielder who had just signed a four million dollar contract was explaining his philosophy of life. On national weather there were clouds over the west, rain over New England, and sun in the south. Then came California and local news, with good coverage of the mayor's press conference. He switched to CBS in time for the local news and carpet advertisements, then ABC for more on George Bush, the mayor, and the weather.

He called the Bay Area Committee, no response. He drove to South Van Ness through clogged and fuming traffic; no one answered the Committee's bell. At a Burger King telephone he tried to find Cyndi Wheaton's number but it was not listed. Don't rush things, he told himself. His meeting with the press had been too late for tonight's news; tomorrow there'd be a story in the *Chronicle*, then more on TV.

When he got home the phone was ringing. "Mr. Murphy?" An anxious, woman's voice. "It's Priscilla Benson. Your neighbor."

"I remember."

"It's really time we talked about your trees. They're getting worse and worse!"

"You're the president of the Sea Cliff Improvement Committee. If you want the trees along the sidewalk trimmed, then fine. Just leave mine alone."

"How would it look with some trimmed and the others left to grow wild, like yours? My husband's a judge, you know, he sees these things from a legal point of view."

THE SILVER PLATE gleamed resolutely in the wavering candlelight, set off against the white damask tablecloth, the rich reds and blues of Royal Doulton, the silver-plated candelabra, Nancy's dark dress and the oval of cultured pearls around her neck. Lyman thought of Kit Gallagher kissing her there, repressed it.

The heavy Kilkenny crystal felt good in his hand. The merlot sparkled, tasted like cooled purified blood. He smiled at Jason sitting across from him with a napkin tucked into his collar, felt it was a false smile, tried to make it true. Jason smiled, winked back.

He smiled at Christina. He wrinkled his brow inquisitively, asking her to smile back but she didn't. He had to admit he hated her, her teenage pout, plucked brows, and straightened hair, the diamond crescents in the ears he'd told her not to pierce.

Nancy glanced at him through the candles. "Look at the grin on Poppa!"

"Just thinking of an old joke." His standard answer, teasing her. Just thinking of what if all of you were dead, and I could walk alone on the hills where no one's ever been.

"Daddy never tells what he's thinking," Jason said.

"Daddy never thinks," Christina added.

"Daddy's buying us a lovely new house," Nancy countered. "So don't you hurt his feelings."

"Daddy has no feelings," Christina answered.

"Goddammit, Jason, can't you hear the phone!" Lyman turned to Christina. "And take those goddamn things out of your ears!"

"They're *mine*, Daddy. I don't have to."

"It's for you, Daddy," Jason called.

As he walked round the end of the table Lyman flicked his napkin hard so it caught Christina just below the ear, making him smile. "Yeah?" he said into the phone.

"I need you to come in, Howie," Curt Merck said. "We've got good news."

"It's my kid's birthday, for Christ's sake."

"You had someone you were looking for, down south?"

"Yeah?"

"We think he just tried to get on TV, in San Francisco, tell his story."

"Shit no!"

"We made sure that no news is good news. But you may want to go out there, discuss it with him?"

"Absolutely. Tell NoCal to stay out."

"I can't, Howie, it's their turf. But I'm telling them he's yours."

DAWN FOG wrapped the house; the foghorn bellowed balefully. Murphy dressed and walked up through the dripping, quiet streets to Geary, dropped fifty cents in a *Chronicle* rack.

Nothing on the front page, nor on page two or three. On page fourteen of the second section he finally found it, a small article in the gutter beside an I Magnin ad for see-through underwear: "S.F. Tourist Claims Army Attack."

San Francisco – A local resident
who had recently traveled to Central
America declared yesterday that US

Army personnel are assisting the Gua-
temalan Army in its campaign against
Marxist guerrillas. Joseph Murphy,
39, also alleged that US troops partici-
pated in a raid against a guerrilla-held
stronghold.

In Washington, a Defense Depart-
ment spokesperson, Joanne Quinlan,
categorically refuted Murphy's claim,
and explained that no US military
personnel "have been in recent years
nor are now on duty in Guatemala."
Quinlan added that Communist revo-
lutionaries trying to overthrow the
country's democratically elected gov-
ernment often dress like soldiers and
commit atrocities against the people,
but that such incidents have been
"on the wane" in recent years due to
the government's military successes
against the guerrillas.

He threw the paper in the trash and crossed Geary
through early traffic to Dunkin Donuts, where a boy with
pimples and a white paper baker's hat served him weak coffee and two jelly-filled rolls coated in powdered sugar.

37

H E CALLED *The Chronicle* but Melissa would not be in until midmorning and the operator wouldn't give him her home number. At nine-thirty someone answered the phone at the Bay Area Committee.

"It's OK coverage," Cyndi said. "The *Chronicle*'s the best in the country for Central American news."

"They didn't *say* anything! They acted like it was made up!"

"Wasn't it?"

"I don't follow…"

"I got a call last night at home, from the DEA. They say you're a drug smuggler and your plane got shot up by the Army and you've made up this story to get them back."

"What'd you tell them?"

"That I didn't know where to find you."

He was waiting for Melissa Maslow when she arrived at the *Chronicle*. When do I get the whole story?" she said. "Now, or when you're in prison?"

"I told you the truth!"

"It's a sign you're guilty, saying that." She led him across a wide low room of people hunched before green screens. The air smelled of warm newsprint, electricity, Coffee-Mate and cigarettes. She took a chair from another desk and put it beside hers, snapped on her computer terminal. "Tell me about the drugs."

"Turn it off," he said. "You tell me."

She flicked off the computer. "After we talked in the Rathskeller I called DC. They denied any US involvement, blamed the Communists." She picked up a pencil, ticked it against her teeth. "By the way, my story was much longer. It got cut, up there," she pointed at the ceiling. "Editorial."

She leaned back in her chair, playing with the pencil. "DEA called last night, wants to talk to you about some drug shipment from Guatemala..."

"That sucks! I was down there looking at El Ceibal, there's ruins all up and down that river." He made himself relax. "What about this General Arena? The Guatemalan grass shipments?"

She ignored him. "And you're just a San Francisco real estate investor, don't even know how to fly?"

"Of course I know how to fly. Taught free of charge by Uncle Sam. That doesn't make me a drug pilot."

"DEA said I should talk to some guy in City prison who just got nabbed with four million in coke. I saw him this morning, brought him photos of ten men, including one of you taken at yesterday's press conference. He picked you out instantly."

"Who is this guy?"

"Normally I wouldn't say, but it'll be in tomorrow's paper. Carlos Bonaventura, originally a Cuban from Miami. Why are you making such a fuss, instead of running for Panama, Colombia? DEA has you *made!*"

He glanced at the room of people clinging crablike to their desks, their hands raised in adoration before the flickering green screens. "You know it's not true, Melissa... What would you do?"

"Turn myself in. Or leave. Fast."

FOR A LOW-PROFILE place you couldn't beat the Oasis. Three hundred units in two long, two-story barracks at the junction of the Bayshore and Monterey Highways, forty-nine dollars cash for color TV and two double beds and a shower with a massage head that sometimes worked depending on the room, with couples coming in and out at all hours, nobody seeing anything but sex or money or getting somewhere down the road. Lyman checked in as Tim Merriweather but left no trace of himself in the room, got back into the Acura he'd rented at the airport and drove downtown, parked on O'Farrell and walked up Polk to a girlie joint, dark and sour-smelling after the bright street. He paid ten dollars for five tokens, locked the door of a booth behind him and put the tokens in the slot. The floor was sticky. A black plastic wall before him slid up and there was a Turkish-looking girl with heavy thighs and purple nipples dancing on a little plate turning around in an octagon of mirror windows. She smiled rotten teeth to welcome him and pushed her cunt against the window. He showed her a five and slid it into the slot and when the little plate came around again she shoved herself up and down his window. The timer buzzed and the black wall came down and he stood waiting for a moment then went out of the booth down the hall to the end through a door marked STAFF ONLY, and up narrow stairs to a suite of offices on the third floor. A fat man in a Scorpions T-shirt was talking on the phone with his feet on the desk. He finished his call. "You again."

"I want a PPK and a hundred rounds," Lyman said, "and this guy's picture and address. And I want you out of my way."

THE PAY PHONE was beat up and didn't work when Murphy put two quarters in it. He walked down California till he found another. "Steele and Friedman," a woman said. He asked for Saul Friedman.

"He's in conference."

"Please get him out. Tell him it's Joe Murphy."

A minute later Saul came on. "Murph, what's the rush?"

"I want you to sell Sea Cliff and every other piece of property I've got in forty-eight hours."

"You fucking nuts?"

"Sell it to CMC, Bayview, anybody, best price you can. Spread it around, not in a lump. Don't tell anybody the whole show."

"You're out of your mind. You're going to get creamed."

"And I need you to hire movers to get all my stuff out of the house by tomorrow night. In storage. And draw up an affidavit that all my stuff belongs to a woman named Dona Villalobos. I'll spell it –"

"I'm not doing this, Murph. Don't jerk me around, I've got a client waiting."

"Who the fuck you think I am, the paper boy?"

"You really want to do this?"

"I *was* a paper boy once, actually, in Texas. Yes, I really want to do it."

"Even the Porsche?"

"Yeah. No, keep that out. That and my bikes, and the Ford three-quarter ton. Sell the rest."

"Why? You're going to get creamed there too."

"I got the kind of problems we always talked about."

For a moment Saul said nothing. "Damn."

"All cash, Saul. Everything. And one last thing –"

"Let me tell my secretary, tell this guy to wait." Saul came back on. "Murph, you gotta think this over."

"Everything sold in forty-eight hours. Then within twenty-four more hours you wire it all to the regular setup in CI? I'll take it from there."

"You're really screwing me up, Murph. I was taking Chris kayaking tomorrow, out at Point Reyes."

"Tell him I'm sorry. Tell him if I ever get out of this I'll take him hunting in Montana, whatever he wants."

"You ought to drop all this, come with us."

"One more thing. You're going to hate me for this…"

"Probably."

"Can you go see a chick named Sherrie Cunningham, 154 Alabama? Write that down – 154 Alabama. She's about twenty. A junkie. I need you to support her if she goes back to school, gets into detox, goes straight."

You shouldn't fuck junkies, man, you'll get AIDS."

"I'm not. Don't go there alone."

LYMAN DROVE out Geary through Golden Gate Park till he was sure there was no tail, then cut across to the Sunset, parked in an Esso garage and stuck the PPK and hundred rounds up behind the Acura's firewall. He took the trolley downtown and rented a Dodge from Asia Rentals with a license and a credit card in the name of Lucian Hayward, registered at the Hyatt Regency under the same name, drove out Mission to Noble's Gun Shop and bought a used Zastava 9mm and forty rounds for four hundred and fifty dollars, using the same ID.

The sun was a thin orange disk sinking into gray beyond the rooftops. He drove down Twenty-fifth Avenue into Sea Cliff, passed by the house, parked two blocks further, and walked back on the far side of the street. The gun was heavy in the holster under his armpit, slippery with sweat. The houses were white and vast, no one in sight. Murphy's house had tall pillars like the Jefferson mansion, no lights. This can't be the guy, Lyman thought. He sat in his car for several hours till a car pulled into Murphy's driveway. It was low and lean but Lyman couldn't see what kind. He started the Dodge and drove past the house as the garage door came down. He idled to a halt. Lights came on in the front rooms. He parked and jogged back along the sidewalk, keeping his left arm against his ribs.

"MURPH!" she said, "How sweet of you to call! It's only been what, six weeks?"

"Lay off, Angelica. I've had a bad time."

"Sorry to hear. Who is she?"

"Can I come over?"

"There's some people here. Little party. What the hell…"

He went down to the garage and started the Kawasaki, let it run for a few seconds then pushed the door button and roared up the driveway, turned left and accelerated to the corner, passing a tall black man who turned around suddenly and sprinted back down the walk. Strange, Murphy thought, never seen him before. He gunned the bike round the curve and up Twenty-fifth Avenue, swung left toward Pacific Heights, burning the lights.

From its curving driveway her house cascaded on levels down through lemon trees, rhododendrons, acacias and palms to a lower lawn with fountains, all overlooking the gingerbread gables of Pacific Heights, the Marina, and the Bay. There were cars in the driveway and up on the street. He hugged her then sat on the kitchen counter watching her green eyes. Music thundered from the faraway front of the house. "Got anything to eat?" he said.

She poured him coffee and set it on the counter with a Sara Lee cheesecake and a bottle of Bushmills. "I've got people to take care of, in there."

"I'll be right in. How's Eric?"

She glanced at the clock over the sink. "He's had his book and he's already in bed."

"Can I go see him?"

"Just for a bit."

He drained the coffee and filled the cup with Bushmills. "You're going to an early grave, Murph," she said.

He lit a joint and passed it to her. "I've already lived longer than I ever thought I would."

"That makes you attractive to women but not necessarily a good prospect." She inhaled the joint, held it. "I've given up waiting for you."

"You've been balling every guy in town while I've been gone."

"My fuck rate's far lower than yours."

"Like that morning in Cleveland when you screwed the Sam Colter Band? All five of them?" He put the Sara Lee box in the trash under the sink. "AIDS will make us all virtuous again."

"There's other ways to whore yourself."

"You should know." When she said nothing he looked up, but she was lighting the joint. "This isn't life, Angie."

"You've always said that. You've just never found anything better."

Footsteps came through the hall and sunroom into the kitchen, a tall man with a black beard and a bit of a belly, black leather jacket and gray slacks. "Murph!" he extended a hand. "When she didn't come back, I should've known it was you."

"Hello, Mitch. Angie's been telling me my fortune."

"Shouldn't take long," Mitch said. He glanced at Angelica. "Just kidding."

"Murph thinks I fuck too many people," Angelica said.

Mitch took a film canister from his breast pocket and tapped some coke onto the counter, scraped it out in a line with a book of matches that said *Enjoy Life... Eat Out More Often.* "Guests first," he smiled.

Murphy shook his head. "How's the new album?"

"She's losing her voice." Mitch bent over the counter to sniff up the line. "Too much coke and Benedictine and parties. Now this album's done, she takes a year off, raises her kid, lives a normal life."

"Fuck you, Mitch," Angelica said.

38

HE CLIMBED the stairs to the third floor, went into Eric's room, the purple glow of a fluid oscillator sliding round the walls, a fish mobile banging his head as he leaned over the racing car waterbed. "How you doin', amigo?"

"Murph! Where've you *been*?"

"Traveling. Had to stay a while."

The boy sat up. "You get hurt or something?"

"Nothing bad. How's you?"

"Doin' fine."

"Feelin' alone?"

"Never."

"Everybody does, some of the time."

Eric glanced at the door. "You don't act so lonely, Murph."

"It's a mask, amigo. A charade."

"What's that?"

"When people dress up to be somebody they're not." He brushed the boy's pale hair, short and crisp. "Pretend they're happy when they're not."

"Mom's happy when she drinks."

"Yeah, I know about that."

"What's drinking change?"

"Makes everything worse."

"Mom says my dad was a lush. I asked Mary what that means and she said a drunk."

"I never knew your dad. But he made beautiful music. Music to make people happy."

"Like drinking does?"

"No. Not like that."

The boy snuggled down. "I was worried about you, Murph."

"No need to."

"Mom isn't going to stay with you, is she?"

He patted the boy's arm, shook his head.

"She never stays with anybody, does she?"

"You and I can still be friends."

"You're awful thin, Murph. You wreck your bike again? You sure you're OK?"

"Guaranteed. You get some sleep now. And Eric –"

"Yeah, Murph?"

"If I don't come around for a while, that don't mean I'm not missing you... I'll be back, soon's I can."

The boy had drifted off to sleep and Murphy went downstairs. The living room was crowded, more people on the stairs going down to the sunken parlor, Guns 'n Roses thudding pyrotechnic solos off the walls. To be able to do *that*, Murphy thought, what the needle gives, pure perception of beauty, untainted? He thought of Sherrie Cunningham, the blue-black marks on the inside of her elbow, of Lila the junkie who'd gone straight then jumped off the Golden Gate.

"Murph!" someone called. "Bring your axe?"

"'Lo, Tiny." He leaned into the man's face to speak over the music. "Not going to compete with this dude."

"He *is* amazing." Tiny gulped a glass of red. "Listen to that shit, how he fills it in, doubles up on the E."

"It's not that, Tiny. It's that he's so *clean*."

"Like Clapton."

"Different. A different vision."

"Heard you had some trouble," a woman bent forward to be kissed. "Down in Costa Rica?"

"Hi, Laura." Her lips tasted like cold cream and raspberries. She shoved against him and he clung a second, nipping her, pulled away. "Where'd you hear that?"

"Paper."

"It was Guatemala. All over now."

A girl came by with a silver salver with lines on it and a silver tube and Laura put down her wine to take one, her face sharp then melting into a smile as the coke hit her.

I'm on the night train,
ready to crash and burn

The girl offered Murphy the tray; he shook his head. "Oh what the hell," he said, sucking in one line, switching sides, then the next. It was a cold blue blade of perception: he could see individual lamé filigrees on the girl's neckline, her big soft tits beneath, nipples poking out the fabric that clung all the way down to her mound and slender thighs, could hear the drummer's quick ripple tossed in for free and the guitarist's fingertips quicksilver down the neck, in and out of blues, playing *for* God, *to* God only, he could taste the wine and the rooty soil and chromium sulfate in it, taste Laura's lipstick on his lips and the lilac perfume of this girl with the silver salver, see every black and silver curly hair of Tiny's beard, smell Tiny's breath of garlic and weed, his armpit stench and the Ban under the girl's shaved pits. Someone knocked over a plant on the glass table by the piano and he saw it fall in slow motion, the awkward frightened leaves, the dirt rushing out when the pot hit the floor, stems snapping like soft wet bones. "Shit!" someone said, stepping back into the dirt, the stems squelching. Someone hit two piano notes, an F and G, discordant, making him look up, but it was just a wine glass, sitting on the keys.

A rocket took his brain straight up, his body far below on the launch pad but still he could feel every cell and the fire climbing from his legs and roaring into his sex and soaring up his chest where every breath was made of ice. He met the girl with the silver salver in the dining room and she gave him two more hits and he held the salver out to her and she did also, and we're completely in touch, he thought, her body absolutely part of his so when he rubbed her breast he could feel not only its soft smooth heaviness but also how the tingle from his hand made her breast feel hot inside, the nipple's stinging need to be touched, touched softly, fingered, could feel the ache racing down into her guts and through her groin to him, her teeth sharp into his lips, her hand around him moving back and forth, and as they went upstairs he raised her dress so he could see her long thighs rising before him, bending at the knee, her crotch in white lacy underpants and he put his hand there as she climbed the stairs, feeling the wet hairs through the silk and wondered is she that hot already or is it from someone else? In Angelica's room he held her against the shut door and shoved her underpants down, her spine against the jamb and her legs around him; he gripped her thighs and shoved into her, her arms squeezing his neck and her teeth hard against his cheek till she came sobbing, leaning back her head, red mouth open, wide large teeth agape with a thread of shiny saliva between them. He carried her to the bed and pushed her legs up around his neck to go in deeper, feeling her every cell, his own, every molecule he breathed.

"I've got to go back," she said. She went holding up her dress into the bathroom and squatted on the toilet. "Barney asked me, keep everybody stoned."

"I could fuck you all night."

"I gotta go back." She wiped herself, holding her thighs apart and looking at the toilet paper. "Barney said he'll get me a part."

He followed her down, sex on fire. "I don't care if he *had* Scuds," a woman was saying. "That's no reason to nuke him."

"We're not getting single time," another said.

No money in our jackets
and our jeans are torn
your hands are cold
but your lips are warm

He went into an atrium of lime and jasmine trees enclosed by a silvery cedar wall overhung with purple wisteria. There was a pool with a rock fountain, a lone dwarf maple stooping over it, red carp in the water. I'm just like them, he thought.

"Lovely tonight."

He looked at the voice. A slim man with spiky hair, an earring and black leather jacket. I'm supposed to know your name.

"You've been out of town, Murph?"

"Few weeks."

"Must be nice to travel. Like that."

"You should try it." He went back inside and met Laura in the hall and she kissed him hard, pushing her pelvis against him, but would not go upstairs. "Sleeping with skulls," he said.

A guy in black jeans and cowboy boots took her arm. "How's your horses?" Murphy asked him.

"You got the wrong guy," the man smiled patronizingly. "I don't have any horses."

"Then what you doing in those boots?"

He was talking with a smaller girl in jeans, sandals with little red-painted toes, her blouse open down the middle. She gave him two capsules of Ecstasy. "The more I reach, the further things recede," she said.

"Don't reach. And everything'll come to you."

She laughed. "Don't be nasty."

You're no good
you're no good
you're no good
baby you're no good

He reached out to the girl's lovely breasts inside the open blouse but she batted his hand away and walked back into the living room.

Downstairs was an enclosed terrace and a redwood tub full of people, and others sitting on the sides with their feet in it. The water burnt his skin; he sat with his back against a nozzle pumping hot vibrating water. There was a noise in his head like a jet landing but it never landed, just kept getting deeper and louder. The people beside him were fucking and trying not to show it, till the girl came and wilted on the man, her long hair down over his shoulder into the frothing steamy water. When she moved up and away from the man Murphy slipped up to her from behind and she was angry for a moment then widened her legs and let him come inside and began to move up and down while the guy watched her. Finally she came again, gasping face down, hands on the rim of the tub, her hair stringy in the water.

The small girl with the red painted toes came in. She had a dark appendix scar across the right side of her belly. "What happened to your arm?" she said. After a while she let him come into her but again he could not come and she took him hand and hand out on the grass under the gentle cool rain and sucked him softly for a long time but

227

he still could not come. With a numb desolation he kissed her goodbye and got dressed and went back up the stairs where two men were kissing, one making little girlish sighs, the other's hand on his crotch.

He started the bike and roared up the driveway, slowed for the sidewalk, the bike skidding. Watch out, he reminded himself, liking how the yellow turn signal flicked, its steady dependable bursts, controllable. Long as you watch out you're fine.

He spun onto Pacific and tore down the block, letting the front wheel go up, feeling the back shimmy. The bike wanted to flip but he wouldn't let it. Keep it under control, he told himself. Then you can have fun with no danger.

He coasted through the Stop and dove down the steep drop of Steiner, engine screaming, up to eighty, let it back off, muffler blaring, the intersection coming up like a head-on collision but he eased the brakes not skidding and there was no one going through the intersection so he made it, sliding sideways down the next block, bouncing slow motion off a light pole, missing a parked Volvo and spinning to a stop.

He looked up ashamed, as if everyone in the apartments nearby had seen him risk his life. The bike had died; he kicked it alive and rolled downhill and swung left on Lombard, beating the last lights and accelerating through the long wide approach to the Golden Gate Bridge, passing a Mercedes that flashed behind him in a blur of shrinking headlights, a Sirocco far ahead whipped past and vanished behind him, the bike screaming the roar of pure truth and he reminded himself be cool, don't let it trick you, saw the needle bouncing at a hundred and forty but didn't dare look down to be sure, the handles vibrating with road ripples, the curve straightening toward the bridge, a patch of mist and moths spattering his face, headlights the other way flying past like comets, wind thunder yanking his hair, the gray concrete wall a blur beside his knee.

The bridge was a rising metal wave, the far tower climbing inside the near one, orange cones separating oncoming lanes and he wove among them; a pickup flashed past blowing its horn. He went up the hill under the Rainbow Tunnel and down into Mill Valley, took the exit to the sea, through rainy hills where eucalyptus scent dripped from the trees and sebaceous snail tracks slicked the road. A white owl flapped up from his headlight, a rabbit in its claws. The night was thick with manzanita and wild roses, thunder and smell of the sea cascading up the cliffs, rain washing his face.

The bike was wild with anger to go faster, screaming up through the long Slide Ranch curve in third, a hundred, hundred and ten, slipping sideways on the dew-wet road but he could hold it, go as fast as it could go, could hold it, the Ecstasy hitting now, bringing everything in one and he loved it all, the speed, the world and all its night odors and sea crashing and all the girls and the engine roaring between his thighs as he tilted into the turn, and there was a cop car across the road and nowhere to cut and he swerved from the edge and the bike went down and soared off the highway and he slammed across the gravel shoulder and crashed into the manzanita.

The world was spinning over and over, slapping him; he stopped tumbling and lay looking at the stars. An enormous noise, the smell of dust and crushed ice plants and manzanitas. He could fall between the stars. He went down to the *Río*, realized he had dreamed her and she was gone, gone for good.

Deuce Harmony had dumped his Triumph in the rain and got decapitated by a Stop sign. Bikers who'd loved speed were spending their lives in wheelchairs. He touched his neck, head, arms and legs, could feel them all, stood carefully. No special pain. Voices and people coming down the hill. He pushed through the manzanita to the edge of the cliff but could not find the bike, climbed up to the highway, saw the CHP car and remembered.

"You crazy fucker!" he screamed, running at a cop.

More cops from all sides. Another CHP car. Cops with guns. "Cuff the son of bitch!" one yelled.

He tried to back up, too late. They pinned his arms behind him, hard metal biting his wrists. "You assholes tried to kill me!"

"Stupid maniac! You were doing a hundred thirty on that curve!"

"I *had* it. I *knew* what I was doing! You assholes! Don't you know *anything*?"

"When you get him to San Rafael," one said, "be sure to do a drug screen."

A plain car slid up, idling hard, a brown Dodge. Tall black guy, three others. "Thanks," he said to the cops. "Y'all have a good evening, now."

"You really want him?"

"C-6. No questions asked."

The tall guy grabbed Murphy's bad arm and yanked him toward the brown Dodge. "Wait a minute," Murphy said.

"Wait nothing!" One of the other plainclothes guys popped open the Dodge's trunk. The two CHP cars revved and pulled away. The tall black man took something small and black out of his jacket. A gun.

"Wait!" Murphy screamed. The black man gripped the gun in both hands and smashed it down on his head; pain exploded inside him and he fell, grateful to be nowhere.

39

THE HUEY FELL in a pocket and he pulled back the collective pitch lever but it didn't respond and he shoved the cyclic to drive it sideways but the ship kept dropping and green tracers leaped up from the tree-tops; he kicked the pedals but the tail wouldn't swing, the Huey spinning as the tracers closed in and he screamed, "Take it!" to the copilot but the copilot was hit, blood spraying everywhere, wounded grunts screaming in the back, the cockpit filled with smoke and the jungle of dark killers reaching up for them.

The ambulance surged forward, the differential whirring beneath him. He tried to change position on the stretcher but found he was bent backwards, wrists pinned to ankles. Not an ambulance, a dustoff. Shot down but the medevacs found us. Tied down so won't fall off. Must be shot in the head, can't see.

Hard to breathe. Not an ambulance. Trunk of a car, this. The car bounced on a bump and pain crashed through his head. *They* hit me on the head. CHP, the tall black guy.

He bent himself harder backwards to reach his ankles, grabbed a shoelace but dropped it, found it again but the knot had tightened. He kicked the shoe loose but it fell beyond reach.

The engine slowed. He gripped the shoe with his toes and pulled it toward his hands, tugged out the inner sole but it was the wrong shoe. He yanked the other off and pulled out the knife, cut the cord round his ankles. The engine roared; the car swerved, dropped from macadam onto dirt, gravel spattering the under-side.

The car was climbing through S-turns, springs jouncing in the ruts. He dropped the knife and doubled himself up to slide the cuffs under his buttocks, tearing his shoulder sockets, the metal cutting his wrists. He slid his cuffed hands forward under his thighs and feet, had them now in front, squirmed round to pick up the knife and held it in his teeth. The brake drums squealed, the trunk's interior glowing from the brake lights. He found his shoes and shoved them on, with one hand squeezed the knife under the trunk lid and popped it open, holding it down with the other hand. The car halted, he leaped from the trunk, ran through a wire fence across a mucky ditch toward a low white building, men shouting, the car's tires shrieking after him, its headlights bouncing over the ditch and he ducked into the white building's ammoniac darkness of screeching chickens, his nose smashed something hard – a perch – and he darted out the back door across a dirt road, sprinting awkwardly with his hands cuffed before him, dogs snarling along a fence, the car gaining as he jumped a corral fence and dashed uphill into an orchard and above it a pasture; the dogs poured out of the kennel and came howling up the hill behind him. There was a cyclone fence; he climbed and wriggled through the barbed wire on top and down to a chaparral slope, the dogs hitting the fence, their fangs clanging steel.

He ran up a rolling meadow, the stars bright above, to the ridge top. Headlights far below wound sleepily along a country road, over a bridge past a cutbank then a small white house with an orange pickup in the driveway, illuminating a stone wall along the shoulder, a yellow curve sign, then slipping around a ridge out of sight.

Voices and dogs coming up fast. He ran downhill and splashed across a creek, climbed through alders to the road as more headlights came up fast behind him. A Ford slid by, a pebble ticking in its hubcap, its searchlight raking the slope and bouncing off the red alder trunks inches over his head. The Ford passed the white house, the pickup truck, the stone wall, and vanished round the curve.

Dogs were baying down the hill behind him; he ran along the road past the white house, up the driveway to the orange pickup, its cab light flashing as he leaped inside. He shut the door, ducked under the steering wheel to cut the ignition wires. Two men were running up the road, a big dog bounding before them. He linked two wires but they were wrong so he tried the first and third, the dash indicators gleamed, he shifted into reverse, the dog crashed into the door as he rolled back popping the clutch, the dog snarling at the door handle, three men spanning the road. The engine backfired and died.

The dog leaped onto the hood beating its teeth against the windshield, a Doberman, the three men running for the truck as he bent again under the dash, found the starter wire and touched it to the others; it caught; he raced the sputtering engine, shifted into first and drove at the men who dove for the shoulder, the dog squealing off the hood and whacking the pavement as Murphy took his cuffed hands from the wheel to shift into second. A spider web of cracks spread across the windshield; there was another *tick* and glass spattered from the rear window down his neck, another star in the windshield, and he spun the wheel weaving the truck. *Tick:* another then another hit the windshield and it collapsed into his face, cold air crashing in; another ping of metal, then only the truck's uneven roar as he peered through the gaping windshield at the unlit road, flakes of glass like snow flicking past his cheeks.

Safely around the first bend he took his hands from the wheel, holding it steady with his knees, and fumbled at the dash till he found the light switch. Valves chattering, transmission yowling, headlights jolting, the truck wound up to eighty-five but would go no faster; ahead was a straightaway suddenly familiar – Olema's scruffy store and few houses. Headlights jumped into the mirror and he shut off the truck's lights, stomped the emergency brake and skidded up an alley behind the store, jumped out and hurdled a fence into a eucalyptus grove as the Ford roared through the Stop southward on Highway One toward Bolinas.

He ran to the truck and cut the taillight wires. The Ford came flying back through the Stop, going north toward Point Reyes. He started the truck and drove fast south, flicking on the lights after a mile. At the Bolinas turnoff he swung uphill on a narrow road into the Coast Range, no guardrail between the edge and the chasm on the right where redwood tops flitted past. Near the top the truck began to gasp then died. It would not start; the gas gauge showed empty. Below, three sets of headlights came fast down Highway One. At the turnoff they split, one continuing south, one swinging west toward Bolinas, the third coming up toward him.

Everything took place very slowly but there was no time. He rolled the truck back, swerved it round till it was pointing downhill, pushed it forward. The car's lights came darting uphill; the truck gained speed. He dived out the truck's door as the car accelerated round the last curve; the pavement spun up and slapped him in the face as the car's tires screeched and the truck slammed into it.

He got to his feet. The awful howling inside his head was the car's horn. He wiped his hands; they were stuck with gravel. He found the knife and ran uphill; from the wreck the Ford's horn wailed like a primeval beast.

He reached the crest. More headlights came up the road and halted behind the wreck. In the columns of light he could see men running uphill, the dark shadow of a dog bounding before them.

Holding the knife carefully before him, he pushed from the road down the far side of the Coast Range, through prickly low firs, stumbling on roots and fallen branches, the needle-thick slope slippery, across a meadow where a deer snorted and bounded away, into a marsh, the dog's bark nearing.

He ran down a steep ledge, Mill Valley's lights two thousand feet below. Now he could hear the dog's fast patter through the brush. Snarling it slammed him down, a horrible Doberman crunching his arm, fighting for his neck. He drove the knife straight up under its collar and yanked; it cried, gurgled, teeth sunk in his wrist, dragging him; it fell dead. He unbuckled its collar and ran along the ledge and threw the collar over the cliff, heard it hit moments later. The brush crashed as the men neared; he ran up the slope above the cliff, dug a rock from the moss and hid gasping under a juniper.

The first man came panting through the trees to the cliff. "Here!" he called. Two others scrambled through the scrub. There was the sound of static, a high, steady beep. "Dog's down there," the first said.

"He ain't moving?"

"He's got him down... Go uphill and around and down this cliff. I'll take the down side, with the receiver. Charlie stay here, coordinate positions. Watch our lights and keep signaling."

The flashlights parted, one moving downhill along the cliff edge, one remaining, another climbing toward Murphy. The light passed, the man exuding smells of sweat and cigarettes.

When the two had climbed down the sides of the cliff they signaled three flashlight blinks up to Charlie. One step at a time, Murphy edged along the cliff toward Charlie, who was scuffing out a place to sit. "Charlie!" one called from below. "Charlie!"

"Yo!" Charlie called.

"Dog lost his collar. It's here, caught on a branch."

Charlie stood, flicked on his light. "I'm coming down."

"Go the uphill way. It's easier."

Charlie came toward Murphy, switching his flashlight to his left hand, parting the bushes with his right.

40

HE HIT CHARLIE with the rock and Charlie fell in a clump, flashlight clattering; Charlie was twitching and moaning; in his pockets Murphy found a gun, a wallet, and a thin aerosol can that made him gasp for breath.

Charlie whined, tried to sit. Holding the spray can in his left hand, Murphy shoved the knife against his throat. "Quick! Why you chasing me?"

"My head..."

Murphy shifted the spray can and squeezed a burst into Charlie's face. Charlie choked, coughed, tried to pull back. "Tell me fast," Murphy said, "or I'll empty this whole can in your face. Then I'll kill you."

"Syndic," Charlie gagged. "Wants you."

"The dealers?"

"No! The *big* guys. Please don't –"

"That place you took me, what was it?"

"The ranch."

"*What* ranch?"

"Congregation, I'll tell you, just don't –"

"Charlie!" a voice called from below. "What's keeping you?" Charlie lunged for the edge and Murphy sprayed the Mace full into his face, up his nose, Charlie writhing, choking, fighting him off. Holding his breath, Murphy hit him again with the rock, grabbed Charlie's wallet and gun, ran away from the cliff, half blinded by the Mace, through the trees and along the meadow and down a great rubbled cirque.

Beyond the awakening lights of Mill Valley, Highway 101 was swelling with early traffic. The Bay gleamed gunmetal under the waning stars, the East Bay hills powdered with lights, their crests stitched with redwood tops against the lavender, orange east.

At a stream he washed blood and dirt from his face, and finger-combed his hair. Charlie's gun was a lousy little Grendel .380, loud and nearly useless. He pocketed the knife and pulled his jacket up over his shoulders from behind and down over his arms to cover the cuffs and gun, holding the jacket against his front as if carrying extra clothing too warm to wear.

In the first street of houses a dog came barking, making him jump, but it was only a Brittany spaniel on a chain. Next came a line of unfinished apartments, the lawns bulldozed and littered with scraps of redwood siding, a pile of uprooted apple trees along the curb. "Early Occupancy", a sign said, "Apple Grove Condominiums".

Cars began to trickle down the streets onto the larger roads that poured into the river of 101 carrying them to San Francisco. An empty *Chronicle* truck idled smokily outside Johnny's Stop'n Go; Murphy ducked under the canvas rear gate, clambered over bundles of fresh papers and hid under plastic and old newsprint near the cab.

LYMAN DROVE FAST up the ridge road past the wreck of the truck and Ford to the top where two more Fords had pulled off the road. A NoCal man came out of one. "They want you on the horn, sir!"

"Let the assholes wait!"

"Whatever you say, Sir. But it's HQ."

"I said *let* them wait," he seethed into the man's face, a kid, crewcut, anxious. "You guys can't wipe your ass without getting it all over you, *why* should I talk to any of you!"

"Regs require response to radio traffic when response is possible, Sir!"

"You little jerk!" Lyman shoved him against the car. "Don't *you* talk regulations! Just take me to where he got away."

The NoCal man pushed himself up from the side of the car where he had fallen, wiping his hands on his pants. "He beat up one of the Syndic guys. The guy's still out there, and another one with him." He nodded at the gun in Lyman's hand. "So be careful with that rod."

The NoCal man opened the car door, spoke into the radio, shut and locked the door and led Lyman through the woods and across a meadow. They came to the top of a cliff where a man was sitting against a rock, his head bandaged, another man sitting beside him smoking. The cigarette drove Lyman wild. "Go back to the car and order up a medic," he told them.

"We did," the NoCal man said.

"Go *get* the medic, I said. I want to talk to this dude." He took Charlie's hand. "Howya doin', big guy?"

"OK. Except my fucking head."

"What'd he ask you?"

"Ask me? Nothing. Nothing, boss."

"C'mon, don't pull my string. I need to know where his head's at."

"I didn't say nothing."

"I *know* that. Just tell me what *he* said. C'mon, good buddy."

"Well, he wanted to know why we was chasin' him."

"And?"

"I didn't say nothing, boss."

"What else?"

"Wanted to know where it was we took him, that's all."

"You told, didn't you?"

"No Sir, I didn't say. I swear..." Charlie strained at Lyman's arm. "That's why he hit me."

"Relax, I'll make it better." Holding Charlie's forehead steady with his left hand, he gripped Charlie's neck in his right and jerked hard. He stood, inspected Mill Valley far below in the blue-golden dawn, and walked back to the cars. "Cancel the medic," he told the NoCal man. "Your boy's had a hemorrhage."

"He's *dead*?"

"It's a homicide now. Give CHP and the Marin and Frisco cops Murphy's full details. Remind them it's C-6. That they are responsible for maximum silence. Say he's armed and very dangerous, probably headed back to San Francisco."

THE *CHRONICLE* TRUCK'S door slammed and the truck lurched into gear, halted minutes later. The door banged, the canvas gate grated aside, a bundle of papers slapped down on the sidewalk; the door slammed again and the truck lurched into gear. After a dozen more stops the truck rattled on to Highway 101 toward San Francisco. It crossed the Golden Gate Bridge, wheezed to a stop for the toll gate, and took the Embarcadero toward downtown. When it stopped for the light at Columbus and Bay, Murphy hopped out and walked up Columbus toward Chinatown, ignoring the occasional passerby who turned to stare at his torn face, the strange way he carried his jacket inside out before him over his clasped hands.

41

CHINATOWN'S sidewalks bustled with housewives carrying straw baskets of fish, vegetables, and poultry on their elbows, with slipper-shuffling old men hugging Chinese newspapers under their arms, with chattering girls in red parochial skirts and solemn boys in blue cardigans hustling to the parochial school of Notre Dame de Victoire.

Up a dead end off Mason was a motorcycle garage. A German Shepherd sitting in the open door wagged its tail as Murphy approached. Inside a man knelt over a disassembled Suzuki. He stood up slowly, put down his wrench. "Did you dump?"

Murphy glanced round the shop. "Anybody else here?"

"Not now. I better be getting you to a doctor."

"Close the door, Ray. You got some cable cutters?"

Ray Lin whistled the German Shepherd inside and pulled down the door. Murphy sat on a car seat that served as a sofa, raised up his arms to let his coat slip back from the cuffs. "Jesus, Murph! Who put you in those? What are you doing with that dink little gun?"

"I need you to get me out of them."

Ray bent over him, checked the bloody wound on his skull, the scratches on his face and hands. He went to the wall of tools and took down a large pair of cable cutters, made Murphy hold his hands on the concrete floor and broke through the hardened steel chain linking the two cuffs. Murphy raised up his hands with a dizzying sense of freedom. "Oh God what I've been through."

Ray sat back on his haunches. "You going to tell me about it?"

"Let's get these cuffs off first."

Murphy stood by a bench vise and Ray clamped the cuffs one at a time in the vise and cut them with an electric hacksaw. Murphy told him about the CHP car blocking the road, the black man with the Dodge, his breakout from the Dodge's trunk, stealing the truck, the man named Charlie, the escape to Mill Valley.

"I don't see why they do all this just because you were speeding."

"Where's Susan?" Murphy said.

"At work."

"Can I go upstairs and take a shower, lie down? I've never felt so bad in all my life."

The phone rang; Ray answered it briefly, came back. "I'll make you some coffee, something to eat while you take a shower, then you have a sleep. When you wake up we'll sort this out."

"That's the problem, Ray. There's nothing *to* sort out."

WHEN HE WOKE rain was falling steadily against the window. The slightest move agonized his head; every muscle and bone hurt miserably. There was a little round carpet on the floor; if I can get my feet on that and stand, he told himself, I'll have it licked.

In the bathroom he took four Empirin with codeine and stood again under the shower, careful not to let it hit his head, till his muscles loosened and the pain became reasonable. Back in the bedroom he could not find his clothes, went downstairs. Over the thunder of Fleetwood Mac was the shriek of a grinder; he waited till it stopped. "Ray!"

Ray came to the foot of the stairs, grinned up at him. "You're one ugly specimen. What happened to your arm?"

"Where's my clothes?"

"Just a minute." Ray put down the grinder and came upstairs. "I washed them, put them in the dryer."

"Thanks. What time's it?"

"Two-thirty."

The clothes were still warm from the dryer. "Hungry?" Ray said.

"I need a drink. Took some of your codeine."

Ray poured him coffee and brandy, went out and came back a few minutes later with three hamburgers and a six-pack of Coke. "Tell me about the Syndic," Murphy said.

"We don't mix with them. They're selling all the coke now, trying to take over the weed."

"*Who* are they?"

"Mostly Cubans from Miami, and the guys that got thrown out of Nicaragua when those Sandinos got in."

"Sandinistas."

"A spic's a spic."

"Ever hear of Carlos Bonaventura?"

Ray shook his head.

"Ever hear of some place in Marin, up by Olema, called the Congregation Ranch?"

"Don't ever go to Marin. No Chinese people up there."

Murphy found the wallet he'd taken from the man named Charlie. Inside was a driver's license in the name of Hector Alvierez, 1449 Paloma Terrace, a scrawny face squinting at the camera. He handed it to Ray. "Ever see him?"

Ray gave it back. "Never." Also in the wallet were a Visa and Master Card from Southern California Federal Savings, a bowling league card, a mini-calendar from Southern California Federal, a Polaroid of a dark-haired, chubby woman and a teenage girl sitting on a floral couch, the camera flash reflecting in the Day-Glo painting above their heads. There was a business card with a federal seal, US Bureau of International Development, Hector Alvierez, Senior Program Evaluator, a condom, and three hundred-dollar bills and seven twenties.

"I got those valves to finish grinding," Ray said. "Susan'll be home at six. We can go up to the Jade Palace."

Murphy stood carefully. "Got to make some calls."

Ray nodded at the living room. "Phone's in there."

"Rather do it from a booth."

"Shoot yourself," Ray said.

THE RAIN had ceased. From a Powell Street booth he called Melissa Maslow. "I never expected to hear from you," she said.

"I need to ask you some questions."

"Questions? You out of your mind?"

There was a drift to her voice that bothered him. "Where you calling from?" she said, offhand.

"I got beat up by some cops last night and put in a trunk and taken to this place east of Olema called Congregation ranch. Ever heard of it?"

"I used to think you were a nice guy. What the Hell'd you do that for?"

"Do what?"

Her voice was on edge, distant. "Kill that guy."

A woman was walking past the phone booth, tugging her little boy by the hand. He was sucking a lollipop and staring at Murphy out of almond eyes. He was wearing shorts and had skinned one knee. Across the street a panel truck was trying to back into a space too small for it. When Melissa had finished he made her repeat it. "I didn't hit him that hard," he said.

"He's dead, Murph. And there's an all-points out for you. You didn't know that?"

"Please listen to me."

"I don't want to get involved, Murph."

"Please, listen to me?" He told her about Charlie, the Syndic. "Do me one favor? See if you can find out about the Congregation ranch, this US Bureau of International Development, find out who got to that guy Carlos Bonaventura in prison, made him say what he said about me."

"You telling me you're not a dealer, Joe?"

"Not the kind that guy would know."

"I'll make you a deal?"

"What's that?"

"I'll go down to the *Chronicle*'s morgue, talk to some news people, check this stuff out for you. On the condition that when you get arrested I'm the only reporter who gets your story."

"Can't you get it through your thick head, Melissa, they're not going to arrest me! They want me dead."

There was the click, across the phone, of her hitting her teeth with a pencil. "Call me at six."

A black and white police car eased down Powell, two fat cops watching through shut windows. He bent down in the booth, pretending to speak into the phone; the car slid by and turned the corner.

WHEN LYMAN checked Murphy's house again there were two moving vans out front and a black BMW in the drive-way. Men were carrying furniture from the house into the vans. A Mercedes and an Olds station wagon pulled up in the driveway; a bearded man in a gray suit came out of the house, shook hands with the people and led them inside.

Lyman strolled along the sidewalk and stopped to watch. After a minute he spoke to one of the movers, then walked on, came round the block, got in the Dodge and drove downtown.

"I could care he's moved," said the fat man at the desk on the third floor over the girly joint.

"He's going to vanish. We need coverage."

"*We*? A day ago you didn' wanna know us."

"You and me, we're supposed to keep distance. You know the drill. But the Congregation needs him. And you just lost one of your golden boys. Don't you *want* this guy?"

The fat man peeled plastic off a toothpick and shoved it in his mouth. "We're just the ugly girl you fuck when there's nobody else."

"You should be so lucky." Unbidden, Lyman sat. "I need you guys to crank out a contact list, spread the ID on his vehicles. There's a Ford pickup and a silver Porsche 944, license MZG 505... I got all the details, but I need *you* to find him before the cops do."

"Cops? The man laughed a raspy smoker's cough. "If you think *they're* going to find him then you're one bright boy."

"And I need you to stay in touch with the media, make sure he's not talking to anybody. We don't want divergent stories."

The man shifted his toothpick. "One truth. That's all there is. Under God. Indivisible."

"I WENT BACK to see Carlos Bonaventura," Melissa said. "But he made bail."

"Damn!"

"No! Don't you understand? Here's this nobody crack dealer, suddenly makes two hundred thousand bail the day after he identifies you for the papers."

"Where'd he get the money?"

"I have no idea. But I'm going to find out."

"Be careful, Meliss."

"We need to talk. In person."

"You're not going to run me in?"

She laughed. "I'll keep my side of the deal."

"Meet me somewhere, then."

"I'm working late. Edinburgh Castle at midnight? It'll be safe for you, and it's on my way home."

42

THE RAIN HAD died; runnels glistened on the streets. Everything was sharp: faces in passing cars, shirts stacked in shop windows, cutlery on tables in closed restaurants, a Sprite can in the gutter. A cruiser tailed him up Polk then veered away like a shark sensing fresher blood elsewhere. A half moon burst through towering black clouds, tainting them silver, vanished. The rain returned.

The Edinburgh Castle faced O'Farrell with its back on a narrow unlit alley where cars crouched along one side against grimy brick walls. Rain beat on cobblestoned puddles where the asphalt had worn away. Stairs with dripping rusty rails descended like gruesome mine entrances. Over the rooftops came the murmur of traffic from Polk and Geary; beyond the dark end of the alley was a Fish'n Chips stand with two distant skyscrapers looming out of the fog above it. The rain hammered his shoulders; his socks sloshed, his feet were numb. A cat scampered between trash cans, something wriggling in its jaws.

A car's lights leaped into the alley, the engine roaring, and he stepped between two parked cars to let it pass. It slowed, tires rumbling the cobblestones; he saw the rectangular Ford grille and dived behind a parked car down slippery stairs to a locked door, broken bottles grinding underfoot, fumbled for the latch but it wouldn't open, and dashed back up the stairs to see the Ford continue down the alley, brake at the end, and turn left on Larkin. He rubbed a scraped elbow and stepped back into the alley. Fool, he cursed himself, even the normal betrays you.

Another car swung into the alley, headlights making him a dancing bear's shadow down the oily cobbles; he stepped aside, waiting for it to pass. It slowed, a searchlight hit his face, a megaphone: "Police! You behind that car! Get out here!" He sprinted along the wall knocking over trash cans and ducked past the cop car as it screamed into reverse after him and he leaped a car's hood onto its roof and up a fire escape, his bad arm wrenched with pain, a cop clambering up behind him, cruiser lights flicking the buildings blue and white. He jumped the parapet and dashed across the puddled rooftop, leaped a gap between two buildings, a ghastly emptiness sucking at him, made the far side and crossed the next rooftop, reached the end and swung over the edge, the cars far below on Larkin casting little cones of light, people like ants on a strip of sidewalk tiny as a ribbon between his feet.

The cop had halted at the gap between the buildings, yelling into his radio, his shiny bulk silhouetted by St Mary's gleaming cross. Murphy dropped free, landed on the top rungs of another fire escape, ran down five floors as more police cars screeched through the Geary red light a block away; he jumped the last story to the sidewalk and slipped into a bar which stank of whiskey and cigarettes.

Biker women in black jackets and chains stared him down as he hobbled toward the johns, reversed his jacket to its pale gray lining, grabbed a yachting cap off the coat rack and ran into a storeroom of aluminum kegs and beer cases. A dead bulb banged his forehead as he stepped into the alley where the blue globes of police cars blinked beneath the fire escape that three cops climbed intently, their flash-lights darting up the walls. As though curious he watched them for a moment, then went down the alley to Larkin and around the corner to the Edinburgh Castle.

In the men's room he wiped his ragged hair and torn bloody hands with paper towels, staring at the stained sink, stinking urinal and carious scribbled walls as if even they would betray him. At the bar he rubbed whiskey into his hands to stop the bleeding, set the yachting cap tighter over his wet hair. Two cops came in, cloaks brilliant with rain. One stayed by the door while the other talked to the bar-tender, who nodded, thumbs in the pockets of his plaid vest, and jerked his chin down the bar at Murphy. The cop am-bled over, splay-footed and chubby, cloak trickling. "Just come in?"

Murphy pulled back his sleeve to inspect his watch. The crystal was scratched. "Jes' little while 'go."

"Got some ID?"

He nodded, as if finding the question confusing, knocked back his whiskey and fumbled at his pockets. With the coat reversed it was hard to get at the wallet; he finally got it out and laid it laboriously on the wet bar, holding it open with one hand, and pulled out the Arizona license in the name of Lamar P. Bultz. The cop took it in pink cold fingers and held it to the light.

Murphy held out his empty glass to the bartender, beck-oning for another, waiting for the cop to put the license down quietly and pull his gun and walk him handcuffed out of the Edinburgh Castle. He imagined Melissa coming in as they left, her astonished look.

The cop put the license down in spilled whiskey and glanced at Murphy's cap. "What's the name of your boat?"

"The hat says SS *Miranda*. But I don't have a boat."

The cops left and he finished the second whiskey and ordered a third. The clock over the crossed guns and sabers over the bar said twelve fifteen; a couple trudged out hand in hand into rain gusting yellow across the lights. Twelve eighteen. Melissa wasn't coming, but in a few minutes the cops would return.

"You're a bit laid back, aren't you?" Melissa sat on the wooden bench beside him, blonde hair dripping down her yellow anorak. "For a wanted man?"

He took her damp cold hand. "Thanks for coming."

"I wouldn't be doing this, except I remember how you were, that one night we met…"

"I was going to call you."

"You just weren't the kind of person to do what they say you've done."

"I *have* flown weed, Melissa. That was my shtick, no big thing. I was going to tell you. What I told you about the village is true. And about the American soldiers."

She leaned against him. "Kiss me, quick. Two cops came in."

Her mouth was small, cold, a girl's. He kissed her again, her hair wet against his hand. She backed away. "They've gone!"

"You're going to catch your death."

"I'm going right home, hot bath."

"What did you find, in the morgue?"

"Not much. A recent *Chronicle* story about the CIA's *contras* getting busted for ten million in coke, funniest part was that federal prosecutors gave the money *back* to the *contras*. Anyway, you asked me about this US Bureau of International Development? I called some friends back east who've done a lot of FOIA stuff, Freedom of Information Act? They said it's been described in classified State Department cables as a CIA group operative."

"What kind of 'group operative'?"

"Formed by President Bush when he was Director of the CIA. He did a bunch of them. Its purpose was to build links with right-wing groups in developing countries, to funnel so-called 'bank loans' to start up commercial enterprises as a cover to channel funds for arms and paramilitary operations, death squads. In Central America it works with fundamentalist Protestant groups, façades. Its top man in El Salvador was Leon Rivera Morales, a close friend of Bush and a campaign manager of Robert D'Aubuisson. He was arrested when his private plane crashed a couple of years ago in Arizona, on its way up from El Salvador carrying four million in coke. After that the Republicans had to stop calling him the Abe Lincoln of Central America."

"And the Congregation Ranch?"

"I asked our Marin correspondent. It's twelve hundred and seventy acres west of Nicasio, a private religious retreat. The Congregational Church of Christ Pentecost, very fundamentalist Protestant. Lots of missionary work in Central America. They've got an office in Guatemala City, Avenida las Americas. Where'd you hear about it?"

"This guy Charlie who told me about the Syndic."

"The one you killed."

"I didn't kill him, Meliss. I didn't hit him that hard."

"Tell that to the Coroner . . ."

"Charlie said that ranch is where they took me."

"Then there's a connection. If the late Charlie was in this CIA front group, and they took you to this Congregation Ranch."

"And the Syndic?"

"I wanted to ask Carlos Bonaventura. But he miraculously posted bail. The Syndic is just the Syndicate – the new word for an old plague – organized crime. The Mafia, that's what we used to call it. It's nobody's secret that the CIA's worked with them for years – like Air America's drug flights out of Laos and Cambodia."

"Air America was the CIA airline in Vietnam, the one that used to ship heroin out of the Golden Triangle."

Melissa rubbed her hands, trying to work warmth into them. What a marvelous gift human flesh is, Murphy thought, how *alive*. "Interesting thing," she said.

"What's that?"

"Southern California Savings and Loan, that's being bailed out after losing three billion in government pension funds. They and Syndicate were laundering money for the Colombian drug cartels."

"That's what banks are for, to launder money."

"It holds the mortgage on the Congregation Ranch..."

An old woman had put money in the juke box, the slow rising strains of a bagpipe surging forth,

I once was lost
but now am found,
was blind
but now I see.

"Southern California Savings and Loan was Charlie's Visa card."

"Don't leave home without it."

"I still have it."

"And the nice thing, the even *nicer* thing, is that Southern California Savings and Loan is in a similar situation to Silverado Savings and Loan in Denver. They're being bailed out to the tune of three billion by the taxpayers."

"Bastards. Crooks."

"And guess who's on Silverado's board of directors? Neil Bush, whose father was director of the CIA. Before he became president."

He stared at the bar, the British colonial sabers and mus-kets, the regimental colors from Scottish regiments, the tar-tans and plaids. "If all this stuff can be discovered, why doesn't the media reveal it? Why don't they *track* this stuff?"

"The American news media is a big cartel that doesn't like to cover what people don't want to hear. They depend, after all, on advertising. That's why when you go to another country the news is so different."

"I don't care about the news."

"And more than a few journalists, well-known ones even, have close ties with the CIA. When the Agency was founded one of its first administrative goals was its media program. There's people with strong Agency connections who've used these connections – access to sources, insider information – to become prominent in newspaper and TV journalism, serving partially as a funnel for what the CIA wants to have said. If you watch the papers over the years you can tell who some of them are."

"All I care about is getting the story straight and pro-tecting the people in Guatemala."

"You're crazy if you go back." Melissa slipped into her raincoat. "What's with Angelica Newton, I thought you were living with her?"

"We couldn't stand each other."

"Drug-dealing murderer throws over famous rock star for woman doctor in darkest Amazon – *that's* the kind of story the media loves." Her cool small hand caressed his face. "Don't be down – we're making progress. Tomor-row I'll interview some Syndicate people, talk to my editors about an investigation of the Congregation Ranch..." She wrote two telephone numbers on a piece of paper. "The first is another number at work, a better one. Just ask for me. The other's my home number." She put ten dollars on the table, "Just hold tight. We'll move on this, fast as we can."

They walked to her red Colt. "You have some place to stay?" she said.

"Thanks. I'm fine."

"Don't take chances." She smiled up. "Take care."

He kissed her again and it was different this time, just a lovely kiss with the promise of more, someday, if there ever were a someday, if he ever wanted. He had a quick sense of how badly he'd wasted the first time he'd met her. How you have to be in pain to sense good. But even though he was the one in danger, she seemed the one needing reassurance, proof that the conventional order is not corrupt, that justice can survive, that evil does not invariably conquer good. Her kiss was salty, her grip against him strong, her body almost offered – yes, offered, unknowingly, in the guise of needing reassurance. I've hurt everyone I get near, he thought, and pushed away.

Her car turned the corner toward Van Ness and the Golden Gate. A passing taxi stirred the curbside puddles. Across Larkin he saw the building where an hour ago he'd run down the fire escape and fallen to the sidewalk, and felt fear again.

He walked through waning rain over Russian Hill, the city lights spread out in the mist below like the answer, the gift, of something at last found and understood.

"I once was lost but now I'm found, was blind but now I see." The Syndicate and the Agency, hand in glove, in San Francisco and in Guatemala, tied to the people that had run the United States ever since John Kennedy was killed in Dallas and his brother in LA – why should that surprise him? If they could kill the Kennedys with total impunity, what could he do against them?

Watching for cops, he walked to Chinatown and let himself into Ray Lin's, and fell warm asleep on the couch in Ray's blue sleeping bag.

Ray shook him awake at eight, pointing at the television where someone was saying that Joseph Murphy, already wanted for the murder of a man yesterday on Mount Tamalpais, was now sought in a second gruesome killing in Pacifica of a *San Francisco Chronicle* reporter, Melissa Maslow, last seen alive with Murphy in a San Francisco bar. The camera closed in on Melissa's red Colt, found deserted at three a.m. on the coast highway south of San Francisco. The camera switched to a silver Porsche owned by Joseph Murphy that had been found an hour later in Pacifica, Melissa inside it with three bullets in her brain.

43

"THEY'RE GOING TO KILL YOU." Ray went to the stove, picked up the coffee pot, came to the table and started to pour it then realized there were no cups. Still holding the pot he got two mugs from a shelf and put them on the table. "They want you so bad, how they're doing this –"

He put the pot on the stove, sat down, picked up his mug, shook his head. "Out of my fuckin mind." He went back to the stove and got the pot, filled the mugs. You was back here long before she got killed."

"She was..." He tried but he couldn't talk about her. "I've never known anything to keep happening. Like this."

"Thinking like that don't get you nothing, man," Ray said.

"She had this cocky way of acting like she was cute but not really believing it. Trying to be tough, but you could tell she *cared*." He walked down the hall, boards creaking, came back and sat. "What am I going to do?"

"You're going to skin your ass out of here."

"No! I mean about her?"

"Murph! You plan to die today?"

Murphy laughed, looked out the light well at stained concrete.

"You better decide, man. I can testify you was here at one a.m. I can testify anything you want, but they're not going to believe me, I'm already on the wrong side…"

"You'll just get accessory, Ray. You'll get ten years."

"No I won't. They'll kill anyone who's touched you. I wouldn't make trial."

Murphy stood, feeling the room's weight on his shoulders. "I've done all this."

"Think of what you did in Nam, man. You never did a thing to hurt people."

"Oh yes I have."

"You even used to even drag in the fuckin gooks! I've seen you run across a fuckin field of fire to pick up some dumb dink."

"You just didn't like the dinks because they've got slanty eyes like you." Murphy hugged him, turned, holding the door jamb. "How safe is this bike?"

"It was wrecked and sold for parts and there's no way to trace it. Calvin Wong doesn't exist."

"Who the fuck is Calvin Wong?"

"He's your friend. The name DMV has it registered to."

NO COPS on the Bay Bridge and none on 580 going south, fields of pale tomatoes to the horizon. At noon he filled up at a truck stop near Coalinga, empty plastic cups sucked along the greasy parking lot by passing trucks, transmission lines like giant mantises across endless rows of beet and cauliflower. He bought a sixpack of Coke, sandwiches, maps, and two five-gallon gas cans, filled the gas cans and strapped one on each side of the bike beneath Ray's blue sleeping bag, spare clothes and poncho.

Highway 46 east was two flat lanes across half-irrigated fields stretching to the smudged horizon where oil derricks rose and fell like the heads of feeding vultures. There were white houses in willow groves and dusty pickups with gun racks, windblown soil and scummy sloughs, the air greasy with herbicides, crude tar and methane.

East of Mojave he emptied the first gas can into the tank, but that made the bike off-balance so he stopped again and poured half the remaining can into the empty one. The cars were beginning to flick on their lights; in the south gray rainbursts slanted across a slug-pink sky. His arms were queasy with exhaustion and his feet stumbled bluntly over the volcanic soil.

Barstow ahead seemed like danger so he dropped south on 395, a straight black line pointing at Mexico, trucks shaking him as they roared north, casting a fine spray that kept him wiping his eyes with the back of his arm. He turned east through Twentynine Palms and Earp and into Arizona at midnight, the cars and trucks fewer now, the stars like points on a great pinball machine.

Mountains and constellations rose and fell. There was just the rumble of the bike, the white lines zipping beneath the wheel, now uphill, now on the level, now going down, nighthawks and jackrabbits darting from the headlight, semis rolling north like dinosaurs, crushed rattlers like red ropes on the highway, once a doe in a mass of blood and guts, remnants of a fawn beside her, saguaros beyond the headlight like shadowy hanged men. There was no feeling in his hands, no feeling in his arms, no sound but this freezing air screaming through his brain, his body locked into the seat by immovable legs, and he moved the bike by leaning only, tipping this way and that through the curves, the white lines flicking under, the tire's tread a continual blur in which endless detail could be seen, the fluorescent green fuel gauge sinking from half to quarter, the speedometer needle jiggling between a hundred and twenty and a hundred and forty... If you hit anything going this fast, he consoled himself, you'll hardly know it.

South of Gila Bend the horizon grew lighter and the ground was rolling waves of boulders and cliffs like bone chips from which the dawn rose like yellow oil. A sign flashed past: *Luke Air Force Bombing Range. Stay on Highway.* Gray rubbled mountains hunched over thorn and cactus and chipped soil. As he floated over a long easy rise with dawn mirages on the pavement there were suddenly two cruisers across the road between narrow cliffs and he hit the brakes looking for a way out, the bike skidding sideways toward the two cops, one running for his cruiser, the other with a shotgun. He spun to a stop and stood, twenty feet away. "You're moving too fast out there!" the one with the shotgun said.

Maybe they don't know, Murphy decided. "Wasn't anybody around."

"*We* were around."

"Sorry about that."

"Let's see your license."

US Air Force was stamped in gold on their cruiser doors. Not cops but MPs: maybe they *didn't* know. He handed them the Arizona license.

"From Flagstaff," the other one said. "Hell I used to live in Flagstaff."

"Where you headed?" the one with the shotgun said.

"Ajo."

"What's there?"

"My sister's ex-husband. We're going hunting."

"Where's your gun?"

"He's got the guns." Murphy dropped the bike into gear. "I'll take it slower."

"We're out here looking for drunk Indians," the one from Flagstaff said. "But we catch you again we'll pull you in too."

He accelerated slowly, watching in the mirror for them to turn and shoot, then for them to leap into the cars and speed after him, but the two cops and the two blue cars diminished in the mirror, stationary in their wobbling shrinking reflection, the sunlit mountains climbing up behind them.

Ahead the road rose steadily into the vermilion sky scented with desert morning; soon he could kill the headlight, in an hour Mexico. In the mirror he caught a flash of blue, cop lights. The two cruisers were coming fast and there was only long straight highway ahead with no place to hide; he stood on the brakes and spun the bike off the road, whanging over the borrow pit and slamming through thorns and cactus. He glanced back to see the cruisers smashing through the brush behind him and he roared up an arroyo to shake them but one kept coming, banging and snarling up through clattering rocks and with a great ping like a ricochet the bike's chain snapped, the engine roaring wild. The bike fell over pinning his thigh to the arroyo rocks, the car smashing toward him as he broke free and ran back downslope before the cop could shoot or turn round, then he cut left across the slope, above the other cruiser, out of pistol range, now out of shotgun range. Looking back he tripped on a saguaro root, needles in his hands, kept running through rolling bowl-like hills, already too hot to breathe, the sun melting over the ridge.

44

HE RAN upslope toward a saddle with a tan peak behind it. The ground was sloshy with lava gravel but open between the desert thorns and cactus so he could run quickly, pacing it, the cruisers now a thousand feet below, and still he could keep the pace, trying to reach the shelter of the tan peak before the planes came.

The arroyo crested into a shallow valley of white boulders, the tan peak above on the right. He ran part way up the valley and then uphill between huge boulders with spiky cactus in the crevices between them. It had been fifteen minutes since the cops would have radioed. Planes could come any time now. If they were fixed wing he could hide among the rocks and maybe they wouldn't see him. If they saw him he could still run, but if they were choppers once they saw him it was over.

The slope turned to lava talus, a furnace of rock. His legs ran with no feeling. He crossed the ridge, looked back; no one had reached the valley below nor its far lower end dropping down into the arroyo. On his left rose the tan peak. To the northwest, back the way he'd come, was purple desert to a crotch of distant dark mountains with raw pale peaks. Behind him, south, stretched a string of ridges with long sweeping saddles between them, boulders, cactus, sun-tortured brush.

Nearly half an hour, still no plane. Now he could put on the miles, stretch out the legs, nothing but running, running and thinking. Running and listening. If I get out of this I will be happy no matter what deaths have happened and how much I'm to blame, he promised. I will force myself to be happy.

There was a tiny airplane whine, a bug maybe. No, a spotter, the nasal blare of its motor as it came upridge hugging the slope. It was still far; he crawled into a clump of greasewood and saguaro and as the plane flitted past it crossed him with its shadow.

It dove over the ridge down toward the valley. He ran as if the land behind him were on fire, down the long sweeping saddle from ridge to tilting ridge, the planes coming and going behind him in widening circles, lazy-sounding as bees seeking honey.

The saddle toppled into a plain of red-flowered cactus widening toward low mountains. All the way across it he stayed ahead of the planes, then up the low mountains through a sharp and craggy canyon with cooler air in pockets in the shade of its great slabs.

From the low mountains a vast chalky mesa tilted southward, millions of cactus pinioned against it, scrub and brush and desert grass and burnt arroyos. He ran in a trance now, knew he could run till night unless his body broke, his heart stopped. Several times there was a white glint of plane behind him, never close. After midday there were no more planes, the land leveled then rose and fell again; in late afternoon he stopped on the bank of an arroyo to look back; still there was no one, no planes, just an immense white land of crevasses and canyons and dry bouldered river beds across the rippled sand.

Standing still made him dizzy so he ran again but could not lose the dizziness till he fell against a cactus and the pain made him sharp. He ran on, the setting sun on his right, saguaro shadows darkening the brush, ran till it was too dark, then walked, watching Scorpio rising in the east to point the way south.

At dawn he could smell smoke and water, day rushing across the desert as he followed a goat trail down into a rocky valley with some palm trees and a stone hut with a palm-thatched roof and shed and a turgid pool. There were fresh goat droppings on the trail. An old woman came out of the hut wiping her hands. "Can I have water?" he said.

She seemed frightened of him but brought a pail of well water and a clay bowl to drink. He made himself stop drinking after five bowls. "Where is this?" he said.

"This? San Jacinto."

"But what country?"

She turned from the ground where he sat. "Felipe! This is what country?"

"It is the Sonora," an old man said, coming out of the shed. He had a knife in one hand and a chunk of cactus in the other. "The land of the San Jacinto people."

Murphy forced his hand from the bowl of water. "It is Mexico?"

"It is not the United States and it is not Mexico. Which one are you running from?"

"I was hunting with my friends, got lost. Two days I've had no water."

"You're going the wrong way. Go north, the way you just came down."

"Can I buy food – *frijoles* – anything? He reached into his jacket for his wallet but it was not there. He felt all his pockets, waiting to discover the wallet so he could relax and stop this horrible sudden fear that he had no money, that he'd lost the wallet when the bike broke or somewhere in between. The wallet was truly gone, only the false Arizona license left in his other shirt pocket.

"We can give you *chiles*," the woman said. "Some cactus *tamale*."

"No thank you," he said. "I have plenty."

"You have nothing and no money," the old man said. "She did not offer to sell them to you."

The woman took the cup into the hut and brought it back with sour goat milk and *chiles* and a cactus *tamale* with beans inside it. He ate the cactus shell last, breaking it in pieces with his teeth. He tried to remember where he might have lost the wallet but could not. He would have to go back, at least as far as the border.

"You should stay," the old man said. "Leave tomorrow. We will feed you."

He drank more water, turned back up the hill the way he'd come, up the goat trail whose droppings were now drier and harder in the sun. At the top of the arroyo he looked out on a wide canyonland of broken buttressed cliffs and rolling stony plateaus. A distant plane buzzed, came nearer. No, a hummingbird at a cactus flower.

This moment would decide his life but he could not tell which way to go. Go back for the wallet and probably he would not find it and probably he would be captured. To go south without money or food or water was death.

The old man was riding a burro up a switchbacked trail on the far slope. Murphy watched him till he crossed the ridge out of sight, then ran back down across the arroyo above the hut and climbed the slope after the old man. When he reached the ridge the old man was far ahead, an atom of black and white among the towering cactus. The trail grew firmer, other paths coming in, became a pair of ruts rolling over a mountain shoulder and down to a barbed wire fence with a gate and a few miles ahead a *rancho* with a silo and metal windmill, thin Brahma cattle standing motionless in its corrals. Next to the house was a creosoted pole with a telephone wire going from the house past the corrals and down the road. The old man was tying his burro to the porch. In the distance were the silver flashes of cars on a highway.

Murphy circled the *rancho* to the south and followed a fence line east and reached the highway at dusk. Swallows were darting after moths; somewhere cattle were lowing. The cars on the highway made a low cadenced hiss.

He followed the highway south to a town. Trucks were parked at a bar smelling of *frijoles* and steaks. He stood in a dark street watching the back of the bar. A boy came out and scraped plates into a bucket. Murphy waited till the boy went inside then crept closer to the bucket but a dog came snarling and rattling its chain, so he went round the bar to where two semis were idling, facing south at the edge of the highway, one driver standing on the ground and speaking up to the other. One was closed up, a refrigerator truck. The other was a flatbed loaded with large shapes covered with blue tarps; he came up behind it and crawled under the tarps; there were huge chunks of steel, pieces of turbine or motor of some kind; he squeezed up inside them. The voices tailed off, someone laughing, "*Arriba!*" The two trucks revved and Murphy's slid forward, bouncing and jouncing over the potholes and onto the road.

45

THE TRUCK rolled endlessly through the darkness, gearing up and down for the hills, tires roaring against the tarmac, the huge iron segments jiggling rustily on the flatbed, the tarp and steel cables whistling in the wind. Murphy was sick from the goat milk the old woman had given him, crawled to the back to throw up over the end when there were no headlights behind. Once there was rain shower and he lay with his head in the open, drinking the oily water that funneled off the tarps.

They went through a big city, lights reflecting on the asphalt, the truck starting and stopping, the iron lurching and squealing on the flatbed. Watching through a crack under the tarp he decided it was Hermosillo. The truck was still heading south.

He woke to a blue-gray light filtering through the tarp, the truck gearing down through sloping long curves, diesel snarling, brakes hissing, tires grinding gravel off the edge. He took off his shoes and repaired the laces that had been frayed by cactus thorns. Again there was a city, stop and go traffic, car engines on all sides, their exhaust collecting up under the tarp. Beyond the city the truck geared down, ground into second and rumbled off the highway across a gravel lot. It pulled into a space where the sound of its engine echoed closely. The engine died; the cab door opened and shut.

He waited what he thought was two minutes but may only have been a few seconds, squirmed to the back and looked out under the tarp. Trucks lined up all around, oil and dust, a distant radio. He could see no one, dropped over the side, walking unsteadily on the pockmarked ground, wandered around and between the trucks till he found a building with a water spigot that said *no potable* but he drank it anyway, long deep cool luscious liquid gulps that made him vomit but then he could drink easily and it was good. A man in boots with pointed toes and worn-down heels, Levis and bow legs, silver buckle and red check shirt, tanned small face with a black mustache and thin black eyes and a black cowboy hat looked down at him. "That's for radiators," he said. You should ask at the café."

"Oh." Murphy stood.

"Where you going?"

Murphy said nothing, watching him. "Why?"

"I saw you get off the truck."

"Going south."

From his pocket the man took a fold of bills, flattened it and pulled one off. "Get yourself a little cleaned up and get something to eat." He gave Murphy a bill. "You'll be OK."

Fifty thousand pesos, a wrinkled blue bill in his palm. "Jesus!" He kept looking at it but it was still fifty thousand pesos. He ran looking between the trucks but could not see the man. He went into the café, steamy and warm and full of the smell of men and hot food and coffee. The toilet was filthy but he washed with water from the tank above the toilet and combed his hair with his fingers till it lay straight. He washed mud, oil and dust off his black jacket and shirt and jeans and shoes with wet toilet paper that left pink shreds. He had tortillas and beans and coffee at the counter for five thousand pesos, found two empty plastic cola bottles and filled them with water, and walked out into the new bright sun.

In late morning the truck pulled off the highway again, halting among others in a huge lot rimmed by hog wire and wind-stunted dusty trees. The driver got down but came back in a few minutes, climbed up and shut the door. The truck did not start and after a few minutes Murphy decided the driver had gone to sleep.

He climbed out the back and walked awkwardly among the other trucks. Most of their cab windows were open, the drivers sleeping on benches up behind the seats. He found a rig with DF plates carrying thick concrete pipes with canvas on each end. He put down his water bottles and crawled up underneath to feel the engine. It was cold. He crawled to the back, picked up the bottles, climbed up under the canvas into a pipe and fell asleep.

After a while the heat woke him and he could not breathe under the hot canvas. The engine started and the truck shook but then it sat for a long time with the engine running. Then the door slammed and the truck creaked out on the highway, the concrete pipes grinding against their chains.

The truck traveled all day. Zacatecas, a sign said, then before dark another, Aguascalientes, where it stopped for diesel and food. Murphy followed the driver into the restaurant, a roly man in sneakers and a yellow Caterpillar hat. The man went into the toilets then sat at the counter and Murphy went into the toilets and looked into the mirror.

Dirty, dusty and sunburnt, thin-faced and hungry: the look that draws cops like sharks. He smoothed and washed off his clothes, his face and scabby hands with their red infections where tips of cactus spines festered. "You look like shit," he said to the man in the mirror, who smiled revealing yellow teeth with brown chunks between them. He brushed his teeth with toilet paper and hand soap, went into the restaurant, ate quickly and paid, watching the roly driver across the counter, returned to the parking lot and climbed back inside the concrete pipe.

Dusk came, dawn went, the air was thick with diesel fumes then thin with the high pine taste of the hills. The truck kept rumbling on, the whirr of the wheels sewing and dismembering, keening and snickering over the curves and downgrades, over the moments and hours that stretched and contracted, appeared and disappeared, phantasms and nightmares, and is this death, he wondered. How can you ever tell if you're dead?

LYMAN sat on the edge of the motel bed watching dawn burn down across the Oakland Hills. Strings of headlights trailed down their sides; below them, square squat buildings were lighting up along the Bay, the Bay Bridge a gray filigree of half-lit steel bearing a serpent of headlights into San Francisco. He made himself a cup of instant and Coffee-Mate and sat on the bed again; it burned his lips.

Soon the coffee was cooler but his tongue kept stinging. He looked down at his naked arms with the tendons and veins sticking out: Come near me if you dare, they said. He stretched his shoulders out and up, arms in a cross then vertical, the sleepy muscles stretching like awakened cats, the pectorals hard as steel. He smiled to think there was not a single thing in this room he couldn't break with one hand. Sipping the cooler coffee, he began to do his wake-up exercises.

The east grew bright; a tallowy fog coated the Bay. He showered, dressed in Levis, work shirt and worn leather jacket, went downstairs to eat, then walked up Market Street to Tenth and across Mission to Alabama Street, entered 154 Alabama and climbed to the second floor. A television roared somewhere behind thin walls, a puppy was squealing. He knocked hard on Sherrie Cunningham's door.

III

House of Fire

46

FOOTSTEPS at the door. "Yes?" A girl's voice.
"Sherrie? It's Steve Williams, I'm a friend of Joe Murphy's. Saul Friedman asked me to come."

Her face in the door. "Saul Friedman?"

"The guy who came yesterday. The lawyer."

"Oh yeah!" She opened the door, looked up at him. He shut the door behind him. She went to the sink, wiped her hands on a T-shirt. "What can I do for you?"

"Can I sit?"

She nodded at a chair. "Sure."

She had on new black Levis and a bright blue sweater that came down to her wrists. "How are things?" he said.

She smiled, a kind of off-sides grin. "They sure have changed."

"Been celebrating?"

She shrugged, shoulder blades up into her long straight hair, sat at the table, smoothing an edge of vinyl tablecloth. "A little bit... I bought some clothes, paid my rent. He sure was astonished, the landlord, to have me paying the rent."

"What'd you do before, give it to him on the side?"

Again she shrugged. "He said that wasn't enough."

"You have enough now, don't you?"

"When Saul gave me the money – that's his name, right? – I couldn't believe it. I sat here a long time, right there where you're sitting, saying to myself, Sherrie, you don't deserve this. You've been mean and hard and you don't deserve this."

"Sure you do," Lyman said.

She looked at him, surprised. "I sure don't. But I've promised myself I'm going to make myself good for it, that I'm not going to let him down."

"Saul?"

"No , Mr. Murphy."

"What else he tell you?"

"Mr. Murphy?"

"Yeah."

"Nothing." She cocked her head, appraising. "You're his friend – you ask him."

"He won't tell me why he did it, just wants me to watch over you, give you a hand. So what's up? Why'd he do it?"

"You a cop?"

Lyman chuckled. "Me? Never." He watched her fingers, nervous on the table top. His own hand rested against his cheek, like a cleaver ready to fall. "Just tell me why he's giving you the money, not just for a quick fuck?"

She looked hurt, then angry, stood. "Maybe I ain't saying." She walked toward the door but he jammed his foot across it, reached up and yanked her down, hand across her mouth. "I *want* you to tell me."

She watched his eyes. He loosened his grip. "He said he was a friend of my dad's, in Vietnam. My dad died. Mr. Murphy wanted to take care of me a little, that's all... I'll give you the money if you want."

Softly he massaged down her slim neck, her breast, felt the little nipple harden. "That's not all I want." He shoved her face down against the sink, her hands on the edge. "One sound will kill you. Otherwise you'll be fine." He unbuckled her belt and pushed down the black Levis and underpants, licking down the inside of her thigh as he knelt to yank her pants off one leg, bent her over the sink and pushed into her; she gasped and he reached up and broke her neck.

MURPHY came into Villahermosa after midnight in the driving rain on a flatbed carrying a yellow bulldozer, crouched under the bulldozer's dripping engine, between its two massive treads, half sheltered by its blade. Roots, creepers and dirt clods hung down from its treads and made a muddy trail of windblown rain across the flatbed's deck. A heavy cold spray came over the blade.

He was hoping it would stop but the truck drove straight through Villahermosa's pale concrete boulevards and cheap international hotels, through the *barrios* stinking of open sewers, the stinging haze of crude distillation, vegetation's sweet rot.

On and on it rolled through the Campeche lowlands. Tree frogs chirped in scraps of jungle; the rain stopped and the moon was a silver stain down the middle of the highway. At dawn roosters brayed from roadside hovels in the gray wool of cooking fires and the smell of asbestos brake linings, red mud and warming asphalt. Once there was a mighty mahogany tree towering over hills of brush and stumps. They crossed a wide river, the bridge shivering under the truck's weight. An hour later the truck rumbled into Escárcega; when it halted in heavy traffic he jumped from the back of the trailer, a woman in a pink Passat staring at him as he stepped round her bumper and walked to the curb. The light changed and the truck lumbered with the traffic toward Campeche, trailing its yellow bulldozer.

He bought tortillas and oranges for three thousand four hundred pesos and walked out of Escárcega in warm morning sun. Where the road went into the jungle there was a blackwater marsh with cattails and egrets; he washed his clothes and himself and dried in the hot sun, then ate tortillas and oranges, woke with the sun in the middle of the sky. He hitched a ride with a small bearded priest in an old hearse all the way to Nicolás Bravo, another on a farm truck to the Chetumal turnoff and Belize border.

He waited till dusk then walked an hour west in jungle along the Río Hondo, past the last trails, swam the *Río*, walked back to the highway and hitched into Corozal.

"I told you this'd happen," Lovejoy said.

"Not like this."

"You was goin' up there with a hardon and you was goin' to get it cut off and handed to you. Yes you *was*. Did'n matter what I said. "

"I didn't have a choice."

"What the Hell did'n you jes' let things be 'lone? What you gotta go makin' trouble?"

"Don't be angry at me, for Chrissake."

"Who else I s'posed to be angry with? Ain' you the one what did it? Jes' like you wen' in Mother Teresa's place breakin' ever'thin' all up. Fightin' with those Americans, Murph when you goin' wake *up*?"

"So you would've said nothing, up in the States?"

"What? 'Bout thet Guatemala stuff? What the Hell good thet do? Other 'n kill some other people an' make *you* feel good 'bout yourself? What difference it make to them Guatemalans how much you talk on American television? You can be a TV star for all they care. You just get yourself kill', thet's all!"

"I made it down here."

"An' you fuckin' lucky! Is'n no thanks to you that you made it, you had the breaks."

"Once I wire some money from CI, I'll be fine."

"You got enough to live on over there?"

"Enough to buy another plane, go somewhere, start again."

"Minute you get a plane they find you. You still tryin' to fock up you life ain' you? And you better get thet money out of the Channel Islands fast before DEA track it down."

"They can't find it."

"Anythin' DEA want to find, it find."

Murphy stood on the terrace watching the stars rise out of Corozal Bay. "Ten days ago I stood here and didn't know what was going to happen. That people would die just because I went up there, trying to tell the truth…"

"What I told you, Murph, is don' walk in death's way. As it is, it goin' come get you far too soon."

"What would you do?"

"I certain would'n go after thet doctor woman. You ain' goin' change *her* mind. You certain ain' bringin' *her* no luck. Shit, I should'n get you any money, then you can't go back to Guatemala."

Murphy smiled. "I'd go anyway."

"Thing about you, Murph, you's the stupidest person I ever seen."

"I told those kids I'd come back for them. Would you leave Desirée?"

"I'm keepin' you damn money."

"I don't need money to get in, Love. It's just safer to have it when you're inside."

You make it sound like ice, Guatemala."

Murphy shrugged, biting his lip.

"I was inside five years, in El Paso."

"I know. For sticking that dude."

"Lucky he lived. So I didn't get life. Thet prison was the bottom of Hell, Murph."

"The House of Fire."

"Wha's thet?"

"The Mayan Hell had six houses. The House of Fire was the worst."

"Them Mayans, they should see Guatemala now."

"Guatemala's a tourist destination, Love."

47

LOVEJOY drove the needle in and out of the ripped knee of his trousers, pulling the thread through. "It's for you I'm worried. Not thet I get back my money."

"It'll clear on Monday from CI to Kingston. There'll be fifty extra for me, for when I get back."

"You ain' goin' come back."

On Corozal Bay the wind was scraping white riffles off the blue water. A string of cormorants laced eastwards. The air was warming and redolent with soil and grass and sea salt and jungle. "Would you leave her, someone you cared about, in Guatemala? Not try to talk her into coming out?"

"Comin' out wit' you? What kind of safety is thet?"

"And that General Arena, he's the *one*, Love! My friends paid him ten grand a month. It was *his* soldiers that shot us up and blew away my village. *He's* the one who sent the word up north, got Melissa killed..."

Lovejoy tugged the thread tight, circled the needle twice through it and bent over and bit it off. "You know thet trail there, goes into the jungle?"

"Out back? Sure."

"Luther Tallow, thet lived up the road, he had a woman in Revelation Town, used to take thet trail through the jungle to go see her. There was this crazy Mexican, Willie the

Fireman, lived back in the jungle, gone crazy on wood alcohol. Willie hated Luther, used to wait for him in the brush with his machete, try to cut him up. I used to say Luther someday he goin' get you, and Luther said he's always too drunk and I ain't afraid of no Mexican."

Murphy stood, stretching his back. "You're so full of shit, Love!"

Lovejoy spread the trousers over his knee, smoothing down the mend. "Willie's dead now. They chase him in the Bay and drown him. After he kill Luther Tallow."

LYMAN sat in his kitchen with a cup of coffee in his hands. The Minnie Mouse clock showed nine-thirty. The dishwasher hummed, amber light on. An icicle clinked as it fell from the window. There were blue sky and white clouds, bare maple branches and the spikes of Normandy firs beyond the double glass. A squirrel ran along a bough, a bluejay called; under Lyman's feet the floor rumbled as the heater in the basement kicked on.

He shivered, in undershorts and T-shirt, bare feet cold on the yellow tile-patterned linoleum. You let Nancy go free, he told himself, she can fuck anybody she wants. At least married she's got to hide it. Say she's not doing it.

He stepped into the shower, let the hot massaging water eat into the back of his neck. Oh Jesus good. He rubbed himself hard with the thick new towels Nancy'd bought for when they'd move into the McCormacks' house. Yellow and green. With Nancy everything had to be yellow and green.

He flipped on CNN but it was just another white face looking earnest about some shit. So sickeningly tiring all these white faces. After a lifetime of trying to be nice, have to admit they suck. Even Kit Gallagher. He winced, seeing Kit Gallagher sucking Nancy's cunt.

The reason I hate them. But I've always hated them, and setting Kit up with Nancy was just giving myself another reason. To see if she would do it with a white man.

Now that I'm older and wiser, I see so many reasons, but where's the *truth*? Was I trying to keep distance from Nancy by enticing her to screw a white man? Or is she right, that I was trying to live out my own desire for Kit through her?

That's just Nancy's psychological bullshit. Marrying Nancy was giving myself another reason, because she doesn't hate whites and even likes some of them. A triumph of integration, Nancy. Bringing up my kids like pigs. Little white pigs.

He dressed in the same Levis and work shirt he'd worn when he'd offed the junkie hooker in San Francisco. Who wouldn't say where Murphy was.

He could see Curt Merck sitting there, his desk, little white penguin feet hanging down. Saw himself standing before Curt in these clothes he'd killed her in. Free and strong as an animal. Smart as an animal. Curt a little white toad as the wolf circles round. Breaking the rule that says you have to disappear the clothes you do a job in. Completely disappear them. Fire and the river. Out to the sea. Never a shred of fabric to recognize. Telling Curt what he was wearing. Watching the little penguin stutter. You're done, Howie, Curt Merck will say. You can cut the grass.

But Curt won't ever let you cut the grass. Doesn't even like to *talk* about the grass. About how he gets his cut, the Agency's. Hilarious that liberals in the States never realize the grass they smoke pays for guns to kill liberals in Central America. How what goes around comes around.

Little white penguin with his Bratislava accent on his little pointed tongue. Little fingers in his pockets. Little white flippers. Who doesn't dream I'd break the silence. If you're not loyal to us, Howie, you're not loyal to yourself. And the moment you tell the story, the Congregation's lifeline drops dead. Along with you, Howie. And a lot of other people.

You hauled us over here in boats, Curt, but it was *us* who built this fucking country. The one you own.

Lyman bent up his leg to put on the running shoe, liking the feel of power round his shoulders and down his arms. Skin like black oil, tendons and muscles rippling. Not like steel – mahogany. Black heartwood.

Curt Merck weighing the odds in his little white paws. Kill me or just send me outside. When you have something on a man, don't let him know. Until you need it. Like a sudden stiletto between friends.

He shrugged into the leather jacket, reminded himself to stand straight. "Keep your shoulders *back*!" his father used to say. Before he'd gone away for good. "You don't have no burden, son, bowin' you down."

He turned to scan the house. Wide rooms and carpets, sense of warmth. Pictures on the piano, everybody smiling. Never trust a smile.

In the garage he revved the black BMW, dropped the window to inhale warm exhaust. A few good breaths is all it takes. Never did anybody that way. But do it right and it has a nice twist: the shame of a man who took his own life. He pushed the garage door button and drove up the street, singing

> *Left my little blue-eyed darlin'*
> *down by the sewer-side,*
> *down by the suicide...*

Curt won't kill you here. He'll send you away somewhere. Guatemala. Like he did to Kit.

He jerked the car off the road, staring across the steering wheel and tinted glass and down the long black hood to leaves and macadam and rough beech trunks umbered by winter and pale grass and cyclone wire and a schoolyard where boys and girls ran in winter clothing. It had been Curt's idea to send Kit down there.

No, but Curt didn't kill Kit; Murphy did. Murphy who's disappeared into the Sonora desert and they think he's dead. But I know him too well, Lyman thought. Only *I* can kill Murphy.

Lyman ran his fingers over the leather steering wheel. But I've got to write it down somewhere. A record. A tape. About the Congregation, Guatemala. About all these things. So somebody can hear it. In case I die in a car wreck, have a sudden stroke. But who to give it to? Who'd keep it for me? No one.

At Langley Merck did not invite him into his office but instead led him up two floors through three coded doors to a place he'd never been, a closed corridor with deep green carpet and polished hardwood doors and wainscoting. He thought of it all being brought up, this antique-style hardwood, to be stuck inside tunnels of iron and concrete.

It was a little room with an oval maple table and maple chairs with plush green arms. The table gleamed with spray polish. There were video cameras in every corner and in the middle of each wall. "Take that one." Merck nodded at the chair where the cameras pointed.

Lyman sat, folded his big hands before him, hating their yellow palms. He reminded himself not to bite the side of his mouth. Sweat trickled from under his arm down his ribs.

"We hear your trip to San Francisco was not an unmitigated success." The voice came through the middle of the ceiling. A Virginia country club voice.

"I didn't find this guy –"

"Not just that. You caused too much commotion."

"It wasn't my fault, the girl!"

"Which girl?"

"That reporter."

"Ah. Then whose fault *was* it?"

"NoCal's."

"*How*, pray tell," said another, slower voice, rumbling out the words, a Brahmin voice, "can you imagine it might have been theirs?"

"They have the people. I don't know *anybody*, out there. And their people got mad when Murphy killed their man, up on that mountain."

"They swear they didn't do the reporter, Howie. And we believe them. That leaves you."

Lyman lurched forward in his seat, looked into the camera. "Then Murphy did it!"

"Murphy's the least likely part of this package," country club said. Lyman could see him as a courtly cragged face, unruly black eyebrows and silver hair, an ancient assassin promoted to top management.

"Murphy's a minor drug pilot," country club said. "He also did two tours in Vietnam, got a Silver Star, two Bronze Stars, and two Purple Hearts. You got through Vietnam without any wounds or medals, didn't you?"

"In those days white guys got the medals."

"Untrue. And how many tours did *you* do?

Lyman got out of his chair and stood at the end of the table. "*You* know how many tours I did!"

Like cobra heads the cameras turned toward him. "We just don't understand your *thing* about Murphy," country club said. "Under other conditions, we wouldn't even mind having him working for us."

"He killed Kit Gallagher."

"We think not."

"Then who did?"

"We're not sure. Maybe the fates caught up with Kit. Maybe he'd drifted way beyond his role, wouldn't change in a changing world. Or he was ad-libbing, like you."

"I've stuck to your script when I can see holes in it for miles."

"Like?"

"Like..." Lyman sat. *This is where they'll have you.* "I just want to do my job." He put his face in his hands, reminded himself not to look through the fingers. "I have this naive, absurd idea that if I just do my job, defend *us* as I would my own family, the rest of my life'll be all right."

"How *is* your family, Howie?" It was a third voice, New York intellectual, professionally interested.

"We have our ups and downs. Like everybody. But I think we're the centers of each other's lives."

"That's nice."

"And I'm trying to move the Guatemalans on this contributions thing, on the Colombians. And I tell them they've got to cool it on this death squad stuff. But they say look, we were tougher than El Salvador and now they've had to have elections and we're still in charge."

"And you've told them?"

"Straight policy. That we don't want to interfere in their internal matters but we're concerned about image. And to stop knifing me in the back every time I start to make progress."

"Maybe they don't want *too* much progress. Maybe nobody does. Maybe you're just not reading things right."

"You know how far it is from Guatemala to Mexico, Howie," said country club. "How'd you like to see a bunch of revolutionaries running Pemex? You think that'd be good for *us*?"

"We all agree on the death squad thing," Lyman said.

"Human rights is the buzzword for the moment," country club said. "It will pass."

"Did you like being in California?" the Brahmin said.

"Sure."

"You stayed in the Oasis, all that?"

"Sure."

"We understand you doubled up on us."

"That's shit."

"We *know* it's shit. And we don't like it."

"I didn't do any doubling up."

"You weren't happy to be Tim Merriweather at the Oasis, with your pretty new blue Acura and your PPK from NoCal's friends on Polk Street."

"*That* fucking cunt joint."

"*You* seem to like it there."

"Why'd you run the double on us, Howie?" Curt Merck said. "The room at the Hyatt Regency and the Dodge from Asia Rentals? How stupid do you think we are?"

"That was *for* you."

"If you don't understand the fault of your own gestures," the Brahmin said, "how are you going to understand our needs?"

"My needs have always been whatever yours were. That's the problem. Yours keep changing."

"Do you want to explore that a little bit for us, Howie?" New York said.

"I wasn't running a double. I was keeping you clean."

"Even in your soul, Howie, we don't want private agendas."

"I don't have a soul. That was the first thing you removed when I came here."

"You had no soul long before that. Or you wouldn't have done us any good."

"When we want soul, Howie," New York said, "we pay for it. And it wasn't in your contract."

"What *do* you want from me, then?"

"Go back to Guatemala. Hold Arena's hand. Try to move him toward some understanding on the contributions thing. About the importance of working with Medellín and Cali. For everybody's good. About removing all this nickel-and-dime competition. These little guys. Remember, Arena's our *ally*: try not to be so judgmental. And let's avoid private agendas."

"Everybody's got a private agenda or two..." He looked into the camera.

The amused Brahmin voice: "Tell us about them."

He could see him there beyond the camera somewhere, an attenuated pale man with nervous fingers. A secret homosexual, unknown even to himself. But probably not to the Agency. Look at a sample of your blood they can tell everything you've ever done, you'll ever do. "I have no idea. No interest. I just want to do my job."

"And what, pray tell, is that?"

"Finding Joseph Murphy."

"If he reappears down there, won't you be the first to know?"

When Lyman left it was after dark, twin lines of taillights trailing away before him in the Virginia slush. God, just to drive to the end of the night, the end of your soul, till you and everything you know is washed away.

48

"IT WAS A WASTE of lives," Dona said. "Everything we do is a waste of lives."

"There was no way to predict those helicopters," Principio said. "It's the only disaster we've had in this sector in over two years. In war you can't plan everything. Even in life you can't."

Dona stared away from Principio's angular features at the dark wall of jungle painted with shreds of firelight. Everything he did angered her, his skinny ankles with their long thin hairs, his sandals and long toes, his clean worn uniform, his fingers folded like a priest's, a priest who has his eyes on people's souls, not on their lives. And what is the soul except an excuse to fall back on when one fails to live? "I won't do combat anymore," she said, wanting to wound him.

"Any of us can go, at any time. But don't blame yourself, not for the accident, nor for wanting to go."

"I do, you fool! You! Acting so holy!" She threw a stone into the fire, realizing it was at Principio she'd wanted to throw it. "Five people we lost! Four rifles, a machine gun." She saw Martín and the others dead and fought the tears, waited till they passed. "What good do you imagine it did, their sacrifice?"

Principio drew up his knees with his arms around them; this infuriated her. "It's the most people we've lost in one fight in thirteen months."

"It makes us weaker!"

"We're getting stronger!"

"That's *mierda*!" She wanted to scratch him, mar his calm assurance, realized she was very hungry and the hunger was making her tense. "We don't even know what we're offering any more! Why die for us?"

"It's not for us we're dying. But for a chance for everyone... free schools and health care, land to grow your own food, enough to sell if you want. No more fear of death squads, freedom to say what you want, live how you want. We've been over this territory, every person in *la lucha*, a thousand times, Dona. You know it all by heart!"

She stood, too angry to stay. "All I know by heart is sorrow!"

ONCE AGAIN Murphy looked down from the clearcut Belize hills to the Río Mopan and the guard post under tungsten lights on the Guatemalan side. It was like going back into a dream where everything had gone wrong but now he could change it, go back into when he'd come this other way, swimming across the river in the night, before then coming down the mountain after the Army truck had let him off, before then the trip from Flores with the soldiers, the cattle truck, the Río de la Pasión, the dugout canoe with the boy who now was surely dead, his hoarse, "Water! God please water!"

He could go all the way back up the Río de la Pasión to the first moment with her, when she'd peered down through the lantern's aureole and he'd thought she was death. But it had gone wrong long before that, when he'd landed on the Machaquilá road, when he'd flown out of San Francisco with Johnny Dio... even long before that, the first time he'd flown for money, the first time he'd flown. But he could not understand how to make it happen differently.

In his mind's eye Dona was looking sideways, to his left, sun gleaming off her Indian-black hair, her smile wide, the slender body strong under the loose shirt. Then her body was naked and he inside her, back down the tunnel of life into the whorl of the universe: all you can do is do what you like, because it's the only message you can trust.

He went down the steep cindery slope in darkness, listening for the hiss of vipers or the rattle of a cascabel. The river seemed impossibly fast and the water too cold. He put all his clothes and his shoes in a double plastic bag and tied it off and shoved it in his shoulder pack and stepped naked into the hard icy water. With the pack on one strap around his neck he swam the river, came out on a sandbar way downstream, got dressed in his dry clothes, squirmed carefully up through the riverside brush and steadily and patiently climbed the mountain.

A wedge of orange moon rose out of Belize, outlining the pine trunks and their knobby roots that jutted like old men's knees up from the needled ground. He reached the ridge, turned south to the saddle where the road crossed it, and followed the road down the long piney slope he'd ridden up in the Army truck. As he walked he tried to count the days and got to twenty-four but knew that there were more since he'd sat in the back of the Army truck and smelled the rare fine scent of the pines and remembered clearly the smell of Texas pines and deer rut and the sweet tang of gun oil, seeing his father's boot heels rising before him, dropping their sharp snow imprints along the long llano ridges.

At dawn he climbed from the road and slept high on a piney hillside at the edge of a clearing where sun shimmered all day on the yellow grass. Bees and hummingbirds fed on rainbows of flowers, hawks and falcons keened far above, the hubbub of birds and crickets constant as an air conditioner. The sun poured into the crack in his skull where the bullet had creased it, into the dent the black man had made with his pistol, into the mended bone of his arm, softening wrenched tendons and bruised skin, relaxing the muscles of his back when he lay face down in the grass, tiny spiders running across his nose. At sunset he ate half his day's rations of bread, canned meat, nuts and dried fruit, waited till darkness then dropped down to the road and walked all night, leaving it only twice when cars came out of the darkness like furious, preying monsters.

After midnight the next night he passed the turnoff to Tikal where a month ago he'd wanted to turn south toward Dona, toward the long straight Machaqilá road through the pine forest beyond the ziggurat hills where once he'd landed the Aztec.

Near San Benito he slept in the brush and walked into town at dawn. Women waded knee-deep in translucent Lago Petén Itzá, unloading corn sacks from dugouts that had come across from Flores. He walked out of town along the dirt road he'd traveled a month ago with doomed cattle in the back of a red Hino truck.

He was hungry and stopped to eat *frijoles volteados* and tortillas in an open café with a thatched roof on four posts, drinking milk from a green coconut with its bottom slashed off and a straw stuck in the hole. At another table a man and woman played happily with a baby; the man got up, went to a blue Jeep parked in the street, and came back with a baby bottle. On the Jeep's front bumper, above the license, was a metal plate:

US ARMY FLYING SCHOOL
Fort Rucker, Alabama

Murphy pushed aside his plate. It was a crime to waste food; he pulled it back. Methodically he scooped the *frijoles* with a tortilla. The man paid; he and the woman stood; she held the baby to her shoulder. "*Con permiso, Señor,*" Murphy said.

The man looked at him, surprised. "*Sí?*"

"You were at Fort Rucker?"

"I was just there. For six months."

"You fly a Huey, then."

"*Sí.*" As the man approached, Murphy saw his face was badly scarred, a map of Guatemala, almost, the Petén high and jagged above his left eye and down his cheek from the ear to Puerto Barrios at the mouth, the Tenangos and the Pacific coast torn and mended along the right side of his chin.

"How is it, this war?" Murphy said.

"Very bad."

"And the rebels?"

"The poor always dream of a better world. It's just a dream."

"You'll win?"

"We'll never beat them, but they'll never win." The man almost smiled. "*Es una tontería, la guerra.* War is stupidity."

There seemed less danger now so he rode in the back of a pickup to La Libertad and then walked twenty kilometers to El Subin, a town that was nothing but a steel bar across the road and a fortified gun tower and a few *tiendas* and children begging money. He caught another ride to Sayaxché as late afternoon fog drifted downriver, blurring the soldiers waiting by a row of armored personnel carriers on which the US Army stars had been painted out. He crossed the *Río* in a dugout with six soldiers; the town came grainily into focus, its streets broken and gritty, garbage and plastic showing the high water mark, the shore stinking of sewage and dead fish.

There was a hotel overlooking the river with four rooms and hammocks with mosquito netting and a WC at the end of the hall with a pipe that dropped straight into the water. He counted forty-seven bullet holes in the door of his room. Up the dirt street was the Temple of God and across from it a restaurant where he ate *pollo* and rice while through a loudspeaker the minister of the Temple promised everyone that the sorrows of this world will be recompensed by joys in the next.

After a long while he gave up trying to sleep and sat watching the black muscled *Río* ripple northwards toward Mexico. If she was dead he would still go through with the other part. No, there'd be no point. If she were dead he could see himself shrinking into how the world saw him – a fleeing killer – no hope, no future, trying uselessly to change into someone else.

With the smell of cooking fires and the ashes of dawn over the *Río* he ate hot tortillas and drank strong coffee in the restaurant, went down to the river bank and rented a dugout with a five horsepower Evinrude from a man named Vaquero, who insisted on five hundred quetzales deposit. "But I'm just going to El Ceibal," Murphy said, "for the ruins."

"The Army doesn't mind if you're a tourist," Vaquero answered. "They shoot at you anyway."

For hours he steered through fog too thick to see the prow, listening for the change of propeller pitch to warn him when the boat neared the shallows. Then the white disk of the midmorning sun burnt through the mist and the river suddenly appeared, a wide tilting sheet of flowing silver edged green with reflected jungle.

A string of ducks rose before the prow, settling ahead till roused again by his approach; a blue heron plodded upriver with steady whistling wingbeats. A log ahead became an alligator that rolled over and vanished with a slap of its tail. The river narrowed, filled with floating islands, sunspangled, vibrant with birdsong; the propeller snagged often, forcing him to tip up the motor and clear away weeds. He came round a bend in the river and ahead was the cove where Jesús had fished from his mother's dugout and where Epifanía had gutted catfish to hang on racks of saplings.

49

THERE WAS NOTHING to come back for, ash and broken pilings of huts and cinders of palm fronds scattered among bones the vultures had dragged from the fire where the bodies had been burnt with helicopter fuel. Digging in the rubble of Consuela's hut he found a twisted spoon and the glob of plastic that had once been her water jug. There were scraps of black jerky on the branches where the soldiers had hung the faces they had cut from the bodies before they burned them. He kicked over a chunk of half-burned wood and saw it was the charred mortar in which he'd ground the corn Placido had brought upriver, that had made the tortillas for the Mass Father Miguel had said before the choppers came.

A macaw shrilled, dipping its scarlet tail for balance and peering at him sideways as it jounced in the unscarred top branches of the yucca under which Ofélia once had played with Manolo's goat in the yellow *flor de muerte*. Stand this, he told himself, and nothing can ever touch you. A flock of blue-crowned parrots argued, shaking the branches of a ceiba beyond the ruined corn where the soldiers had shot Conchita down, her red cloak flying in the choppers' wake.

As he poled the dugout from shore a buck broke from the brush and bounded high-antlered into the jungle. The sun sank below the tallest western trees, casting shadows across the water, lagoons of coolness where flycatchers swooped after the first mosquitoes of evening.

Night fell with the malevolent yowl of howlers from the lowering hills, the slap of fish tails against the steely water, and encroaching mist from which herons glided like heralds of an afterlife, the rabid chortle of spider monkeys, the lament of wood owls, the dipping chittering whirr of bats, the surprised snarl of an ocelot fishing belly-deep in the shallows. Trees merged into fog, only the horizon of their peaks still visible, then all was black.

He switched gas tanks and traveled all night, till a chill downriver breeze cleared the fog, the vast star-blazing river sinking northward toward the Great Bear, a violet stain widening in the east.

The banks steepened, closer. Under widespread *bolocante* boughs was the mouth of the narrow creek where he'd left Jesús with the old man, and where round-faced Pollo with the dead monkey had come to take him upriver to Dona for the last time. He cut the motor and poled up the creek, its leaves lashing his face. At the place the old man had tied up his canoe the root was still velvet green where the rope had abraded it.

He followed the path through the bracken and up the mountainside. It led to a corn and bean patch with a thatch hut where, in its shade, a woman was weaving at a stick loom.

"I'm looking for *la doctora*."

She smiled. "*Está bueno*."

"She's well?"

"*Está bueno*."

"Where is she?"

"*Está bueno*."

He spoke louder. "Do you know Spanish?"

"*Tixtxol castiy*," she smiled.

"You could learn Kekchi." Behind him a woman, pointing a rifle. M-1. Young, Indian, short-haired, jeans and sandals.

"Don't shoot! I haven't done anything!"

"That won't keep you from getting shot."

"I was at San Tomás, brought the boy here, Jesús."

"Why are you back?"

"The *doctora* –"

"You don't belong here."

"She's OK?"

"I have no idea." She shouldered her gun and led him round the corn and bean patch up into the jungle and a steepening valley walled by reddish cliffs, her feet rising steadily before his eyes, clods of dirt and leaves breaking under her sandals and skidding past his wrists down past his feet. She laughed when he rubbed mosquitoes from his face. "Too much meat you're eating! It attracts them!"

"Please tell me how she is!"

"Where we're going someone might know."

The valley peaked in a wide saddle of sparse tall trees. She led him across the saddle and turned down another canyon of rumbling wind and water, down between dark escarpments to a spattering stream of gloomy tall trunks. Three men in bandoliers nodded as they ascended the trail; wood smoke came up from below. Trogons were gathering in the high leaves, croaking and scolding. By a fire pit a camouflage tarp linked three trees, with four bodies on raised stretchers beneath it; beside it stood a woven sapling table with instruments on a white cloth. A stone scuffled, a small thin woman coming up the trail.

"You!" he said, seeing the joy and pain in her face at seeing him. And seeing it was love.

STUCK IN TRAFFIC, Lyman drummed fingers on the steering wheel, punched the Platters into the CD player and popped them out again. Couldn't be worse to have a cigarette than breathe this shit.

He reached for a Marlboro but his pocket was empty. Seven days without nicotine. Forty days in the desert. My bound and bloody wrists. At five hundred and eighty thousand dollars Nancy was calling the McCormacks' house a good deal, sure to appreciate. Getting it from them at a loss. What Nancy knew about white people and about money could be put in a very small space.

The cars ahead inched toward red and blue flashing lights. He glanced across the road, thinking of going back, but there was too much traffic the other way and no way to turn. The accident grew closer, its boxy ambulance and massive fire truck like two animals feasting on a third, a baby-blue Thunderbird upside down in the ditch, a blanket-covered body on the grass, a Raggedy Ann doll *flump-flump* under his tires. No seat belt – how could anybody be that dumb? He would not think of Joshua's red frothy pool under the cement truck. He would not think of it, clenching hard fingers on the leather wheel, thinking of a cigarette, of Nancy in Kit's arms, her coming twice, one right after the other, when with him she never came more than once. Or did she come at all? Was *that* a lie too?

The accident eased past, the traffic took a breath and hurried onwards, back to business. Lyman punched in the CD

> *heavenly shades of night are falling,*
> *it's twilight time,*
> *deep from the dark your voice is calling*

He should have been a singer, riding up and down the harmonies like this. He could sing as good as these guys. Why hadn't he?

"YOU CAN'T just walk right in and kill him," Principio said to Murphy. "There's a thousand soldiers around him all the time."

"And when he goes to his *hacienda*, like Dona said, down on the coast?"

"You'll never get close, not even then."

"Even with a helicopter?"

"What helicopter?"

"The one I steal and fly in there."

"It's been years since you flew one," Dona said.

"I can fly it in my sleep."

Principio scratched at mosquito bites on his ankle. "And you would do all this, probably get killed, just for Arena?"

"It's not *just* for Arena. It's for the people who've been hunting me. Here and in the States. This Syndic... Anyway," Murphy pulled back, not wanting to push, "there's no need to get killed. With the chopper we'll be out of there before they know what's happened."

"It's not your battle."

"It was *my* village. When I was nearly dead in the jungle they saved me. You don't think we owe debts like that?"

Principio recoiled; Murphy sensed he'd wounded him, that Principio thought of almost nothing *except* what he owed to those who'd died. Principio smiled, and Murphy saw his upper front teeth were gone.

"Also the reporter in San Francisco," Murphy said. "The Syndic killed her."

"Over a hundred journalists have been killed in Guatemala in the last five years," Guadalupe said. "She was just doing her job."

"And my friends who were killed when my plane was burned, to you they're nothing because they were drug dealers. But to me they were good people. And one was a friend."

"To avenge the murders of all the good people in the world you would be very busy," Principio answered. "You would have to be God."

Murphy leaned across the fire, brushed a coal from his knee. "These were *my* people."

"You mean if you'd never come down here they'd all still be alive?"

"That too. That most of all."

"After Vietnam," Principio said, "what did you do?"

"Took all my pay and sat in the Sonora desert for six months."

"That is where you learned such good Spanish? Then what?"

"When the money was gone I went back north and worked on a cattle ranch in Montana. For a couple of years the oil thing was good and I worked on drilling rigs in Oklahoma. When that gave out I drove trucks, Salt Lake, Boise, Billings, went to San Francisco and worked – how do you call it, 'jackhammer' in English – the thing that breaks up stone?"

"*Uno martillo.*"

"I went back to Mexico, down the coast. One day I started flying again. San Francisco was wide open – I flew weed out of Mexico, Belize, made good money…"

"It's a crazy scheme," Principio said.

50

HOW THEY irritated Murphy, her patients. Craving, in pain, dying, taking up her time, leaving none of her for him. Boys spilling out their guts, women with breech births, babies slated to die under a chopper's guns in the middle of the river. Couldn't she see sooner or later they'd all die?

She came back, putting on her camouflage jacket against the night's chill. "How are they?" he said.

"One will die but the others are getting better."

"That's good."

"That's *good*? The one who lies dying there, he's an engineer. A chemical engineer! What happens to a country that kills its best?"

"It's something we all do. I don't understand why."

"And now you want to kill some more."

"Only one."

"You don't think others will die when you go for him?"

"I'd kill any of the soldiers who attacked my village. You wouldn't?"

She crouched beside him at the fire; he sensed she saw more clearly than he ever would. "Most of those soldiers are farm kids." She squeezed his wrist. "Like the boy from Texas who went to Vietnam."

He took her hand; her fingers laced quickly into his. "I don't ever want to cause another death," she said. "I told Principio I'm against your idea."

"I don't want you in it."

Her two hands came up his ankles, warming her fingers. "I'd go away with you right now. No killing, nothing. Just go."

"Going away with you is all I've dreamed of. For weeks." He eased his fingers back through her hair, massaging her neck, felt the muscles soften and bend. "And now I see we can't."

"I don't care they're after you." She smiled. "I'm used to being hunted by the Americans."

He sensed her naked, skin to skin, her lips opening, he could taste her, breathe her in. She drew back, reading his eyes, his face. "We're going where I can be a doctor and you can do whatever you want."

"I have enough money. You don't ever have to do anything."

"I'm a doctor. It's my life."

"We're not going anywhere."

"I've already told Principio." She held his face in her small, chilled fingers. "I can't do it anymore. Even without you, I'd go."

She returned to her patients; he could see her moving like a doe among them; one raised his hand briefly to her and it seemed a benediction.

Before dawn the chemical engineer died, he who had raised his hand; the others slept. She lay beside him in the hammock, silent, curved within his arms. He felt strangled by a horrified joy, that of a man who thinks everyone in his family dead in an accident, then finds one is still alive.

The stars were fading through the distant canopy. Three times she had been up to check the wounded; each time he'd gone with her. Sleepless, he dreamed of the past, seeing the young bodies tossed into his chopper, bodies that had laughed and hoped just hours before, boys who last night had sung "Blowing in the Wind" to a cheap Taiwan guitar and had smoked too much grass and drunk too much Jack Daniels, who wore peace signs on their dog tag chains, but when you yanked off the dog tag the peace sign fell lost into the mud and blood; battle-spent boys who didn't know why they were there, who'd just written home, "Don't worry, I'm not seeing any action."

LYMAN rose stealthily so as not to wake Nancy, got dressed and went outside into the new snow. It caped the Norway firs and lay on the maple branches and twigs and halfway down their trunks. It squeaked softly underfoot, like mice. He shook it from his loafers, went back into the kitchen and took five slices of bread outside, tore them up and tossed them on the snow, but no birds came.

DONA came upstream with two men carrying shovels. They carried the chemical engineer's stretcher up through the trees to a flat place with seven mounds. The two men dug and when one was tired he gave Murphy his shovel. The soil was soft and damp but corded with roots that were difficult to slice. Sweat ran down his chest, attracting the mosquitoes. His arm ached too badly and he gave the shovel back. When the hole was three feet deep they took the tarp off the chemical engineer and laid him in the hole. He wore a white T-shirt and his chest bandages were soaked with blood. His eyes had turned up into his head and his mouth was open, showing a silver filling. There was a wedding ring on his finger and a cross around his neck. More *compañeros* came and one read from Ecclesiastes: "'For in much wisdom is much grief, and he that increases knowledge increases sorrow.'"

Dirt pattered like rain on the body. Going back to camp one of the men took a banana from his shirt and gave it to a wounded *compañero*.

"IT'S STUPID to risk good people to kill Arena," Principio said. "When Arena's dead there'll only be another."

"But it's justice. If you won't help me, I'll do it alone."

"Even that we oppose. If you are successful it will lead to great reprisals. They'll kill hundreds of people. Women and children, students, nuns, nurses, catechists, teachers – anyone they have a grudge against."

Murphy looked at the dirt he crumbled in his hand, little flecks of mica or quartz in black duff. Again he saw the dirt falling on the chemical engineer's chest. "That changes everything. I hadn't thought of it."

"Every year for the holidays Arena goes to his family *hacienda* in the south, near El Salvador. He keeps a chopper there." Principio turned to two others, Guadalupe and Pablo. "What if you captured him?"

Guadalupe, tall and slender, with an upturned nose and haughty eyes, was the kind of person, Murphy decided, you instantly don't like; she had a way of preparing the world for each step she took. She tossed her head to one side, a rejection.

Pablo was chewing a twig under his mustache. "You think we could get in, and get him?"

"He goes dove hunting. Out of season. Riding by himself in the brush."

"Why not just go in there on foot?" Murphy said. "Why use the chopper at all?"

"To get him out. Or they'd have us in hours."

"To take him where?"

"A place would be ready," Principio said. "It's nine days to the Feast of the Dead. He'll be there then, Arena, for the Feast. At his *hacienda*."

"How much is he worth?" Murphy said.

Principio's delicate fingers slid down his trouser seam, as if the answer could be harried out, like lice. "Hundreds of people."

"I'd rather kill him. But seeing that's impossible, that it would lead to reprisals..."

"Like your village," Dona said.

". . . then I'd be willing to steal a chopper and fly in there, to get him. To *try* to get him."

"Right now," Principio stood, "we're just working with an idea. A lot depends on people elsewhere. If there were an operation and you were in it you'd learn little about it. It's probably impossible."

"If you were tortured," Guadalupe said to Murphy, "how long could you hold out?"

"Probably not at all."

"If such an operation were done and at any point you might be captured you must kill each other. It's absolutely standard practice. If, despite that, you *are* captured, the rule is to hold out forty-eight hours. That gives other *compañeros* time to realize what's happened and make adjustments. Under torture, forty-eight hours is an eternity..."

"And you know all about it?" Murphy said to her.

"Yes."

An animal scurried through the brush. Overhead the leaves lisped; a spider danced across a web in which a single star was caught.

THIS NIGHT was colder. The burlap poncho covering them crawled with centipedes and chiggers. He dreamed he was surrounded, put Dona's rifle to his temple but could not shoot. "Do it!" Guadalupe hissed. "For your own good!"

The burlap was soaked with dew, the stars sharp as stiletto points between the high tiny leaves, the universe clear
and cruel, nourishing some and crushing others.

A shape moved past and knelt beside another sleeper,
who rose, took up his rifle and departed; the first lay down
in his place. Another came and changed places with a different sleeper who shouldered her Galil and stepped away.

A scream made him jump, then he realized it was only
a *jaguarondi* hunting; he thought of Father Miguel perhaps still alive in an Army torture house. If they got Arena,
Miguel was one who might go free . . .

The *jaguarondi* called further west; it must have crossed
the stream. Was it calling for a mate in a world where there
are no more *jaguarondi*? He thought of Epifanía and Jesús
walking steadily before him in the shallows of the Río de
la Pasión. If he died here trying for Arena he'd never come
back for them as he'd promised. Maybe that would be the
biggest sin of all?

Beside him Dona turned onto her shoulder. He had an
instant's repressed vision of her turning in the grave, getting
comfortable, laying her face to the earth.

Between the trees a lighter darkness. There were footfalls, the snapping of twigs, someone blowing on a fire, a
bony face tinged by bronze as the coals caught.

51

A-37 JETS stood in sun-bright silver rows when Lyman landed at Flores Airbase to catch the Army propjet for Cobán, each plane with twin pods of jellied death beneath its wings. Like the weeds in the fields, Lyman thought. You break them and the seed spreads on the wind.

He saw a napalm pod as it would strike the earth, its onrush of fire, people running coated in flame. America's backyard barbecue.

Vodega extended a hot wet palm. "Murphy's back."

"Where!"

Vodega raised his hands, in crucifixion or ignorance, it wasn't clear. "Shit!" Lyman screamed.

"A *patrulla civil* recognized his photo."

"Why didn't you *grab* him?"

"My dear Colonel, you *just* sent us his picture! Anyway, we heard you'd got him, in San Francisco."

"That's crap! Who told you that?"

Again the smarmy shrug. "It's a small world."

"Advise all the *patrullas*. Spread the photo, the checkpoints –"

"Every drunken civil guard in the mountains has his lousy photo."

"Put a hundred thousand quetzales on him."

"Yours, Colonel? Or mine?"

The propjet climbed fast to avoid fire. The refracted sun off the Río de la Pasión blinded Lyman but he would not turn away, nor look at Vodega. To the south the hills were like storm omens, steepening dark waves. Murphy's down there, he thought. If I can figure why he's back I'll have him.

MURPHY WENT DOWN to the *riachuelo* and drank. The water tasted of rocks, moss, cool sand, the humus of leaves. Water spiders skittered away; black beetles chugged along the bottom raising tiny trails of silt. A water snake uncoiled past his hand and slid like a slender twig downstream.

Naked he scrubbed his body with silt, sitting in the stream to wash it off, lying back drinking the cold water as it flowed over him. It was sweet-tasting from the guavas that had fallen from a tree; the tree's blossoms floated on the surface.

He stood on the bank letting the sun dry him. How long have I lived in buildings and walked on concrete, he wondered, yet spoke of being down to earth, of having my feet on the ground?

"WITH your knowledge of helicopters it is a very unusual chance," Principio said. "But we should never do it with such short notice, not knowing you."

"And I don't know you," Murphy reminded him.

"You're more danger to us than we to you."

"Perhaps."

"We're willing to study it. We think the four of you should go down to the coast as two happy couples, you and Dona, and Guadalupe and Pablo. Quickly. If it seems possible, to do it."

Murphy watched the stream roil round its polished stones, tiny flies shifting before it in skeins of light. Caught by the current, a fern frond ducked and rose, tugged constantly downstream, constantly reasserting itself. Till one day it would break.

IT'S ACTUALLY in the Bible and you've missed it. Not that you cared about the Holy Book. But you knew what it said.

Outside Lyman's window a large buff spider with a yellow belly sat in the center of a web full of dead insects. As each new insect landed the spider leaped on it, bit it to death, and returned to the center.

The walls were barracks yellow, the door and trim dark. There were voices in the hall; he hoped no one would knock. He shoved the Bible into a drawer and shut it. The Bible just another handbook for mass control, social management. A storehouse of tactics. Like any effective tool, it had to have enough truth or it wouldn't sell. But when it says, "Thou shalt not kill", is *that* what it really means?

THEY WALKED SOUTH all day, a hundred yards apart: Lupe in the lead, then Dona, then Murphy without a rifle, then Pablo. The trail was rarely visible through the jungle understory. After sunset they crossed a ridge with the jungle falling away in a great sweep to the south. Lupe looked at her watch, shifted her rifle. "We have to close up, move faster."

"Christ! We've done forty klicks in seven hours!"

"More," she smiled. "Nearly fifty."

"How many to go?"

"Sixty."

"When you escaped through the desert, *hombre*," Pablo said, "you didn't walk like this?"

It *was* like the Sonora desert, but jungle. Running all night through the thick, tangled, humid blackness, seeing only rarely Dona's shade flitting before him, or Lupe's before her, hearing occasionally Pablo's soft pad and steady breathing behind him. Each time he fell he rolled to his feet and kept running, Pablo slowing, giving him slack, then closing up again.

"Four-twenty," Lupe said. He could smell her and Dona and Pablo, and himself, each separately, hear his own heartbeat in his temples and their hearts thumping in their chests, the whistle of breath in his windpipe and the rush of their lungs.

"Christ!" he said, bent over, holding his knees, needing to vomit, to spit, but nothing would come out.

"Well done, *niña*," Pablo said.

Lupe moved against him, whispered something, they kissed. Pablo turned to Dona, kissed her on each cheek, turned to Murphy, his hand coming out of the gloom. "Well done, comrade."

"You're going?"

"Just stick with them." Pablo moved on ahead and took a trail breaking to the right. They went straight, slower now, for two hours, till dawn cut in nearly horizontal layers between the tops of the trees. In the distance a rooster crowed; a truck was climbing a hill. The trail grew clearer; Lupe picked up speed, her black mane bobbing far ahead, Dona's behind her, Murphy angry now, trying not to fall back.

They laid up, panting, in a cave on a rocky jungled slope with a tan glimmer of a road cut visible above through the trees. "Bathroom, whatever you have to do," Lupe whispered, "do it now. We don't move outside all day. I'll take first watch, till noon, Dona till three, then Gringo, then me."

HE WOKE to the sound of a car coming along the road. It was dark. The car paused and seemed to come downhill toward them, stopped. "Let's go," Lupe said.

The car waited, no lights, on a trail below the road. Someone was there. "*Listos, amigos?*" he said. It was Pablo.

Lupe drove with no lights, her rifle slanted loosely across her chest. The road was narrow and terribly rutted and pot-holed. Trees had been dropped in it to fill the biggest holes, and the car jounced and clanged miserably over and around them, slithering, stuck then stuck again as they pushed knee-deep in mud, the wheels spraying them, the blackness harsh with the smells of overheating radiator, crushed vines, and oily mud searing on the exhaust. The road climbed a plateau where she drove faster, branches and boulders clanging and clunking the fenders, rocks pinging on the chassis, brush and trees ducking past, thorns screeching at metal; the transmission kept popping out of fourth so she held the gearshift and drove one-handed.

"Chopper!" Pablo yelled; Lupe skidded into the brush and they dove out scrambling for cover. Lupe ran back to slam the doors and kill the dome light. The roar loudened, three choppers in formation slid across the stars, a beacon slashing up and down the road. They rumbled westward, their thunder dying in the mountains.

"How the hell you hear that?"

"Natural selection, *hombre*. Those who don't hear them die."

"We were very dumb," Lupe said. "About the light."

"Before this it didn't work," Pablo said. "I thought it was cut, but we must have bumped the wires. I'll take out the bulb."

"And the brake lights?"

"Already I've taken out their bulbs."

They drove back down the ridge into forest. Then Pablo walked ahead, holding a cigarette for Lupe to follow its light. They crossed a stream on foot which Lupe drove through fast, then climbed a mountain and broke out on a savanna studded with thorny trees, the grass barer, the calciferous soil like a tilled graveyard.

There was a thump and a body rumbled underneath. "Damn," Lupe said.

"*Jabali*," Pablo said, then to Murphy: "Mountain pig." "No," Lupe said. "Armadillo."

Three times they stopped so Pablo could scout forward for soldiers or civil patrols, and drove on cattle tracks around each checkpoint. After midnight Pablo drove and Lupe slept, her head thumping against the window.

DAWN hinted in the east, ahead lay the lights of a town. "Fifty kilometers to Guatemala City," Lupe said. "We've circled the last checkpoint."

The road coiled ahead through gray hills tinged with reddish green daybreak and loud with chattering birds and roosters. People were walking on the roadsides – women balancing bundles of corn or water jugs on their heads, old men and boys with tall firewood stacks slung from tumplines around their foreheads, a naked little girl with a black puppy on a string. The air stung with the smoke of green hardwoods, smoldering rubber and burnt diesel from the trucks laboring up the hills, the seared asbestos smells of their brakes and clutch plates deepened by the occasional stench of pig manure where a family fence ran close to the road.

At sunrise they crossed the Río Las Vacas bridge into La Ermita and the Guatemala City smog, turned up Calle Martí behind a rusty red truck whose back doors clanged their chains each time it jerked forward.

Lupe drove through the city and across Río Barranca down a long slope of packed shacks, the river valley falling off steeply below. The road turned to garbage and mud thick with citrus skins and cardboard, the air bitter with charred litter and plastic, naked children and bony dogs staring from the tin and cardboard huts. She parked amid broken cars and trucks where a man with a Galil kept guard, and led them down the slippery stinking slope of a dump where people lived in caves burrowed out of the garbage and trash, alleys loud with the music of competing tinny radios, the voices of strangers calling each other.

In a lane of rotten detritus and reeking urine Lupe banged on a plank door hinged by two rubber straps to the corner post of a chicken-wire shack covered in newspapers. There was no answer and she opened the door. "Stay here," she said to Murphy. "If no one comes by dawn tomorrow, go home."

52

INSIDE in the igloo-like light he could read the advertisements on the newspapers of the ceiling and walls. Flies
clustered on a black stinking fluid that percolated from
under a wall across the floor; there was a crucifix and a
God's Eye over the door.

He tried to lie where the black stream would not touch
him. Exhaustion was thick as vomit in his stomach and his
eyes would not stay open. He thought of eating some of the
newspaper to slow the gnaw in his stomach. As the sun rose
higher the hut grew hot, the smell horrible. He went outside
and sat in the half-shade of an upturned truck seat; three
boys were playing soccer with a shred of tire; a woman
brought a skinny rooster out of her hut and cut off its head
on a car fender, catching the blood in a chunk of coconut
bark.

He had diarrhea and tried to find a hidden place among
the walls of trash; there was nothing to drink and his tongue
stuck in his throat. He went back into the hut and slept,
curled in a corner in the reeking heat.

"Let's go!" Dona was shaking him. It was dark. They
went up through the aisles of trash to the car. She wore
sports clothes and carried a handbag.

"I've had enough of this," he said.

"It's just you and me." She gave him the car keys. "Take the Periférico."

"Where are Lupe and Pablo?"

"We'll see."

He drove up the long hill of garbage. Kerosene lanterns glowed on faces in the crowded huts. "Where we going?"

"I have a Mexican passport. You are this American – Lamar Bultz – where do they get such names, these people? We're on vacation... Listen, now, we must practice the story of what we're doing here."

The traffic was light – a cattle truck with two men in the back holding M16s, a Jeep, a BMW with dark windows, the dim roadsides empty of life as they rehearsed past times and presents, lives in which she was María Iturbo of Oaxaca and he was still Lamar Bultz of Flagstaff, and they were in love.

She directed him south on Central America Nine toward Villa Nueva, past Lago Amatitlan flat as mercury under the moon, black buttresses above one shore.

Sickness was a snake in his stomach. One by one the checkpoints passed, at each Dona pretending to wake, rummaging sleepily in her bag for her Mexican passport while the soldiers thumped their rifle butts on the ground. The road narrowed, slinking through curves in rolling hills silvered by the setting moon, no lights in passing huts and villages, occasionally a truck or car the other way. Several times he pulled off the road and waited, twice doubling back, but no one followed.

The moon fell down, sea smell in the air. She pointed him down an overgrown lane through miles of dunes and salt-brush to a village square with an adobe church. They left the car in a grove of wind-stunted cypress behind the church and went down to a narrow beach and a broad estuary scattered with stars, beyond it a hump of sand spit and the shuddering roar of the sea.

"We have three days," she said. "I'm not supposed to tell you, but now you know."

"I don't like having the truth dribbled out like this."

"How else would *you* do it? The less we each know –"

"I won't be pushed around by Lupe."

"We have three days. Let's just live with that."

They took off their clothes and washed in the estuary's liquid silver; it felt like a magic shield they could wear; he drank the salty algal water and it felt good in his stomach.

At dawn a boy took them in his dugout across the pale estuary reflecting pink tumbled cumuli. The church tolled six, the bell's sound quavering across the still water. A line of snowy egrets undulated away like a broken necklace. The dugout crossed the inverted reflection of the sand spit's palm huts, and grated ashore. Beyond the huts was a streak of platinum that was the sea, then the lightening blue pit of space. "Twenty centavos," the boy said.

A woman in a black dress was cooking *frijoles* on a chunk of tin over a ring of stones. Smoke from the driftwood fire contorted in the breeze. A man came out of a hut scratching his chest. "*Sí*," he said. "I have rooms."

It was a hut with a plank door, a driftwood floor and palm frond walls, two woven willow sleeping mats raised on posts, a wooden chair. Beyond the door was the curl of the beach then the great blue shoulder of the sea. "You want breakfast?" the man said.

It was coffee from fresh beans heated over the fire then crushed with a rock and boiled in a black pot, black *frijoles* covered with green salsa, bright yellow eggs from hens run wild, tortillas charred on their edges. When they could eat no more they took their coffee cups out and sat on the newly warm dune going down to the waves that hissed and darkened the sand with foamy wet fingers.

A bony lion-colored dog burrowed in the sand trying to escape his fleas. A salt-corroded red and white sign, *COCA COLA DA MAS CHISPA!* banged in the wind. Gulls cried, blown eastward; blue waves slapped the strand.

The sun reddened her black hair. "How did he die," he said, "your fiancé?"

She raised her head from the sand to look at him. "That doesn't matter now."

"It always matters. It never *stops* mattering."

"He was one of seven people captured by the new IBM that Mossad gave the Army to watch the flow of water and electricity in Guatemala City. They found them all in one house, and shot them the day the Pope came."

The waves broke suddenly and late against the steep beach, shaking the dunes so that sand avalanched down them.

"I was such a kid," she said. "Twenty-three, first year of medical school. Wild with studying so hard and trying to keep my head above water, working in the hospital from midnight to six as an orderly to pay for my room and food. Diego was so bright, alive, a cardiology intern. He thought that if we've learned how to heal the body we can learn how to heal the soul."

Looking southward the beach was pure as cocaine, stretching out through blue sea and sky to a horizon of low clumped trees hazy at the world's edge. In both directions the line of white sand fled beyond the ends of the earth. "I wish I'd known you then. I wish I'd always known you."

"Silly!" She pushed him. "Then you'd be bored with me now."

"I've always wanted to walk this beach. From Alaska to Chile. Funny to realize you'll never do the things you always thought you'd do."

"Down there's El Salvador. You'd never get through."

"El Salvador," he said. "The Saviour. Who said do unto others what you would do unto me?"

She put a finger over his lips. "Let's try to live through all this, and raise children, get old and tired of each other, like normal people?"

He smiled, pillowed in the warm dune, tasting the sand the wind blew into his face. The sun like a hot abrasive sponge seemed to cleanse his skin. "Better to die for something than nothing," he said dreamily.

He must have slept, woke remembering a vision of atoms, atoms uniting in paramecia, ants, bears, humans, each a coalition of atoms defending their union from dissolution, all hungering to continue.

53

T HE HUTS were a tiny hump on the beach behind
them. The sea slung cool foamy tentacles round their
ankles, crabs scurried sideways along the waterline.
Far ahead a pebble became a thatched shelter, a blue-paint-
ed dugout drawn high up on the sand below it at the edge
of the dune grass.

The shelter was empty, the windy sand trackless. The
other side of the dune went down to a fringe of thick trees
along a *riachuelo* paralleling the beach, with flat low jungle
behind it. Her ankles and the rolled-up cuffs of her jeans
were white with fine sand.

A tern slanted across the cobalt white-capped sea, its cry
familiar as a language he'd forgotten. When they went further down the beach they could not even see the huts or the
shelter and blue boat in the misty distant silver curve behind
them; ahead the tree-topped cape of El Salvador seemed no
closer.

They swam through the warm salty froth beyond the
waves, down to kelp raising willowy arms like drowned
men, the water turbid, colder. In the shallows the waves
washed cool silk between them, lightening and lubricating,
welding them to each other and to the soft sea, the sand,
the sun.

"We should be more careful," she said. "It's here the choppers drop lots of bodies."

"They won't bother us."

"It's the sharks. They've learned a taste for human flesh."

Carrying their clothes they walked naked, the breeze like warm water against their salty skin. Terns dived crying over feeding mackerel. Along the water's shifting edge, countless millions of tiny embryonic creatures wriggled up the damp sand, battling the swell, trying to reach dry beach, most already dead, here and there one succeeding till the next wave bashed it down, the universe crammed with worlds hungry for life; from time to time, he thought, one survived, but not for long.

They grew thirsty and went back to the huts, sat with bottles of mineral water at a rough-sawn table. The sun had sunk past the thatched veranda that a pig was shaking as she rubbed her pink flank against a corner post. Loose fronds of thatch tossed in the breeze like a woman's long blonde hair.

Beyond the hump of beach they could not see the shore, only the sea rising and sinking like a sleeping woman's breast, the casual rumble of each wave drowning the chatter of Radio Tropicana from a portable radio that hung on a beam. He realized he could see the earth's curve in the wide arc between sea and sky, thought how small the earth was, and how many people were on it. "*Hay qué vivir,*" sang a Mexican love song, "*Vivir el momento...*"

The sun sank round and scarlet into a sea of blood. A fisherman was mending a net, a web of gold that shimmered as his fingers moved across it. The sun's last blaze ignited a strip of red plastic half buried in the sand, the scuttling shreds of paper, strands of thatch, the riffled dunes. Gulls slid by; the sky thinned, magenta to crimson, violet to emerald, to manganese, to the copper-gray of ashes thrown on snow. Between their toes the sand was rivuleted by infinite tiny capillaries of sea, as if they flew at a great height over a land of many rivers.

The man, Felipe, brought them *morrachos* grilled with lime over palm fronds, rice with *chiles*, raw white cabbage with tomatoes in salt and lime, tortillas, and El Gallo beer. The *morrachos* had transparent needle bones. "They're from the river," Felipe said, pointing to the estuary. "Now it's sweet water, but at midnight, when the tide comes, it's salty."

The woman, Carlita, sat with another by the fire; children swung in a fishnet hammock hung between two beams. Felipe chopped green coconuts with a machete and tossed the chips to the grunting butting pigs. Murphy borrowed Felipe's cracked Mexican guitar and played, and the children came closer. After a while he could feel the music start to go out of him, out of his heart and down his arms through this beaten old guitar to the end of the night where all music goes.

"Jesus, that's beautiful," she said. "Where did you learn that?"

"It's just the blues."

"Do again that part that goes down and then way up."

"It's all I've ever wanted to do, this," he said. "Sit on the beach with you and play the guitar."

"Your fingers move so fast! *Madre*, it is beautiful!"

"You should hear the good ones. The ones who know how to play."

"I am getting drunk with your music and your beer."

"We're going in the hut to make love."

"I won't let it happen yet. First I am going to drive you crazy."

"You already drive me crazy."

"We are going to get drunk and crazy. We are going to be like normal people, with all the time in the world."

The slim moon had risen, silvering a great dark cloud that lay far over the sea, low in the middle and raised on each end, that looked like the crouched form of Chacmool, the Mayan messenger between the worlds who, holding his tribute of fresh human hearts, ferries his burden of poor human souls across the great divide.

In the main hut a candle flickered against the thatch and beams. They went into their hut and hooked the string of the door behind them and took off their clothes, his jacket folded for a pillow with Dona's .357 beneath it.

54

H E WAS TRAVELING through rough country and kept looking for water but all the streams were dry. Even the cactus were dead; he pushed one and it snapped and crashed to the ground. It wasn't the cactus banging but guns; he snatched the Magnum and shoved Dona to the floor; someone scrambled over the wall and he fired, the sound enormous in the tiny dark room; a cat snarled and rushed away; there was another boom and a rattle of guns; he yanked open the door and sprinted for the beach pushing her before him; they dived into the dunes as another string of shots erupted and he saw across the lagoon that it was fireworks, their bright cinders twirling down.

"Good God we're stupid." She stood brushing sand from her stomach. "The Night of the Dead – that's all it is."

"I shot at that poor cat."

"Perhaps the shot just scared him."

Inside the hut he lit the candle and found the burnt hole of the bullet high up in the thatched wall, went outside but could see no blood. "Felipe, he's going to be pissed."

"He doesn't care. We'll tell him we brought our own fireworks."

"We have no dead to feed tonight."

A curlew called, morose from sleep. A baby cried; the sea rose up and slapped the beach, recoiled, rose up and fell again. The moon strode glittering over the waves. He re-tied the door string and put the gun back under their heads.

When she slept he held his hand warm on her warm cheek, feeling the soft skin. How magnificent life. How can it die?

How deep love, how absolute. Her skin so smooth, her forehead clear, how soft the fine hair of her eyebrows – all so holy, pure, and death so present, the awfulness of it when there's so much to lose.

He'd never thought of it when it had seemed far away, death. But it was never far away – it's always here; we're always dying. It isn't going to happen some day; it's happening now.

You could see the skull beneath the smooth soft skin, the sockets behind sleeping eyes, the gaping jaw within the lovely lips moving so gently now in a dream. The awful aching endless silence of death.

Her coppery face seemed loving, without care. The peace that passes all understanding. Oh Lord make me understand, he prayed. Do this and I will love you always. Give me a chance to understand. One hand beneath his head, his wrist against rushes and hemp, the other arm round her shoulders, he watched the hewn rafters and their burden of crossed saplings and thatch, each frond lashed to each alternate sapling in the simple harmony of Indian handiwork. Each of us contributing his or her handiwork to the structure of infinity. Harrowing a meaning, order and pattern, a shelter for the future, for others and ourselves.

THERE WAS COFFEE on the rough-sawn table in the cool morning breeze off the sea. Up and down the beach, forever, the hot sand and wet waves. El Gallo in the evenings, too many, laughter coming out too easily from under the stone of his heart, while he knew he couldn't afford to laugh and told himself not to care. When she laughed her small nose wrinkled and the sides of her eyes crinkled, her laugh both deep and high as if two bells rang at once. To make her laugh he told her stories of Texas rabbits big as coyotes, drunken hookers in the Oklahoma oilfields, forty-five below in April on the Montana Highline, carrying newborn calves into the ranch house to warm in the bathtub, all the truck stops to get sick at between Elko and Salt Lake. Deliberately exaggerating, he played the joker, anything to see her smile, hear her laughter as he'd always heard it down inside a part of himself that had been deaf and dumb.

She told him about bringing the goats up to pasture in the early mornings with Venus going down over the Sierra Madre, the cold spring between ancient carved pillars where a black jaguar sometimes slept on the low broad branch of a *chicozapote* tree with a deer carcass beside him, the magic plants the old women used to heal the ill, liven the spirit, and even, in the case of some, look forward into time.

"Did you ever do it, take them?"

"I tried the mushrooms, when I was fourteen."

"And?"

"After all the laughter and fun I suddenly realized I was able to look into my own brain. How it worked and where the pieces are. In medical school, years later, when I finally opened one, it was exactly as I had seen, way back then."

THE PRIEST had an odor of old cloth and tobacco. The veins on the backs of his hands were distended and blue. Although his left hand was still, his right kept twitching, as if beckoning Murphy closer. "Come back in an hour," he said. "Bring Felipe and Carlita."

Murphy took the dugout back to the sand spit. In the hut Dona was brushing the salt out of her hair; it hung way down her back. "Do I look all right?" she said.

He could not speak. It came upon him now, the wonder that she would be his wife and this lasted forever, because it is part of the Mass, the Sacrament. And the Sacrament is that which cannot be undone.

"Carlita says that after we have children we must come back here so that they can grow up in the countryside."

"Felipe told me the same thing."

"It is kind of them to do this, they don't know us."

"It does them no harm, a quick trip to church."

WITH Carlite and Felipe they took the dugout across the lagoon. The priest threw open the church's eroded plank door. Inside was musty and chilled, dead fragrances, incense, and candle wax. "You have the rings?"

"Jesus," Murphy said. "I never thought –"

"I will not do it without them. Quickly, go see the old man, Pepe Domingo, in the last street by the dock. I hope he's there."

He ran through town to the last street, sweating in the sudden sun. Pepe Domingo had a purple snake tattooed round his neck. He lived in a hut whose rush walls had been coated with clay and whitewashed. He had a window but it had no glass. He made Murphy wait in the path then called him inside. He had seven rings in a rusty tin can. Fresh dirt clung to the can. On the wall behind him a Day-Glo Saint Michael, face full of hatred, was spearing a dragon.

"*Con prisa!*" Murphy said. "*Hurry!* I'm getting married!"

"No need to rush."

He tried on the biggest. It pinched but he could wear it. He picked another smaller one. "How much these two?"

"They are gold, very expensive gold."

"How much? How much!"

"Well, that one it is white gold, the most expensive. Twenty-two thousand. And the other, well, it is fine gold, but, well, eighteen thousand."

He put them in his pocket and ran back through town, dust flying under his feet. The church door was open but no one was inside.

He ran out into bright sun. "The falcons took them," said a woman in a *tienda* across the dirt street.

"The *what*?"

"The death squad. Your woman and Felipe and Carlita and the Father. In a black Jeep with a Guatemala City license." She was weeping. "What are we going to do," she said, "without a priest?"

He fell on his knees, looked up at the sky, the yellow tower of the church. Somewhere birds were singing.

"You should never have bought rings from Pepe," the woman said. "He gets them from the cemetery. From the dead."

55

H E RAN to the car but had left the keys back at the hut. He ran to the boy's dugout and poled to the sand spit, smashed down the hut door, grabbed the keys, their things, raced back across the lagoon. "*Which way?*" he screamed at the old woman.

"Toward San José. But you won't catch them now."

He drove like a madman, dust, rocks, trash and coconuts flying from his path, turned toward San José, down the middle of the road as fast as the Nissan could go, other cars and trucks screaming at him as they dodged out of the way.

"No," said the advance guard at the San José Paratroop Base. He looked nervously back at his comrades in their machine gun nests on both sides of the road. "I haven't seen a black Jeep coming in here."

"You're sure?" Murphy grabbed money from his pocket. "Here, I'll give you fifty thousand – anything – you tell me –"

"Sorry, *Señor*. I cannot take your money. And I haven't seen a black Jeep."

"Panchito!" somebody called from the machine guns.

"I got to go now, *Señor*. You too, or we have to shoot you."

He stopped only for gas, at Escuintal, making the four-hour trip to Guatemala City in an hour and forty minutes.

Before the towering stone gates of the Army Headquarters four soldiers with Uzis manned the barrier, machine guns to each side. He parked halfway down the street and shoved the Magnum under the seat.

"No," said the first man with an Uzi. "You can't go in there."

"I have an appointment, with General Arena."

The soldier had a dark face with flat cheekbones and black eyes under heavy brows. His finger caressed the trigger. Murphy thought of the heavy bullets, how they smash through you. Happening to her now. He jammed his hands into his pockets to keep from grabbing the Uzi.

The soldier stepped inside the stone gates. The others watched Murphy without interest. Cars and trucks rumbled and banged on the Avenida. A chopper came up from the south and landed inside the Base, rotors clattering. Again he thought of shooting his way through them but there was no way to make it to the machine guns and if he made it to one he'd never get across open ground to the other and even if he did they'd close the gates and shoot him to pieces from the walls. The soldier came back. "You make a big mistake. No General Arena here."

"You don't know where he is?"

"I don't know of any general like that. Anyway, you not stay here. Go."

"I'm a reporter, American. I need to see the commanding general."

"No commanding general. You're getting in trouble now. Why not just go?"

"Listen, I *have* to see him. I have information, on the guerrillas –"

The man's head jerked back. "You better go to your own embassy for that. Up the Avenida, to Ocho Calle."

"I have to see the CO!"

The man stepped back, dropped the Uzi. "You're exactly one meter from death, *amigo*. Step forward and you get erased."

He returned to the car, feeling their gun barrels aimed between his shoulder blades. He drove into the back streets and sat. He could see it all, the guns, the knives, what they were doing to her right now, each second.

In a corner drugstore he borrowed the phone book and found the Iglesia Congregacionale del Cristo Pentecostal, 112 Avenida las Americas. It was a two-story white building in a palm garden. The ornamental iron fence around it was topped by barbed and electric wires. He rang the bell. "*Sí?* a woman said through the interphone.

"I'm Will Daley," he said in English, "from the Church in Marin."

"Marin?"

"Near San Francisco."

"Just a moment."

The interphone went silent, then a man's voice: "*Who are you?*"

"You want a conversation on the sidewalk? Open up!"

A crewcut man in black horn rims opened the door. Inside was a square vestibule with three blank white doors and two television monitors high on the walls. "Explain," he said.

"The folks at CCCP in Nicasio sent me down about a flying job."

"This is a *church*, fella. We don't have flying jobs."

"Bullshit. I did two thousand hours in Nam, I'm rated from dusters to jets and I came down here to fly in and out of Petén."

"Our office in Marin *told* you this?"

"Of course. What's the hitch?"

"Stay here." The man went through the middle white door and came back three minutes later. "Nobody's ever heard of you."

"I fly all the way down here and now you guys jerk my chain!" Murphy snatched at the door, spun round. "Let me talk to the top guy, we'll sort it out."

"There *is* no top guy. This's a church, remember?"

"I was promised a job! Listen – I flew for Renamo, Angola, what more you want?"

"Calm down!" The man spoke up into a TV monitor: "I'll take him uptown." He led Murphy through the left-hand door and down a white corridor with no windows or doors to the rear of the building. There was a Van Gogh print on one wall, beached boats with an arched stone bridge and women washing clothes. The man took a plastic card from his wallet and slipped it into a slot beside the rear door, punched a code into the keyboard above it. The door opened. They went down the stairs to a walled alley and a white Plymouth Aries with diplomatic plates. "One," the man told the driver.

"I've got information," Murphy said, "about the guerrillas."

"Kill it," the man answered, nodding at the driver.

They went north on las Americas round the Costa Rica oval, crossed Ocho Calle in front of the US Embassy, and pulled into the driveway of a three-story beige building with a forest of antennae on the roof.

The driveway was guarded by a burly man in a red blazer and an Uzi, and by four Guatemalan soldiers who saluted hurriedly as the car drove down to the basement garage, bulletproof steel doors opening then shutting behind it. In the garage were several new cars with diplomatic plates and three Suburbans with dark windows and Guatemalan plates. They took an elevator to the second floor then down another white empty corridor into a little room with no window. There was a gray steel desk and chair and two gray metal folding chairs before it. A big man with a rectangular red face, his lavender tie undone and his sleeves rolled to his elbows, came in and sat behind the desk. He snuffed out his cigarette in a glass ashtray on the desk. "So what's up?" he said.

"He says NoCal sent him down for Southern Air, out of Petén."

The big man looked with interest into Murphy's face. "Impossible."

Murphy stood. "You guys've really screwed me up!"

"Hold it, trooper!" the big man rumbled genially. "You got to start from the States if you want to fly for Southern Air."

"Listen, I got data, too, on the guerrillas – I need to talk to somebody."

The man rubbed his jaw. "What *kind* of data?"

"I'll make a trade – I need to interrogate someone who's just been captured, on another matter, I'll trade some data…"

"What other matter?"

Murphy looked into the friendly, blank face. "Drugs."

The man looked back at him, and Murphy saw the black widow he'd seen in the chopper pilot's skull in the jungle so long ago. It was big and very black and moved on dancing cables from side to side. "Nobody trades info here, trooper," the man said. "I'm beginning to think you're in a real bad place."

Murphy stood. "Then you're just wasting my time."

"You can't hop down here, just run all over us. You got to play by the book, trooper. Channels, like anybody else. Who you think you are, Galahad or something?"

Not waiting for them Murphy took the white corridor and down the elevator to the main floor, to an anteroom guarded by Guatemalan soldiers with MAC-10s and Uzis. There was a steel box at one side with a woman answering a telephone behind bulletproof glass. "What *is* this place?" he said.

"*This?*" she had a pleasant Alabama accent. "Why this's USAID. ROCAP."

"What the hell's that?"

She looked at him in surprise. "We're foreign aid. We organize urban work, agricultural self-help, educational projects."

Behind him Murphy heard the elevator open. He went out the front door and down the marble stairs guarded by Guatemalan soldiers and through the electric sliding gate.

In the shade of great trees on La Reforma Indians were selling flowers, blankets, and willow baskets; chubby men in hundred-dollar running shoes jogged past skinny kids hunting the sidewalks for butts and gum, past lovely fifty-dollar girls and hobbling old women, the road full of flashy cars and Microfé vans with their windows crammed with faces. There were rattling smoky buses tilting their ragged human burden, children pushing bicycles stacked with Coke crates, black-windowed Jeep Wagoneers and Chevy Suburbans, symbol and tool of the death squads.

56

A CINDERY sediment was silting down between the buildings that wobbled in the ochre heat. He drove across the Río Barranca and down the slope of shacks and garbage, left the car and ran through the dump with the caves of rotten garbage and the trash huts, found the chicken wire shack where he'd stayed. It was empty; he climbed up through the trash to the next hut and knocked on the wall. A skinny little girl looked out, up at him.

There were two babies on a blanket on the floor, no one else. The girl did not know where her mother was. He went to the next hut, recognized the woman who had killed the rooster, days before. "I don't understand you," she said. "There's no *compañeros* here."

He tried three other huts, then in an alley asked a wiry girl with a scarred face. "Don't talk about it," she said. "Go back to your hut and wait."

He stood by the plank door of his shack, out of the way of the flowing sewer. After perhaps an hour Lupe came. "If you've lost her I'll kill you," she said.

His hand itched to take out the Magnum and shoot her. He told her about the priest, the rings, the death squad. "You're insane," she said. "You deserve to die."

"What are they doing to her?"

Lupe clasped her face in her hands, her back to Murphy. She knelt down on the ground and he did not know if she was crying or praying or simply thinking. "They're torturing her," she said. "When she tells them everything they'll kill her. Unless she figures out how to kill herself first."

"We can still get Arena, and trade him for her, the others!"

She shook her head, her face a mixture of pain and fury. There was perspiration, or tears, in her eyes. "It's too late, now. You were supposed to meet others."

"Let's go, meet them!"

"It was for this afternoon. By now Arena's on his way back to Guatemala City."

"We'll meet him here then."

She stood. "Stay here." She went out the door, came back. "You're just worrying about her! Don't you realize every word she says will cost a life!"

"So hurry!"

She vanished up the path and he stood at the end of the alley watching the hazy sun sink behind black pillars of trash smoke, the first breeze of evening rising through the dump of huts and tunnels, bearing the chatter of children, a woman's laugh, the odors of garbage and tortillas, the wistful songs of radios and seagulls, and the chirr and swoop of swallows after flies.

He realized he was incredibly thirsty. Hungry. The world of your body goes on, he thought sadly. Each step, everything that had happened, he could see how he'd done it. Even the rings. Each step had made sense at the time and each had led to ruin later.

After midnight Lupe came with a bottle of water and two tortillas. "Sorry, this's all there is."

"What next?"

"You have clean clothes?"

"In the car."

"Go up and sleep in your car. In the morning wash and shave with some of this water and change clothes. Make yourself presentable."

"And?"

"Wait."

Where the car was parked the sewers from the City above had backed up into pools where mosquitoes bred, so he had to sit with the windows rolled up, sweating, barely breathing.

At dawn he washed and changed. At ten Lupe and Pablo came down the hill behind him and got in the car. "Drive," Pablo said.

He drove back across the Río Barranca into Guatemala City. "*No critiquemos Guatemala!*" screamed a yellow billboard above a highway abutment.

"Get out on the next corner," Lupe said. "Three corners ahead you turn left on La Reforma and walk to the El Camino Real Hotel. It's a big building on your left in one kilometer. Use your Arizona license to register. They don't file room booking data by telecom so there's no danger for forty-eight hours. Take a room on the south side with a clear view of the pool, at least four floors up. Don't take *any* room that doesn't meet all three of those qualifications. *Stay* in the room. *Don't* go out. When you're hungry use room service."

"What the hell for?"

"Someone'll get in touch. If in three days nothing happens, go home."

FROM THE WINDOW of Room 708 he could see the long turquoise pool and its ramps of sunbathers like dead seals flayed over deck chairs, others sprawling under palm-frond umbrellas, white-coated waiters wandering among them like medics looking for survivors on a battlefield. Beyond the pool a thick wall shut out La Reforma. Between the buildings the noon sun hung thick as lead.

The room had two king-sized beds and a color TV and a red telephone and a desk and a bar with a small refrigerator. On the coffee table was a bowl of fruit and fresh orchids and a fan of brochures for the hotel sauna, coiffeur, massage, manicure, tennis, room service, luxury shops and chapel. In the bathroom were double sinks set in a long pink marble slab, a pink marble bath and a separate marble shower with a rubber floor mat, a bidet, toilet and white telephone. There was a complimentary kit of shampoo, a shower cap, laundry bag, shoe polish, sewing supplies, toothpaste and tanning lotion. Over the faucets a sign said "Purified Water" in English.

He turned on CNN, stories of death in the Middle East. He pushed a button and a college football player was speaking about today's game: "It's life and death for us." The player leaned down to speak into the microphone, his shoulder pads blocking out the light. If it's college football, Murphy decided, it must be Saturday.

A man in a red jacket and cap brought him eggs and bacon and tasteless white bread and a thick steak with coffee, orange juice, milk, and a lime pie. He slept till three, ordered newspapers and magazines from room service. *GUATEMALA KILLINGS RISE,"* said a *New York Times* headline, *"BUT OVERALL GAINS NOTED."* El Grafico listed yesterday's twenty-one known deaths of the death squads, another article on a visiting US official:

"The democratizing process operating in Guatemala is extremely significant," said Democratic Congressman Stephen Solarz of New York yesterday after visiting the Armed Forces Chief, General Mejía Victores. *"It is imminent and sure the US government will extend new*

military loans to Guatemala…"

On an American game show, housewives groveled for kitchen accessories. The phone shrilled.

"*Sí!*"

"*Señor* Bultz? In the man's accent it sounded like "Bullets".

"No. *Sí!*"

"This is reception," the man said. "May the maid clean away your lunch?"

He held the Magnum hidden under a towel when he answered the door. The maid was a little Indian woman with a bowed back and a smile. He went into the bathroom and put the gun back in his belt under the shirt. In the mirror it swelled his stomach.

He switched back to CNN. The city of Ponchatoula, Louisiana, was burying its pet alligator. A thousand citizens, many weeping, marched in the funeral procession. A new alligator had already been caught to replace it.

He paced the room, twenty-seven steps from bathroom door to far window, round the beds and coffee table and back again. She could be dead now. Maybe they just shot them and didn't torture them. You could always hope for that. Whatever Lupe and Pablo were doing they'd better do it fast. Or what? What was he going to do?

The daylight failed like a bad dream. Car lights were like snails' eyes on La Reforma.

Three sharp knocks on the door. He ducked into the closet beside the door aiming the .357 through the wall. Again three knocks. "*Sí!*"

"*Señor* Bultz? It's Guadalupe."

He let them in, Lupe and Pablo, she in a short silky pink dress and black stockings, he in a tuxedo. "Arena's downstairs," she said. "He may be coming up with me, to another room one floor above this."

"That's nuts!"

"You have to wait up there, outside the window. There's a little ledge, you and Pablo."

"We'll never..."

"He's here often, the bar's full of Americans from the Embassy. He likes the hookers here, always likes new ones; he's never seen me before. If I can get him to come to the room upstairs, we'll try to take him out the window, down to this room, then down to the car. We're keeping you with us, in case we need the chopper, a way out..."

He backed away, to see them better. "You've been working this all out, never letting me know?"

She brushed his hair forward, almost affectionately. "What *good* would it have done, except cause you more suffering if they ever catch you? And other people too."

"I won't do it unless I know what's going on."

"She's told you what she can, *hombre*," Pablo said. "Take it or leave it. We're not even sure we need you."

"Where's Dona?"

Lupe took his face in her hands, looking right into his eyes like a mother with a beloved belligerent child, and he saw with shock how beautiful she was, how deep her jade eyes, how her presence glowed through her skin. "We don't know."

"You *must*!"

"We think she's been taken to Cobán for interrogation. The three others we think were found this morning near Escuintla."

He could hear his own words through a thick fog, as if he were alone in the room. "You think?"

"There's been over twenty found today. Most of them don't have heads."

There was no air to breathe. "How do you know she..."

"There've been only five women. They all were bigger."

He couldn't move, couldn't speak, seeing the five headless women found today, thinking of their lives, thought how willing we are to trade others' lives for those we love. "She's dead. You just haven't found her yet."

"The people who took her, they'd have identified her right away. Just bringing her in is worth ten thousand quetzales."

Everyone was ordered to hold out for forty-eight hours after capture to give the *compañeros* time to adjust, but no one could. Very soon you told your interrogators everything, *any*thing, to stop the pain. They'd know she was trying to hold for forty-eight hours and would find a quicker way to break her. Right now. Right this very second. Every second.

Lupe opened the window. "Let's go! You still have bullets for the Magnum?"

"Eleven."

They took the stairs up one floor to Room 809. Lupe opened that window. "Wait on the ledge, here. Watch carefully. Come in when I call you, not before. Remember this: if I don't call you, don't come in. If Arena is here, do nothing. His bodyguards will be waiting for him outside the room door. If anyone comes in, I will pretend to faint if there's danger. If I do that then shoot everyone you can except me and Pablo."

LYMAN WATCHED the chick come down the wide stairs into the bar, with her short pink dress showing lovely long legs in black stockings. There was something about the way she walked that let him imagine her cunt right there, moving under the silk as she walked, and he could feel it warm in the hollow of his hand.

She gave the room a professional glance and sat at the bar behind him. "*Gin y tonica*," she said, a girl from the *barrios* trying to sound chic. He felt his penis throb like a thick rope.

"And also, the bulls of Finca las Golondrinas," said General Arena, "will outperform all others in Guatemala, for wisdom *and* for speed. That I have proved, have I not, Deputado?"

"The General always said the bulls of Izabel are best," Deputado Calejes Cruxiero said to Newbury, "until he bought this *hacienda* down by the coast."

Newbury jiggled the ice cubes in his glass. "Management. All depends on management."

Arena's hand slapped the table. Lyman shifted his eyes from the girl in the pink dress to Arena's fat dark fingers with the gold Citadel ring biting into one. "Management," Arena said.

"That's why I'm here," Newbury said. "I want to improve *your* management."

Lyman snickered. "Progress's our mos' importan' produc'."

Newbury cracked a grin. "That's why I asked Howie to join us, always says what he thinks. He's your advisor and he wouldn't recommend that you contract for this matériel unless you need it."

"But isn't it the Japanese who progress," said Deputado Calejes Cruxiero, "while the Americans consume?"

"I talk to many people about my bulls," Arena said, "but I am the one who decides what to do with them."

"And Howie's one of our people."

"How much is *he* getting?"

Newbury's chin rose. "Getting?"

"How much does *Señor* Lyman make on delivery of five hundred of these RPG-7 launchers and ten thousand rockets which he thinks I need?"

Lyman sat forward. "I don't get nothin'."

"Come on, *Señor* Lyman. I've been to your house. I see what you drive. You don't do that on GS 14 Agency pay."

"Expanding infrastructures," Newbury said. "Electricity, roads, getting them to watch television, controlling information properly, gaining unanimity through dependence: that's your task here, General. This will help you do it."

"Give 'em a good tit to suck on," Lyman said, "and few people ever raise their heads to look around."

Deputado Calejes twirled his cigar against the ashtray, breaking off an even section of ash. "It's those few…"

"Give them a little more tit to suck on," Lyman answered, "and they'll be eating out of your hand."

"So your manual says."

"And it's good advice," Newbury said. "So listen up. Same way Howie's telling you, invest in these launchers – you won't regret it."

Arena pushed out his lower lip. Like a bull's, Lyman thought. Put a ring in it. "My problem with your matériel," Arena said, "is that I have to pay for it."

"Life's a bitch, General."

"I need more credits." Arena was watching the bar. A tall gangly man in a too-tight suit was trying to talk to the girl in the pink dress, but she was facing away. Grabbing for her wrist he spilled her glass.

"And the ones that won't suck on your tit," Newbury was saying, "them you just have to excise. Sounds cruel but you really have no choice. Kindest thing, best thing, for the society as a whole."

"You tried that," Arena said. Lyman noticed that his voice made the table shiver. "Don't you remember," Arena said, "Vietnam?"

The girl snatched her drink and handbag and moved to the next stool. The man followed, tripped, tugged her arm.

Arena moved like a cat in one motion up from the table across to the bar. "You want to talk to this guy, *Señorita?*"

"Absolutely not."

"Then, *hombre*, why are you here?"

The man looked at Arena's medals and stripes, his bull neck and round thick face with its crushed-in wide nose and tiny merry eyes. "She's here to be taken."

"Apparently not by you. You have ten seconds."

The man scowled drunkenly. "You don' mean it!"

Arena glanced at the soldiers guarding the door. "Assuredly I do."

The man steered a course for the door. "*Gracias, mi General,*" the girl smiled.

"You're expecting someone?"

"No. I just told *him* that, to make him go."

"It wasn't working, your strategy. May I sit?"

57

MURPHY SLID his back slowly up the wall. Between his feet on the tiny night-lit pool eight stories below a swimmer trailed a threadlike silver wake.

He reached slowly for the truss between the side girder and the ledge above; it was too far. Wind came up, rocking him; against his fingertips the concrete was smooth, cold and damp.

There was a rush of air out the window of Lupe's room, the curtains wavering. Through them he saw Lupe come into the room and speak quickly with Pablo. She crossed to the window and leaned out. "He's coming up! *Stay* here!" She ducked back into the room, checked the Uzi under the pillow, went to the door unzipping the side of her dress as Pablo slipped out the window and crouched beside Murphy on the ledge.

"Ready, *amigo?*" Pablo smiled, patting Murphy's arm. Murphy's heart went out to him for caring about another's fear more than his own.

"We're going to do fine," Murphy said.

"We've got one chance in ten," Pablo said. "*If* we watch it."

ARENA leaned over Lyman and the others, jiggling the table. "Making a couple calls," he said. "Be right back."

Newbury was waving for the waiter. "Order you another round?"

Arena shook his head. Ugly as a bulldog, Lyman thought. "I'll get a fresh one when I come down," Arena said.

"I'm serious about this deal, General," Newbury said. "I'd like to wrap it up."

"Put some money on the table," Arena said. "You don't expect *me* to pay?"

"The guerrillas are your problem."

"No, Mr. Newbury. The guerrillas are *your* problem."

"She's a nice little piece," Lyman said.

When Arena winked it seemed to Lyman like an anus closing. "We'll see if she can fuck," Arena said. He motioned to two of his bodyguards and they followed him out of the room.

THROUGH the wavering curtains they saw Lupe move to the door. She stood by it speaking, then opened it. A tall broad-shouldered man in a greenish suit came in, then a second in blue slacks and gray windbreaker. They spoke with her and she waved behind her at the room. They looked under the beds, in the bathroom, the closets. The tall one stopped at the door, feeling her up. She backed away tossing her head. They went out; Arena came in. She closed the door and slid the chain across. He tossed his jacket on the coffee table and opened the minibar and took out two glasses, ice, a bottle of gin and a bottle of tonic. She went to the bed, turned round with the Uzi in her hands. He was busy making the drinks and looked up suddenly. His hands flattened on the bar, he glanced at the door; she shook her head, speaking fast. Pablo slipped through the window and checked Arena for weapons while she held the Uzi on him.

Pablo took a small silver pistol from Arena's coat and made him put the coat on. Lupe put her high heels in her handbag. They came to the window, Lupe speaking gently to Arena as if counseling him. "You're going to be just fine, *mi General*. Just do what we say. We intend to trade you. You'll go free, so don't worry."

"They'll give you nothing for me." He shook his bearish head. "You're lost."

"Please listen. You're going with us out this window and down one flight to another room. There's a rope so you can't fall. If you try anything silly, or breathe a sound, we instantly kill you."

Lupe came first out of the window, over the girder and down. Arena stuck his head through the window, drew back. "You're going to push me," he whispered.

"If we were going to kill you," Pablo said, "you'd already be dead."

Lupe reached the seventh-floor girder, grasped the rope, leaned out and looked up. Arena squeezed through the window, flinched when he saw Murphy and twisted himself against the wall, away from the edge. "No."

Murphy single-cocked the .357. "Quick!"

Like a seal sinking back into the water, Arena slid over the edge, rope clenched in his great paws. Pablo then Murphy followed him down. Murphy climbed back up to untie the rope round the eighth-floor girder, slid the door shut and went back down after Arena and Pablo along the ledge and into his room, 708. He shouldered his backpack and took a last glance round the room, strangely anxious to stay.

"We'll have three guns on you all the time, *mi General*," Lupe said, "plus others on the stairs and in the lobby and outside. At the slightest wrong move, even with your eyes, it's over."

Pablo draped his tuxedo jacket over his arm, holding his Colt inside it. He went out and came back. "It's clear." They walked Arena down the corridor. At the elevator an old woman waited, her head perched like an ancient bird over a nest of diamonds. They went past her to the service stairs, a bellboy coming up with a tray of drinks. "Too long to wait, the elevator," Pablo said to him.

Windblown grit scurried in the stair corners. They entered the gleaming lobby, other bellboys advancing then turning away with fixed smiles when they saw there was no luggage. They went out of the staff door into the parking lot, the .357 sweat-slippery in Murphy's grasp under his jacket, Arena's arms hanging straight at his sides.

It was the Nissan, shiny with polish. Lupe drove, Murphy in front, Pablo with Arena in back. In a dark street Lupe stopped and made Arena change into a brown suit and hat. With a tube of glue she fixed a broad mustache to his face. "Remove this and you're dead," she said.

She drove east toward La Ermita. "You have a wallet with two hundred and twenty quetzales in your left coat pocket," Pablo told Arena. "There's a driver's license that says you are Arturo Valdes Moraga; you're fifty-four, born 21 January. Your wife's Jazmín Elena de Sevilla, you have two boys, Arturo and Alejandro. You have an insurance office in Jalapa, 2-47 Calle Doce. You specialize in life insurance. You live with your family in an apartment over the office. Now let's go over it, fact at a time, till you get it right."

Arena's lips smacked as he talked. Beyond La Ermita the traffic was thin, feeding out into the dark of the hills.

A string of lanterns blocked the road. Lupe geared down, clamping the Uzi between her legs. "Pretend you're asleep, *Señor* Valdes," Pablo said. "Wake up slowly, just act natural. If there has to be any killing you're the first to die."

"Four guys on the right," Lupe said. "Pablo takes them. One in the middle of the gate. Murphy takes him, then helps Pablo with the ones on the right. Two on the left by the guardhouse and two beyond. They're mine. Make sure, Pablo, that Arena gets it first."

"No one's going to get it," Pablo said.

A soldier yanked open Lupe's door. "Where to?"

"*Solo* Zacapa."

"Better hurry!" He slammed the door. "Or you'll miss curfew."

Beside the road the Río Motagua coiled and uncoiled in the starlight. Cactus on the hills seemed to be waving their arms like furtive *compañeros*. The moon rose, bigger than two nights earlier at the beach, Murphy thought, the Night of the Dead, when we too should have set out a share of our sustenance for our dead.

Lupe turned up a goat road into the hills. It was the same one they'd come down, Dona and he and Lupe and Pablo, and now it was Arena instead of Dona, and to Murphy it seemed a hideous barter he'd somehow deserved, and knew he'd never know why.

58

"WHERE were you going with this American?" Breathe deeply, steadily. Don't look what they're doing. Steadily. Don't look. She was ready but it made no difference, the electric agony darted up her arm crushing her lungs, seared into her skull. The air afire; tears boiling in her eyes, every last cell begging it to stop.

"I'm no torturer, *compañera*. But I need to know..."

The current burned faster, a white atomic flash eating through her at the speed of light; air exploded in her cells, her bones screamed. The words were in her throat but she couldn't choke them out.

"I'm trying to *save* you. Once DTI gets you it's over, *compañera*. They'll really *hurt* you. Just give me something, dear, please? So I can keep you out of their hands?"

The G-2 man sighed. His chair legs banged down in front of her face. "Drop the juice, Hermanito. She's cooked."

His boot came down on her neck as he reached for an instrument on the table. By the sounds of the instruments against the table she could tell them all apart, the electric probe with its soft thump, the knife that rattled, the bigger one that didn't, the long needle that tinkled, the other long needle with the wires attached, the other wires, their clamps, the drill, its different bits, the cigarette lighter – just a little butane lighter, anybody'd have one.

The G-2 man handed the instrument to Hermano. "Index left, Hermanito. Come come, *compañera*, don't ball your little fists! That's it, Hermano, get a good hold, twist! Twist! Side to side, do you like that, *compañera*? Gently, Hermano, not too fast! Now, *compañera* – who's the American?"

Cyclone of pain, jaws of agony crushing her arm, a train wheel riding into her body as Hermano in his big white uniform took a better grip on her fingernail with the yellow needle-nosed pliers that said "Case" on one side, agony exploding inside her, and she must have deprived them terribly, these men, for them to do this, just block the synapse, you can do it, it's only integument separating from the lunule, membranes splitting, cells ripping down their walls, electric cries up the ganglia, my brain converting them like a speaker does electric signals, Oh Jesus please help me *Oh Dear Father*.

"Harder now, Hermanito! You should see her face..."

The fingernail was coming out now and she begged it to hurry, realized she was choking and made her neck relax against the chain clamping it to the metal frame on which she lay, felt the warm relief of blood welling down her knuckles.

"This grieves me, *compañera*. I'm sick. I hate a world that's forced to do this. Please help me – please?"

The boot that smelled so sickly strong of cordovan polish lurched back from her sight and came zooming forward but she'd made allowances, told herself stop screaming the cheekbone's not broken, her stupid nose pouring its weakness on the ground – stop pulling your arms back, it chokes the chain. His boot crunched again into her jaw, and she begged *Dear God let me die please do it quickly*.

HILLS jumped up startled from the Nissan's headlights, a sawmill's dark windows flickered past, a white goat gleamed red eyes in a town named Matanzas – Massacres. The road climbed north into fog then rain, pines teetering out of the black. Even with the windows open the car smelled of Arena.

A man and burro shied from the lights. A few huts, flash of dog's eyes, then jungle, frenzy of tree frogs, thunder of rain pelting billions of leaves, water chanting in ditches, pines moaning in the wind. Another town leaped from the mist – Niño Perdido – Lost Child, a few huts miserably ragged in the rain, brown runoff sluicing between them.

Beyond Cobán, Lupe turned east away from the Army Base and picked up the road to San Pedro Carchá, up and down through cutover jungle, skunks and raccoons scuttling from the lights, down a long hill and left over a bridge, a river and banana trees below, through the main square where topiary shrubs threw leaping shadows across the façade of the ruined cathedral, down a soggy alley of shuttered shops and rats loping for cover, two men arm-in-arm shielding their eyes from the lights, then a weedy track past bedraggled huts and into a stone shed with a tin roof and a rusty garage door.

Lupe shut the door and lit a candle on an upended engine block. She and Pablo gagged Arena with her pink silk scarf and took him outside to piss. They tied his wrists behind him and Lupe blew out the candle.

Outside the stars were afire. Lupe walked uphill and Pablo led Arena and Murphy down to the chilled mushy riverbank. The *Río* churned round a half-sunk trunk cab, in its lee a tethered canoe, river chill up their thighs as they climbed in, Arena in the middle, Pablo poling downriver, the stars bobbing on the current, black sandbars sparkling, a chain of cormorants scattering white wakes ahead, occasionally the smell of drying fish, humans and ordure where a hut stood by the bank.

The smoke of morning's first fires came upriver, the river dropping into a deep *cañon*, the jungle cut to raw slopes, lights scattered among huts.

Pablo poled ashore and ran them up a slippery steep trail to a tin-roofed shack and unlocked the padlock. Murphy pushed Arena ahead of him into the room and shut the door. Holding a flashlight in his teeth Pablo dragged bundled banana clumps from the middle of the floor, under them a trapdoor with a rope ladder down to a pit hollowed from the earth, rootlets like white earthworms down its walls, on one side a mat and red blanket and a white plastic pail.

Pablo lit a kerosene lantern. He made Arena sit on the rush mat then tied his wrists behind him to a thick root. Cross-legged on fat thighs, Arena rubbed his chin against his shoulder, hunched forward, straining his bonds. Pablo loosened the pink scarf and held a bottle of water for him to suck.

Arena drank some water and spat the last on Pablo's leg. "Kill me now," he said. He ran his tongue over his upper front teeth, grimaced. "They'll give you nothing for me."

Pablo retied the gag. "If he does anything, shoot him in the head." He climbed the rope ladder, opened the trapdoor, stepped out and shut it.

Arena hunched over his fat legs, trickling sweat, eyes prowling, trouser knees stretched tight, feet big in muddy river-soaked shoes.

He jerked his chin: come here. Murphy went closer. Arena mumbled through his gag, nodding his chin down, pointing with it. Murphy moved back, shook his head. Arena growled louder, eyes wide.

The .357's grooved trigger felt nice against the inside of Murphy's finger. "Just give me a reason," he said.

There were footsteps and the door lifted, daylight dropping in. Lupe came down the rope ladder. "Go up," she told Murphy, ignoring his eyes.

59

PABLO was not upstairs. Through cracks in the walls Murphy watched the daylight grow between the mountain avocados contorted like frozen dancers round the shack, torn garments of silver sphagnum hanging from their arms. From one side of the shack he could see the gray sparkle where the river rounded a brown abutment of cliffs. Below were the glossy crowns of riparian trees, uphill a red-muddy slope, and beyond it a few huts trailing thin smoke, a woman with a burro going down to the river.

White sun flamed through the boughs. From below a rooster called; another answered from above. A mule brayed disconsolately. The air grew hot. A huge black beetle rattled in cornhusks in the corner of the hut. Flies sparkled through shafts of sunlight. Blackbirds chattered, toucans croaked. The tin roof creaked as the sun bore down. Acaris called, "*Fe-liz, fe-liz*"; the incessant wail of tree frogs like the river's steady rustle faded in and out of mind.

Lupe came up and Murphy went down. Arena squatted like an apostate buddha on his mat. The floor above creaked as Lupe paced it. The air stank of kerosene; the dirt walls sweated in the lantern's light.

There was motion upstairs and Lupe came down. Murphy went up and Pablo was there. "We'll see," he said.

"They *have* her?"

"Don't know. She's on our list – the ones they have to give us."

"Will they?"

"If they don't find us first. Dona didn't know this place. She didn't know this part."

"You mean they can't torture it out of her."

"That's what I said."

Lupe came up. "He wants to use the bucket."

Murphy and Pablo went down. Murphy loosened Arena from the wall and he stood suddenly and jerked off his gag, rubbing his face and mouth with his big flat hands, swinging his head from side to side. He bent to untie his ankles. "No," Pablo said. "Use it like that."

Arena pulled the bucket to him, unbuckled his trousers and squatted down on the bucket, his urine spattering in, then great soft plops. Murphy held his breath. "You have no hygienic paper?" Arena said.

"No."

"Pigs!" Arena stood and hitched his trousers, smacked out the lantern and knocked Pablo into the wall and Murphy slugged him with the Magnum and Arena punched him in the crotch and the gun boomed, smashing his ears, flames darting up from the spilt kerosene. Daylight leaped down as Lupe jumped into the pit and whacked the Uzi on Arena's head and he fell grabbing at her, and she hit his temple and he eased down onto his face, blood pumping from his thigh.

"We're cooked," Lupe said. Pablo threw Arena's blanket over the spilled kerosene, relit the wick. He retied Arena's wrists behind him; he and Murphy turned Arena over and Murphy cut off Arena's powder-burned trouser leg and slit it for a compress, wrap and tourniquet. Arena's thigh was thick as a man's waist, mottled brown. His broken femur crunched.

"He hit the gun," Murphy said.

"We should go now," Lupe said.

"Not till night," Pablo answered. "How you going to move *him*?"

Lupe went up. Arena's head hammered the floor, his other leg quivering, teeth grinding. "That was very foolish, General," Pablo said. "Now you will probably die."

With two planks from the trapdoor Murphy splinted the thigh. He wrapped it tighter. "Can you hear, pig?"

Arena gasped, nodded. Murphy loosened the wrapping. "That better?"

Arena nodded. Murphy wrenched it tighter, Arena's teeth bared. "No!"

"San Tomás – up on the Río de la Pasión – who attacked it?"

"N'not mine – General Blandia's –"

Pablo stood over them. "General Blandia's in Santa Cruz."

Murphy clenched his hand to keep it from punching the wound. "I'll twist this leg right off..."

"Go easy," Pablo whispered.

Murphy waved him away. "Tell me quick, San Tomás –"

"I don't know. I didn't oh please God stop this pain. You have anything, please anything, stop it?"

"The Americans with your units – who are they?"

"No – oh God Jesus – no Americans!"

"We have *aguardiente* – want some?"

Arena nodded, eyes wide, sweat and tears pouring down his cheeks. Pablo uncorked the bottle.

"Wait." Murphy took the rum. "Tell me right, the first time. I know most of the story, just need you to fill me in. Tell it right the first time and you can have rum. Tell me one lie and I pour it down the hole in your leg."

"You're not even Guatemalan."

"The Americans – *who*?

"*Me duele mucho*! Wait!"

"*Who*!"

"Advisors, Jesus!"

"*Who*?"

"Counterinsurgency. The Agency. You know this!"

"Who burnt my village?"

"God it hurts." Spittle ran down Arena's chin. "Want to know who burned your lousy little village, wherever in hell it is? *You* did." He coughed; it sounded like a laugh. "Your *own* country. God did, then – maybe you like that better?"

"I want the *names*."

"*Who* pays your taxes? *Who* votes? How many times have we been invaded by *your* Marines? Who changes our government like a whore changes underpants! Who changes your own government, whenever it wants? Kills your president and his brother and gets away with it?" Again the croaked laugh stiffened by pain. "It's fools like you, make the world such a dangerous place."

"Tell me. Or to hell with it all I'll kill you."

"Easy, *amigo*," Pablo said.

You really *are* a fool," Arena gasped. "Don't you *know*, what really runs things?"

"Who's telling you to hit the drug flights?"

"Can't you see – same answer... snuffing the independents."

Wind guttered the lantern; the trapdoor opened and daylight dived down. "Pablo!" Lupe whispered.

"SHE'S NOT in here." Lyman shoved the folder of photos back at Vodega. "Not the one who trapped Arena."

Vodega opened a new dossier, tossed another photo across the table.

Lyman sipped his coffee. Beyond the window soldiers

were doing an arms drill in the yard. The photo was a young woman, hair cropped, face and lips puffy, eyes bruised, nearly closed. "Not her, either."

Vodega smiled. "This one we've got. Murphy's *chica*."

"The *doctora*? Lyman dropped the photo and stared at it. "Just think – his whole world's come down around his ears. She was all he had left –"

"Sad."

"– except Arena."

"They want a Mexico exchange. Theirs released first."

Vodega peeled down a fingernail, gnawed it.

"Tell them legally you can't. Offer them close to the border."

Vodega smiled. "If it's provisional Mexico will get very pissed."

"Fuck them. Don't you want Murphy?"

"Not like you do. I think you have a screw loose about this dude."

"We *all* need him dead, Angelo. He's in everybody's way."

"Yours more than anyone else's. Why?"

Lyman looked at Vodega. Yes, he thought, sometimes you can be frank even with people you don't like. "I want out, Angelo. The Agency won't let me go until the pilot's done." Lyman tipped up the photo, smiled at the swollen gaze of one who knows all that's coming is unending agony then death. He felt his sex stir. "Do you suppose he knew her, from before… ?"

"He was shot up, she fixed him. In that village where we got the priest."

"He never gave you much, that priest –"

"He's not done yet."

She could have been pretty, the one in the photo. Nice small tits, slim waist, nice hips and long legs with one thigh raised trying to cover herself. Sweet bruised skin. Key to Murphy's heart.

THROUGH A CRACK in the shed wall Murphy watched the patrol coming house to house down the hill. "Three more below!" Lupe said. "No, five."

"We'll tell them to pull back," Murphy said, "or we kill him."

Pablo came up, took the Uzi. "Beat it!"

Lupe looked at Murphy distractedly, back at Pablo, gripping his hands. "At the end, please, let them take you? You'll be on the list."

Pablo clasped her face in his hands for an instant, like a prayer. She reached for him but he pushed her away, toward the rope ladder. "Go!" he told Murphy, his eyes fierce.

"Better we cover them from here."

"There's a tunnel down there and you're taking him through it. Go!"

Beneath the ladder Lupe had pushed aside the dirt to a second trapdoor, a black core down into the earth. "You're going to have to crawl one-legged," she yelled at Arena. She turned angry eyes on Murphy. "You first!"

"What about Pablo?"

"Somebody's got to stay behind, cover this up, stall them."

With a roar Murphy leaped back up the stairs. Pablo was watching the soldiers climbing from below.

"Get down there!" Murphy yelled. His chest was shaking, he couldn't breathe. "I'll shoot you! Get down there!"

Pablo ran to the other side of the shack, peered at the soldiers coming down through the huts. "We've got two minutes."

"You son of a bitch I'll shoot you!" Murphy's gun was shaking badly and he held his right wrist in his left hand to steady it.

Pablo looked into his eyes. "Perhaps it's better."

Lupe went first, Arena dragging his leg and moaning through his gag, then Pablo. Murphy shut the trap and shoved the loose dirt and straw back over it, scattered dirt and straw over Arena's blood.

"*Hola!*" A man's voice. "Anyone in this house come out!"

Murphy went up, shut the top trap. "Men!" The voice called, "I'll count ten then you fire on the hut. Cut it apart! One..."

Smooth snicks of steel as the soldiers readied their guns. Murphy dragged the first banana clump back over the trap.

"Three..."

He threw them one on top of the other.

"Seven!"

"*Hola!*" Murphy yelled, stacking the last ones, "*Hola! Hola!*"

"Get out here!"

He shoved the Magnum into the banana clumps and opened the door. Hands up, he went out into the bright hot sun waiting for the bullets to hit.

60

"YOU'RE NOT going to believe this!"

"Not if *you* tell me, Howie."

"We have him."

"Fantastic! Safe?"

"Not Arena, goddammit, Murphy! His chickie, too."

Merck said nothing, then, "Where?"

"Right under my feet."

"Where the hell's Arena?"

"Murphy may know. Where we got him there was a tunnel. We think some others, maybe Arena, went out it."

"Where?"

"Goes uphill to empty houses."

"You mean you didn't *secure* the area?"

"I wasn't *there*, Curt. Be happy with what you get."

"What's he said?"

"That he was hanging out in this deserted hut."

"Crush his fucking nuts!"

"He's holding."

"He made us a lot of trouble in San Francisco, this guy."

"Soon as we finish talking with him it's over."

"We *need* Arena back, Howie. They took him right from under your nose."

"I'm not his bodyguard."

You *trained* those two guys! And they're jerking each other off while your friends go out the window with Arena. How you think that looks up here?"

"I'm not your PR guy, either."

Merck caught his breath. Like a puppy, Lyman thought, that's been tearing at something. *Pant pant.* "For now be happy with what you got," Lyman said. "You got Murphy, his chickie. She's one of their best doctors, a fucking surgeon."

"I don't *care* from no doctors, Howie. I certainly don't care from no pilot. What I *care* about's Arena. Think what we've invested. What we have to gain. He's too good to lose, and *you* lost him."

"He's not lost yet."

"Even if he isn't, you gotta give up a whole lot of people. People you ain't finished with."

"Not if we get Arena first."

"If you *do* have to trade, Howie, don't fight too much about the numbers. If they want two hundred people then give them two hundred..."

"Lotta people they're asking for don't live here anymore."

"Give 'em others. Go get new ones and give them to them. Trick is, get back Arena. We get him back we can ride a sympathy vote in Congress to more appropriations."

"I don't know what's worse, Curt. The guerrillas or the Hill."

"How we talking with the ones who have Arena?"

"Pay phones to pay phones. They're moving too fast to catch."

"Think of what we been through, this Soviet Union thing. Think what *I* been through, my family. Seventy years of lost lives, millions of lost lives. All because back in 1917 we didn't grab ourselves by the balls and jump in!"

"Like Nam?"

"We *took* Nam, Howie! For over ten years we kept the wheels turning! Kept a stable balance."

"I thought the idea was win."

"Win? That's what we got now, Russia, all that. You call that a win?" Merck stopped, to sip his coffee maybe, three thousand miles away. "Nam taught you all the wrong lessons, Howie. You go slow where you should run, and run where you should hide. I wonder maybe the Agency's too *into* you. Maybe I shouldna given you, you know, such a hand up?"

"It's your nuts I'm saving down here. Long before this Arena thing. This pilot thing."

"You're not saving anybody's nuts. You could lose yours. It happened under *your* nose. You playing for *their* team?"

"You're beginning to piss me off."

Merck laughed. "Being pissed off counts for nothing in this world."

IN THE PINE GROVE was a spring between black rocks where blue *sayune* flowers, violets, and red wild begonias grew. There were water spiders on the spring and the water was achingly cold and the cool resiny air rose up the bronze trunks into the golden day.

"*Tell* me," said the first G-2 man. "Where are Lupe and Pablo?"

"She's stalling again," said the other. "Let's do some teeth."

"YOU FLEW SLICKS for the United States of America! That's your *country*! What you doing tied up in *this* shit?"

He was tall and very black, trace of southern accent, Levis, muddy running shoes, a work shirt.

"You're the one that hit my village. I know you. You're the one."

"Man, you're not making *any* sense."

"The whole village. Little children, old people, everybody." Murphy pulled himself along the bars till the chain stopped him. "The people in the river. A woman and a brand-new baby and a fourteen-year-old boy..."

The black man drew up a stool in the corridor, tilted his head to see between the bars. "I don't know you from Adam. I know nothing 'bout no village and people in no river. I'm just Second Secretary at the American Embassy, and *I'm* the one gets called when some American gets his ass in deep shit. But to get you *out* of this very deep shit you're in, I first need to know why you're *in* it."

"There was an old woman, Consuela. Little children..."

"You getting crazy 'gain, brother. I don't know *anything* 'bout none of this old woman stuff." The black man leaned into the bars. "But I do know you're in some very deep shit up in the States, in *addition* to the very, very deep shit you're obviously in down here. So what the fuck you *done*?"

"Who *are* you?"

"I told you."

"You don't even *know* who you are! Oh yes you do."

"I know I got to hustle to keep the Guatemalan Army from just *wrecking* you. That's understandable, they want Arena. But instead of ripping you apart they might be persuaded to free you, wherever you want to go, with some money to go on. If you help them find Arena."

61

THERE WERE THREE and they wasted no time. They tied her hands to the steel bar behind her. They stretched her tight between the bar and the wires round her ankles and two held her mouth open while the third took a Black & Decker drill and drilled into the root of one lower molar. He curled the end of an electrode and shoved it down into the root. He went behind her and drilled a second hole into the base of her spine and twisted an electrode into it. They locked down her head so she couldn't shake it and snapped on the gray US Army field telephone clamped to the electrodes, and turned up the current.

"I JUST TALKED with the top guy here," the black man said to Murphy through the bars. "They've got your doctor lady in custody down in Antigua. They were going to let her go – you should've kept your mouth shut. Now they know she's with you, that she's part of this Arena thing."

"Let her go. Then I'll tell you whatever you want."

Two soldiers unlocked the door and the black man and a smaller younger man in a maroon blazer came in, trying to step lightly in the muck. "This's Carmen here," the black man said, "he's the Embassy translator. My Spanish ain't so great..."

"Jesus," Carmen said, "what they do to you?" He bent down, looked into Murphy's face. "Oh my God Jesus, what they do?"

"We gotta move quick," the black man said. "They're going to ruin him."

"Pigs." Carmen bit his lip. "Goddamned pigs!"

The black man knelt down. "Listen, pal, you gotta come straight." He shook his head. "Otherwise I can't help you."

"Have to get him out of here." Carmen glanced round. "You!" he said to one of the soldiers. "Get a stretcher. We're going to move this man upstairs." The soldier backed away, shook his head.

"I've tried," Lyman said. "The Guats say no. Their jurisdiction."

Carmen leaned near. "You want me to tell them not to hurt her? To be ready to let her go, with you? That you're going to tell them where to find Arena?"

Murphy's words were like chunks of splintered stick coming out of his mouth. There was cool air all over his skin, as if he were going to faint. After a while, he thought, pain is its own drug. "First let her go."

The black man's face came at him. "Tell *us* and they'll send you and her to Mexico, Cuba, anywhere you want. They do it all the time, these trades."

"They'll even broadcast an amnesty," Carmen said, "so your friends can give up Arena without bloodshed. So they can go with you."

"No one knows who you are except us," the black man said. "We're the only friends you have."

"Guatemala's gone through too much," Carmen added, "it's on the road to democracy now, doesn't need this suffering, this reminder."

"I'm afraid they're going to hurt somebody else," said the black man. "I've seen how these people work. If you don't talk."

"They've got somebody," Carmen said. "Somebody you know. You probably shouldn't have told them about that village, where you were... Now, I'm afraid, they're going to do him harm."

"They killed everybody there."

"When it comes to torture," the black man whispered, "the Guats can't be touched. For thirty years now they've been trained by the best. Can make you suffer endlessly and never die. Remember your Revelations: *you'll long for death, but death will elude you?*"

THEY DRAGGED HER from the white soundproof room down a cement corridor of white solid steel doors through a cellblock where naked, beaten women gripped the bars whispering but she could not hear, down another corridor of mould-green damp concrete to a rancid stone room with a steel door in the center of the floor. One knelt beside her. "Last chance. We need *names.*"

She looked up at him, and at the end of all things she understood, *him*, the agony he could not expiate. "That is the problem. I have no names."

He yanked open the steel door, dragged her over the edge. Her head fell into the hole; she scrambled for the memory that was *all*, that made it all true, tumbled down and slammed head first into icy muck, thought the steel door shutting was the noise of her head hitting. Her head was under; she pulled it up. There was air, mud cool against her skin. Oh God, she thought, I'm saved. I've got away.

THE PAIN was bigger than his body, than this corroded sweating room. He saw the curve of the earth from the sand spit – the pain was bigger than the sea, the earth, filled all space, erased the stars; you could scream it louder than the universe but it would never go away.

They asked him questions and were very angry and others came and asked the same questions and he begged them for answers to give them, the answers they wanted, these men with their crisp uniforms and white coats and hard hands, but he didn't know the answers they wanted and wouldn't tell the ones he had, thinking they won't know, but they knew, they kept knowing, even when he did not say they seemed to know.

The black man came in. "One o'clock," he said in Spanish. He rubbed his face, a whiskery sound.

THE DARKNESS was absolute, the air like mud. A gurgle of new sewage cascaded into the pit; Dona held her breath, wiped the muck from her face. The sides of the pit were too slimy to climb, even if her hands could do it.

Something moved, a snake, in the sludge. Kill me quickly. Moving – an arm? Yes an arm, a face. Long hair thick with muck. "You," Dona said. "Speak to me!"

A hand touched her face, the pain intense. The woman mumbled.

"Who are you?" Dona said.

Again the mumble.

"Can I move you, help you?" She slipped her arms under the woman's, pushed her up. "You've been here how long? Tell me!"

"—"

"I can't understand you. Here, let me feel your mouth, it's clogged with mud." She wiped muck from the woman's face; there were no eyes. The woman's head jerked back as Dona felt inside her mouth: no teeth, no tongue. Dona skimmed water from the muck and washed the woman's face, brushed back her hair. "I will ask you questions, yes or no questions. Make a sound if it is yes. You are Quiché? No? Ladino? Yes?" She tilted back the woman's head, cleaned the mud from her ears. "Not long will they keep me here. So tell me what I can do for you."

62

THEY TOOK HIM to a cell with plywood walls. A child sat on a wooden chair, two men in black hoods behind him. Dark hair, skinny arms, one bright with burns. Ankles and arms clamped to the chair. Jesús.

"You wouldn't do this. Not even you."

"It's their turf," the black man said. "Kid's not American, nothing we can do. Only you can stop it."

"Even *you* wouldn't do this."

"We need answers," said a man with a thin mustache and sideburns. "You're making us do this. You're the evil one."

TWO MEN came down the sewer on ropes and tied another rope under Dona's arms. "Bring *her* up too!" she said.

"Who?"

"Her! This woman whose tongue you've cut out, she's still alive."

"There's no one here but you, madwoman."

They hosed her down in a bright tiled room. One pinned her to the floor while the other felt up inside her, back and front, pulled down his pants, his flesh like stone inside her.

They chained her to the wall and left. Sperm dribbled down her thigh. They came back with a stooped, portly man in his sixties in a white lab coat. He shut the door softly behind him, checked a clipboard, shined a small flashlight in her eyes. "So! The young doctor!" He had a conscientious manner, smile wrinkles at the corners of his eyes, wire-rim glasses, a little gray mustache and a kindly mouth. A bureaucrat, she wondered, prison inspector, anything, there's hope... He nodded at her, her torturers, glanced at his watch. "Pick up tempo," he said, and left.

"ARENA'S in a warehouse above Carchá. An adobe warehouse with a tin roof, banana trees."

"There's no banana trees above Carchá, Mr. Murphy. The elevation's too high. We will now spoon out one of the boy's eyes. *You* choose, Mr. Murphy: right or left?"

The man with the thin mustache and sideburns held up the spoon like a magician ready to perform a well-known trick. A soldier unclipped the electrodes from Jesús's fingers and tipped back his chair, the boy's head rolling; the man took it one-handed and with a flick of his wrist dipped the spoon into and under the boy's eye; the boy sat up screaming. "Tell us?" the man said.

He told them how he'd flown down, stumbled on the village, the boy'd done nothing, knew nothing, just a kid, but they wouldn't listen, refused his lies, refused his truths because they weren't enough, didn't go all the way. The man with the thin mustache spooned out the other eye too; it hung down Jesús's cheek on its connective tissue like a baby squid, Murphy's wrists bloody from trying to break the cuffs, his arms nearly torn from the sockets, but it did no good, nothing did any good. Die, Jesús, he prayed, urging him along, it's not that hard, child, die quickly now, die from shock, die from pain, die. Over the boy's upraised pleading face the man with the thin mustache slid his plastic bag, the boy's mouth sucked it taut, his ribs heaving.

In the corner of the floor was a scrap of red Indiana, a Kekchi girl's bracelet. On the plywood wall were splashes of blood and the words *Boise Cascade*.

"It's on *your* soul," said the man with the thin mustache. "This death."

WITH RIFLE BUTTS they beat him along a corridor into a cell. It was too small to stand or lie except diagonally across a sewer hole. Wind down the corridor swayed a bulb hung by its wires, the shadows of the bars sliding back and forth.

From the other cells came moans, weeping, a far-off solitary cough that made it seem for an instant this might be a hospital. In the next cage a man lay with legs bent, an emaciated, white-bearded face. He shoved himself up, wiped dribble from his mouth and squirmed his hand through the bars. "My God! It's you!"

Murphy took the frail, wet hand. "*Hola, compañero.*"

"Don't you remember? It's me, Father Miguel!"

"YOU GOT nine hours."

"The Guats'll stretch it."

"*Can* you find Arena in nine hours, Howie? That's the question."

"I'll do my best."

"You know what I think of people's best? It's never good enough."

"That's a problem with you, Curt. You're too tight on people."

"You call this tight, Howie? We ask you to carry on Kit's work, and you don't succeed in raising contributions. We ask you to explain to Arena the tactical value of pulling in the Colombians, and you've seemed to fail at that too. Then Arena gets kidnapped on your watch."

"I wasn't assigned to *watch* him!"

"He's your *baby*. How many times I have to explain this with you?"

"Explain it *to* me, Curt?"

"Call it how you like. But you don't find Arena before noon, Howie, things are going to be bad on you."

"You threatening me?"

"You know what I'm doing."

"You don't want to, Curt. Not like you did with Kit. I'm ready for that. You'll all get hurt. Badly hurt."

"You're back in your private agenda again, Howie. Your private traumas. You got nine hours to find Arena. Safe and sound. Any hope you ever had of getting out of the field depends on this. You don't get Arena back, Howie, you're stuck with us forever."

Lyman put down the receiver and lit a cigarette. Nine minutes past three a.m. First one of the day. Still keep it at ten. Twelve yesterday, eleven before, but most of last week ten. Normal, for your hands to shake like this. Too cold. Cold in here.

Three eleven. Feel the smoke like brandy in your soul. Rising fire in your brain. Lovely scented leaf with the power of the sun.

He locked the MACRO room door and went through the three sets of doors and outside. The night hung heavy and cold, the stars like Christmas lights.

"YOU'RE LUCKY," Father Miguel said. "It's better to be shot right away."

Down the aisle a man was coughing, shallow and repetitive. Picking blood from his stubble Murphy watched a cockroach select its delicate way across the sewage on the floor. "It's pathetic, the way you try not to hate."

"We've had our time for hating and wanting and running around. Now it's time to thank God and live in peace with what's left. You know that."

"Who the hell is that coughing? Why doesn't he stop?"

The cough was like a pendulum: *cough-cough... cough-cough.*

"It's an old man, Santana. They're shooting him too."

Through the canopy and rotor blur the Mekong sky is porcelain blue. Five thousand feet below are the verdant evil hills. Okie scanning right, chewing gum. Always chewing gum. Okie's black helmet with the Grateful Dead on one side and the Chicago Bears on the other.

Back on the deck three grunts, an ARVN intelligence man and a US Special Forces captain with a woman prisoner and a little girl. Slick riding the thermals, appreciative flutter from the blades, Okie popping gum. The US Special Forces captain shoves up between Murphy and Okie. "These people don't have no feelin's," he says.

The US Special Forces captain has tears in his eyes, from the wind. "I been asking her some questions, me and Dao here, and Dao was holding her kid out the door, you know, to make her talk? The stupid fucker drops the kid and the woman just sits there, not a change in her face. Fuckin animals!"

"Take it," Murphy screams at Okie. He unbuckles and climbs through to the deck. "You did what?"

"He dropped her by accident, Dao did. Don't get unbent."

Dao holding the woman by the hair, a .45 against the side of her face. She is looking out the door.

Murphy takes out his pistol; the Special Forces captain shakes his head. "You're getting out of line, trooper."

Dao speaks in Vietnamese, turns the .45 on Murphy. The grunts stir, reaching for rifles. The captain steps back.

That was it. The moment it all went bad, the moment that led to this. When you should have shot him and didn't. Then came the court martial but they won, so they sent you into the very worst, every time you and Okie, Okie chewing gum, every time a jet was down and Charlie was waiting, every hot LZ, till Okie got it, and they gave you Searles, and then Finkelstein, and when he got it and you got wounded for the second time they gave up and sent you home.

63

"IT ISN'T WRONG," the priest said, "to try to make a better world."

"I wasn't trying to make a better world," Murphy answered. "I was trying to please myself."

"We all do that. Even God did that, inventing us. Though why I'll never know. Or perhaps I shall." He coughed; it sounded like a laugh. "You took on too much: the Army, your own government. That's like trying to battle God. I use that word too easily, God. I'm not sure I believe in God."

"Then why are you a priest?"

"Because here it was the best way to do something, to make a better world. And because I loved Christ, believed in what he said, about how to live and how to treat each other."

"All I've learned is that the world is evil..."

"You were like a bird caught in a hurricane, there was nothing you could do. There was your government supporting a fascist dictatorship as it nearly always does. And you were smuggling drugs, a role they didn't want to share with anyone but the Guatemalan Army and, as you say, the Colombians. So your intelligence agency, with the help of your Mafia, hunted you down, killing a lot of Guatemalans in the process."

"That's what I've learned: every attempt to do good only brings more evil. But I wasn't even trying to do good. I cared more about my so-called love than the person I loved."

Again the priest coughed. "That's love. Even God does that."

Footsteps echoed down the stairs to their cells. The black man positioned himself before Murphy's. "I can stop them," he said. Murphy dropped his head, uninterested. "I can get your woman."

Murphy looked up. "You could have stopped them long ago. You always could have."

"I was home in bed with my wife when this village of yours got hit. If it ever did."

"That's not true." It was an old, worn voice, Guat accent, the next cell. A small skinny man, hair tangled and white. "You *were* there, when his village got attacked."

"Who the hell are you?"

"*I* saw you. Don't you remember, the helicopter? When you kept the one named Angelo from kicking out my teeth?"

The black man peered down at Father Miguel, chuckled. "That's what comes of good deeds. I should've dropped you out the door."

"But you didn't. You stopped him from kicking me. Why?"

"Might have needed you later. You turned out not to be worth much."

The priest smiled. "Most of us aren't. How about you?"

Lyman laughed. "Not much, either. Call it fate."

"It isn't fate. You don't have to live this way. None of us does."

You won't much longer." Lyman leaned back against the far cell, arms crossed. "And after you're dead there isn't even going to be a *trace* of you."

"Think back over all the years and all the pain it's caused you, think of all the love you've had to throw away."

"I'm down here to ask *him* one last time..."

"There's no good in asking. You know that."

"For *his* sake. Can't you see you've made your rules too strong?"

"The rules of goodness are inside you. That's why you fight them so hard. The rule never to hurt people is engraved right on your soul. And every breath you take, you can feel it."

Lyman stretched, arms behind his head. "I'm going upstairs, get some sleep. They'll wake me when you're dead."

SANTANA'S incessant hack through the bars. A man snoring, another gasping in a dream. From somewhere upstairs came faint moans and begging voices. On the cell's concrete back wall so many names carved in the khaki-colored slime: José María Montejos, 4-4-51—11-11-90. Gloria Casales, 19-10-57—4-91, Jaime Aidaño, how many others, names with new names carved atop them, names old in the stone?

He could leave his own body and stand beside them, *in* them, think their thoughts and feel what they felt as they carved the day of their deaths into the damp cold stone. Brothers, sisters, we are all the same body and the same blood. For there's only two human families, prisoners and guards. He saw them with sweaty numb fingers digging their names with a piece of metal into the stone, as they imagined how the bullets would feel.

Tick tick ticktick tick water dripped from the ceiling into the muck of the floor. Did you stare into the muzzles? See the flash?

Curious but timid, a rat ducked its head through the bars, darted over his foot and down the sewer hole. She said to live a good life you have to do as much good as you can.

He folded his fingers, felt the pulse between them. Blanched frightened skin.

A rooster crowed but it couldn't be dawn. Wakened by a weasel, something. Santana's cough was like a man trying to remind you of something. There's no time, Santana, to be reminded. It doesn't matter, your cough.

Stuck on a car fender, little kid. Father gets you down. He could see it, feel the bees stinging, rough grass. Walking by the road, skipping rocks across it. Fingers stuck with cold to the rifle barrel, whitetail diving over the ridge, crack of the Winchester splitting the sky. Girls in the back seat pulling down their underpants, windows of frozen breath. Gulls over the sand spit, scream of the sea. Rites of love all come to nothing. Man just another seed eating out its heart to populate the stars.

A truck, starting. Couldn't be. You can live it all in the next two hours. The whole thing. Live it fast. Don't be afraid. Accept it's coming and be ready to meet it.

Bell. Two. Three. Four. Five. Let it not be six, Lord.

Six. Somewhere a generator shuddered, took life. Boots tramping, wail of a gate. Pure water of Montana's Sun River off the Chinese Wall through lodgepole and meadow, down in swirls of light, red-gilled trout, grass tan like elk hide. Sonora cactus *cañons*, the air a hot knife. Dawn rising over the world at fifty thousand feet. Scents of love and flowers and blood, fresh blood of a kill and old blood between a woman's legs and dried blood of people lying on the ground, one's own miraculous blood spreading over the dirt.

Pain travels at the speed of light.

AN OFFICER and soldiers came softly down the aisle. They opened Santana's cell and led him out, confused and disarrayed. Then Father Miguel. "So you're really going to do it," he said. They tied Murphy's wrists with rope and led the three of them back up the oily green stairwell that Murphy could not remember descending. He saw everything clearly, every grain of concrete and flake of rust, the scintillating windows and the stars dying behind them, years passing in a moment, a marred boot heel rising on the stair before him, Santana's threadbare sandal *slap slap*, when he had looked into her eyes and in them had seen the sun in his own. The wall, a cold rail, brushed him, click of opening door, snap of rifles, long lean wall of pockmarked concrete cavitied with stains, three wooden posts before it.

One soldier came close. "You want the blindfold, *hombre*?"

He shook his head. "Where do you shoot?"

"Straight for the heart."

"*Amigo* –"

"*Sí?*"

"Don't shoot me in the head."

"You'll feel nothing."

"It's a joke," Santana said, beside him, "to end this way."

Beyond the soldiers checking their magazines was another concrete wall with a tiled roof and above it the early blue of day, the cries of birds and the distant morning clatter of the town, roosters and dogs, a donkey calling. "It's a shame," Father Miguel said, "a Goddamned shame." A fly buzzed round, warming his wings in the new sun. He rose like a diamond up over the parade ground and flashed away; rifles clicked as the soldiers brought them to their shoulders, but there was still time for the world in all its glory, *her* flesh soft scented and sinuous, the apple, the wine, the core of the tree red like a beating heart, as we go down the tunnel of our love back to the first days, the first day of all, before time.

Black muzzles pointing with little black eyes. Black hard steel. "Bless us O Lord for these Thy gifts," he heard himself saying, "which we are about to receive." He realized he was saying grace, the oldest prayer, felt a warm scarred hand grip his shoulder.

Flame spit from the guns, the thunder in one hideous long roar. There was nothing; he floated in an ether of pure perception. It's true, he thought, you just don't feel it.

He would find Clint now, tell him about Sherrie, how she was going to be fine, that Saul would steer her straight, good Saul with his beard and calm reflective manner, he would find Dona now as soon as she passed over and darling come quickly, it's better here.

A loud bang made him jump. An officer with a pistol moved from Santana and fired again, this time into Father Miguel's temple. Blood hissed over the dirt; chunks of Father Miguel's brain stuck to Murphy's face. The officer jabbed the hot barrel into Murphy's temple. "We haven't shot you yet. Want to live?"

The soldiers were lining up again, reloading. A flock of multicolored parrots burst from a tree.

"We give you one last chance," the officer said. "Give us *names*!"

His mouth was too dry to speak. He tried to look into the officer's face but the world was dancing. There was the smell of blood and excrement and dirt and sweat and anguish and burnt powder and seared oil, the calls of men and birds, the soaring music of the sun, the brilliant sky in which all the worlds were coalesced, blood crashing through the streams and canyons of his body. The pistol whacked his jaw. "Want to *live*?"

64

THIS TIME they did not take her to the interrogation
block but to a long low basement room with full-
body human targets on a sandbag wall. Two of them
held her wrists; a third took out his pistol but she would
not flinch nor close her eyes, and the shot crushed her hearing and her stomach caved in monstrous pain, awful agony
each instant worse as she writhed in circles on the floor
begging them to kill her. "Kill you?" one mocked. "You're
going free!"

BACK IN HIS CELL he stared through the gritty rusted
bars. The other prisoners watched him suspiciously now
that he had returned from the dead. *La vida es sueño*, Consuela had said, and death a dream also, for we're dead and
dream ourselves alive, hold these bars in our hands and
think they are real.

If I could only tell you now, my love, all I've learned,
how much I've learned from you, how I've always loved
you from the first moment, the moment I was born, from
long before. If I could only tell you, it was *my* mistake, my
wanting you, my coming back for you, my thinking I could
free you, that's what cost your life. That it's all been wrong

since I didn't kill him, the Special Forces captain in the Huey over the Mekong. Because I've always tried to keep a foot in both worlds I've never stood in either.

So long I've wanted you, before I knew you; when I was a child I wanted you, have always loved you. I tried to bend the world to my hunger but the world never bends.

Darling, it's charade, acting with our minds *sin saber por qué*. Beneath the charade the heart beats, the body sings, air feels new in our lungs, we touch each other, die.

THE SOLDIERS came raging as if they would kill him now, banging rifles on the bars and whacking him with the butts, pushing him and three others down the corridor and up the greasy stairwell to the killing ground. Green GMC trucks stood in two lines; they shoved him up into the back of one, other prisoners crying out as he fell among them. "*Qué pasa?*" he screamed.

"They're going to shoot us," a woman said.

A soldier shut the back. The truck lurched forward, bouncing and grinding, the roar of the other trucks following. Through a space between the canvas and steel he could see a parade ground, then fortifications, then a long road and jungle.

"Who are you?" someone said.

"Just a gringo, got mixed up in this."

"Sad. Now they're going to shoot you too."

The grinding gears and diesel smell were the same as his trip on trucks down through Mexico, these injured people he didn't know were just like the injured anywhere, Nam or Guatemala. Death was coming just like any other death.

Still the trucks did not stop. "This is the Sierra de Chamá," a man said.

"We're going to Chisec," the woman said. "That's where they'll shoot us."

Chisec came and went, huddled hovels in ragged jungle under the downpouring rain. A few minutes later the truck slowed again, the others closing up behind. It swung left, the others following. "Xuctzul!" someone called.

There was a smell of wood smoke and river and the rattle of a bridge as the truck crossed over it; they followed the side of a canyon, the stream roaring below, down and across another bridge then up through the hills on a muddy track, the truck lurching and groaning, then down the other side. The trucks halted, canvas sides slapping.

"It's the Usumacinta," an old man said. "They'll throw our bodies in the river."

One by one they climbed over the back. The rain had cleared; drops still pattered from the trees. The soldiers tied them in a line and walked them down the slippery trail through wet branches and grass, the roar of the river rising to meet them.

When they reached the river the soldiers untied them. One of the prisoners from another truck came running, calling, "Is anyone here a nurse, a doctor?"

"I'm a medic," Murphy started to say, then stopped. Everything you've done's gone wrong, he told himself. Don't start again.

"You?" the man said to him. "Come then, we have someone dying."

"Let him go in peace. We're all dying in a minute anyway."

"She's in pain. Come then, it won't hurt her to see you."

"Let's go!" a soldier cried. "Down to the river!"

Murphy followed the other prisoner to a huddle of people and a body on a bloody poncho, and saw that it was she.

65

S HE SAW dugouts drawn up along the shore. The men carried her down to the water and rowed her across, then lay her by a fire whose smoke settled on the afternoon air between the *palo pinos* and *pimentijos*, a fire of *palo sano* bright as youth, moss on the mottled gray bark flaring with flame, the russet grain of the *palo sano* like a burning heart, blood to ash. And she saw that change is not evil but only change, and death the end, but no matter, for even nothing ends, and no Heaven exceeds one loving touch, one graceful act, one moment in which another's loved, the gift of love is more momentous than time.

They were so gentle, moving round her. I can write a book now for you all, she thought, on the mystery of death, the symptoms of its censure in the body and the brain, but why do we always speak of symptoms and never of the heart? We're so wrong, dear Lord, not to be satisfied with love.

Wood owls called, a blue-crowned motmot tolled the ending day. Smoke sank on the damp air, far away a chopper passed, those men of wood whittled by the Creators, pale-fleshed men who used the Earth but did not revere the Creators, so the Heart of Heaven drowned them in a rain of tar and soot.

How true the legends. I go back now. To the early days. My father's knee in its striped wool suit. Bony: when I sit on it his kneecap shifts. He pushes his glasses up his nose, his smell of pipe. Back to the jungle our mother, the scent of leaves and soil and slumber.

He was there. She held his hand and felt his warmth, could clamp her fist in it when the pain was so bad it made her scream. He was beside her speaking in his rough soft voice like that of a man who has drunk or cried too much, his body warm beside her, not like this fire that glows but does not heat. You, my Utzíl of Panimache who crossed far hostile lands for his beloved, saved then lost her and dived from a cliff to drown in Atitlán. But *you* will live, you and the child Jesús whom you saved, and a million like him, live to form the new Guatemala. Utzíl my love, my Guatemala, my beloved quetzal singing from the sacred *amate*.

"Where," she said, "where are the soldiers?"

"Across the river. I was in the last truck. This is Mexico."

Another *compañero* bent over her, a boy with long dark hair and sad eyes. "The soldiers," she said again.

"They're gone," he said.

"They're never gone!" she pleaded. "Give me a gun?"

He smiled to hide his anguish, the lack of guns. "I'll give you my knife, *compañera*." He took a combat knife from a sheath around his neck and slipped it into her pocket.

"We're safe now," Murphy said. "Just hold on."

"Truly?"

"Lupe and Pablo, the others. They traded us for Arena."

"How many?"

"Sixty-three, plus you and me."

She closed her eyes. "We won..."

"Arena was injured, but he'll live."

"It doesn't matter. Perhaps he'll change. It's suffering that teaches us to love."

Fire shadows danced in the companionable chatter of
wind in the leaves and ferns, of water trickling down trunks
and lianas. They lifted the four corners of her poncho and
carried her up the slippery slope toward the trail to Saint
Elena and the road the Americans had built to keep out the
guerrillas, where the car was waiting that would take her to
the clinic at Caribal.

The trail came up from the river canyon and there was
a broad steep meadow with a white car above it and they
carried her up it toward the setting sun, the wind-bent grass
red, the far line of trees and sky of blood, his torn shoulders aching with her weight but no pain could stop him
now, and over the river's rumble came another that was
four choppers fast over the ridge and down on the meadow.
With Dona in his arms he ran for the line of blood-red trees
but saw he would not make it, ran back toward the river
but the soldiers were there too, Dona crying, "Drop me!
Run!"

The tall black man jumped from the lead chopper,
ducked low under the blades. "Put them in mine!"

"This is Mexico!" Murphy screamed. "You can't!"

"*Pronto!*" he yelled at the soldiers. "Get them in the
chopper."

They beat Murphy down and lashed his arms and ankles
and threw him in beside her, the cargo deck slippery with
her blood, the ancient steel rattling as the Huey took off,
nose dipping, tilting back toward Guatemala. "I'll always
love you," she said, her face drained of all but the red sunset
through the open cargo door. "I'm going now, it's a hemorrhage. Take this." She slipped him the knife as he tried to
lie beside her but the soldiers forced them apart, and he
watched her die quickly, her face relaxed, her lips opened,
her chest no longer moving beneath the bloody shirt as the
wind toyed with a lock of her hair.

The scar-faced pilot seemed familiar, as if from Nam, as if time were compressed, and everything that had happened there would happen over and over forever, its images serving as lessons to a mystery he would never decode. The last sun sank beyond the mountains of the Río Ixcan, the jungle fading to umber greens, the sinuous headwaters of the Río de la Pasión silver and carmine in the south.

The ancient Huey wailed on an evening downdraft, the rotor shaft grinding at its bearings. He watched the gap between the Jesus nut and the shaft, wondered could he shove the knife into it, break it loose. The tall black man was talking with the other officer, the one who had been Carmen the Embassy translator. Turned away from them Murphy cut the bounds round his wrists, pulled his legs beneath him and freed his ankles. Keeping the knife and his unbound wrists hidden, he looked up at them. "I know you," he said.

The black man grinned down at him. "Search me, and know my heart? Try me, and know my thoughts?"

"I mean *him*." Murphy nodded at the other.

"Carmen?" the black man said. "That was just our little joke."

"His name's Angelo."

"What makes you think that?" Carmen said.

"I heard it from an American, a guy named Gallagher. Just before you cut his throat."

The black man looked at Angelo, at Murphy. "When was that?"

"The night he wasted my plane, killed my friends. When this all started. Didn't it, Angel?"

The black man took out his gun. Angelo shook his head. "You're not going to believe this shithead?"

The black man raised the gun, nodded at the cargo door. "Go."

"I won't let you do this!"

"I'm not going to hurt you," the black man said. "But I want you over there." Watching Lyman, Vodega edged toward the door.

He's the one, Lyman thought. All along. *He* killed Gallagher and blamed it on Murphy because the Guats don't want to pay their share. Because he likes to kill. We've all been used, all of us who fight, by people who move us back and forth, to kill and to be killed. Nancy was right: I'm everybody's dupe. Especially my own. I could let Murphy go, make amends. But not Angel.

Holding the safety strap, Angelo approached the open wind-sucking hole of the door but when Lyman fired he fell into the corner screaming. As the black man went to kick him out the door, Murphy rose up behind him and drove Dona's knife into the perfect place between the shoulder blade and spine, straight into the heart; he fell gasping and Murphy grabbed his gun and saw the scar-faced pilot was climbing back from the cabin; he shot him in the face, then the copilot at the controls.

He stood in the cargo door and the jungle was very soft and far below: you could jump but you would never hit. You would float, far away, not thinking, no longer feeling. Epiphany, all pain gathered into one.

Epifanía. The Huey began to drift then drop. The black man slid out the door. Murphy stepped over Dona, dragged the pilot free of the crew aisle and climbed into his seat, tipped the cyclic forward and swung the Huey around in a long easy descent back to Mexico.

THE END

The opening pages of

The Last Savanna

by Mike Bond
Published by Mandevilla Press

"A manhunt through crocodile-infested jungle, sun-scorched savanna, and impenetrable mountains as a former SAS man tries to save the life of the woman he loves but cannot have." (Evening Telegraph)... *"A gripping thriller from a highly distinctive writer."* (Liverpool Daily Post)... *"Exciting, action-packed... A nightmarish vision of Africa."* – Manchester Evening News

With Africa's last elephants dying under the guns of Somali poachers, ex-SAS officer Ian MacAdam leads a commando squad against them, to hunt what for him is the only decent prey – man. Pursuing the poachers through jungled mountains and searing deserts he battles thirst, solitude, terror and lethal animals, only to find they have kidnapped a young archaeologist, Rebecca Hecht, whom he once loved and bitterly lost.

She escapes the kidnappers, is caught and escapes again to risk perishing in the desert. MacAdam embarks on a desperate trek to save not only Rebecca but his own soul in an Africa torn apart by wars, overpopulation and the slaughter of its last wildlife.

Based on the author's own experiences pursuing elephant poachers in the wilds of East Africa, *The Last Savanna* is an intense personal memoir of humanity's ancient heartland, its people and animals, the lonely beauty of its perilous deserts, jungles, and savannas, and the deep, abiding power of love.

1

THE ELAND DESCENDED four steps down the grassy hillside and halted. He glanced all the way round the rolling golden hills, then closer, inspecting the long grass rippling in the wind, behind him, on both sides, and down to the sinuous green traverse of acacia, doum palms and strangler trees where the stream ran. The wind from the east over his shoulder carried the tang of drying murram grass and the scents of bitter pungent shrubs, of dusty, discarded feathers and glaucous lizard skins, of red earth and brown earth, of old scat and stones heating in the afternoon sun. He switched at flies with his tail, twitched his ears, descended five more steps, and stopped again.

Thirst had dried his lips and eyes, tightened his throat and hardened his skin. Already the rain was drying out of the grass and soil pockets; here only the stream remained, purling between volcanic stones, rimmed by trees and tall sharp weeds. He circled a thorn bush and moved closer several steps, his spiral gray horns glinting as he looked up and down the valley from north to west, then south, then up the slope behind him.

The shoulder-high thorn bushes grew thicker near the stream. The downslope breeze twirled their strong, dusty scents among their gnarled trunks; the sour smell of *siafu*, warrior ants, prickled his nose. He waited for the comforting twitter of sunbirds in the streamside acacias, the muffled snuffling of warthogs, or the swish of vervet monkeys in the branches, but there were none.

Licking his dry nose with a black tongue he raised his head and sniffed the wind, batting at flies with his ears, dropped his jaw and panted. There was truly no bad smell, no danger smell, but the wind was coming down the valley behind him and to get upwind he'd have to cross the stream and there was no way but through the *commiphora* scrub, which was where the greatest danger lay. He glanced back over his shoulder, gauging the climb necessary to regain the ridge and travel into the wind till he could descend the slope at a curve in the stream and keep the wind in his face. The sun glinting on the bleached grass, bright stones and red earth hurt his eyes; he sniffed once more, inhaled deeply, expanding the drum of thin flesh over his ribs, and shoved into the thorn scrub.

A widowbird exploded into flight from a branch on the far side of the stream and the eland jumped back, trembling. The sound of the stream pealing and chuckling coolly over its rocks made his throat ache. The heat seemed to buzz like cicadas, dimming his eyes. Shaking flies from his muzzle, he trotted through the scrub and bent his head to suck the water flashing and bubbling over the black stones.

The old lioness switched her tail, rose from her crouch and surveyed the eland's back over the top of the thorn scrub. She had lain motionless watching his approach and now her body ached to move; the eland's rutty smell made her stomach clench and legs quiver. She ducked her head below the scrub and padded silently to the stream, picked her way across its rocks without wetting her paws and, slower now, slipped a step at a time through the bush and crouched behind a fallen doum palm part way up the slope behind the eland, only her ears visible above it.

Far overhead a bearded vulture wavered in its flight, tipping on one wing, and turned in a wide circle. The eland raised his head, swallowing, and glanced round. Water dripping from his lips spattered into the stream. He shivered the flies from his back, bent to drink and raised his head, water rumbling in his belly. He turned and scanned the slope behind and above him; this was where he'd descended and now the wind was in his face and there was still no danger smell. His legs felt stronger; he licked his lower lip that already seemed less rough from the water filling his body. He trotted back through the thorn scrub past the fallen doum palm, bolting at the sudden yellow flash of terror that impaled him on its fierce claws, the lioness' wide jaws crushing his neck as he screamed crashing through the bush. With one paw the lioness slapped him to the ground but he lurched up and she smashed him down again, her fangs ripping his throat, choking off the air as his hooves slashed wildly, and the horror of it he knew now and understood, dust clouding his eye, the other torn by thorns; the flailing of his feet slackened as the sky went red, the lioness' hard body embracing him, the world and all he had ever known sliding into darkness.

The lioness sighed and dropped her head, the stony soil hurting her jaw. After a few moments she began to lick the blood seeping from the eland's throat and mouth and the shoulder where her claws had torn it, then turned and licked her left rear leg where one of the eland's hooves had made a deep gash. Settling herself more comfortably among the thorn bushes, she stripped back the skin along the eland's shoulder, licking and gnawing at the blood and warm flesh beneath.

Crackling in the brush made her lay back her ears; she rumbled softly, deep in her throat. Heavy footsteps splashed through the stream and she growled louder, her rope tail switching. The male lion came up to the eland, lifted his lip and snarled.

Still growling she backed away slightly, lowering her head to grip the eland's foreleg. The male sniffed the eland's shoulder, crouched, ears back, and began to chew it. Then, gripping the shoulder in his jaw, he dragged the animal sideways, the lioness crawling after it, still holding the leg. Baring his teeth, the male leaned across the eland's shoulder, bit down on the foreleg and pulled the eland over to get at its belly and flanks. Carefully the lioness edged round the carcass, reaching tentatively for a rear leg. With a roar the male flicked out a huge, flat paw that caught the side of her head. Her neck snapped loudly and the lioness tumbled back into the thorn brush, one rear paw trembling briefly.

The Samburu warrior rose from his hiding place among the rocks high up the slope, stretched his stiff legs and picked up his spear. From the shade he watched the lion's thick black-maned head burrow into the eland's belly. Since dawn, when the Samburu had begun watching the two lions, the young male and old female, they had mated nearly three times ten, but now he had killed her, giving the Samburu a possible solution to the problem that had been bothering him all day.

2

T HE SAMBURU WARRIOR climbed to the ridge, keeping out of sight of the lion a half mile below, his bare, thick-soled feet soundless on the raveled, stony earth, his goatskin cloak soundless against his slender limbs. Once over the ridge he broke into a run, down a long, wide valley with a *laga*, a dry sandy stream-bed, against a line of umber cliffs bloodied by the afternoon sun. Where the cliffs became a scrubby talus slope he ascended to a large, spindly desert rose bush with red flowers. He waited till he'd caught his breath, unsheathed his *simi* and began to draw its blade up and down the head of his spear, till both edges glittered and easily shaved the few hairs on the back of his wrist. He sheathed the *simi* and knelt beside the desert rose, cut a downward slash in its stem with his spear, and waited.

Soon a bubble of white sap had collected on the slash. He fitted together the two halves of his spear, thunking the shaft against the earth to seat the top section firmly in the steel haft of the lower one. Then very carefully he drew both edges and the tip of the spearhead along the bubble of sap. He went back down the slope, careful not to touch the spearhead against the brush or bring it near himself.

A gerenuk standing on hind legs to munch at the twigs of an umbrella acacia dropped to all fours and scampered away, halting to look back over her shoulder, but the Samburu ignored her. He reached the *laga* and turned north, walking fast but not running, stepping once over the groove in the sand where a puff adder had crossed his earlier tracks, and he reminded himself to be watchful among the bare rocks warmed by the afternoon sun.

He climbed out of the valley to the ridge and down part way, smiling when he saw the lion was still there, far below. The lion had dragged the eland's intestines, stomach and lungs to one side, eaten the liver and both rear legs and flanks, and was now lying belly down and holding the eland's head and chest with his paws as he ripped strips of muscle from its neck.

The Samburu checked the sun now a forearm's length above the western hills. He sniffed the wind, which had scurried round and now came upstream from the lion, toward the thick scrub below him. But once the sunlight had climbed above the streambed this would reverse, and the cooling air further upstream would begin to descend from him toward the lion.

Again he estimated the distance from the lion and the eland carcass to a single doum palm standing upstream of them, whose first fork could be reached quickly and whose trunk was strong enough to withstand the lion's lunge and too vertical for him to climb. And again the Samburu felt doubt and fear and once more estimated the distance between the lion and the tree.

Keeping the spear point well ahead of him, he crept on hands and knees down the slope, into the failing wind. Thorns caught on his skin and sank into his palms and he extracted them noiselessly, breathing as quietly as possible, holding the spear free of the ground so it would not clink on stones, always conscious of the pressure of the wind against his face.

With a crunch of bones the lion severed the eland's foreleg from the shoulder. The Samburu moved closer, fearing the pounding of his heart, hearing the rip of connective tissue as the lion pulled muscle from the eland's ribcage and, muttering contentedly, gulped it down. Ahead of him the Samburu could see the doum palm rising above the scrub; the wind in his face died, his pulse thudding in his ears.

On hands and knees, weaving the spear point ahead of him through the thick and tangled thorn scrub, holding down one by one the blades of pale bunchgrass as he moved across them, detaching each finger-length thorn that sank into his skin or cloak, keeping as much as he could to the fiery but quieter stones that seemed to whisper into the soil as he placed his weight upon them, he reached the doum palm as sunlight left the valley floor and began to climb the slope.

A touch of wind ran up his back and he tensed to run, but the lion did not snarl or charge, must not have caught his smell. More insistently the breeze returned, flowing down the stream as the sun dropped it into shadow. The Samburu stood, spear drawn back, the sap-coated point beside his eye. Twenty paces ahead, the lion's shoulders rippled huge and tawny as he stripped connective tissue from the eland's ribs, his back muscles flexing down into his thick back legs, his triangular ears kittenish above the mass of black mane. The Samburu darted forward, hurled the spear and dashed back to the palm, his cloak sailing as he scrambled up the scaly trunk to the first fork and the lion crashed roaring against the trunk and leaped up it, a bough above the Samburu's head snapping with the lion's impact on the trunk and spinning outwards and splashing into the stream. All this the Samburu saw clearly, slowly, as if it took no time, was timeless, the lion's huge white teeth, red tongue, yellow furious eyes, the impossibly broad square jaws framed in its colossal black mane nearing as the lion thrust himself up the trunk, his front paws the size of a man's belly, their yellow curved claws shattering bark as they dug into the wood. The Samburu snatched his *simi* and leaned downwards, as if to cut this forepaw wider than his thigh, seeing now the spear hanging from the lion's side, its head sunk between his ribs.

Unable to hold his weight the lion slid back down, wood chunks showering him. He growled, deep and disconsolate, turned and snapped off the spear with his teeth, padded back to the eland and darted a few steps after two black-backed jackals that fled through the bush. He glared at the Samburu, sniffed the eland, and streaked through the scrub to collide again against the doum palm. The Samburu lost his grip as the trunk snapped down then whipped back, his *simi* flying, bark slipping through his fingers, but he clenched his ankles round his branch, a huge paw whistling past his head as he twisted back up, grabbed the trunk and stood on the branch. The lion slid back to the ground.

Again he chased the jackals from the eland. He seemed to trip, righted himself, jerked his head round and began to lick at his wound. This did not satisfy him and he squirmed to lick beneath his tail, plodded to the stream, drank, fell down climbing the bank, returned to the eland and resumed eating. After a few moments he stood as if hearing something from afar, jerked spasmodically, and fell. He dragged himself on forelegs toward the stream, wavered to his feet, turned his wide-maned, bitter face in a roar of rage at the Samburu, toppled over the lioness, and lay still.

Sunlight had fled to the upper eastern slopes. To the north, across vast, empty Suguta Valley, the sky shifted steadily from cobalt to blood and lavender; doves called from the candelabra euphorbias, "And you too? And you too?" A honeyguide fluttered past the doum palm, alit on a higher branch, and cocked its head expectantly down at the Samburu. "Come with me!" it twittered. "Honey! Honey! Come with me!" A string of puffball cumulus trooped across the eastern sky, nose to tail like elephants, sunset reddening their flanks, as if they'd been rolling, as elephants once did, in the ochre desert dust of the Dida Galgalu.

Furtive, then more assured, the jackals returned, barking their alarm calls at each bird's flutter or whisper in the wind, glancing often at the motionless lions while they chewed hurriedly on the eland.

The Samburu slipped down the doum palm, found his *simi* and edged closer to the lions. He threw a large rock that thumped against the male's head, making the jackals bark, but the lion did not move. The jackals did not back away, one standing proprietarily atop the eland's ribs. An owl called from the downstream darkness.

The Samburu threw several more rocks but the lion seemed truly dead. Gathering up his cloak and holding his *simi* before him, he moved closer, the lions now a single fawn-colored mass in the gathering gloom. He poked the *simi*'s point into the lion's eye: yes, he was dead.

It took all his strength to roll the lion on to his back. With the *simi* he slit down the center of the lion's lower jaw, down his neck, the center of his chest and belly and back to his testicles and the root of his tail, and started to free the skin on both sides from the stomach and ribs.

The moon rose yellow as maize, deformed like a melon that has lain too long on one side. On the ridge beneath the moon a clan of hyenas yodeled like demon children; the Samburu paused to wipe his *simi*, looked up but could not see them. He dragged the male lion's carcass free of his pelt, went to the dead eland and sliced long strips of skin and sinew from the two unchewed legs, folded the lion's pelt, lashed it with the sinew, and carried it on his back to the palm. With a long strap of sinew sections he pulled the pelt up into the fork of the tree, returned and began to skin the lioness.

The hyenas had circled from the east around the southern upper end of the valley, crossing his trail. Now they were coming fast along the west side, halfway up that slope. Soon they would pick up his scent again, and the eland's, and begin to close in.

Hurriedly he gathered dry leaves from the base of a thorn bush, and with his *simi* cut thin strips of bark from a small tamarind tree. These he piled near the lioness; then he ran to an umbrella acacia and snapped twigs from the edge of its canopy where giraffes had browsed the leaves and killed the branches. Something black moved through the gray scrub silvered by moonlight – a low, hunchbacked scurrying silhouette, the lead hyena, scouting him. They were silent now, smelling his fear.

He ran back to his pile of leaves and tamarind bark, but the wind had scattered it. Brush whispered as the hyenas drew closer, a moon-pale eye blinking. He scuffed together the leaves and bark as best he could, crunching down the acacia thorns with his hands. Wiping the blood on his shins he unwrapped a small flint from a fold of his cloak and struck it hard against the edge of his *simi*, the hyenas whining appreciatively as the smell of his blood reached them.

Like a small planet flung from its orbit, the spark flared across the darkness and ebbed against its bed of leaves. The wind fanned it; it burned a hole in its leaf and dropped through, went out. Claws ticked on rocks; more than lion, leopard, even more than buffalo he feared and hated hyenas, skulking, elusive, afraid of man until he's alone, at night, without fire, when they attack in hordes and tear him apart alive, crush his still-living limbs in their jaws, as they had his cousin Oaulguu's father-in-law, caught alone in the desert near Ilaut. The Samburu knew now that they would have him too, not just his lion skin; faster and faster he struck the flint, a hyena snickering at its flash, the sparks dying on the wrinkled leaves. He flung a boulder at the closest hyena, who barked sharply and retreated, the others clacking their teeth in anticipation. With his *simi* he dug more rocks from the soil and threw them till there was only one hyena between him and the doum palm and he charged it, screaming, swinging his *simi*; the hyena backed away, snarling, then pounced at his heels as he clambered up the palm tree and crouched, breathless, on the limb beside his lion pelt.

In the clear blue moonlight he watched the hyenas circle the eland and lioness, draw closer, then suddenly swarm them, yipping and snarling, crunching bones and ripping flesh. For a while they clustered round the eland, fighting and dragging it first one way then the other, till more hyenas appeared one by one out of the dark scrub, deposing several of the first group who then, growling and whimpering, turned their attention to the lioness. With regret the Samburu watched them, his hand descending often to check the sinew binding the male lion's pelt to the branch beneath his feet. He who takes more than his share, *N'gai* says, ends with nothing. This big black-maned lion was *N'gai*'s gift, to pay the year's school fees for his sons. He would not spurn or squander *N'gai*'s gift.

3

LONG BEFORE THE STARS DIED the birds began to sing – cool rippling doves, loud cheery starlings, the long lilting trills of warblers and thrushes. The hyenas has ceased snarling and yipping around the eland; against the paling stars the Samburu could see the tiny gliding spots of the vultures that had come before dusk and circled all night.

Dawn raced like fire across the savanna. Three hyenas still lay with their heads inside the eland's bared ribcage; another was chewing fleas at the base of his tail; the lioness' pelt was shredded, her head severed and half-gnawed in the scrub. The first vulture skated down on wide, whistling wings and landed near the eland, cocking its rubbery red head; a hyena ran barking at it and it lumbered off, flapped above the hyena and circled back. A second drifted down and roosted in a thorn bush; another hyena raised its muzzle from the eland's belly and growled.

The Samburu lowered the lion's pelt on its sinew and slid to the ground. He steadied the pelt on his head, grasped his spear and trotted eastwards up the slope into the full raiment of the sun.

The lion pelt was still heavy with fat and blood and the lion's heavy fur, heavier than the stone-heavy *podocarpus* boughs he had carried often from the banks of the Ewaso

N'giro to his mother's *manyatta* when he was still a boy and the desert had not yet come. He should stop and skin the pelt cleaner so he could carry it with less exhaustion, but as he crested the ridge he realized the hyenas had left the eland and, yowling, had taken up his trail. Further north, along the stream, the others answered. Glancing back as he ran, the Samburu tried to unsheath his *simi*; a stone shifted underfoot and his ankle snapped loud as a dry stick in the bright morning air, and he fell face down among the rocks. He lurched to his feet, raised up the pelt, and hobbled forward on the spear; the pelt tumbled from his head, skipped and rolled, spinning awkwardly, downhill. The four hyenas checked their lope to watch it slam into a thorn bush, knocking loose a weaver's nest that bounced over the rocks and vanished in the scrub.

The Samburu cut a strip from his cloak and wrapped his ankle but could put no weight on it. Using the spear as a cane he sidestepped down the slope; below, the hyenas drew together round the pelt and halted on their haunches, watching him descend. He drew his *simi* and waved it, yelling, but they did not retreat.

Single file the other hyenas had cleared the scrub along the stream and were hurrying upslope. The Samburu reached the pelt, shaking with pain; the four hyenas glanced back at the rest of the pack and trotted toward him, haunches down, ears back, jaws grinning. His back to the pelt and thorn bush, he fitted his spear together and held it in his right hand, the *simi* in his left. The pack of hyenas joined the first four, now numbering the fingers of three hands. Whining, eyes darting side to side, long jaws gaping with delight, as if imploring him not to fear, this would all end quickly, they circled him, sniffing the bloody pelt, his fear.

He backed tighter into the bush, its thorns pricking his back and thighs, blood trickling down his spine. The hyenas split up; he sensed some coming up behind, their claws rattling the loose soil, the branches twanging in their wiry fur, their anxious panting. As the three before him darted in, low and fast, he caught the first in the shoulder with the spear, the second across the skull with the *simi* but the third gashed his calf and, leaping past the *simi*'s swing, ran to the others and sat licking the blood that spotted its muzzle. Whining, the speared hyena backed away; the second, slashed across the head, crouched beyond reach, ears back. A big female sniffed his bleeding head and, turning her curious, affronted eyes on the Samburu, bolted at him. She leaped back from the *simi*, then tore his knee and bounded aside as he spun to spear another from the left. He swung the *simi* at three more coming straight, one leaping for his throat, the massive female soaring at him with jaws outstretched, her breath hot in his face as he drove the spear shaft down her open jaws, ducking, flung her past him, the spearhead going with her. He chopped another's spine with the *simi* as it tore into his ankle, jerking the blade upward to slice another's throat as it snapped for his face, lashing sideways to bare another's shoulder before it screamed and dove away.

In this moment of death he felt a great calm. Panting, tongues hanging, the hyenas gathered to watch him bleed. He glanced behind the bush, but the spearhead was out of reach. One darted in but sprang back when he raised the *simi*. With his good foot he rolled one dead hyena toward them, then the other. The big female, bleeding from the mouth, eyes ablaze, slunk nearer, sniffed the first body and as she turned to the second the Samburu jumped forward and cleaved her neck halfway through. But he could not pull the *simi* free as the others charged him, howling, his *simi* jammed in her vertebrae by the angle of her neck. He flailed at the others with the broken spear till he could yank the *simi* free, and the others fell back, watchful, angry.

His feet slipped on the soil muddied by his blood. Sun drummed on his head; the land spun round and round. Attentive and eager, the hyenas crouched cheerfully on their haunches, nostrils and jaws wide, as if it were a game, he thought, about to begin again. He glanced at the blood sliding down his shins: staunch it soon, he thought, or die. Again he saw his bones crunched by them, and he bared his teeth.

The huge sun slid overhead, whitening the desiccated sky and searing the sulfurous soil, the tortured barren scrub. Flies buzzed at his blood; a hyena stood, stretched, sniffed the changing wind, and trotted swiftly northwards, angling downslope. One by one the others rose and followed. Unbelieving, the Samburu waited by his bush, but they were gone, gone away, a new wind raising dust devils and scuttling dead leaves like vipers under the thorn scrub, drying the blood on his lacerated legs and sucking the last moisture from his throat.

He gathered up and re-shafted his spear, looked across the undulant, afternoon-hazed bitter brush wavering with heat, but could not see the hyenas. Baffled, he tore apart the rest of his cloak and tried to wrap his legs; it was difficult to walk with this flesh and muscle hanging in strips down the narrow white bones, with his broken ankle lurching sideways at each step, driving impossible pain up what was left of his legs. But *N'gai* had favored him still with life, this magnificent life with its aromas of bush, soil and wind, its bird songs and buzzard cries, its hum of flies and ants and butterflies and all that composes the cosmos in perfect harmony. And because his youngest sons needed their school fees *N'gai* had willed that he should live to carry back this lion pelt and it must be done as *N'gai* willed, to find a way to raise this pelt, steady it atop his head, to lean forward, take a step with these legs baring their bone beneath flags of muddy flesh, to raise this bandaged foot and place it on the crumbly soil, then bear the weight so evenly on the spear shaft, bringing forward the other foot, and all that mattered was to make each step possible, carry it through, then another, then another. He must cross the dead savanna of Lailasai, but if *N'gai* had spared him the hyenas it would not be to kill him in Lailasai, but to lead him home, where at the *duka* of Mohammed Amin Sala he would receive four hundred shillings for such a pelt, enough to send the boys to school, and with each step he repeated this thought, under the weight of the pelt and the heat of the sun.

Each time he fell the sun's heat woke him, and he dragged himself to the pelt and, kneeling, raised it to his head then forced himself up, steadying his stagger till he could again step, then step again, then step again, toward the ridges of the Ol Doinyo Lailasai hovering before him in the late afternoon heat.

Again the sun had died. How cool the land, how soft the violet light, as he crested the last rise and Ol Doinyo Lailasai towered before him like the entrance to an immense mystery he was beginning to understand, in the clarity of pain and early starlight, when the birds are silenced by the sudden wall that falls between day and night and in the very far distance the rock mountain where *N'gai* was born guarded his *manyatta*. If the hyenas did not come he'd reach it before the sun grew hot tomorrow, if he walked all night, and yes, *N'gai* was good to him and his sons for he would reach it now, and taking a deep breath of this dry, chill sunset air he did not understand nor realize the shocking, crushing force that suddenly separated him from the earth and hurled him in scattered awareness among the bushes whose thorns no longer hurt, the pelt's weight no longer bearing him down, and he tried to remember why he was carrying it, then could not remember what it was, remembering then, only, *N'gai* has been good, *N'gai* has been so good.

Finger still on the trigger of his AK47, the young Somali slipped from his cover in the euphorbias and, hugging the dark places between the brush, crept to the Samburu lying gape-mouthed on the tousled sand. He was truly dead, this barbarian; the Somali wondered at the power of the rifle, seeing how the bullet had entered the Samburu's chest just above the heart, and had come out the left eye, which dangled down his cheek on a trace of tissue; the impact of the bullet had forced brains like the insides of snails out the Samburu's ears; a pool of near-black was spreading round his head.

An uneven clump, clump-clump of hooves approached; shouldering his rifle the Somali turned to another leading a camel. "Ho, brother! Did I not shoot well?"

The other smiled. "Yes, Warwar, it was well done. Now let's load your pelt quickly. The shot was loud."

"It's a shame to share this with the others."

"You would live alone?" The other dragged the lion pelt from the bushes where it had tumbled. "Check there's no money on him."

"Him?" the young Somali scoffed. "It's a barbarian in rags—an old *simi* and a worn spear."

They lashed the pelt atop the camel and continued leading it south as the last rays of sun receded across the lilac sands. Just before dark they crossed a furrowed trail coming from the northwest. Warwar knelt, fingering a round, deep print. "It can't be!"

His brother walked alongside the tracks, noting the different sizes and strides. "Three females, one old. Plus a calf." He scanned the back trail, the rough scar in the earth's reddish eroded crust shadowed by the fading horizontal light. "The last of the northern herds. Driven by thirst down out of the mountains, headed for the Ewaso N'giro."

"How many days?"

"Weeks. We won't catch them till the river."

"Perhaps they'll find us a bull."

"Hush, you dreamer! Don't bring bad luck."

"Since when would it be bad luck," Warwar laughed, "to come home loaded down with ivory?"

4

B Y READING, MacAdam realized, he had enlarged his awareness but impaired his vision. Now to see the world clearly he was forced to look at it through a wall of glass.

He unbuttoned his shirt and wiped dust from his spectacles, watched the camels milling in the paddock where the Rendille woman had driven them. Not even eight o'clock and already the sun hot on the back of your neck. The grass underfoot not too brittle for December: so far the short rains had been good.

Under a thorn tree by the paddock the dismounted cab of a Land Rover served as a shed from which he took two bottles of hydrogen peroxide and a large antibiotic tube. This probably would not work but was better than that mixture the Rendille woman used that killed four camels last year.

A string of Samburu kids lined the stockade, their fuzzy hair paled with dust kicked up by the camels shuffling nervously and swinging their heads to snap at flies along their haunches.

The Rendille woman climbed the stockade and jumped in, her head barely to the camels' bellies. With a switch she drove one into the chute; Isau, the Samburu foreman, dropped the gate behind it. MacAdam slipped a noose of sisal round the camel's knee and as it lurched forward against the front gate of the chute he yanked the noose tight, jerking up its knee. It brayed and tried to pull back, tautening the noose that he then tied off against the stockade. He threw a halter rope around its head, tossed the end to Isau who looped it once around a beam and held it tight.

With the camel neighing and jerking at the halter MacAdam washed a large boil on its neck with hydrogen peroxide, took a knife from his pocket and sliced the boil open. The camel screamed, craning its neck, green grass spittle frothing its yellow teeth and pale gums. MacAdam squeezed the boil, blood and pus running down the camel's rough, dusty fur. Wiping pus from his fingers on to its neck, he screwed a syringe top on to the antibiotic tube and squeezed some into the wound. He slipped the noose from its knee; Isau tossed free the halter; MacAdam opened the front chute gate and the camel trotted, swinging its head angrily, into the pasture. The Rendille woman drove another camel into the chute.

It was nearly noon when he finished. Dust and sweat caked his face; blood and pus streaked his shorts and knees. He thanked Isau and the Rendille woman, who nodded, her eyes on the savanna, as if he had not meant his thanks and therefore to accept them would further demean her, or that neither his thanks nor he were significant. For an instant he saw himself as they must see him, an easy-smiling, hearty man with a booming voice and nothing to say, with a fine home and wife and possessions that inoculated him against others' joys and sufferings and his own. A gregarious fake. *Oi meninisho k'kiri nememe*: flesh that is not painful does not feel.

He put the last half-bottle of hydrogen peroxide back in the Land Rover shed, rubbed his hands clean with dust and walked past the thatch-roofed sheds where several ancient Land Rovers rusted calmly on blocks in the tall grass, past the long stone barn with its galvanized roof, toward the slate-roofed house under flame trees, frangipani, bougainvillea and jacarandas, a candlestick euphorbia towering cactus-like on either side.

Dorothy was not downstairs. He entered the parlor cool and dark after the blast of the sun, poured gin and tonic water into a glass and wandered into the kitchen for ice, then out on the veranda, sipping gin and watching the heat seethe over the wide golden savanna; behind it, blocking the horizon, the blunt, vast bulk of Mount Kenya was cloaked in clouds.

On the equator the days pass one like the next. You come here young, marry, raise a family, die, and leave no tracks. Occasionally you go "home", to London and the Cotswold mists, the old streets of Cirencester, the city's bookshops, movies, pubs, museums, the facile English conversations. After a few weeks you wake up one day and decide to go back to Africa – the rest is just a game.

Like malaria, Africa. Once bitten you can never shake it. They used to call acacias "fever trees", thinking malaria came from them. Now they "know" malaria comes from mosquitoes. Some day they'll realize malaria comes from the continent itself: Africa is a fever. For Africa there's no chloroquine. No matter if you leave it, it's engraved in your blood.

Yet Africa is dying, taking the fever with it. Have no attachments, MacAdam knew the Maasai said: see the world as it passes, not siding with lion or gazelle. A century ago the whites came, ploughed and fenced the savanna, cut the forests, grazed their ignorant cattle where the wildebeest had roamed. They killed the warriors and made the docile ones clerks, told them we nailed God to a tree because He threatened to free us of our sins. "What are sins?" the Maasai answered. "God is the land, the trees, the mountains, the animals, the sky, the rivers and the rain. How do you nail this to a tree?"

Now the land, the trees, the animals are gone; the whites were right—God's not so hard to kill. And most of the whites had gone, too, leaving behind them a plague to finish off what they began. This plague, MacAdam had reflected so many bitter times, was medicine without birth control. It allowed the weak to live, populations to explode, the limitless savannas and jungles cut into tiny *shambas* where swollen families burnt and hacked the vegetation, then clung to the malnourished soil till it eroded to bedrock. Without the grass and trees the soil dried, the rains died and you could see a man coming miles away by the dust he raised.

But don't see a lion's killing a waterbuck from either side, he reminded himself. He should not try to attribute "good". Learn not to care, again and again he had told himself, about the death of Africa.

Dorothy's footsteps upstairs. Africa, that still enslaved the black woman, in MacAdam's experience wore the white one down, made her either passive or hard. In the first years of their marriage there'd been friends, other ranchers, with a common longing for an England whose mirage grew ever more entrancing as the reality was forgotten. But now the neighbors and her own children were gone, Dorothy couldn't stop talking about going "home".

The Samburu distinguished between house and home. A house was what the Europeans had, here in Africa. It was not their home. Home was where the family lived, generations, the familiar soil. A place which had no written history because it was in their bones, as their bones were in the soil. The Mau Mau had come because the Africans got tired of waiting for the white man to go home.

When MacAdam and Dorothy went down to Nairobi she perked up, but said she hated it. As the other white ranchers left the Lerochi plateau, Kikuyu politicians had bought their ranches and resold them in tiny parcels whose buyers could not make enough from them to live. Their goats tore up the last grass; the rains scoured the broken topsoil into dirtied streams that gnawed gullies through parched valleys. Now MacAdam and Dorothy were the last whites on the plateau. When the rains were good their cattle prospered. When there were no rains he cut the herd to two hundred heifers and a few bulls, and wandered northern Kenya with them like a Samburu nomad.

Dorothy's tread was listless on the stairs. When they were young there'd been so much passion, joy in each other. Now they were old friends and passion a trick of memory. He felt himself turning into sinew. "Take a second wife," Aiyam the Samburu elder had counseled. "Look at me – at more than seventy years I have four wives – I keep them happy!"

He'd take no other wife. Once yes, with a joy that bordered on abandon. But those days were dead. Dead and buried. The other wife had never been his own, and they'd been right to kill it. But when he dared to think honestly about her, he saw that only then had he lived down to the bottom of his soul, with a joy so hot and bright it cut him to the bone. He'd acted like a fool, he would tell himself, a teenager lost in visions of himself. It never would have lasted; he would have ended just as badly off as he was now.

In the kitchen he took three ice cubes from the fridge and plunked them into his glass. How soon they start to melt, he thought. Have I reached the age when nothing is enough? What else *is* there? When you're young it's so easy: you love danger. Look for it. But once you test yourself, face fire, you never have to doubt again. Then you see that courage is so little. In any case I've got no danger now. No risk means no joy.

He tucked the gin bottle away and hid his glass in a corner of the sink as Dorothy slippered into the kitchen. "Hullo," he smiled, hating his smile and the timbre of his voice. "Another lovely day."